THE NIGHT BEFORE

The Queen

ISBN-13: 978-1-7336442-5-9

For information regarding special ordering for bulk purchases, contact:
Queendom Dreams Publishing - www.queendomdreamspublishing.com

Queendom Dreams Publishing

THE NIGHT BEFORE

The Queen

Queendom Dreams Publishing

www.QueendomDreamsPublishing.com

CHAPTER 1

Being a social media influencer and model for several years provided me with many unique experiences to rub elbows with some of the "Who's Who" in the entertainment industry. My lifelong friend Jeanette was the one who talked me into becoming an Instagram model. I started it thinking it would just something fun to do. Never in a million years did I think it would turn out to be such a lucrative career move.

A couple of years into our Insta careers, while Jeanette and I were at a music producer's party, in walked who struck me as the ugliest guy on the face of the earth. His upper torso made it evident that he worked out a lot, but his legs were exceptionally short for his body. His head looked a bit too big, his forehead went almost to the top of his head, and even at a distance I could tell one of his eyes was larger than the other. When I say he was black, he was black-black. Hell, I'm a Hershey's milk chocolate-black, but him, he was a midnight-blue, no-stars-in-the-sky black.

However, the thing about him that caught my attention when he entered the party was the many women who flocked to him, along with the sparkling diamonds that blinged from his hand, his neck, his ear, and even his belt buckle. My immediate thought upon seeing him was, "What in Satan's world is that?" As a matter of fact, those were the exact words I spoke to Jeanette.

The crazy thing is, the more Jeanette and I discussed the pure ugliness of this guy, the more intrigued I became. I wondered what it was about him that had those women throwing themselves at his feet. Meanwhile, the room was filled with attractive men who were getting no play whatsoever.

The party was in a two-story penthouse, which covered half of the top of a converted warehouse. The windows wrapped all the way around the penthouse, providing spectacular views of all of greater Atlanta. Most of the décor was purple and gold. The place was huge, but sparsely furnished, and the sitting area was roped off. Not only were the furnishings sparse, but so was the number of bathrooms for the hundred-plus people on that first level of the penthouse. Men and women had to share a total of three bathrooms.

There were plenty of tables to stand at, but not for sitting. The place was well-lit, making it easy to see who you were talking to, or to read the many business cards being exchanged. At the entrance to the penthouse, there was a beautiful curved waterfall wall lit in alternating purple and gold, preventing one from seeing inside the space from the doorway. Security stood posted at the bottom of the steps, only allowing select people to go up to the second level. While hors d'oeuvres were being served downstairs, people were coming from the upper level with whole plates of food.

From time to time, Jeanette and I would separate to go work the room. I knew I had it going on and turned many heads with each step I took. I wore a white sheer catsuit covered with Swarovski crystals creatively designed to cover certain areas. I had a bit of— not much—work on my body and loved showing it off each chance I could. The problem with these events was that most of the other women in attendance also had some work. It was like a competition of who had the best work done—who looked the most natural. I always had plenty of natural boobs, but just wanted them to sit up better for when I opted to go braless. I also had a decent sized ass, but I got some of my belly fat transferred for enhancement. I had height on my side, so I stood out in a way the others didn't, and it looked as if I was all natural. I am five-eleven without heels. Jeanette is five-nine, so when we entered a room together, you could hear the whole room come to a hush.

"Asha, why are you still staring at that ugly motherfucker? Every time I look over at you, I can see your eyes stuck on that troll," Jeanette asked with a laugh when she came back to where I was standing.

I hadn't realized I was staring so hard.

"Girl, I'm just trying to figure out what it is about him that got these bitches going crazy and laughing extra loud. He's like a hiccup away from being a dwarf. I look at him and imagine this is what Satan's minions must look like. He must be important, because even the guys are running up to him like he's somebody."

"Hmm, girl, I see you sizing him up to fit in your plan to be married with a baby by the time you hit thirty." Jeanette laughed.

Her words knocked the wind out of me, delaying my response. From as far back as I can remember, I was always talking about how I was going to have a wealthy husband and a baby by the time I reached thirty. Actually, I wanted either two girls or two boys, so they'd be able to be like best friends. Since thick women ran in my family, I couldn't risk having more than two, because I wouldn't be able to lose the weight.

"Jeanette, don't make me beat your ass up in this place. I would die if I was impregnated by that. Hell, I'd die if that creature even touched me." I shivered at the thought.

Jeanette continued. "These dumb bitches see all that bling and they lose their minds. He's probably broke as hell, spends each of his McDonald's paychecks on some new piece of ice, and then shows up to these parties to front like he's got it going on."

"Kind of like how we do?" I laughed.

I laughed because that's exactly what we did to get started. Jeanette had just started community college part time and worked in different restaurants, hoping to one day get discovered. She'd use school money to buy expensive outfits to be able to get into different parties. I had an administrative assistant job to supplement my few community college classes. Jeanette and I rented an apartment together with my first cousin, Sylvia, to help us cut down on our expenses and be able to afford our clothing habits and cosmetic surgeries. We called it an investment.

"We might have started like that, but look at us now." She wore a black catsuit that was similar to mine. She twirled so I could take a good look at her. "My momma always said, 'Never despise humble beginnings.'"

I high-fived her. I had to agree. In just that one year, we were doing quite well financially. Better than I could have ever imagined. I even often wondered how.

"Eew! He's looking over this way," I said after taking yet another peep in the ugly guy's direction.

"I guess so. He's probably wondering why you keep staring at him despite all the other men in here. Stop looking at his ugly ass. Hell, I'm trying to figure out if he looks more like an ape or a toad."

I rolled my eyes before cracking up laughing.

She pressed her lips together. "He must have a King Kong-sized dick, though."

"I was thinking the same thing. He walks with a bit of a limp, like his dick might be in the way. Or maybe he just has super-sized testicles."

Jeanette shook her head. "Please stop. You're making me nauseous. Don't make me imagine him without clothes on." She pretended to be gagging. "Even worse, look at how he's tearing up that plate of food. Damn slob!"

"Are you serious? You're the one talking about his King Kong dick."

"Whatever! I'm about to walk around. You need to get your ass out and be seen. That's why we're here, remember? You look cute near this lamp, but you need to keep it moving."

"Yes, I agree. Let's walk."

My walk was short. I ended up parked once again, and Jeanette was off in the crowd, being Miss Social Butterfly. As I stood near the large window that overlooked a phenomenal city view of Atlanta sipping on a glass of Chardonnay, I heard, "I wouldn't be able to live with myself if I didn't come over here to meet the baddest chick up in this joint."

I loved the words spoken, but the voice almost caused me to laugh out loud. It reminded me of a broken buzzer. I turned to the voice and had to look down at the top of the ugly guy's head, which came up to my surgically lifted breasts.

"Aw shit now!" he said as his eyes made direct contact with the rainbow-colored Swarovski lips design around my nipples. "Now that's exactly where I'd like my lips to be. You mind if I put my lips there to see if they match the design?"

As much as I wanted to smack the hell out of him, I laughed. He wasn't the first to say something vulgar regarding the design that night, but it was just the fact that it was his ugly ass saying it.

He looked down at the design covering the pubic area. "Now that's what the fuck I'm talking about! That's where I want to put my tongue," he said, referencing the opened mouth with the extra-long tongue design made with the crystals. "I like your style. What's your name?"

I debated if I wanted to tell him or not before answering, "Asha."

He took my hand without the drink and kissed it. "Hi, Asha. I'm Anthony. I couldn't help but check you out. I noticed you were checking me out too," he said, looking at me like a hungry man ogling a steak.

"Oh! I'm sorry, I didn't mean to stare. It's just I recognized most of the people here, but you didn't look familiar."

"Nah, I'm not from around here. I live in Jamaica. I'm international, so I get around."

I looked at him in disbelief. "Jamaica, like the island? Or New York, Jamaica? I don't hear any accent."

"I said I live in Jamaica. I didn't say I'm from Jamaica. Well, actually, I am from Jamaica. I grew up in Jamaica, Queens, in New York. I bought a mansion outside of Kingston, Jamaica."

"Wow! Really?" I asked, trying to not sound overly impressed by the word *mansion*.

"Yep! Hopefully, I can get you to come visit me sometime."

The more I looked at dude, the more I asked myself if I could dare gather the ability to fuck him. He looked even more hideous up close, with a grain of rice still stuck to his chin. His teeth were extra small compared to his gums, and he had a funky-looking rash on the back of his head. However, I couldn't stop imagining his super thick tongue actually licking my pussy. His tongue appeared too big for his mouth. As disgusting as the thought was, it also aroused me.

I chuckled as I shook my head. "No, thank you. I'm not trying to be a part of anyone's entourage or harem, and I see you already have a hefty one."

"It wouldn't be like that if you came to visit me. You say the word, and I'll make all of them disappear."

"Oh really?" I laughed. "You don't even know me."

"I don't need to know you. I like what I see and that's all that matters. I want you and can make you a very happy woman. I'd even take you around the world with me."

"How exactly are you supposed to make me a happy woman?"

"I got an anaconda. I can look at you and know that's what you need. You're nice and tall, so you won't be complaining, talking about 'it hurts' or 'it's too much.' Looking at your outfit, I can tell you like to be licked down there. I can definitely do that to you."

The mere thought of being licked down there caused my va-jay-jay to quiver. I laughed. "Oh, so you're already trying to bed me? Damn! You waste no time."

He held both of his short arms up to the side. "Hey, when I see what I want, I don't believe in beating around the bush. Life's too short to be bullshitting."

"So, no dinner or anything. Let's just get to fucking, huh?"

"I ain't got no problem feeding you. I'll fly you out to my palace and feed you like a queen. You ever been to Jamaica?"

"Plenty of times."

"A resort or a palace?"

"A resort. Why does that make a difference?"

"If you let me fly you out, you'll see. There's a huge difference."

Jeanette made an ugly face as she walked up behind Anthony. I tried not to laugh at her expression.

"Hey! What's going on?" she asked.

Anthony turned and looked Jeanette's body up and down.

"Damn! Ebony and ivory! How's a brother to choose?"

"Who's ebony and ivory?" she asked offended. "This is all-natural dark chocolate right here and silky milk chocolate right there." She pointed toward me.

"You're wearing black, and she's wearing white, right?"

"Oh yeah. My bad." She giggled. "Anyhow, I'm Jeanette, and you are?" She switched into flirt mode, which was something I always hated about her.

He took her extended hand and kissed the back of it instead of shaking it. She used that moment to knock that persistent grain of rice from his chin. "I'm Anthony. Nice to meet you, Jeanette. I was just here trying to talk your friend into letting me fly her out to my mansion in Kingston and having dinner with me. Maybe we could get you to join us."

"He ain't just talking about dinner. He's over here talking about his anaconda and how he thinks it'll make me happy." I laughed.

"Shit! An anaconda? For real?" she asked, raising an eyebrow while slightly biting down on her manicured index finger.

"It is what it is," he answered smugly.

"I ain't trying to fuck you, but hell yeah, I wanna go too. We go everywhere together."

"Consider it arranged."

I held up a hand and pulled my neck back in disbelief. "Hold up! How the hell you just deciding for me?" I asked Jeanette.

"Girl, stop playing. You know the minute he said the word 'anaconda', your bags were mentally packed." She cracked up laughing.

"Whatever! Don't play me like that." I laughed as I rolled my eyes. She was partially right, but I was still struggling with his ugliness.

CHAPTER 2

I don't know how I let it happen, but two days after the music producer's party, Jeanette and I were stepping off a plane in Kingston to see Anthony's mansion. He had his car service picking us up from the airport.

"Girl, you know this dude is a drug dealer or something. You talking about how you looked him up and he's into some international rubber or plastic sales. This shit looks like international drug sales. Look at this place," Jeanette nervously whispered as the SUV pulled into the compound.

Instead of answering, I just held her hand to ease both of our fears.

There were armed military-looking guards all around that had me questioning my own sanity for being there, even if I had brought backup. It wasn't like Jeanette was capable of saving me if something went wrong. I've seen plenty of movies that didn't turn out too well for the drug-dealing homeowner, and Anthony's place looked like a scene from one of those movies.

As we got out the car, we noticed several women strutting about, butt naked in heels, and suddenly fear had us wondering if we had just walked into a prostitution ring. A huge guy met us at the car and walked us into the beautiful mansion. The bright twenty-bedroom mansion was huge, containing beautiful and unique hand-carved doors throughout. The big guy showed us to our individual rooms on the second floor of the four-story home and instructed us to come back downstairs after we freshened up from the trip.

We toured the large property, had lunch, and lounged by one of the private pools. We had yet to see Anthony.

"Girl, there's so much eye candy here, I can't decide who or what I want first. Thankfully, you'll have your anaconda." Jeanette laughed as she sipped her tropical concoction the bartender named, The Sailor.

I pulled down my sunglasses and looked at her like she was crazy before rolling my eyes at her.

"I wonder where he's at. He's probably somewhere getting cute for you." She laughed hysterically at her own joke.

I was sooooooo mad that I was expected to have sex with the ugliest guy on the planet, while we sunbathed in the midst of a collection of gorgeous specimens.

"Shut the whole fuck up! You make me sick." I rolled my eyes again, trying not to laugh.

Jeanette laughed so hard she choked on her fruity frozen drink.

"Good for your ass!"

I wanted to enjoy the absolutely amazing tropical experience, but I cringed at the constant thoughts of Anthony eventually showing up. While Jeanette blatantly looked at the gorgeous array of chocolate that was all around, I kept my eyes closed behind my shades to avoid gawking.

After a while, one of the servants brought me a note served on a silver platter. It was from Anthony. He said he wouldn't be able to make it back that night and for me to enjoy anything I wanted. I was ready to do backflips.

My joy was short-lived.

"Girl, don't you fall for that shit. You know he's somewhere lurking and watching you from one of these cameras. He's probably watching your wandering eyes behind those shades."

I subtly tried to look around at the various cameras. "You think?"

"You think he just flew us out here and ain't watching his investment? Hell yeah, he's watching—and if he's not, someone else is watching and reporting."

Her words of warning frustrated me even more. On the one hand, I was enjoying our little getaway, but when I thought of the purpose, vomit came to my throat.

Our assigned servants got us formally dressed for dinner in the gowns that were provided for us, as well as styled our hair and applied our makeup. There was a photographer snapping pictures as we made our way down the elaborate set of stairs. However, when we made it to the dining room, it was just me and Jeanette. We looked at each other and shrugged.

The cuisine was amazing. It wasn't only Jamaican food, but an assortment of international dishes. There were eight tall, serious looking men who stood around in black suits with black shirts but weren't allowed to sit at the table for dinner. I wasn't sure if that selection of men was for me and Jeanette to choose from, but I saw at least two who piqued my interest. The scene was scary and exciting all at the same time.

After dinner, we were pulled into a nearby ladies' room for a makeup refresh and then escorted to a lounge for cocktails with the bossy, little, elderly photographer following. He was constantly shouting at Jeanette and me to, "Look natural!"

To our surprise, there were other people of all nationalities there in the lounge. There was also an abundance of drugs, which really had me nervous about what we had gotten ourselves into. Jeanette and I had already pre-decided to not accept any drugs or smokes, and to never let our drinks out of sight. Although there were women at this cocktail party, none could hold a candle to Jeanette and me. The people were friendly, and many seemed to want to network. They came from all walks of life. There were diamond dealers, movie producers, oil brokers, and businessmen from every industry. The funny thing about it was I felt a little bit more impressed with Anthony. I still didn't know much about him, but I was definitely impressed by what I was seeing. I even tried to imagine if I could ever love a man who looked like him if it meant I would be set for life. But in the next thought, that gunfight scene from the movie *Scarface* had me trying to shake that thought.

As usual, I let Jeanette do all the talking because she had the gift to gab. I'd just smile and look cute as she instructed. When she spoke, she made our occupation sound just as important as any of the people we shared the room with. She was also sure to collect plenty of business cards. I had none. That was our norm: she'd always collect cards and I'd question what I felt was a foolish waste of trees. I'd collect numbers if they were cute and I wanted to talk to them again, but I'd store them in my phone.

We stayed in the lounge for a little over an hour before an escort came to collect us and hand us over to our servants to go prepare for the pool party. Although we brought our own cute matching bathing suits, we were provided with the bathing suits we were expected to wear. Basically, Jeanette and I were walking billboards. There was some famous designer there, and Jeanette and I were his designated models and didn't know it before arriving. I'll admit, it was great for our portfolio and social media. It was like the swimsuits were designed for us. They were monokinis. We weren't allowed in the water. The designer didn't want to chance any disasters, so we just walked around and mingled with that crowd as the guests would carefully examine the swimsuits.

By midnight, we were being changed and ushered to yet another party within the compound. I noticed each party had different people. It was exhausting.

The last party was at two, and we could finally wear our own clothes and let our hair down. The music was great. The drinks were on point. The people were cool. The whole vibe was what it needed to be. I felt like I was really in Jamaica, compared to the previous parties. I would get a bit nervous when different guys would come and dance up on me, because I felt Anthony had to be somewhere lurking. I couldn't imagine him flying us all the way out there, thoroughly entertaining us, and then being nowhere to be found.

Jeanette was having the best time of her life as some of the women taught her to authentically wine, Jamaican style. I also wanted to learn, but I was worried about making a fool of myself. I thought I could twerk, but those women made my level of twerking look like child's play. Jeanette tried it, but she looked like a damn fool. She was having fun, so it was all good. It also didn't matter to all the guys who desperately tried to grind on her ass. Eventually, I faded into the background, as usual.

While standing off to the side, swaying to the music and watching Jeanette have a good time, I felt eyes behind me, burning a hole in my soul. I could smell his cologne tickling my nostrils, causing a sensual drunkard feeling within me. I subtly turned around and spied this tall gorgeous chunk of chocolate standing less than ten feet away. I'm five-eleven, and with my heels, it put me at six-three. He appeared a hair taller. He wore a dark suit without a shirt. It was dark, but he had shades on. I didn't want to keep staring, especially when I couldn't see his eyes, so I turned away from him to look back at Jeanette.

As quickly as I turned from him, I felt his breath behind me. I didn't know what was happening, but I felt my nipples harden. He was so close, I could feel the heat from his body. I was ready to turn and kiss him, not giving a damn about Anthony.

"Is that your friend?" he asked, standing about six inches off of my ass. He had an accent. A sexy as fuck accent.

"Uh . . . yeah. Yes . . . Yes, that's my friend," I stuttered.

"How can I meet her?"

I stopped swaying and stood momentarily shocked by his words. I was certain that this man, who was literally standing mere inches up off my ass, didn't have the audacity to ask how he could meet my friend.

That shit had me HOT, and I don't mean in a good way. *The nerve of him.*

I took a step to the side and used my hands to demonstrate the path for him to walk. "My friend."

"What does that mean?" he asked.

"That means, if you want to meet her, you get up off of my ass and walk your ass over there and meet her. That simple."

"Oh, okay. Thanks," he dryly responded, rubbing his hands together and nodding his head.

He flashed what would have been a dazzling smile if I wasn't so angry. In that moment, his gorgeous smile made me even angrier.

I could feel my blood boiling. I was ready to go. I was feeling resentful toward my best friend. As I thought more, I realized that Jeanette had always been the life of the party, and she had no problem mingling and meeting new people on her own. As such, people naturally gravitated to her. The only time they seemed to gravitate to me was when I was next to her—or if they looked like Anthony.

"I'm Vincent. What's your name?" he asked, giving me new life.

"My name is Asha."

"What's your friend's name?"

I rolled my eyes. "Are you serious?"

"What? I just asked your friend's name." He shrugged innocently, as if he had no clue.

Just then Jeanette happily danced her way over to us. "Ooh, I see someone's having herself a good time."

I rolled my eyes. "You ready to go?"

"What's the matter? I know this sexy specimen is not over here boring you," she said, rubbing her hand on his bare chest. "Damn! All dis sexiness for no good reason. Lawd hav' mercy," she tried to say with a Jamaican accent.

I also resented her problem with boundaries. What if I was trying to be with dude? She was just making moves for herself. She had this habit of running up on me whenever she saw me talking to any guy, and she'd seem flirty.

"Good, all that sexiness is just for you," I snapped.

I squeezed past the guy and tried to quickly leave before the formed tears fell. I was really in my feelings. I was in them even more when I realized Jeanette didn't run after me to see what was wrong. When I turned to see where she was, just that fast, she was hugged up and kissing the dude as if she'd known him forever, his hands all over her ass. I was half tempted to go snatch her from his arms. I couldn't believe her slutty ass. I couldn't believe how angry I was. Particularly when the plan was for us to fly down so I could experience *the* anaconda, while she found her own anaconda to experience.

I left Jeanette and found my way to one of the swimming pools to lounge by. The night breeze was delightful and just what I needed to help clear my head. We were supposed to stay in Jamaica for a couple of days, but I was ready to leave right then. I was even feeling jealousy, thinking about the likelihood of Anthony laying up with some other woman—or women—somewhere else.

"Is someone sitting here?"

I heard the voice behind me and closed my eyes to say a two-second prayer, hoping he was fine as hell and this would turn into some happily-ever-after romance. I turned around and figured the devil must have intercepted my prayer. He was a taller, skinnier, malnourished looking version of Anthony, with a mouthful of extra teeth. He looked like a grown-up version of a needy child from a Feed the Children advertisement.

"No, but I was just about to leave. I'm super sleepy, and I need to get back to my room."

"Why don't yuh haff a drink wit' me? You are so lovely. You are my favorite shade of brown. An absolute beauty."

He took a seat on the lounge chair next to mine, smiling his hideous smile.

"How could you tell what shade of brown I am and it's night?"

"I can tell dese t'ings. Please, haff a drink wit' me."

"Uh, yeah . . . NO! I said I'm tired," I snapped as I sat up from my lounging position.

Unmoved by my abrasiveness, he said, "Well, let me wok yuh to yuh room. I haff to know yuh."

"No. I'd rather you didn't. I am here to see Anthony. I don't think that would be a good idea," I said, trying a different approach.

"Yea mon, I kinda figured that. Dat's my cousin. He not here, ya know. He ballin' in Rio."

"What?! He's doing what in Rio? Like Rio, Brazil, Rio?" I asked, jumping up from my seat.

"Yea, mon!"

"Wow! How fucked up is this shit? I need to go pack. This is some bullshit!"

I was really fighting tears then.

"Why leave? Hang around and make the most of your opportunities. He got some really great t'ings planned for you and yuh friend tomorrow."

Frustrated, I sat back down and let the tears escape. He moved over to my lounge chair to console me.

CHAPTER 3

I don't know where the breakdown came or when the drinks started that had me waking up with the sun hitting my eyes and a luscious tongue in between my thighs. I lay there, trying to recall where I was and how I made it there with someone I didn't know. As I became more and more receptive to the mind-blowing oral stimulation, I prayed it was Vincent and not Anthony's ugly-ass cousin, whose name I didn't recall knowing. I didn't remember talking to anyone after him. I vaguely remembered him consoling me, and I kind of remembered a hostess conveniently walking by with a tray of drinks. That's the last I can recall.

In between the electricity that shot throughout my body from the wonderful tongue assault, I tried to open my eyes to determine if I was even in my own room. I wanted to fight the orgasmic feeling and figure out where I was and who was underneath the covers, in between my legs. When I tilted my head downward and noticed the mostly dried up, white residue of cum on my exposed brown breasts, running off to the sides, I knew this little party was about to come to a halt. I mean, it was a lot of cum. And as my senses were returning, I tasted cum in my mouth.

I clinched my thighs together to signal that the party was over. He tried to persist, but I was more forceful in pushing him from between my legs. I was no longer feeling good. I was feeling violated. I felt even more violated when the guy emerged from underneath the covers, and it wasn't anyone I recalled seeing or meeting the day before.

"Oh, hell no! What the hell are you doing, and where did you come from?" I yelled, startling him.

"It was my turn."

My eyes widened. "Your turn! What the hell is that supposed to mean?"

"You picked deh guys yuh wanted and said yuh would only take one at a time."

I was starting to hyperventilate as I held the covers tightly to cover my nudity. "Oh my god! Oh my god! I can't breathe." I fought to catch my breath. "How many were before you?"

"I don't know for sure. Yuh just told me who I was after."

I started crying. "Please leave me. I don't want this. I don't want to be here. I want to go home."

The partially dressed guy collected his remaining clothes and started dressing. He looked remorseful. I felt really bad because this particular guy was cute. I mean, *really* cute. He reminded me of that Jamaican singer, Shaggy. He was the one person I would have voluntarily chosen to sleep with, without hesitation. It was just the whole violation thing that had me all confused.

"Would you like me to get yuh some'in or call anyone for yuh?"

"I need to find my friend so we can leave."

"I saw her leave sho'tly before I come in deh room."

"What! What do you mean *leave*? Like with her suitcase?" I was really about to lose it then.

"Nah, she left wit' a guy name Vincent. I saw dem haffin breakfast and den dey leave out."

"You're lying! She wouldn't do that. Jeanette was partying last night and she wouldn't be out anywhere without getting some sleep. She would not be up this early, had breakfast, and out the door already."

The guy looked at me puzzled. "Early? It's almost one ah clock. Dat's why I offered to get yuh some'in. I figure yuh might be 'ungry."

I cried even harder. He looked like he wanted to run to console me, but stayed near the door.

"Someone drugged me! I don't sleep late. I'm up early every morning."

The guy looked sad, but he didn't deny that I might have been drugged.

"Would yuh like me to get yuh back to deh airport, or did yuh wan'ta wait on yuh friend?" he asked sympathetically.

Everything in me wanted to leave Jeanette. I couldn't believe she would leave out with that strange man and not bother to check on me.

"I have to wait on my friend. I can't leave her like that."

"Okay. Would yuh like me to get you some'in in the meantime?" he asked with a hand on the doorknob.

I shook my head. I wanted to ask his name, but I didn't want to give the impression that I was okay with him violating me.

It was as if he were reading my mind. "By deh way, I'm Ricardo. I wish we met under different circumstances."

I forced a smile. "Do you know where Anthony's cousin is? That's the last person I remember talking to last night."

"An'tony's cousin?" He chuckled. "Nah, mon. Almost everyone here call demself 'An'tony's cousin,' but I actually am his cousin."

He pointed to his chest. "His fadda and my madda were first cousins. All the rest of these characters just like to ride An'tony's boot. I ain't gonna lie; it has its perks, but most of dem are just playing a role."

I closed my eyes. I desperately wanted to know how many guys were passing me around. "He looked a lot like Anthony. I don't even remember him telling me his name. I remember being upset when he came and sat near me."

"Hey, I don't mean to be curt and cut yuh off, but I'm going to step out so yuh can get cleaned up and dressed and I'll be waiting downstairs. We can get yuh some food and talk."

I nodded my head, and he left the room. I was thankful to at least be in my room and not some other random part of the house.

I sat on the bed for the longest and took a good look around the grand room and wondered exactly what it was that Anthony did that afforded him such an extravagant mansion and lifestyle. I couldn't wrap my mind around a rubber or plastic salesman living like this. That website I found had to be a front. Aside from the sexcapade that I had no memory of, I wanted that lifestyle. I wanted to jet set around the globe and have homes all over. If I could have a piece of the lifestyle with Ricardo, that would be just as wonderful.

When I left the room, I felt paranoid with each guy that looked at me, wondering if they had been with me while I was unconscious. My paranoia had me thinking all the women servants I walked by were snickering. I was tempted to run back in my room and wait for Jeanette to return from wherever, so we could leave.

In the time it took me to get myself together, Ricardo had gotten himself all cleaned up and sat on a chair at the bottom of the steps, waiting for me. He smiled as I made my way down the grand stairway with the hand-carved railings. I momentarily paused, again taking inventory of my surroundings. I wanted it. I really wanted it.

After a delectable brunch, Ricardo took me out around Kingston. I felt pride being with him, seeing how well respected he was. But on the other hand, he was well-wanted. The women didn't concern themselves with my presence. Most were rude and seemed to be talking bad about me in my face, but I couldn't make out anything they were saying. He'd tell them to behave and would attempt to politely check them.

He introduced me to a few people as his lady. For some reason or another, that made my day. That simple word made me want to finish what I awoke to with him. From time to time, while we'd be walking down the street, he'd hold onto my hand, but mostly his hand was on my ass.

Whenever he wasn't looking, I'd steal a good look at him. If I looked as good as he, I wouldn't dare tell anyone that Anthony was related. Ricardo was six-foot-three. He was what I'd say, more on the yellow side, and he had a good grade of hair styled in a kinky curl with his edges shaped up perfectly. His smile was to die for, because it boasted a perfect set of teeth. He wore his beard neat. His cologne had my entire body tingling, and his subtle accent added the "s" to his sexiness. For the most part, he sounded like he came from England, but a few of the words he'd pronounce sounded more Jamaican. However, when he got around other people, his Jamaican accent was in full effect, and it sounded like he spoke a completely different language.

I reluctantly accepted his invitation to stop by his house. I was curious to see how and where he lived, but I was afraid because I had no way of communicating with Jeanette, and no one knew where I was at. I kind of figured he'd try to finish what he started when we arrived at his house. I was still feeling funny about the whole awkward situation, but I ultimately gave the green light.

We pulled up to a large, beautiful home surrounded by acres of lush greenery. It wasn't a mansion, and I didn't see any water nearby, but it was nice enough to have me packing my mental suitcases to move in. There were several nice cars parked on the property. I wasn't sure what to make of it until we actually went inside and I got to meet his family. An elderly brown-skinned woman with white hair came from the kitchen and greeted us both with a kiss.

I was again paranoid because I was wearing short shorts, exposing legs for days. I didn't want to meet his family looking like that. I would have worn a skirt. Or better yet, I wouldn't have agreed to come.

"Gran'madda, dis mi sistren, Asha. She's from deh States. Asha, dis my grandmadda."

"Your sister?" I asked, wondering why he would try to pass me off as his sister to his grandmother.

He chuckled. "My friend. Sistren is friend."

I wanted to tell him to say that shit in English so I could understand, but it wasn't like I was in America. I couldn't help but wonder why he didn't refer to me as his lady, as he had when we were out. A downgrade, just that quick.

Grandma might have given me a hug, but her look was icy. She even looked as if she rolled her eyes and turned her nose up after looking me up and down. Maybe she knew my smile was as fake as I knew her hug was.

Lawd! I suspected we were coming for sex. I didn't know I was coming for a damn family reunion.

Not only did Grandma come from the kitchen, but six other family members emerged from different parts of the house. They were all seemingly pleasant, I think. The two he identified as his sisters did this teeth sucking thing as they looked me up and down before speaking with a somewhat fake looking smile. There was a petite woman named Jocelyn, who Ricardo identified as his sister-in-law who was married to one of his brothers, Desmond, who wasn't present. She seemed very timid, giving a half-ass smile with no teeth. The heavyset one he called his auntie also gave me a hug, but she didn't look nice at all. Even worse, she grabbed hold of my wrist, turned me and looked at my ample behind which was barely covered in my short shorts, before saying, "Dick gul." I didn't know if she was trying to call me a ho or fat. Either way, it didn't sound like a compliment.

His father was out at work, and I learned that his mother, the one who was related to Anthony, passed away several years ago.

His sisters and sister-in-law were setting the table for dinner.

"Yeah, uh, Ricky, yuh all be eating?" one of his sisters asked.

Ricardo yelled out, "Yea, Kara."

I wasn't sure if they were speaking about me, but the delightful aroma had me hoping I was going to have an invitation to the table. I was hoping he didn't let on that we had just eaten less than three hours prior.

I couldn't help but notice the awesome body on Kara. Her exposed abs were flat and muscular, and I couldn't remember having a waist as small, even when I was a kid. However, she had a hell of a rack on her and an ass that would surely make a man cry. I wondered if she too had some surgeries, but everything on her looked firm and muscular.

After he showed me a washroom to clean up for dinner, I got to sit at the large table made for twelve. Although there was a cover, I could see the sturdiness of the table was unlike any regular table I'd seen. That table looked sturdy enough to withstand a hurricane, earthquake, and a tornado. Sadly, my mind thought of all the freaky things that could happen on such a table. The thought had me tightly squeezing my thighs together.

Once everyone was seated and the prayer was spoken by one of Ricardo's brothers, their aunt Lucy piled the food on almost each plate. I found it odd that Ricardo was seated on the other side of the table, instead of next to me or directly across from me. Grandma was seated at the head of the table and Lucy sat at the opposite end. I was seated near the end of the table closest to Lucy. Jocelyn sat to the right side of me with Irene next to her and Winston seated to Irene's right. There was an empty seat after Winston, near the end where Grandma sat. Kara sat directly across from me. Ricardo was seated next to Kara, and Clifton next to Ricardo. There were two empty seats after Clifton, near where Grandma was seated, yet I was seated on Lucy's end instead of near Ricardo.

"How old are yuh? Yuh look like a baby?" Grandma asked with her icy stare that would make someone think she'd immediately know if they lied to her. She wasn't eating, but just sat staring at me with her hands folded at the head of the table. Hell, that initial hug made me think I was already in there with Grandma, but everything after, had me feeling like she already decided I wasn't good enough for her grandson.

I nervously responded with a smile, "I'll be twenty-two in three weeks."

"Eh now!" She laughed before the other women followed her lead. "Ricky like 'em young, eh?"

It occurred to me in that moment that I never asked his age. Looking at him, I figured he was no more than twenty-eight, which I didn't see as a big deal. He looked a little tired around the eyes, but I attributed that to his lack of sleep.

"Fadda! Mi haffi always tell 'em." Kara dramatically laughed.

"Dat a mi bredda. Like ta make da ladies t'ink he young. He ah old mon." She hysterically laughed, and Aunt Lucy gave her a mean look before trying to swat her.

"Hush eh no!" Lucy fussed.

"Hey! Weh yuh tell dat lie fa? Galang 'bout yuh business. I don' trick no one."

I struggled a bit to make out all that they were rudely saying, and what I was able to catch was eyebrow-raising. I tried to playfully look over at Ricardo, waiting for him to tell me his age.

"Ba did I lie to yuh? Yuh never ask me," he reasoned, trying to look innocent.

I looked at him as if he were crazy and chuckled.

"Weh yuh come from?" Lucy unpleasantly interrogated as if I was some intrusion, while sucking the remaining life from her cob of corn.

I wasn't sure if I should say the United States or Georgia. Well, technically, I'm from New York but grew up in Georgia. "I'm originally from New York, but now live in Atlanta, Georgia."

"Uhm!" She looked at me in a disapproving manner, before switching her eyes to Kara, and then the two of them laughed.

Oh my goodness! How friggin' rude!

I was hoping Ricardo would stand up for me or chastise his aunt's behavior, but he was too focused on his plate that Lucy had piled extra high. Come to think of it, everyone's plate was piled high but mine. I guess she figured I needed a diet-sized plate.

"How'd the two of you meet?" Winston, one of the brothers, asked. I was extra appreciative of him speaking a clear English that I could understand.

"She's a model, and dey come in fa An'tony's event." Ricardo's face came up from his plate to answer before I could. He spoke with a mouth full of food, which I think is absolutely disgusting.

I guess he was worried about me telling exactly how we did meet.

Lucy leaned to her right to look down toward my hips with a twisted face before rolling her eyes and sucking her teeth, as if she wasn't buying it. "Uhm!"

Grandma didn't say anything, but her expression matched Lucy's.

Kara sucked her teeth and pouted. "Weh yuh can ever get mi invited to anyt'ing?" She turned her attention from Ricardo to me. "Ash', yuh shuh insist I attend dis evening."

Oh, now the bitch's ready to be nice to me? First, she was trying to make me feel like some random thot. Now she wanted my help. I smiled and tried to look polite. "I would love for you to attend. I'm just not sure who I'd have to ask."

She sucked her teeth and rolled her eyes, making it clear she felt I was worthless to her. "Ricky, gimme Ant'ny's number. I call and ask for mi-self," Kara demanded as she hit Ricardo on his arm.

"Lef mi nuh!" Ricardo scolded as he continued to gobble. "Nuh bodda mi."

"Aye! I wanna go!" Ricardo's other sister, Irene, pleaded.

"No! Don't let dem go," Ricardo's brother Clifton warned. "Dem a wan no good bunch. If dey're not drinking too much, dey're fighting. Yuh always cause too many problems and we haffi leaf ta get yuh home." He was very animated when speaking.

The sisters did the eye rolling, teeth sucking thing again before laughing, validating Clifton's statement.

"Big Bredda 'as spoken," Ricardo said, pointing to Clifton.

I made eye contact with Clifton in that second, and it was an uncomfortable feeling. I wondered if he was at the mansion the night before and knew I was supposed to be there for Anthony. I was also uncomfortable because Clifton was very attractive. He was seated on the same side of the table as Ricardo, but nearer to Grandma.

Just then, Grandma slammed her hand on the table and yelled, "Nyam!"

She looked super angry. I wondered if she picked up on my eyes flirting with her other grandson.

I had no idea what she yelled until Ricardo responded, "I'm eating. Dem boddering mi."

After our meal, Ricardo took me upstairs to show me his bedroom, and told me how it is common for families to reside together in Jamaica. I wasn't sure how I felt about that long-term. The room wasn't as impressive as the rooms in Anthony's mansion, but the décor definitely reminded me that I was in the Caribbean. We were seated at the foot of his large poster bed. I definitely didn't feel comfortable when he started deeply kissing me and rubbing one of my breasts, knowing all his family was right there in the house. Despite my coochie tingling, I stopped him.

"Wait! You never did say how old you are. You seemed to skip right over that." I really wanted to chew him out for letting his family be so rude to me—that was, until they wanted me to help get them a party invite.

"How old you say I am?"

I looked at his face for any signs of aging, and took into consideration the hints his family had given away. This man was freaking gorgeous. I was already envisioning what our babies would look like. "Hmmm, I'd say about thirty."

His eyes stretched as he laughed. "Tohti?! Wow! Dat's a compliment. I look in deh mirror and see an old man."

"Old? Not at all." I leaned over and pecked him on his lips.

"No, darling. I faati." He laughed again. "Hopefully, that won't change anything."

I jumped up from the bed. "Forty? Did you say, forty?" He nodded. "Get the fuck out of here! You are not that old. Well, if you're forty, how old is your grandmother? She looks about sixty, sixty-five."

Ricardo laughed so hard. "Gran'madda would love to hear you say dat. My fadda is sixty-five. Gran'madda is his madda. She is sehv'nti-nighn. She was a young bride when she had him."

"Did you say, 'seventy-nine?'" I knew damn well he couldn't have said that.

"Yep!"

I was amazed. I was envisioning his grandmother as a young bride, having a child by the age of fourteen. Looking at Ricardo's almond complexion and his grandmother's mocha complexion, it seemed that there was definitely some Caucasian blood coming from that grandfather. I didn't want to offend anyone by asking, so I just left it alone.

"I think I heard you say Clifton is your big brother. How old is he and how old are your sisters?" I tried to ask casually to hide the fact that I thought his brother was sexy as hell.

"Yes, Clifton is faahti-eight. He's deh first child. Kara is deh youngest. She's tohti-six."

"Did you say she's thirty-six?" I had a confused look. Surely, that couldn't be the case. I thought I was probably older than she. He must have said twenty-six and I didn't understand him.

"Yea, mon. She a crazy gal." He laughed while shaking his head. "She dancehall compete and always get into a fight, ready to cut someone."

I desperately wanted to ask if that was her natural body, but I didn't want him asking if my body was natural. So, I just asked, "How many are there of you in all?"

"There are twelve of us in total."

"Twelve!" I gasped. "You're bullshitting."

"Nah. I have six sisters and five bredders. Most of dem are scattered now, ya know."

"Do you plan to scatter someday, or is this where you will be for life?" I asked, hoping and seeing if there was a future for "us" to consider.

"I go back and faaht' with travels, but I wouldn't want to live anywhere else. Dis is home for me."

"Is this where your children are?" I asked presumptuously.

He laughed, seeming to know I was probing. "I haff four children. Two in deh States and two in Jamaica. My eldest da'ghter is in college. She attends Grambling."

"Something tells me that she's my age, right?" I got a sinking feeling in my heart.

Instead of answering, Ricardo simply stood from the bed and hugged me. He said nothing.

The trip was turning into one disappointment after the other. I felt myself fighting tears. "I'm ready to head back and catch up with my friend," I said, still trying to mask my disappointment.

"Sure. But just know, I don't want yuh to feel hurt or anyt'ing. I really wasn't trying to deceive yuh or anyt'ing. I actually like yuh. I haff enjoyed spending deh day wit' yuh, and my family seems to like yuh."

Now that seemed to be a far stretch. They seemed like they couldn't stand me. I decided to skip over that family lie and smiled. "Thank you. I really did enjoy my time with you, and I'm glad I took the time to get to know you better." Just as we were about to leave out of his room, I turned and asked, "Okay, I have to ask: when we first met, you seemed like you spoke perfect English, but as the day went on, it's like I've had to struggle to understand everything you were saying. What's up with that?"

He laughed. "Does dis sound better?"

I just rolled my eyes and laughed at his attempt to sound proper.

CHAPTER 4

When we arrived back to the mansion and I saw Anthony wearing a jeweled crown on his huge head, a cloak on his back, and a gold and jeweled scepter in his hand, I was beyond disappointed with myself. Especially since during the ride back, Ricardo told me that Anthony was forty-six years old. Vomit rushed to my mouth when he quickly rushed to claim me from Ricardo. The more I looked at Anthony in the light, the more it hit me that he was beyond ugly. Hideous. I couldn't understand what form of insanity would cause me to agree with the arrangement.

"Ah, here's my queen. I was getting worried. I had your attire for the evening laid out in your suite."

"Anthony, we need to talk. What you did was not okay," I challenged him, and watched as Ricardo cowardly eased away without another word to me.

"I know, my love. I had something come up at the last minute. Hopefully, my staff made you and your friend comfortable while I was away."

I was angry but too embarrassed to tell him about the events from the time I left the pool to the time I woke up with Ricardo licking between my legs. I decided not to say anything. I also didn't want to get Ricardo in any kind of trouble.

"Yeah, whatever! That shit wasn't cool. You got us all the way down here and poof—you're nowhere to be found."

Anthony reached up for my head, pulled it down to meet his lips for a kiss. "Don't worry, Big Daddy is here for you now, and I'm going to make sure you are totally happy."

My eyes searched for others walking by that would have witnessed my lips touch Anthony's. I couldn't believe it myself. He patted my ass and then called for some woman to take me to my suite to help me get ready.

When I arrived to my room, I found a rack of clothes that I was going to be modeling that evening. There was this gorgeous white sparkling gown and a crown. I was hoping that it wasn't an indication that I'd be taking photos with Anthony. That would kill my poor career before I could fully get it off the ground.

As expected, the white gown was for photos with Anthony posed in his white tuxedo. After that set, I had to change into dinner attire, which was a gold beaded mini dress. I won't lie, the outfits had me feeling like I was moving up in the modeling ranks. I had more featured shots than Jeanette. We were in an unspoken competition, and I figured with my two extra inches in height, I had an advantage over her when it came to modeling. People were applauding and even talking to us about future gigs. That helped Anthony become a bit more attractive to me. I felt like I could go places with him if I could just get past his ugliness. We did a few bathing suit shots, with Anthony being very vocal in ensuring the shots were classy.

I wasn't sure what was going on, but I noticed Jeanette didn't seem to have much to say to me that evening. She seemed as if she was angry with me. At first, I was just going to ignore her, but then I thought she had a lot of nerve.

I decided to pull her away from the group of people she was chit-chatting it up with, like Miss Social Queen.

She followed me into a deserted hallway, which was like a gallery filled with art pieces hanging and enclosed in cases, and a bench. I took a seat on the bench, but she remained standing with her arms folded, rocking one shoe on its heel, looking annoyed.

"Is there some kind of problem I should know about?"

"Why, do you feel you did something that I need to tell you about?" she answered.

"You seem like you have an attitude with me and only me. I see you're nice with everyone, but act like you have nothing to say to me. I've been worried about you all day, and then you act like you have an attitude with me. What's that all about?"

She laughed. "I have an attitude? No, you seem to have the attitude. You don't think I've noticed how you've been trying to outshine me during the shoot? You kept trying to take a step in front of me and even requested more shots of you without me. We've always worked as a team, and tonight you're acting like you're mad about me even being here. If anyone should be mad, it really should be me, because of how you ditched me last night. I mean, everything worked out, but you didn't know that, nor did you concern yourself."

"Well, where is your Mr. Sexy? I haven't seen him. I thought you went out on the town with him today?"

"On the town? Uh, no. He has a wife and a bunch of children. I think he said nine. He couldn't dare be seen with another woman in public. I'm here to have fun, so I grabbed one of those security guys and had him and the driver take me out on the town."

Still angry, I stood from my seat. "And you couldn't even concern yourself about if I was okay or not?"

"Did you concern yourself with my well-being when you left me last night? Remember, you left me. I didn't leave you. And speaking of which, why did you leave in a huff? What did I do or say that had you treating me as if I did something wrong?"

I shook my head when I thought about how foolish I was behaving and sat back down. "You're right. I was behaving like an ass. Dude comes up to me, all up on my ass, acting like he was trying to talk to me, and instead asks about how he could get to you. That pissed me off."

"Are you serious? That was rude."

She finally sat down next to me. Guess I seemed less threatening in that moment.

"Exactly! That's why I was pissed."

"Okay, I get that he pissed you off, but you still should have said something to me. I would have given his rude ass the boot. Why would you leave me with that rude motherfucker?"

I skipped over her question, still mindful of how she just came up and made a move on him, not knowing what I was going to do with him. Instead, I asked, "Did you fuck him?"

Jeanette tried to hide her face, not really wanting to answer.

"You can be honest," I probed. "Hopefully, it was worth it."

She got giddy. "Girl! That shit was everything. I mean fucking epic! I don't mean to sound like I'm bragging, but since you asked. And then his ass kept trying to get out of wearing a condom. Hell, his wife only has two of his nine kids and six other women have the other seven. Guess he thought I was willing to give him number ten." She laughed. "But that shit was so damn good, I was half tempted. Like I said, epic."

I wasn't the least bit amused. I rolled my eyes. While this bitch was having epic sex with the guy I wanted to be having epic sex with, I was passed out with different random men having epic sex with me. I stood up and walked toward one of the art pieces in the case to keep her from seeing my anger and hurt.

"Well, at least you got your anaconda for tonight." She laughed.

I turned to face her. "Please don't remind me. So, what you plan on getting into tonight, or should I say, who you plan on letting get into you?"

"I saw this one guy that I'd like to try on, but if that don't work out, I'll try on another. I'm going to make the most of this experience. What happens in Jamaica is going to stay in Jamaica. I ain't going home with any regrets."

"Yeah, just make sure you keep yourself protected."

She smiled without saying anything. I wanted to ask if she also fucked the security guy that she left out with, but I was pretty certain she did. Probably the driver as well. As concerning as that seemed, I was most concerned with what was inside of me the night before. At least her whoring was consensual.

Again, the parties went on nonstop late into the night. It was insane how I had to wait off to the side as Anthony played the host. It was like everyone needed to speak with him in private. I decided to venture off to a man-made beach on the property.

I was startled and about to turn away when I saw a couple working it out in the sand. I was intrigued and continued to watch as my eyes adjusted to the darkness with the help of the moonlight. I was devastated when I was eventually able to make out my best friend and the man who was licking in between my legs just that morning.

I was hypnotized and wanted to cry. I felt so betrayed by Jeanette, although she had no knowledge of me and Ricardo. I wanted to beat the hell out of him, because he did have knowledge. Since returning to the mansion, all I could think about was how I'd work out some arrangement to be with Ricardo.

That was the first time I had ever witnessed Jeanette getting busy, and the way she slow-rolled on top of Ricardo had me jealous of her skill. Every now and again, she'd bend to kiss him, but then straighten her back up to keep riding. I watched as Ricardo lifted her, flipped her on her back, threw one of her legs up to align her body, and dove deep inside of her ocean. He fucked her mercilessly, and I wanted every bit of what he was doing to her done to me. The more I watched, the more I hated her. I watched until both their bodies became limp. I snuck off into the darkness, crushed.

I slipped off into my suite, wanting to avoid Anthony. I really wasn't in the mood for his grossness. I still wanted to be with Ricardo and was fixated on finding a way to make it happen. I was kicking myself for not taking advantage of the opportunity I did have with him at his family's house. I couldn't imagine Jeanette letting him out of her sight if that was the guy she spoke of earlier, and I couldn't imagine how I'd be able to get away from Anthony to steal a moment with Ricardo. The thought of Ricardo being so low down to take Jeanette to meet his family the very next day was deeply disturbing.

I had just hopped out of my shower and I heard a tapping at the door to my suite. I threw on a spa-like robe and went to the door. Not sure why I was hoping it was Ricardo to come and tell me what a dreadful mistake he made. Instead, it was Anthony standing in a long silk robe, holding a bottle of champagne and two flutes. My mind raced for an excuse to get out of laying with the creature, but I could think of none. I stepped back and allowed him access.

"I didn't want to leave you hanging again, so I had to drop by to properly tuck you in tonight."

I turned away to roll my eyes.

He set the bottle on a tray that was on top of the dresser and brought the tray over to a sitting area with two Caribbean blue chairs. He rested the tray on the beautiful seashell shaped coffee table.

"Anthony, I don't want to upset you or anything, but I'm really not in the mood."

"You haven't been enjoying yourself?"

"No, not really."

"I know you were expecting to see me last night, but I really was taking care of unexpected business. I would have never invited you here and then not be here. That's not my style. That's why I tried to find other ways to make it up to you and your friend," he said, handing me a glass of the champagne he poured.

I took the glass but set it back on the table. "I woke up this morning with someone I didn't even know in between my legs. Then I learn that there had been a trail of guys before him. Someone who claimed he was your cousin obviously drugged me, and I have to now deal with all of that."

"Are you serious?" Anthony's expression looked beyond angry. "They told you they were my cousin? Do you know around the time or area? Because I can easily find out who it was. I don't get down like that, and I don't believe in making people do what they don't want to do. Sure, there are many women walking around this property naked, but that's just what they choose to do on their own. They make good money doing what they like to do.

"Asha, I want you to know that I am very disturbed by what you just told me. I even had a security team set up to keep an eye on you and your friend, so I'm bothered about where they were while all this was going on. All that aside, I'm gonna be one-hundred with you; you seem like a young lady trying to play a role that you're not exactly comfortable with. I'm not trying to victim blame or anything, so please don't get me wrong. The role seems comfortable for your friend, but you seem like you're still trying to find your way. And to be really real, you seem like the type looking for a husband more than someone to play around with. Am I far off?"

I looked away and thought about his words. They cut me, but they were truthful, and I was living the life Jeanette had created for us. I couldn't really find fault, because I did enjoy the lifestyle we were afforded. Probably how Ricardo enjoyed the lifestyle Anthony paved the way for. I also appreciated Anthony's genuine concern for the events of the previous night.

I shook my head and shrugged my shoulders. "I don't know. There's some truth in there, but I'm not trying to run off and get married tomorrow. I still want to have fun, but I wouldn't mind meeting the person I might eventually marry. I would like a long engagement."

"And there's nothing wrong with that. I like your honesty. But I'm going to be honest with you too. Looking at your social media pages, you seem like you're selling sex. That outfit you wore when I met you screamed, 'Come fuck me!' I mean, you have the right to wear whatever you choose, and no one should touch you if you don't want it, but if you're trying to attract a potential husband, that ain't the way to go. If you noticed, the things you have been modeling the past two days, they were to upgrade your image. You are a very beautiful, tall, statuesque goddess, and you shouldn't sell yourself short. I know I ain't the most handsome looking fella, but you need to ask yourself, if you weren't attracted to me, what made you hop on a plane to come sleep with me? It wasn't like you knew anything about me when you accepted my offer."

"I was intrigued. You seemed cool. I liked that out of all the women you had with you, and all the people you had around, you still pressed your way to me. That meant a lot to me. If it hadn't been for Jeanette, I would have definitely had way more phone conversations before flying out here."

"Do you follow your friend all the time? What do you do to take the initiative within your friendship?"

That was quite embarrassing. I couldn't think of anything where I took the initiative. While growing up, Jeanette was the leader and I was the follower. Even my cousin Sylvia, who lived with us, did her own thing and was capable of taking the lead when we'd all get together.

"I don't know. I think Jeanette has always been like a safety blanket in our relationship. I always had sense enough to not go down bad roads, but I can admit, she's always been the leader."

"Not saying I'm a bad guy or anything, but you don't see hopping on a plane to go see someone you knew nothing about, in a country you hardly know anything about, as possibly going down a bad road? I have daughters, and I wouldn't be okay if they told me they were going to see some random dude in another country. The laws here are very different from the laws there. I'm not trying to scare you, but I just want you to think for yourself. If you are the type to have more phone conversations first, then do that. Don't follow. Be who you are."

I started drinking the champagne. I couldn't put my finger on it, but there was something about Anthony, below the surface, that I was finding really attractive.

He stood from his seat. "Well, I'm going to get up out of here and let you relax. I'll be around tomorrow if you want to go see Kingston or just hang out. I'll have to pull out tomorrow evening. A prior engagement."

"You don't have to leave. I enjoy chatting with you."

He smiled and sat back down. "I can hang for a little while longer, but I'm going to have to bounce in a minute. I've been up most of last night, and been on the move all day. Eventually, I'm going to nod off and I don't want to seem rude or anything."

I nervously twiddled with my fingers for a minute and then said, "You can lie on the bed if you want. At least you could be comfortable while keeping me company."

"You sure about that? If I fall asleep, I don't wake up that easy." He laughed.

"It's cool," I said, holding my glass for him to refill.

"Are you going to stay seated over here? Because then I won't be able to hear you speak. I'm not trying to make you do anything you don't want, but I'm just pointing out the obvious."

I stood from the chair and made my way over to the large bed. He was behind me at a safe distance.

"Oh, I should also let you know, I have nothing on underneath this robe. If I fall asleep, something might fall out."

"There's nothing underneath my robe, either," I said, trying to sound seductive, while my mind was screaming, "WHAT THE FUCK ARE YOU DOING?"

"Interesting." He chuckled and turned the big light off and turned on a smaller night light on the night table. "Would you like some music on?"

"Uhm, I don't know. I guess."

We both laid on the bed. He laid toward the foot of the bed, while I laid toward the head of the bed. While we made small talk about life in general, I felt myself getting more and more aroused. I wanted to be touched and caressed, and I had yet to see his anaconda.

"Can I see it?"

"Huh? Can you see what?"

"Your anaconda. I want to see it."

He laughed. "Oh, you really wanna go there? I think you need to give it a bit more thought first."

I lifted up from my leaning position and opened the top portion of my robe. His eyes stretched to match the smile that he wore.

"Damn! You for real! You sure it ain't the champagne?"

I then lifted onto my knees and removed the belt that held the robe closed, permitting a full-frontal view of what I was offering. The champagne probably did have something to do with it, but it only made me want to do what I was already curious to do.

He approached me on his knees, crawling on the bed. His mouth went directly to my breasts and his fingers began to massage my shaved genitals. I closed my eyes to block out the image of the hideous creature I knew was stimulating me. I parted my thighs to allow his hand to explore further, and I liked it. He wasn't rough nor did he act desperate, as I kind of thought he would. I figured a guy with a slew of women wouldn't be as deliberate with his touching. His touch showed appreciation. His mouth alternating each nipple made it clear that he wanted me to derive pleasure. His fingers didn't rush to penetrate me. They stayed outside the entrance to gently rub and caress. He teased enough to cause my thighs to tremble and my breaths to be taken away. His free hand peeled the robe completely from my body before nudging me to lie on my back. When I did, his mouth went to my navel and he licked while one hand gently squeezed a breast and the other hand continued to tantalize me below the waist.

As I felt the room spinning, I tried not to think of Anthony, but instead tried to focus on the image of Ricardo. That aroused me even more. I lifted a knee with my foot on the bed to part my thighs. I wanted him to explore inside. He was taking too long to get in there. I moaned because it was difficult for me to speak, and I moved my hips to communicate to him that the inside of my pussy needed to be touched.

He made it clear that he was going to lead the performance. He lifted his body up and rolled me onto my stomach. When he did he positioned himself to sit on the back of my knees and he massaged my ass. At first gently, and then rough. He'd slip his thumb in between my buttocks. Sometimes he'd go shallow, and then he'd go deeper, sending shockwaves throughout my body. He lifted himself from the back of my knees and parted my thighs, but continued to use his thumb to tease me. Then he lifted me to my knees as he remained behind me. That reminded me of our huge height difference, but I tried to block out that and what he looked like from my mind as I anticipated his next move. He leaned me over into a doggystyle position. I was hoping that he wasn't going to just try to stick his dick in me without finishing up the foreplay, the way I needed it.

He bent his face down behind me and used his fingers to help find his target. He licked in a teasing manner at first, and then switched to a hungry man who just found the buffet. He lifted his face up long enough to push my shoulders to the bed, allowing him better access to my cave. His hand parted my ass cheeks, as his tongue found its way inside of me. His tongue was thick and pleasing. It would go in and out and then it would push up deeper to suction the liquid treasure. From time to time one of his hands would let go of my ass cheek to massage my throbbing clit. My face was buried into the bed, as my hands searched for a pillow to scream into. Anthony had me feeling all kinds of good.

When he lifted his torso, he allowed his fingers to finish the exploration, and I felt like I had just transported to heaven. His fingers were thick, but not long. He started off taking his time, but then picked up the pace after inserting three fingers inside of me. He was finger fucking the hell out of me as I continuously begged him to fuck me. I had yet to see what his dick was looking like, but I desperately wanted it inside of me.

He spread my thighs apart a little more, bringing my ass lower to the bed. I felt him working his rod up in between my crevice, and eventually inside of my hole. I screamed out in pleasure. It wasn't anaconda big, but it was big enough to get the job done, and my pussy was happy for it. He held onto my hips and thighs as he pleasured himself with my pussy. I tried to block out the annoying animal sounds he was making, so I buried my head underneath a pillow. My pussy was soaking wet from the goodness he gave me. I wanted to change positions, but at the same time, I didn't want to have to look at his face. I was able to alternate imaginary images of the person fucking me from the position I was in. One thing I have to give him credit for, he definitely had plenty of stamina. He seemed to be going like an Energizer battery in that same position. When I felt his thumb start massaging my asshole, I was hoping that wasn't his next move. Jeanette told me how great that was, but I wasn't willing to venture down that road. His finger went inside and it felt good, but still, I wasn't trying to have a dick inside of my ass. I could tell he was sweating up a storm, because every now and again, I'd feel his heavy drops fall on me.

Without warning, he just stopped. He stayed positioned for a minute, but was at a standstill. Then he pulled out of me and turned me to my back for the next round. I tried to keep my eyes closed. I really, really, really didn't want to look at him. I wanted to enjoy all the pleasure he had to give. He munched on my breasts for a hot minute before pulling his train back up into my station. That time he rested his sweaty body on top of mine. I could feel his body on top of me making this weird movement, almost snake-like. The feeling was really weird, but I loved the thrusting it caused inside of me. I wondered if that was his signature "anaconda" move. He smothered my chest and neck with kisses and would lick my sweat. I kept trying to keep my face turned to limit any mouth kissing. As he laid on top of me, making me feel so good, my legs wrapped him to bring his body deeper into mine.

"Damn! Your pussy is so fucking wet. You like this big dick, don't you?" he asked in between thrusts.

"Yes! Hell yeah! Fuck me! This shit is so fucking good!" I'd alternately yell when I could catch my breath. "Oh my god! I'm coming! I'm about to come all over this big dick!"

"Yeah, I want you to come all over my dick, baby. Fuck this dick!" he said, getting more excited.

"Yes! Yes! Yes! Oh yes! Ohhhhh!" I yelled as the earth-shattering orgasm gripped my entire body and locked my thighs around his waist.

He continued to stroke once my contracted thighs allowed him movement again. I was ready to roll over and go to sleep after that one. I guess my body must have expressed that signal, and he took that as his cue to finish himself off. He picked up his pace and had himself quite the workout, providing me with mini orgasms in the process. I lifted my thigh all the way up, to allow him even deeper access as I threw my pussy at him as hard as he was throwing dick. Finally, he yelled out for all of Jamaica to hear. I know we joked about him looking like King Kong, but his scream rivaled King Kong's growl.

My legs trembled for the longest after he rolled off of me and fell unconscious next to me. I laid wide awake, kicking myself for not having on any protection. I was also bothered because I never got to see what he was working with. I decided to enhance the night light a bit, so I could take a closer look at the object I just allowed inside of me, raw. The first thing that disgusted me was seeing it was uncircumcised. It had a deformed shape. Kind of like a boomerang. It was limp, but it did have a good length and width to it.

Like it knew my face was nearby conducting an examination, his dick began jumping while he slept. It became erect, causing this disgusting looking red tip to emerge from the excess foreskin. I didn't sleep around too often, but I had never seen a fire engine red penis head.

Eventually the thing was full grown, standing to attention. I quickly turned away and turned the light back down. I even tried to move over away from him on the bed. I was so disgusted with myself. There wasn't condom the first in sight, not to mention I let him cum inside of me. I was so angry with myself, but when I felt him move up behind me with that erection, I didn't have the willpower to stop him from taking me from behind and making me feel good all over again. I ain't gonna lie—I was really digging this ugly dude and wondered what my life would be like with him all the time. I was digging him so much, I eventually found myself sucking that fire engine red tip like my life depended on it.

By the time he left that next evening, I was seriously sad. I was also mad because I learned Ricardo did in fact take Jeanette to meet his family and they treated her wonderfully. Nonetheless, I didn't want Anthony to leave. I really liked him and he made me feel special during my time with him. I didn't even care when he told me he had sixteen children that he knew about, in different parts of the world, ranging from the age of one-year to twenty-seven. When he asked me about possibly having one of his children, I even contemplated it. I wasn't sure if he was just joking or not, but I thought how it would help get me a piece of his lifestyle. He told me he didn't want me doing any more trashy modeling. He wanted me to take on gigs that would refine my image and allow me to be a role model for other young women.

Although the modeling and hosting gigs rolled in from that point, that was the last time I got to physically see or be with Anthony.

CHAPTER 5

Jeanette was still who I called my best friend, but over the six years that followed our Jamaican adventure, life took us on various journeys. While I was getting modeling gigs and building my brand, Jeanette achieved her dual Bachelor's degree in business administration and finance. She continued seeing Ricardo for almost a year before calling it quits, but she had no knowledge of my "revenge" trip to see him.

I know it was wrong, but technically, he was mine before he was hers. His sex skills were okay, but not halfway as good as Anthony's. I made that trip four months after the trip with Jeanette. I took my cousin Sylvia to keep Jeanette from suspecting anything. We stayed at a hotel and Ricardo met me there for a quickie. Sylvia didn't like what I did to Jeanette, but I tried to use that "family loyalty" line and pushed the fact that I had Ricardo first, but Jeanette took him without any regards for my feelings. I left out the part about Jeanette being in the dark about Ricardo and me.

Sylvia also completed her degree. Actually, degrees. She earned her J.D. in law and was on track to becoming a lawyer. Somehow stuck at 47 credits, I had yet to finish the associate degree I started long before meeting Anthony.

Anthony introduced me to a lifestyle that made me want more than what I felt a college degree could provide me. Although he no longer called or tried to get with me, he did continue to follow my social media pages. Not only that, when some people called about gigs, they would say Anthony sent them in my direction. The distance he put between us was hurtful to me, but I didn't let it keep me from using my imagination to satisfy the urges between my legs.

I thought a lot about how he told me that night that I was Jeanette's follower, so I decided to live life on my terms. My terms included plenty of random dicks, because it momentarily satisfied an emptiness inside of me.

Even though Jeanette was doing her business stuff, she was still hot on the social media circuit. She used her business knowledge to build her brand in a more professional way and was able to book speaking engagements after publishing her first book. A part of me resented her—well, not just a part of me—because life always seemed to work out better for her. In her defense, she did offer to help me with my business brand, but I didn't want to live in her shadows anymore, with her always telling me how I should do this or that. And I certainly didn't want her building up her portfolio off of my sweat, treating me like she was my pimp and I was her ho. Basically, I was cutting off my own nose to spite my face.

Jeanette, Sylvia, and I bought a really nice three-bedroom condo in Buckhead, which significantly increased in value since. Our plan was to eventually use it as an investment, renting the space however we could. The place was spacious enough for us to not get in each other's way. We were rarely home at the same time, and when we were, we thoroughly enjoyed our time together. At this point, we made other friends, but our various circles didn't seem to mesh, so we often entertained them separately.

When I met Brandon a year after we bought the condo, Jeanette wasn't all that supportive of our relationship. He was wealthy and owned multiple businesses, was only thirty-two, and had no children. He was gorgeous and dressed well. The sex was super and plentiful, when we had it. That was the pros. The cons were that he lived way on the other side of town in a really nice house and had a bunch of guy friends that tried to keep him away from me. Even when he, Jeanette, and Sylvia got together to throw my surprise twenty-eighth birthday party, which also turned out to be our engagement party, his friends kept trying to get him to leave and go elsewhere.

After I met Anthony my modeling career took off. I was getting paid very well. I wanted to let him know how much I really appreciated everything he had done for me. I was tired of the impersonal comments on my posts, so over the past few months, I tried to DM him, saying I wanted to see him. He'd generically respond that he'd get back with me, but never would.

Anthony knew about Brandon from my social media. When Brandon would attend some local events with me and we'd be photographed together, Anthony would like my posts. I wasn't sure why I couldn't seem to get Anthony out of my system. Probably because he seemed to still have a hand in my life. I wanted to believe that meant he really had feelings for me, but was just consumed with everything else he had going on in his life. All the men after him were unable to satisfy me the way he did that night. Despite the great sex, not even Brandon could make me feel as Anthony did.

I think what really triggered my recent urgency to speak to Anthony was my uncertainty about marrying Brandon. I wanted Anthony to realize that I was the one he wanted to be with for the rest of his life. Not only that, the fact that Anthony had been photographed with the same woman for the last six months wasn't sitting well with me. I saw that her name was Corrine. She was attractive. Very light complexion, perhaps biracial, with blue-green eyes. Her long, sandy-brown locs looked to be natural. I even tried to study the curves on her body to determine if she too had work done. She appeared to stand just about a foot over Anthony, the same way I did.

I tried to convince myself that she was just the flavor of the month, but now that it had been six months, her presence was irking me. I needed to know more about her and why she's been hanging on for so long. There were photos of them together in different countries around the globe. She was always draped in expensive looking jewelry and fine clothing. That should have been me, but Anthony seemed to friend zone me.

I'd look at the photos of him with this Corrine on his various social media accounts and laugh to myself, saying she must be one desperate bitch to want his ugly ass. Yet, I was jealous. What did that make me? I was so jealous, I started following her, using one of my catfish accounts I created to stalk people's pages without them knowing.

"What are you doing? And who is Rachel?" Jeanette asked, sneaking up behind me while I was on my laptop at the dining table.

"Oh shit! Girl, you scared the shit out of me. Don't be sneaking up on me like that." I tried to ease my laptop closed as I turned to greet her. "When did you get back in town?"

"I just took a Lyft from the airport. But I wanna know, who is Rachel? Why you using fake names? You trying to see what Brandon's up to?"

"He's always claiming to be with the boys," I partially lied. "I wanted to see if he's still trying to get with other women."

Jeanette cracked up laughing. "So, you've resorted to catfishing?

Girl, you better go get your life. That's ridiculous. You think he's seeing someone else and you're wearing his ring on your finger? Maybe you need to give it back to him."

"To be honest, I don't know." I got up from the dining table to go plop down on the sofa where she settled at.

"I'm going to tell you like this, Asha—if you have to be doing all that, you have no business trying to be engaged or marry him. Find you someone else."

"You never did like him. I thought since you helped with the surprise party, y'all might be cool now."

She scoffed and rolled her eyes. "Girl, girl, girl! Trying to keep the peace for your sake and liking him are two very different things. But, regardless of how I feel, the fact that you're creating fake social media accounts to stalk people is some silly shit. It's juvenile and petty. However, I saw you on a woman's page when I came up behind you. You looking for threesomes or trying to play for the other team? She was cute." Jeanette looked at me suspiciously.

"Hell no! I just saw a nice outfit on a different page, and I clicked on her page," I lied. I didn't dare tell her I was stalking Anthony's new girlfriend. Anthony's name hadn't even been spoken between Jeanette and me in maybe four years. She had no idea I was still pining away. She also didn't know that the majority of my modeling gigs were courtesy of Anthony. I wanted to give the impression that I had carved out a career of my own, since she went and finished college and had carved out her own career path.

"How come you're not with your man right now? Is he out of town or out with his boys?"

"He's out of town. He'll be back tomorrow evening. Why, you wanna hang out and cut up like we used to?"

"Girl, I'm so exhausted, I can hardly make it off of this sofa. I need me a hot shower and my bed. I'd prefer a bath, but I might fall asleep in the tub and drown."

"Well, you ain't even gonna tell me about your trip? How was it? You meet any new guys?" I asked, excited.

"When I'm out there handling my business, I'm not thinking about any guys. That shit gets played out after a while. However, the trip went well. Checked out a couple of nice restaurants. Food was great. Had a good turnout at the conference. Pretty routine," she answered, shrugging her shoulder.

"Aw man! That sounds boring. I wanna get out and go somewhere. I don't wanna go out alone."

"Where's Sylvia? She can't go with you? Don't you have other friends you be hanging out with sometimes?"

"I haven't seen Sylvia in about a week. Sometimes I'll see that she's been here, but I haven't actually seen her. She probably got a new man or something. And you know how this modeling business is; there are no friends."

"Ah, yes! How could I forget?" she responded. She seemed to look directly at me and rolled her eyes. She often would bring up my little rivalry behavior while doing that bit of modeling in Jamaica. This time she said nothing on the subject.

"I don't know when you're going to get over that shit. I said I'm sorry a million times. Look how great your life turned out since then. Shoot, I'm still trying to get you to manage my career so we can both get paid big time."

"Oh, I get paid big time already. Guess you forget how many times I've offered to help you build your brand and you refused, huh? Nah, you're doing fine. You don't need my management services."

I was getting annoyed with the conversation.

"You see why I don't like trying to help you? Did you see how quick your attitude just got ugly with me? You don't like to hear the truth. What you need to do while you're earning money from modeling is finish your damn degree. You can't do that shit forever. Your ass is twenty-eight years old. You'll be thirty before you know it, married with a baby, and they'll be looking for the next hot twenty-two-year-old. Not only that, it looks like you might have put on a few pounds. Have you? And your boobs look way heavier, but I know you didn't have any new surgery."

"Wow! That's really fucked up. So now you're calling me fat?"

Jeanette stood from the sofa and shook her head. "Okay, I'm done with this. I'm going to my quarters. Now you're hearing shit and making up shit I didn't say. No one called you fat. You'll probably be out in the morning, and then with your man, but I'll be heading back out of town tomorrow evening. I'll catch up with you whenever."

"Whatever!" I waved my hand in a shooing manner as she walked off near the door to retrieve her luggage and then headed to her room.

I grabbed my laptop from the dining table and headed to my bedroom to finish checking out Anthony's new girlfriend's latest photos. I got back on just in time to see her live video.

"Hey, mi lovelies! I just wanted to let everyone know to get that passport ready. If you don't have one, go get one. If it's going to expire, go renew it. Do what you gotta do, so you can join me for my twenty-second birthday in Rio. Yes, that's right, Rio de Janeiro, in Brazil. It's going to be epic. I'm giving you seven months' notice so you can book your hotels and flights. Be sure to stay tuned for more details in the next few days. Right now, I'm trying to get my party on with my girls, and I'm already tipsy and feeling good." She turned the camera to her friends as they all waved to the camera before she ended the live video.

She appeared to have a lot of friends. But then again, it could have been people she'd just met that night. She had an accent with a hint of British. I figured she must have been from one of the islands. I had it bad. I watched her various videos over the next few hours, until I finally fell asleep.

I woke up briefly to go to the bathroom and to the kitchen for some water, and finally caught a glimpse of Sylvia just as she was about to leave.

"Damn, girl! I was wondering if you still lived here. I don't ever see you anymore. When are we going to hang out?"

"Hey, cuz! Between working and studying, I stay on the move. I'm already running late. But I am going to have to find a moment to sit down with you and Jeanette. I'm going to be moving out, and we need to figure out how we're going to handle this business arrangement."

"Sylvia, are you fucking kidding me? Move out? Where? When? Why?"

"Asha, stop tripping! You knew this day would eventually come. Hell, you're engaged, so I'm sure at some point you were planning to move. I just feel like it's time for me to move on and get my own place now that I've finished with school. It's not comfortable having company when I know at any minute one of you will be walking in the door. Then I have the only room that doesn't come with a private bathroom, so it's really awkward to have company."

"So, you're trying to leave us just so you can get dick? That's ridiculous."

"No, Asha! I'm leaving because we've outgrown this arrangement. I'm leaving because we've outgrown each other. And you forget that I remember what you did to your own best friend a few years back. No, I don't feel comfortable having company around you. Either of you. While I was in school, it wasn't a biggie. I'm about to take my bar exam, and . . . like I said, it's time for me to move on."

"Okay, but we bought this place together, as an investment. What are we supposed to be doing with it? Are you saying we all have to move because you're moving, or will you be paying the mortgage here and someplace else at the same time?"

"I really didn't want to get into all of this right now because I have to get to work, but I figure I could either get a person to rent my room or you and Jeanette could buy out my portion, based on current market value. I'm not going to be paying for this place and I'm not living here. The third option would be for all of us to move. You're planning to move soon, right?"

"I don't know. I can't even get Brandon to set a wedding date. I don't want some strange roommate in here."

"Like I said, we'll all have to get together and chat. I'll text you both so we can set a time to meet. If we have to meet via Zoom, then so be it."

"This is some bullshit, Sylvia, and you're foul for bringing up that Jamaica shit."

"What Jamaica shit?"

Sylvia and I turned, surprised to see Jeanette walking into the kitchen, still half asleep.

"I gotta go. I'm late," Sylvia said, excusing herself from the conversation.

"What's going on? What did I just walk into?"

"She was just telling me that she plans to move out now that she's finished school. She said she's outgrown this arrangement and feels she can't ever have company if she wanted."

I expected Jeanette to be just as appalled as I was, but instead she simply went to the refrigerator and pulled out a bottle of ginger ale.

"Did you hear what I just said?" I snapped.

"Don't start with me this morning! I just came in here to get something to settle my stomach. I'm not here for the foolishness. It's too damn early for this mess. Maybe we do all need to move and make money off of this place."

"You too? How are y'all just talking about moving like it's nothing? Neither of us have ever lived on our own. You know how hard that's going to be, and how expensive?"

"Asha, you're making all that money from modeling. You'll be all right. Move in with Brandon."

"I'm not moving in with Brandon. I can't even get him to set a date for our wedding. You talked to him about this whole engagement thing before he proposed. Did he give you some kind of idea of when he actually planned to marry me?"

"You make it sound like we had a whole bunch of conversations about your engagement. No, we didn't. Actually, we had zero conversations about your engagement. He asked about our plans for your birthday, and when we said we were trying to plan a surprise party, he invited himself into the festivities. He didn't mention the engagement part, or else I wouldn't have let him join in on the party, period."

"I have to ask, are you jealous of my relationship with Brandon? I'm trying to understand why you have such a problem with him."

"Okay, got my ginger ale that I came for." She held up the bottle of soda, looking offended. "Time for me to crawl back into my bed and avoid the drama. But before I go, I will agree that maybe we have outgrown this rooming situation and it's time for us to move out. I ain't with the drama, and seems like you got plenty of it lately, *Rachel*."

She walked out of the kitchen before I could respond. I guess it was good that she did, because I think things would have gotten really ugly, since I was still stewing in my anger toward Sylvia.

I went back to my room to call Brandon again, but he still didn't answer. That was the biggest problem I had with him—when he was away on his business trips, he could never seem to talk, Face Time, Zoom, or anything. I made up my mind in that moment that I was going to force him to give me a date to take place within the next six months or so, or I was walking. I needed to make plans for my own living arrangements, and I couldn't have him stringing me along with a long engagement.

CHAPTER 6

I talked Brandon into getting married in Rio—the same week of Corrine's big birthday bash. He agreed, but he refused to help pay for the wedding, talking about we could've had something simple in Georgia, but I wasn't going along with that. I know I was wrong, but I had become so obsessed with seeing Anthony and couldn't understand why. Once Corrine publicly broadcasted all the details of her birthday extravaganza, I quickly booked my wedding at the same hotel.

Jeanette and Sylvia moved out of our condo, and there was still a bit of unspoken tension, but they agreed to attend my wedding. I had about twenty other family members show up. No one from Brandon's family attended, talking about they couldn't afford the trip. It bothered me that Brandon wouldn't at least help his parents buy a ticket. He claimed he wasn't, because we should have had the wedding in Georgia. However, he said he'd pay for a small ceremony back home at a later date.

I hadn't told Anthony about my plans, nor did I let on that I had knowledge of Corrine's event. I was troubled that Corrine managed to hang on in his life for a little over a year up to that point. I desperately wanted to run into him and have a final fling before I said, "I do." I was hoping I'd be disgusted just by looking at him up close again, and that would help me not crave him anymore. Then again, I was hoping he'd leave Corrine and save me from Brandon, the man I was rushing to marry, to fit my perfect timeline.

Two strategic days before my wedding, I was camped out in the lobby after breakfast catching up with a few of my cousins, minus Sylvia, on the prowl for any sign of Anthony. Although we didn't have a long flight from Atlanta, I was still feeling jetlagged and wanted to get more sleep, but I had yet to see the Anthony or Corrine.

"Hey, lovelies! Are you here for my party tonight?"

Lo and behold! I looked up and it was Corrine, in the flesh. She was with three other snooty looking bitches that stood off a bit at a distance.

"Got damn! You are fine as—Whoo! Damn, girl, you fine! All of y'all," one of my older cousins, Pete, exclaimed. "Count me in. I'll be there."

I tried to play dumb. "Party? What kind of party?"

"Oh, I'm sorry. I heard your American accents and thought you might have come to Rio for my birthday party this evening. Forgive my presumption. Actually, it started yesterday. Tonight is the event here in the hotel, and tomorrow we have part three in a different location," she shared. "But if you're not doing anything this evening, you're more than welcome to attend. I'd just have to get your names to put on the guest list. Everyone else had to register online."

"Oh wow! Sounds really nice. We came just in time," another of my cousins, Sandra, said. "We're here for our cousin's wedding. She's getting married day after tomorrow." Sandra pointed to me.

"Aww, how lovely! Congratulations! You been to Rio before?

'Cause you can't let your groom-to-be wander." She laughed.

I gave a fake smile. "Thank you. This is my first trip. I wanted my wedding day to be special. I didn't want to have a typical wedding in a boring place," I told.

"Your accent, where is it from?" my cousin Jackie asked Corrine.

Corrine smiled. "Barbados is my original home. Now I spend a lot of time in Jamaica. I also travel to Europe a lot. I have lots of family there I'll go see when I have modeling gigs."

"Oh, you model? No wonder you so damn fine. My cousin here models, also," Pete said as he pointed to me. "I take it you got those pretty eyes from your European family, huh?"

I was so embarrassed. "Pete! Don't do that! That is so not cool!" I scolded.

She laughed. "I don't mind. It's the truth. I was born in Barbados, but my family came from Europe. My father was in Cameroon before moving to the UK to study. My mother had family in Barbados, so they moved there before I was born, and that's where I spent most of my time growing up."

I noted how she didn't even inquire about the fact that I also model. Hatin' ass bitch!

"You ever been to Africa?" Jackie asked. "I always wanted to go there. This is the farthest I've ever been from home."

"Yes. We go often. Maybe three times a year."

The more she talked, the more I hated her.

Is that a fucking engagement ring on her finger?! I asked myself when I saw the sparkle as she waved her hand, making my ring look like a prize from a Cracker Jack box.

"That is a beautiful ring. That sparkle is blinding," I said, hoping to get an explanation.

She blushed big time. "Thank you! I got it last night. My boy—I mean fiancé proposed to me last night at a private black-tie affair. I was so shocked. Obviously, I said yes." She giggled, holding her hand up to show off her ring.

I fought to keep a smile on my face.

"You set a date yet, or you haven't had the time?" Sandra asked.

"Trust me, we haven't had time yet, if you know what I mean." She laughed. "No, my baby had to fly out early this morning."

"He's not going to even be here for your party?" I asked in disbelief.

The way my family turned to look at me made me realize I must have had too much emotion tied up into the question. Corrine looked perplexed by my tone. She hesitated before responding. It was obvious she was annoyed. It kind of looked like she rolled her eyes at me before fixing the smile back on her face to respond.

"He won't be here tonight. There's going to be over a thousand people attending tonight. He wanted me to enjoy and mingle instead of being stuck up underneath him. He'll be back for tomorrow's event."

How'd she get over a thousand people to attend her event? In another country, on a different continent, at that. Turning twenty-two is not even a big deal. I could hardly get thirty people to attend my wedding. I would think getting married is a bigger deal than some stupid birthday. But since Brandon wasn't helping to pay, I couldn't have the lengthy guest list I wanted, filled with names of superficial people I only affiliated with for business purposes.

"Corrine, can we go now? We have things to do," one of the ladies she was with rudely asked from a distance. She had a similar accent to Corrine.

"Okay! I'm coming," she shouted to them. "Well, I have to get going. Did you want me to add you to the guest list?"

"Hell yeah! Count me in!" Pete said.

"Me too!" Jackie added, as did the other family members sitting with me.

"Waldo!" she called to a large man standing not too far away and waved for him to come near. "Could you be a dear and get their information to place on tonight's guest list? I have to get running."

Waldo came over pulling a small notebook from inside his jacket pocket.

Corrine beamed. "Well, it was really great chatting with you. I'll see you tonight," she said before walking over to join her friends. Once Waldo got our names, the whole entourage departed.

I wondered who Waldo was supposed to be since he wasn't dressed like the other obvious bodyguards, yet he looked very serious. Was she supposed to be living so large and important that she needed a bunch of bodyguards? Then again, I remembered Anthony's failed attempt at trying to assemble a team of bodyguards when we went to Jamaica that time.

I tried not to look at the back of her as she walked away, but when Pete said, "Damn! Look at all that beautiful ass walking away. I know that must be one happy dude stroking that ass every night."

"Please! It's probably some old dude with a little dick, needing some Viagra to keep it up," I bitterly spoke. "Besides, I'm sure she bought that ass here in Brazil."

"Stop hating on that girl, Asha, like you ain't go to the Dominican Republic for yours," Jackie said with a laugh. "She's cute though, with her little blonde locs. It looks nice on her. She must have them kept up regularly."

Pete narrowed his eyes. "I wonder if her tits are real. They looked real. I was trying not to look too hard, but they were calling out for attention."

"Pete! Get your mind out the gutter. Gesh!" I laughed. "That's all you ever talk about—ass and tits."

"Shit, I'm almost fifty-years-old. You make that sound like a bad thing. Matter of fact, you need to start worrying about where your fiancé is at. Rio has a smorgasbord of ass and tits in all different shades."

"Yeah, where is Brandon?" Sandra asked. "We haven't even had time to really get to know him. Is he trying to avoid your family 'cause he know we're gonna get all in his ass with a microscope?"

"Y'all better not give that man a hard time, and then he leaves Asha at the altar," Jackie said.

"Ha, ha! Very funny. He has a separate room until after the wedding. He knows I'm spending time with my family. Hell, I have the rest of my life to spend with him."

I didn't want to tell them that my darling fiancé was already out in the streets of Rio with his boys. Although his family wouldn't make the trip, Brandon wouldn't dare make moves without his friends. Matter of fact, he wouldn't agree to the wedding in Brazil until his friends were on board.

Later that night, Brandon sent me off to the party without him. I was pissed, but I didn't want to get into a fight and have him call the wedding off, at my expense. I was also pissed when he rejected me for sex, talking about we should wait until after our wedding. I didn't want to believe that he was running around Brazil, sticking his dick inside anything with a hole. Yet, I was becoming even more determined to find a way to fuck Anthony that following day or night.

I didn't trust Brandon, which made me constantly question why I was marrying him. Everything in my gut told me he was messing with someone else, but as long as I got him and she didn't, I wasn't going to stress myself about it.

I was also questioning why Jeanette would make the trip, and she seemed as if she still had an attitude about the moving out situation. During our meeting, since I wasn't okay with having two new roommates, we decided to wait until I moved in with Brandon. Then we'd rent the entire condo to a family or couple, for a profit, of course. Although Jeanette didn't move out right away, she was forced to pay her share of the mortgage for the past three months, in addition to the mortgage for her new home. That didn't sit well with her. Since Sylvia had dirt on me, I agreed to pay half of her portion of the mortgage. I made that arrangement behind Jeanette's back. I didn't want her to then expect me to pay a portion of her bill.

Jeanette declined the invitation to Corrine's party, saying she was still feeling jet-lagged. I thought that was bullshit, since she had been out all day and was just fine. Sylvia did hang out at the party, since most of our family was going.

I thought for sure Corrine was exaggerating with that "thousand people guest list," but it seemed like more than that. The place was packed. The bitch made this grandiose entrance. She was carried in and onto a stage by six shirtless men in a Cinderella looking carriage. She got out wearing a sky-blue Cinderella looking ballgown. And just as I wondered HOW she planned on partying in that thing, a person to her left and one to her right grabbed hold of the dress and ripped it off. The crowd went crazy. A scant, sparkly sky-blue dress appeared from underneath the oversized ballgown. She twirled around so everyone could get a good look at her dress, and then she took a microphone being handed to her.

"Oh my gosh! I can't believe so many of you came out to help me celebrate my twenty-second birthday. Thank you so much! I know some of you are wondering who makes a big deal when turning twenty-two. I do! That's who!" She laughed. "But really, I believe everyone should make a big deal about each opportunity they get to see another year of life."

The crowd thunderously applauded.

She continued. "I'm going to try to make my way around through the crowd, so I can personally say hello to each of you, but if I don't get to you, please don't take offense. It is not my intention to shun you. Once again, thank you, and be sure to eat and drink up. I love you, my lovelies!"

Again, the crowd cheered and applauded.

As long as I had been following Corrine on social media, I never saw what her talent was, other than modeling. She didn't sing or dance to my knowledge. I was having difficulty trying to understand how she became so much more popular than me. I had obviously been in the game longer. I booked gigs and got paid well, but I didn't have half the following that Corrine had. She had millions of followers, and I didn't know why. Although some of her photos bordered on nude, they were tasteful and her privates were concealed. The photos of her doing a split were also artistically done. Nothing raunchy.

"Why have you been staring at that girl all night?" Sylvia asked, catching me off guard. "It's like you're mesmerized by her or something. I heard about earlier, when you were acting kind of funky."

"I wasn't acting funky. That silly-ass Pete was asking her inappropriate shit, and I told him not to do that. Truthfully, remember the guy Anthony I told you about?"

"The short, ugly guy from Jamaica?" she asked.

I looked around to see if anyone else may have heard what she said. Everyone was in their own glorious worlds.

"Shh, don't be saying that so loud."

She repeated it in a whisper and then laughed.

"Whatever! Well, that's his girlfriend."

"Oh my goodness! He's here? I'm gonna finally get to see the dwarf in person?"

Again, I looked around to see who heard as she laughed.

"Would you stop that? She said he flew out this morning because he wanted her to be able to enjoy her party. She said he'd be back tomorrow."

"Okay, so is this why we're in Brazil? Did you plan all this just so you could run into him? He was like five or six years ago. Wait! Almost seven years. What the hell's the matter with you?"

"Huh? What are you talking about?" I asked, trying to play dumb. "I had no idea about him being here until she approached us in the lobby this morning."

"Did you let her know you had a quick fling with him almost a decade ago?"

"Of course not! Why would I say something like that?"

"Well, how do you know that's his girlfriend and he's not here with her and you just met her this morning without him?"

Sylvia was acting every bit of the attorney, and it was getting on my nerves.

"He and I still follow each other on social media. Hell, he still sends gigs in my direction."

Her eyes widened. "What? Are you serious? I thought you were getting all those gigs on your own?"

"I do," I lied. "Sometimes I go on one gig and it leads to another. That has nothing to do with him.

"Have you invited them to your wedding?"

"Hell no! First, I didn't know they were going to be here. Second, I don't know how he might feel about me getting married."

"Your social media pages say you're getting married this weekend, and he doesn't know? You said you follow each other's pages. That makes no sense. Maybe he saw it and that's why he's not here tonight—because he sees that you're here."

"I doubt it. I think she said he had to fly out on business tonight but will be back for her continued celebration tomorrow. She told us they got engaged last night."

"You think she told you because she wanted to flaunt it in your face? You think maybe she knew who you were and tried to play like she didn't know you? I mean, you're in more magazines and ads than she is, right? I don't recognize her from anything."

"It's dark in here. How can you really see her from way back here? I don't think she was trying to flaunt anything in my face. I noticed the sparkle from her ring finger, and I complimented her on her ring. That thing is huge."

"I heard she was gorgeous. How does that make you feel?" Sylvia asked, looking at me as if taking a jab.

"How does that make me feel about what?"

"She got your man! He put a whole ring on that." She laughed.

"Bitch, please! Ain't nobody jealous. He was not my man. That was a one-shot deal, more than six years ago. Come to think of it, I was just about to turn twenty-two back then."

"You think he knows anything about what you did with his cousin a few months later?"

"I could care less. He got his harem of women. What can he say? The only feelings I was concerned about was Jeanette, but she seems to be acting funny lately."

"Maybe she knows what you did and is waiting on the right time to drop her axe."

"How would she know? Did you tell her? I'm sure Ricardo didn't tell her."

"I didn't tell her. I wanted to at least a thousand times. I ain't ever really like her ass. I tolerated Jeanette for your sake, and it helped put money in my pocket."

I laughed. "Well, if you didn't tell, and I didn't tell, then she doesn't know, and I'd like to keep it that way."

Corrine was making her rounds and getting closer to us. She was surrounded by four big bodyguards.

"Damn! She's tall. I didn't realize how tall she is from that stage. She's about our height," Sylvia said.

"Duh! She's a model. You would expect most models to be tall."

"Oh yeah. You should invite her to your wedding. That's the least you could do, since she invited you to her birthday."

"No, I don't think that would be a good idea."

"Your jealous ass!" Sylvia laughed.

Corrine got to us before I could respond.

"Hello, lovelies! Thank you so much for coming out for my birthday celebration. Is this your first time in Brazil?" she asked us, as if she didn't recognize me from just that morning.

I couldn't stand her with that "lovelies" bullshit. I was like old enough to be her auntie. Hell, I should've been calling her young ass "lovelies."

"Yes, this is our first time. My cousin here is about to be married in a couple of days."

"Oh, how wonderful!" She fake clapped. "Congratulations! A lot of people are here getting married. You're like the fifth person in here that came to Rio to get married. Anyhow, thank you again for coming. I have to keep it moving. I have to say hello to everyone.

Eat! Drink! Be Merry! Enjoy!"

And then she moved right along as if we hadn't even registered on her radar. Bitch!

Sylvia shook her head. "Damn! She's a funky bitch. Cute, but funky. I should have asked how she got that little dress to stay up on her boobs like that."

"Fuck her!" I responded. I was glad I had my cousin there with me on my team.

I decided to cut the evening short right when they were about to sing Happy Birthday to her. There was no way I was going to fix my mouth to wish her happiness on anything. Sylvia stayed with our other cousins.

The crowd was everywhere outside of the ballroom. As I waited on the elevator, I caught a glimpse of what appeared to be Ricardo and two of his sisters. Although I couldn't remember his sisters' names, I started to go speak to them. Before I could make it over there, some young girl came and attached herself to Ricardo, giving him a quick kiss on the lips. I stopped in my tracks. They all walked away with his arm around her waist and his hand resting on her ass. I snickered to myself, wondering if she was feeling special that she got to meet his family.

I got back to my room and tried to call my own fiancé and couldn't reach him. He didn't answer his room phone, and his cell phone was going straight to voicemail, because he most likely had it turned off while out of the country. I was frustrated and horny.

My parents, Joy and Arthur, never married and pretty much lived their own separate lives, but even they were getting their swerve on, acting like they were on a honeymoon. My mother was seventeen when I was born, and my dad was twenty-seven. She was sixteen when she became pregnant. I always wondered how he didn't get locked up for statutory rape, since she was a minor at that time. He's another one who loves young women. Pete is his first cousin, and they typically get into mess together, but my mother wanted her plumbing fixed on this trip, and my daddy was more than willing to oblige.

I sometimes wonder if I am truly my mother's child. I say that in the sense that seven years later I couldn't seem to get over Anthony. After twenty-nine years, my mother hadn't gotten over my father.

He left her before I was born. Well, technically, they were never in a real relationship. My dad would see a nice ass and tits on a young girl and hound her until she gave in. I spent the better part of my life growing up on welfare because my father would only help out "when he could." He was a truck driver, but never seemed to make enough to pay a full child support. My mother would tell the welfare people that she didn't know who my father was so she could receive benefits and they wouldn't go after him.

I was about fourteen when my father started taking more of an interest in my life. Ironically, he was most bothered about my figure being so developed, concerned that some older guy, like himself, would come along and take advantage of me. Despite being the deadbeat dad that he was, my mother was always happy to welcome him back between her legs. I honestly don't remember ever seeing any other guy around. I was kind of hoping that this wedding would cause my father to finally decide to settle down and propose to my mother.

Aside from Sylvia, my mother was the only other person who knew what I did with Ricardo after he was supposedly in a relationship with Jeanette. My mother's not too fond of Jeanette, so she agreed that I had every right, since I was with Ricardo first. My mother and Jeanette's mother used to be friends. I can't remember what it was, but my mother nicknamed Jeanette's mother "The Backstabber." Not sure if it had anything to do with a guy or not. Sometimes I think it might have been about my father, since I don't know of my mother trying to date other guys. Nonetheless, their issues had no bearing on my friendship with Jeanette.

Jeanette's parents were from New York, like my parents were. Her father never left, but despite the distance, he wasn't a deadbeat. He made sure she was provided for while growing up and she made frequent trips to visit him. Sometimes, they allowed me to accompany her.

My mother relocated us to Atlanta when I was just over a year old because my father had already moved, and she thought it would help her—us—have a full-blown relationship with him. It didn't. If anything, it made it that much more painful to know my father was close by, yet unavailable.

My father had some family in Atlanta, and they did embrace us. That helped my emotional well-being to some degree. That's also how Sylvia came into my life. She's the daughter of one of my father's sisters. She was actually born in Atlanta into an educated, married household. Her father, who was originally from Louisiana, did a lot to help fill the void my father left.

My mother and Jeanette's mother met when we were in grade school, and bonded on both being from New York. Sylvia was the same age, and we were in the same grade, so we somehow became a trio from then on.

I was about to hop in the shower but decided to pour myself a glass of Crown Royal. I would rather turn up in my room alone with foreign music I'd never heard, than I would continue to be down there celebrating Corrine's bitch ass.

I had stripped off my clothes but then realized I needed some ice. I put my clothes back on, grabbed the ice bucket, and left out to search for some ice. I was pissed that I had to go one floor down to find it. However, I was glad I'd have an excuse to pass Brandon's room.

I was a bit put off when I saw the "do not disturb" sign hanging from his door. I knocked, but there was no answer. I decided to creep past one of his friend's room, and there was a "do not disturb" sign on that door also. Just as I shook my head and laughed at myself for tripping about the hanging tag, I noticed another of his friends heading down the hall in the opposite direction, looking real cozy with some random chick that he was obviously about to sex. That had me really wondering where Brandon was at, if he wasn't hanging with his boys. After I got my ice, I walked back to Brandon's door to see if I could hear anything. Still, there was no sound, nor any answer when I knocked again.

CHAPTER 7

The following morning, I was awakened by a knock on my hotel room door, despite my "do not disturb" sign. I figured if everyone else was going to have theirs on, I might as well do the same. I dragged myself from the extra, extra-firm bed to see who it was.

I glanced through the peephole to see who was bold enough to ignore the sign. "Brandon!" I said, lighting up and swinging the door open.

Oh, I needed him soooooo bad. I wanted to inquire about his whereabouts the night before, as well as that sign on his door, but I didn't want to say or do anything that would get him angry enough to call off the wedding.

"Come on and let's go get breakfast," he said when I stepped back to let him in.

"Huh? You're not coming in?"

"No-no! I told you, after our wedding. I already know what you want me to come in for."

"Oh, this is ridiculous. Come on, I need you. Please, Brandon."

"NO!"

I flashed him a breast.

"We're in Rio. That ain't gonna work." He laughed.

"What's that supposed to mean?" I asked, hoping he wasn't suggesting what I thought.

He was.

"There's naked tits everywhere like it's no big deal. We can go out after breakfast. You'll see."

"Why would I wanna go out to see tits everywhere, especially while I'm with my husband-to-be?"

"Let me ask: why'd you even want to come to Brazil? You've been pretty much stuck in this hotel the entire time. You're supposed to be so big on social media, I figured you'd be out and about, posting pictures of your adventure. And then you want me to come in and be stuck up in a room, while we're on an entirely different continent. That's insane. Get yourself together and let's go out."

My feelings were hurt, but I did as he said. I probably should have just stayed at the hotel. Aside from the fact that it felt like the temperature outside was at least two-hundred degrees, watching Brandon's neck almost break with each passing set of barely covered tits was unnerving. Each time, he'd ask me, "You think those are real?" or he'd ask, "You think she had work done?" From time to time, we'd pass some cocoa looking Brazilian sisters with super long "good hair," and he'd ask if I thought their hair was real, causing me to feel self-conscious about my weave that he long ago claimed to have no problem with. I was also annoyed each time we came upon a store and I expressed an interest in something I wanted, and he would just keep us moving right along. Aside from the snow cone he bought me, he purchased absolutely nothing for me. I somehow convinced myself that he must have gone shopping for me the day before, which was why he was being so fiscally tight. That thought made me feel somewhat better. However, another thing that bothered me was the fact that he wouldn't hold my hand. The couple of times my hand would find his, he'd somehow ease it away.

Since I felt he was treating me like a roommate, best buddy, I called myself trying to give him a dose of his own medicine. "Wow! You see the bulge on that guy? I wonder if he has an implant or something? What you think?"

"Who cares?" was his response.

I tried it a couple more times, and he wouldn't bother to come down to my petty level. Instead, he cut our day out short, returned me to the hotel before lunch, and was back off with his boys. I was kicking myself for behaving so foolishly and not acknowledging the fact that he was trying.

By that time, I couldn't find any of my family at the hotel. Jeanette was gone also. Everyone was out enjoying MY joyous occasion but me. I grabbed a book from my suitcase and took it down to the lobby to pretend to read. I say "pretend," because it was almost impossible to read in that large, busy lobby. There were tons of people. The pool and beach areas were even more congested.

As I sat pretending to read, I heard a commotion. It was the damn paparazzi breaking their necks when Corrine made her way through the lobby. And who was she with? Anthony. They looked as if they were headed to someplace with water. Within close proximity was Ricardo and some other guys. She was steady waving and smiling and would occasionally stop to pose for a photo. For as long as I watched, not one time did I see Anthony act ashamed to be with his woman, the way Brandon behaved with me. Even Corrine seemed proud to be with her ugly-ass man. I watched as they and their entourage crowded into three SUV limousines. Long after they pulled away, I was stuck sitting in the lobby with unwanted visions running through my head of them having sex—the way he sexed me.

"Why are you sitting here pretending to be reading? I know damn well you can't read with all this mess going on. Did you see your boy, Anthony?"

I looked up as Jeanette took a seat across from me.

"Anthony? Jamaica, Anthony?" I asked trying to play dumb.

"Girl, stop! Why don't you just admit, you missed that anaconda he put on you?" she said with a giggle. "Hey, maybe you can get you some more before you say, 'I do.' 'Cause we all know Brandon's getting his in."

"Don't even go there," I snapped.

I hated how Jeanette always portrayed Brandon as a misogynist and a cheater. And despite him gawking over Brazilian tits, I wasn't trying to hear or believe that. They didn't have anything to offer that I wasn't able to give him.

"I thought you were supposed to be happy about my marriage. Why are you still trying to make him out to be a dog? I didn't ask him to marry me. He proposed on his own. I only pressed him for a date, AFTER he proposed. I was trying to figure out living arrangements, since y'all started putting pressure on me about moving."

"Hey, you're the one that gotta live that life. Don't say no one warned you."

"Girl, go on with the foolishness! Where are you coming from, anyway?"

"Ricardo's here. Figured I'd get in a little for old time's sake."

"You screwed him? Just now since we've been here at the hotel?" I asked in disbelief.

Jeanette laughed. "Uh, yeah. Why, is that a problem? He even invited me to go hang out with them at some private beach. Did you know Anthony got engaged? That girl he was just with is his fiancée. They just got engaged the other night during her birthday celebration. They're having a part three of her celebration tonight at the place they're headed to right now. That's by special invite only. Did you get an invitation?"

I didn't like the way Jeanette was looking at me. It was as if she was suspicious of me. I couldn't help but wonder if she remembered Corrine on my computer screen months back. She also had a smirk, as if she was asking to be sarcastic.

"No! Hell no! Why would I wanna go?"

"Damn! Why you tripping? You still hung up on Anthony, for real. I thought he was a good friend. It ain't like you haven't kept in touch over the years. I'm sure if he knew ahead of time that you'd be here, he would have definitely invited you."

"No, thank you. Anthony and I have not had a whole conversation since Jamaica. All of our generic communications have been via social media or text. Sometimes he'd comment on my posts, and that's that."

"Well, why are you so angry? I'm sure Ricardo's going to let him know that you're here. Are you going to give him all this attitude if he stops by to say, hello, or maybe introduce you to his fiancée? You can introduce him to Brandon. Just think, had you played your cards right, all this could have been your world." She laughed as she waved her hand to demonstrate the elegance. "He bought his woman a gorgeous eighteen-carat diamond on eighteen-carat white gold for their engagement."

"You ask me why I'm angry and then try to throw shit up in my face. What's up with that? For your information, I was bothered about something that happened earlier, that had nothing to do with Anthony or Anthony's world," I partially lied. "Brandon doesn't want to have sex until after we're married. This is like bullshit. We get married tomorrow evening and leave the day after. I was hoping this would be a romantic trip for us."

Jeanette cracked up laughing.

"What's so funny?"

"Did you seriously think changing the location was going to change his trifling ass?"

"He's not trifling!"

"Asha, look up 'trifling' in the dictionary and you'll see Brandon's picture. You're so stuck on that married-and-first-baby-by-thirty bullshit. Do you even know how he's going to take care of you and a baby when you have to give up your modeling career? You haven't bothered to finish your degree, and you're getting closer to twenty-nine. What career will you fall back on? The girl Anthony's with—now that's a real modeling career. Everyone knows her name. Do they know yours? You're sitting here in a lobby, and not one person has approached you yet. Where's your paparazzi? Lately, you've been just doing gigs. How long you think that's going to carry you?"

I closed my eyes and counted to ten to keep from going ballistic on my supposed best friend. "I see you're trying to come up with more garbage for one of your self-help books, huh? Don't try to sit there and judge my life, like yours is doing so grand. I'm happy, and tomorrow, I'll have a husband. What will you have? A bunch of casual flings with exes?"

"Whoa, Asha! You really went there?" Jeanette laughed, shaking her head.

"You took it there first—insulting me, my fiancé, and my career."

"Nah, I was just trying to get you to wake up and take better charge of your life. And as for my coins and my books, I'm banking seven figures a year now. Where you at? Remember, I just purchased my own, brand new house with plenty of land. What? Where's yours? Hell, you need me to help you pay the mortgage where you're dwelling. Not the other way around. And the reason I never told you about my finances was because I didn't want to make you feel inferior or anything. I was sitting back in the cheering section, trying to cheer you on, so you could get yours too. How many times have I tried to help boost your career over the years, and you talked shit, just like you're doing now? Believe it or not, all of THIS, could have really been yours if you would have accepted my help. As for a husband, I'd rather be alone and wait than to have a shady one like yours. You can trust and believe, any husband I ever have will be chasing me, and not the other way around. Even when I tried to tell you to look at all the writing on the wall about that shady, bum ass, you accused me of being jealous of you. Why? For what? What prize do you have? Sex? That bum is perpetrating like he actually has something, while his dumb-ass friends are laughing at you for paying for this whole wedding and trip by yourself. Heard them with my own ears. And you can also trust that when I get married, my husband's entire family will be present, and I won't shell out a single dime. Where's your husband's family?"

I stood to walk away. I was pretty done with Jeanette and her bullshit at that point. Tears had already started falling. Jeanette quickly stood up and grabbed hold of me to hug me.

"Asha, I'm so, so sorry. That was way low-down. I shouldn't have gone there. I don't know why I took it there. Let's fix this. This shit's been building for a long while, and we really need to talk shit out. Can we do that?"

I looked Jeanette in the eye with pure contempt and snatched away from her to head up to my room. In that moment, I could care less if she attended my wedding the next day. It wasn't like my family would grieve over her absence.

A part of me wanted to have that clear-the-air talk with her. It had been brewing since the night we were in Jamaica and that one guy asked me how he could get with my friend, and then I saw her screwing the man I wanted to be with that next night. But how do you tell your friend the crime they've been deemed guilty of, they had no knowledge of ever committing? To help me get along with Jeanette and keep our friendship intact, I'd try to convince myself that it wasn't her fault and it wasn't like she knew I wanted the guy who wanted her. I thought going back to Jamaica to sleep with Ricardo behind her back would somehow level out the playing field. It didn't. He didn't leave his relationship with her to be with me. Nope! He stayed with her until she decided she wanted to move on to other things. And to now hear her say they just finished having sex? That was the ultimate slap in the face to me.

My room floor was kind of high, but not so high that I didn't see Sylvia walking from the beach with my fiancé and his friends. She was walking next to him, and it almost appeared as if his hand was briefly on her lower back. His friends walked behind them. My imagination went all the way from zero to sixty in a nanosecond. Then I shook it off, convincing myself that he must have run into her and my family while on the beach, and she just was casually walking back to the hotel with him and his friends.

I left the window to go take a good look at myself in the mirror. I laughed, because I started thinking I was my own worst enemy—the author of my own confusion and destruction. I was a loner, an introvert trying to be a big-time celebrity. I was like a square peg trying to fit into a round world. As quick as I laughed, I began crying from the same thoughts. Jeanette's question took root in my mind—

about how would Brandon and I manage without my occasional income once I became pregnant. Brandon was a businessman, but I really wasn't sure about the logistics of his business, nor did I know if it was successful enough for me to be a stay-at-home mom for our future children. I often wondered how being pregnant would impact my scar-free, perfect milk chocolate skin. I already had a bit of thickness to my thighs. No doubt a pregnancy would increase them. I wondered if I'd become a victim of stretchmarks, forever ending my modeling career.

I often thought of Jeanette's admonishment about finishing my degree, but since my mother was not so fond of Jeanette, she'd be in my ear, telling me to not let Jeanette tell me how to live my life. That would make me think of what Anthony said to me, about being a follower. So, I'd cut off my nose to spite my face and reject Jeanette's sensible advice to avoid being in her shadow. Furthermore, I wasn't sure what I'd want a degree in. I was hoping my modeling and occasional commercial assignments would ultimately lead to some real acting or speaking parts. If I were to take classes, that's what I'd be doing. As I thought more about Jeanette's words, I couldn't really recall any conversations with Brandon about my career desires. Well, I might have mentioned I wanted to act, but we never had any conversations where he'd sit down with me and map out a game plan, the way Jeanette would have done if I had allowed her in.

I opened my door, ready to head back out of my room and found Sylvia about to knock.

"What the hell is going on with you? I hear you're biting heads off. Are you having second thoughts about getting married? Is that what got you wound up?"

"Whose head am I biting off? I just feel sometime people disrespect me and can't handle when I stand up for myself."

"Jeanette said you tried to tear her all the way down, and she thinks it might have something to do with Anthony also being here with his new fiancée. Don't bite my head off too, but is he the real reason we coincidentally happen to be in Brazil at the same hotel, at the same time?"

"What? How ridiculous you're sounding!"

"Whatever! I'm not Jeanette, and I'm gonna keep shit one-hundred here. When you first set the date, it seemed so very odd. You chose seven months and not six months or a year. Not a June or Valentine's Day wedding, not even a Mardi Gras wedding, but an April wedding in Brazil. I thought to myself, why wouldn't she just wait two more months and have a June wedding near her birthday? You know what I did this morning? I went online and looked up this girl, Corrine, and I see she's been posting for months that she was having a huge twenty-second birthday celebration here in Rio on this particular date. You know what else I saw on her page? All the evidence that she was in a solid relationship with Anthony. So, I have to ask, is Anthony the reason we're here? Are you still salty because he friend-zoned you after giving up the ass?"

"Sylvia, if you only knew how stupid you're sounding right now. Please go on somewhere with that shit."

"Asha, you think when I was strolling along that girl's page, I didn't take notice of her announcement coming before you and Brandon even set a date? Brandon didn't want to have a wedding in Brazil, where his family couldn't even attend. But that wouldn't even faze your tunnel vision. I could see if you had your wedding in Atlanta, and then came here for your honeymoon. No, you got us all involved so you didn't look like the thirsty, rejected chick while you stalk that man's life. Dude doesn't want you. Get a grip!"

"Oh my goodness. Are you still talking? 'Cause I wasn't listening to shit you had to say. I had better things to think of, such as my wedding about to take place tomorrow."

"It's not too late to call off this wedding. You don't even love this guy. You can't love him the way you're still hung up on Anthony. You don't even know Brandon."

"What! Are you fucking serious? I've been with him for almost two years," I yelled.

"Doesn't mean you know him or should be with him. What's his favorite color? What's his career goals? How does his family really feel about you—or do they even know about you? What's his favorite food? Where's his favorite place to go or thing to do when he's stressed? What's his greatest sex fantasy?"

"Okay, that's enough. You need to get the hell out of here. If you don't want to be a part of my wedding tomorrow, I'm cool with it. I don't need y'all anyhow. I see family only makes us blood, 'cause it damn sure don't make for loyalty."

"Don't talk to me about loyalty. I've kept your dirty little secret for years. How you think your best friend will feel if I drop those jewels on her right now? She'd probably beat your ass for the principle of it."

I got quiet. I hated Sylvia for always having that hanging over my head.

"Yeah, I see your ass is quiet now. And let me add, it would be really, really tragic for someone, let's just say, your fiancé, to find out why he's in Brazil and his family couldn't attend his own wedding. Oh, and before I go, let me drop one more jewel of loyalty on you: Trust and believe, Brandon is not in love with you, at all. Not even a little bit. I'm not sure why you can't see it. Everyone else can. He thinks you're rolling in dough. A fucking meal ticket is what you are to him."

I went into the bathroom and locked the door to avoid beating the hell out of Sylvia. I desperately needed my mother right then, but I couldn't call her until Sylvia left.

"See you at the rehearsal dinner," she sang out to taunt me before leaving.

I sat in the bathroom long after she left, wondering about the answers to the questions she asked me about my fiancé. The truth was, I really didn't know the answers. Reality was sinking in; I really didn't know Brandon. Most of our time was spent having sex and watching television. We'd eat whatever I had a taste for. We'd go wherever I bought tickets for. The bulk of our late-night phone conversations were sexual in nature.

I can recall meeting his mother once, early in our relationship, and she acted indifferent with me because I said I was a model. She thought it was a joke, questioning when did they start letting dark skinned women become serious models. So, I didn't care about not going there again. The couple of times that Brandon would offer, I'd decline.

I didn't like going around him when he was with his friends either, even when his friends had their women with them. He'd seem more focused on his boys, or he'd treat the other women as if they were super intelligent, making me feel left out or stupid. I tried to be a good girlfriend by not imposing limits on him spending time with his friends, but he seemed to be with his friends too damn much.

I often had thoughts of him cheating on me, but I'd shake it off. After all, it was me he proposed to, not whoever he was cheating with.

However, Sylvia's words about me being a meal ticket stung. I thought about how much I put out financially during our time together, that might have given him such an impression. As my mind raced, I realized I paid for almost everything, despite him supposedly being wealthy. Even my engagement, slash birthday party—Sylvia and Jeanette paid for it, and he injected himself in the planning, but not the payment.

My emotions were all over the place. I was particularly perplexed about how Sylvia would have known all that. I thought back to them crossing the street from the beach and wondered just how cool they really were.

I sat on the bathroom floor for over an hour while my mind raced and I contemplated attending the dinner or not. I was getting cold feet about marrying Brandon, but then the realization of my twenty-ninth birthday approaching was disturbing me. I needed to be married with my first child on the way by thirty, and I only had a little over one year to make it happen. I couldn't imagine walking away from Brandon and finding a financially secure man within the next few months to marry. I pulled myself together and made up my mind that I was going to that altar tomorrow.

I got up from the bathroom floor and took my laptop to relax on my bed, once again obsessed with what Anthony and Corrine were doing. There was no new information posted, so I decided to stalk Ricardo's pages with my catfish profile. There I found one post saying, "Damn! My big cuz is doing it all the way big for his queen's birthday. Love you and proud of you Cuz." THAT pissed me off all over again.

I decided to scroll to see what else I could see. He even had a few photos of him with Jeanette. One was from just this morning.

She was wearing the spa robe in his hotel room, laughing as she tried to block the photo. Some were from over the years. The more I looked, I saw he had a lot of pictures of her, often referring to her as his baby. One of the photos was from one of her conferences in New Orleans, and she was on the panel. He had a couple of pictures of her during that event, but he wasn't in any of them. He was just bragging on her, talking about how proud of his baby he was. As I recalled, that conference was long after they supposedly broke up.

I sat up from my lying position when I saw a photo of the two of them together at a restaurant in Atlanta, dated less than two years ago. I couldn't help but wonder if he had ever been in the home we shared back then. It was obvious that Jeanette had never stopped seeing Ricardo, but for some reason or another wanted me to believe she had. *Why would she lie about something like that?* Although he made it as if they were a couple in love, Ricardo had several photos of other women, referring to them as his baby or his girl, just the same. He was shameless, and didn't try to hide his doggish ways. Instead, he had women on his page begging for the opportunity to also be his girl.

The more I thought about the day's events, the more I was feeling the need to just distance myself from both Jeanette and Sylvia. I would only deal with them on an as-needed basis. I wasn't sure how we'd even gotten to that point, because growing up, no one could ever tell me we would. All those photos Ricardo posted showed how untrustworthy Jeanette was and had me wondering how many other things she'd done over the years to stab me in the back. Her mother's nickname came to mind: The Backstabber.

CHAPTER 8

Our rehearsal dinner was awkward. I had an opportunity to fill my mother in on the latest, so she automatically gave shade to both Sylvia and Jeanette every chance she could. Brandon hardly behaved like he was about to marry me the next day. He seemed so distant, but he was enjoying himself with my father, male cousins, and his friends. Watching my father interact with Brandon as a best buddy annoyed me. I wanted my father to be a firm, put-his-foot-down type with Brandon, so he'd know to never try to mess over my father's baby girl. The thing that bothered me even more than that was watching Sylvia act like besties with Jeanette. I figured she was doing that to piss me off and make me worry about her telling.

I wanted to get away from the group and back to the lobby to see if there were any updates with Anthony. It was almost nine o'clock. Surely, they wouldn't still be at the beach when they had a black-tie event to prepare for. As if reading my mind, Jeanette administered the next kick in my gut.

"Hey y'all I'm out. I've been invited to a black-tie party and have a limo coming to pick me up shortly. I gotta go get dressed," she announced, throwing up happy hands.

Everyone oohed and ahhed. I could hardly believe my ears.

"Is it the lady who had the birthday party last night?" my cousin Sandra asked.

"Yes. They had another party at a private beach earlier. I passed on that one. I wasn't sure if I'd be able to make the event tonight, because I wasn't sure what time I'd be done here. It's still early, so I got plenty of time to make it."

"Will you be safe? You're in a completely different country. You shouldn't be going off by yourself like that," my cousin Leslie asked.

Jeanette waved her off. "Oh, it's not the first time. I was left on my own when we went to Jamaica a few years back," she said with a smile, knowing it was directed to me. "I made out just fine. Actually, the party is with some of my good friends I made from when we went there. They always look out for me and take good care of me."

Leslie shrugged. "Well, if that's the case, go have yourself a good time."

"I wanna go," Jackie pouted. "How can I go? Shoot, all we gonna do now is just hang out in the lobby or in a room."

"Damn! We never did plan a bachelorette party, did we?" another of my cousins chimed in.

Pete laughed. "Well, that's too bad, because we're on our way to the bachelor party now."

"You going?" my mother asked my father and he nodded. "Wow! Okay, we're going to find us some fun tonight too."

Everyone laughed except me. I was really in my feelings. I even had it in the back of my mind that someone might have planned a surprise bachelorette party for me, and I was learning that wasn't the case at all.

The group seemed to scatter after that, and I found myself searching for a familiar face in the busy lobby. I couldn't believe everyone just left me like that, and I was supposed to be the star of the show. I sat in the seat I claimed as mine earlier in the day. It offered a perfect view of different directions. However, I stood up with my mouth wide open, when I later spotted Jeanette emerging from the elevator wearing a beautiful turquoise formal gown and her hair eloquently pulled up. She looked as if she had a personal stylist dress her. I watched as she sauntered off to the awaiting limo outside, accompanied by two bodyguards. It was almost as if Anthony had made the arrangements, because I know she didn't have that gown when we arrived in Rio. That REALLY angered me.

I was ready to pay the world back. I was angry at my family for not preparing a celebration for me. I was angry at my father for being more attentive to Brandon than me, his daughter. I was angry at Brandon for not forsaking the guys' night to be with me. I was angry that my mother would somehow disappear with my father's family, forgetting all about me at a time when I needed her most. And the bulk of my rage was reserved for Jeanette. How dare she? Her cutting my celebration dinner short, so she could run off with Anthony and Ricardo? That took the cake.

"She was stunning, wasn't she?"

"Huh?"

I looked and some guy sitting on another chair nearby.

"The lady that just left in the turquoise dress—she was stunning. I saw you stand to get a better look. That made me stand also. You think she's someone famous?"

"Look, mister, I'm not trying to be rude, but I could care less about her or her life. So please don't ask me questions about her."

His eyes stretched and he held his hands up in surrender. "Oh! I'm sorry. I didn't mean to offend you. Is it okay if I ask questions about you, like your name and if this is your first time in Brazil?"

I took a deep breath and exhaled to help me simmer down.

"Sure," I answered. "I'm Asha and this is my first time."

"Hi Asha. I'm Teddy and a good listener if you would like to vent. Could I order you a drink or something? I notice you don't have anything, and it would be quite rude to sit and talk while I have a drink and you don't."

I smiled. I did want a drink, but that moment gave me flashbacks to Jamaica, when one of Anthony's self-proclaimed cousins got a drink for me. I didn't see that guy have an opportunity to drop anything in it when he grabbed it from the tray and handed to me, but somehow that was the last I remembered of that night.

"No thank you. I need to stay sober."

"Well how about a bottle of water or a juice? Something?"

He was persistent, which made me even more nervous.

"I'll take a bottle of water, but I don't want it opened."

"Ah, I take it you've had a bad experience," he said empathetically.

"Yeah, something like that."

He flagged down a hostess going past and ordered the water for me, and a Scotch refill for himself.

I must have been truly desperate for someone to talk to, because we sat there for about an hour as I poured out my troubles. I even became comfortable enough to order a Mojito, but I still wouldn't allow him to take if from the hostess's tray. Once my drink came, he offered to show me a quieter area away from the lively lobby.

There was another seating area on the third floor. Well, the elevator didn't say third floor, but it was three floors up from the lobby. It was definitely much more peaceful, and there was also a bar on that level.

"How'd you find this? I've been here a couple of days and didn't know it existed. It's beautiful."

"So is my company." He smiled.

That comment came off a bit creepy, but I dismissed it as a lame attempt to compliment me.

Over the next couple of hours and three more Mojitos, I learned Teddy was in Rio, treating himself for his fiftieth birthday. He'd been divorced for a year, after twenty-six years of marriage. He had two adult children, a son and a daughter, plus a stepson. He had one granddaughter. He was an engineer in Huntsville, Alabama.

Somehow, during my fourth drink, the conversation switched to his bedroom skills and how well he would lick my pussy. Although he was black, he said he'd never in his life had sex with a black woman. By my fifth drink, I was in his room, taking him up on his offer, wanting to break his "black woman virginity." I couldn't blame it all on the alcohol. I just needed the alcohol to give me the courage to do what I wanted to do, with anybody at that point.

We carried on a bit before making it into Teddy's room. As quickly as we made it inside, his hand was underneath my miniskirt, snatching the thong off my ass. I mean, dude had the whole thing off in one snap of the wrist. I was still standing while he got his face down underneath my skirt, throwing one of my thighs over his shoulder. He was down there slurping and groaning like a hungry man. He'd used his fingers to part my lower lips, giving his tongue better access.

Ooh, my lord. I was certain I felt an ovary move while he was down there licking and sucking. It was a good thing the wall was helping me to stay in an upright position, because my poor leg kept trying to give on me. Maybe it was the alcohol, or maybe I was just seriously horny, but Teddy had every bit of the skills he bragged.

After a while, he came up for air long enough to usher me to the bed. He laid me back and continued his tongue assault, that time spreading my thighs in opposite directions. My body kept trying to escape, but he would mightily grab my thighs and bring my ass back closer to the edge of the bed.

He ate my pussy endlessly. I wondered when he would take off his clothes and actually fuck me.

"Teddy . . . Teddy . . . Stop. I have to pee. I need to go to the bathroom," I pleaded in the midst of the assault.

"Let it out," he answered.

"Huh? Let it out? My piss?" I asked, hoping he wasn't suggesting what I thought.

He didn't respond, but instead started focusing his suction on my urethra, trying to coax my piss out. I swear I was trying to fight it and actually pull away, but he had my thighs locked in the fold of his arms, and eventually, to my dismay, I felt the endless hot stream being released. He continued to suck as if sipping on a milkshake, while making animal noises. When he finished siphoning out all the urine, he continued on the fluids spilling from my pussy. Hell, I didn't know whether to be turned on or disgusted. He released my thighs long enough to lay on his back on the bed. Then he flipped me in a position to sit on his face. Again, he latched onto my thighs. I wondered if I was too heavy because he sounded as if he was struggling to breathe from time to time.

I looked at the clock on the nightstand, and it read 1:37. It seemed as if an hour had passed since we entered his room, and I was still waiting on some dick so I could hurry up and skip my happy ass back to my own room. He had yet to open my blouse and attend to my breasts. Hell, they wanted to be sucked also.

This dude was taking way too long to get whatever gratification he needed. I had come about five times already, and I was getting bored. So bored, I started itching to go online to find Jeanette hanging out at Corrine's swanky shindig. That thought irked the hell out of me. I felt like Jeanette was betraying me by hanging out with Corrine.

Ted abruptly stopped. I looked down at his wet face and he appeared unconscious. I jumped off of him saying, "Oh shit! No!"

He wasn't. He smiled. "You liked that? You want some of that down there?" he asked pointing to the bulge trying to come out of his pants.

"Why'd you do that? You scared the hell out of me. I thought you were dead or something."

He sat up on the bed. "I noticed you seemed to not be here anymore. You just stopped moving and wasn't making any sounds anymore. I stopped to see if you'd notice. Where'd your mind go? I was really enjoying you, looking forward to getting up inside of you." He grabbed hold of my hand and rubbed it on his groin. "You want that?" He used his other hand to open his pants and release his swollen cock from his pants.

Man, he had a fat dick. I mean *fat*. I couldn't even imagine how that thing was going to squeeze up inside of me without breaking my pelvic bone. That thing made me think of a newborn baby's head.

"Damn!" I said.

He smiled. "You like?"

I remembered Anthony talking about his anaconda. No, THIS was an anaconda.

My hand gripped it. Actually, I needed to use two hands to grip it. I had never seen or felt a dick that fat. I couldn't even believe it was real. While I gripped and inspected it, he finally got around to opening my blouse and freeing the girls from my bra.

"Wow! These are beautiful. I've seen some in porn movies or on television, but never this close up and in real life." He inspected my chocolate breasts in awe, the same as I inspected his fat dick in awe. He seemed just as amazed as I was. I still was having difficulty believing he'd never experienced a black woman in a strip club or something, but the way he examined my breasts and nipples was more like a science project than for sexual purposes.

Lord, I was so happy when he finally began licking and sucking on them. I helped him peel my clothes off finally, and then his clothes. I was kneeling on the bed, slightly bent to his face, so he could nurse on my needy breasts. His hand ran up and down my thigh before finding its way between my thighs and into my wet wonderland. I held the back of his head for dear life as I felt another orgasm about to erupt, while my other hand squeezed the pre-ejaculate from his log.

I was feeling super desperate and horny and ended up becoming aggressive. I moved his hand and made my way to straddle him, while slightly pushing him back to help me position myself to allow his dick easy entrance into my pussy while it was well soaked. It was a bit of a struggle, but eventually, it got up in there. I could feel it quivering inside of me, but riding up and down on it wasn't quite giving me what I needed. I hated to have to say the words, but I think his dick was too big for me. I tried to grind on it, and that gave me some stimulation. I turned my attention to him and he seemed like he was thoroughly enjoying himself. Definitely more than I was getting out of the deal. He continued to fondle my breasts, every once in a while, moving his mouth up to lick one or the other.

My mind wandered to the clock again, and it read 2:18. A part of me was ready to call it quits, especially since I was sobering up, but I needed a climax—not just an orgasm, but a climax—in the worst way, and I wanted it to come from his super fat dick.

I climbed off of him and laid on my back with my legs open, pulling his hand for him to climb in between. He squeezed back inside of me. Although he was all the way inside of me, I realized he wasn't hard. It felt like something large and blob-like inside of my pussy. He was thrusting, but I wasn't getting anything from it. He held one of my legs in the air, as he tried fucking me at different angles. At that point, I was in "fake it" mode, so he could hurry up and be done so I could leave. For a brief moment, he got still and I felt this hot gush inside of me, and then he started pumping again and I could feel hot liquid pouring out and down the crack of my ass.

"Did you just pee inside of me?"

"You liked it? It felt good, didn't it?"

I was ready to die. I was sooooo done.

"Okay, you know what, Teddy, this ain't working. I need to get back to my room now."

He pulled out of me and looked hurt. "You didn't like that? I thought it would feel good to you. I didn't mean to offend you. I was enjoying you so much."

He bent over to kiss on my breasts, while I was still lying on the bed. I was lifted up onto my elbows. That time he used his hand to stimulate my pussy, and I ain't gonna lie, he did a damn good job. Good enough to get me to turn over onto my knees and let him work his log back up into my pussy. He raved over the beauty of my chocolate ass, saying he'd never seen anything so beautiful and delicious looking. Between the dirty talk, his finger playing with my asshole, and the occasional fondling of my breasts, I was getting closer and closer to that climax. That helped me to start throwing my ass at him and twerking it, which he loved. I would shift back and forth from doggystyle to raising upright on my knees. It was feeling good, and his dick felt hard inside of me.

I wanted to try other positions, but it wasn't that simple. His dick was super fat, but it was average length, meaning it would slip out easily. He got such a kick out of my twerking that he wanted me to stand up from the bed and dance for him while he rubbed his dick. He wanted me to pleasure my body as he watched. Actually, that got me off more than his dick. From time to time I'd go sit on his lap and grind on him, either facing him or away from him. I'd smother his face with my tits and he'd try to grab a nipple in his mouth as I teased him. When I bent to hold my ankles and twerk my ass cheeks, he came up behind me and inserted fingers into both openings, while kissing my butt.

Somehow, I was in there having a totally good time and lost all track of time. The next time I looked at the clock, it read 4:47. I was totally exhausted and ready to pass out, but I still needed more. I couldn't get enough, even though he ate my pussy some more, finger-fucked me a few times, and would pound that log inside of me. I gave up at 5:23. I dressed and returned to my room, where I showered and masturbated.

My wedding was planned for six that evening, but for some reason or another, I had no regrets sleeping with Teddy. I just wished I could have reached that climax I needed. I was about to doze off when the thought of Teddy pissing inside of me entered my mind. I cracked up laughing as the thought sent a volt of electricity to my pussy.

"Eew! Disgusting!" I said out loud, and then I conked out.

CHAPTER 9

here have you been? I've been worried sick about you."

I could hardly see out of my one opened eye, but I knew my momma's voice as she scolded when I opened the door. I dragged myself back to the bed and fell onto it. I had no idea of the time, but I was hoping I still had plenty of time to catch some more z's.

"Asha! Get your ass up! I'm worried."

"Mom, I'm fine. I'm right here in the room you just came to find me in. Please let me get some more sleep. Wake me up in about an hour."

"Your father never came back to the hotel last night. It's almost ten a.m. Where could he be?"

That got my attention. I turned over and sat up on the bed as my eyes continued to adjust.

"What about the others? They went out together, didn't they?"

"Brandon and his friends returned last night, but your father didn't return. Oh, and Pete. I'm assuming they're together somewhere." She paced back and forth, sat down, got back up, and paced some more.

I didn't want to have to say what I was about to say. "You think maybe they're out there getting their freak on and lost track of time?"

"Bullshit! He wouldn't dare."

I left the subject alone.

"Well, did Brandon say where they went last night? What time did they return?"

"Brandon said they were back by midnight, and he was trying to find you."

Those words caused me to fill with panic. I had no idea where to say I had been or what I had been doing. Right in that moment, my eyes gravitated to a business sized envelope on the floor near the door. I thought it might have been the hotel bill, but it was too soon for that. I got off the bed and went to pick up the fairly thick envelope. It was a sealed hotel envelope.

My mother had gotten comfortable on a chair. "What's that? You think that's about your dad?"

"No, I doubt it. I just noticed it on the floor. It didn't just come. Maybe Brandon slipped it under the door last night when he returned."

"You never did say where you were last night," she persisted.

"I was hanging out in the lobby at first, and then I found this other lounge on the third floor. It was really nice up there. I didn't even leave the hotel. I did get to see Jeanette leaving out the hotel last night looking like she was going to the Oscars or something."

"That bitch had the nerve to be out there hanging with your ex?"

"Exactly! I don't care if she makes it back for my wedding. I'm kind of ready to wash my hands of her."

"I don't blame you. But I gotta find your father. I don't even know where to begin looking."

I picked up the phone to dial Brandon's room.

"Who are you calling?"

"Brandon. Surely he would have an idea of where they went."

A groggy woman's voice answered the phone. I immediately hung up.

"What happened?"

"I must have dialed the wrong number. A lady answered."

"What?" she asked, jumping up from her seat.

I dialed the number again, trying to be a bit more careful. That time Brandon did answer, sounding wide awake. I was immediately relieved. I signaled for my mother to relax.

"Hey, babe. I just dialed the wrong number and was about to lose it. My mom is sitting here with me, and even she was about to go crazy."

"Crazy about what? What are you talking about?" he asked.

"A woman answered the phone."

He didn't respond.

"Anyhow, my mother can't locate my father. Do you know where he might have gone?"

"Yeah, but I didn't really wanna tell her. I would think he'd be back by now."

My mother's eyes looked at me, waiting for me to tell her something. I wasn't sure what I'd tell her. To avoid her eyes, I picked up the envelope and opened it, because I wanted to let Brandon know I received it, just in case he asked. Shock caused the phone to drop from my ear, and the envelope and contents to drop from my hands onto the bed.

My mother started shouting, "What's wrong? Asha! What's the matter?" Instead of her looking at the fallen contents of the envelope, she grabbed the phone. "Brandon, this is Joy. What happened to my—I mean, her father?"

I quickly assembled the contents back inside the envelope as my mother was focused on what Brandon had to say.

"A brothel? What the hell do you mean? Why would he do something like that? Him and Pete? That motherfucker! I hope his dick fall off!" she yelled before slamming the phone down. She rushed towards the door. "Asha, I gotta go! I can't believe his ass. Why would he do some shit like that to me?" she cried as she rushed out the door.

I was greatly concerned about my father's whereabouts and even wanted to call Brandon back for more information. However, I had an even more pressing matter to deal with.

I pulled the contents from the envelope again, and it was nude photos printed out on regular paper. Each page contained four different photos of me performing various sex acts, to include me sitting on Teddy's face naked and another while my clothes were still on, making it obvious of the night the event would have occurred. There was a note saying, "I'll mail you the rest of them when we get back to the States."

The worst part was, in the photos, it appeared as if I was looking directly into the camera. I ran to the bathroom to vomit. I couldn't believe it. I sat butt-naked on the bathroom floor, contemplating suicide. I couldn't believe the mess I had just made of my life. There were no demands being made, but for someone to take all those steps to find the perfect photos, print them out, and slide underneath my door that early in the morning, for my fiancé to possibly find . . . I knew there was more in store. I jumped up from the floor to reread the note, questioning if I saw him say he would "mail" something to me. I never gave Teddy my address. I don't even remember telling him my last name. I told him I was a model, but I know there's nothing on my social media pages with my address. I was planning to move in with Brandon and had no idea of when to expect the other photos.

I threw some clothes on and rushed to Teddy's room to let him have it. The housekeeper had his door wide open, and it looked emptied out.

"Where is the person in this room?"

She shrugged. "No English."

I closed my eyes, forgetting I was in a foreign country and didn't know a bit of Portuguese. I went in the room to look around, trying to figure out where Teddy could have had multiple cameras posted up without my noticing them. As I looked around the cleared out room, I vaguely remembered him saying he did photography and videography as a side hobby, saying it helped him relax. He said he made good money from it also. I was hearing an alarm going off inside my head, as I thought of him trying to make money from my photos. I also recalled him elaborating on his engineering career, having to do with robotics. I wished I took heed to the alarm when I first met him in the lobby and insisted on drinking just a bottle of water. Or better yet, I should have just got up and left right then. My mind honed in on the word, "video" and I again filled with panic, wondering if he might have one of those as well.

I rushed back to my room after thinking about where else I could run to. My mother was going through her own crisis. I couldn't talk to Jeanette or Sylvia. I contemplated just confessing to Brandon, but for all the thousands I spent to make our wedding happen, I couldn't chance him calling the wedding off. Maybe if he had time to process things, he would get over it and still marry me, but we were only hours away from being married.

The saddest part of it all is, despite all my grief, I decided to further torture myself by going onto Facebook to see if there were any updates from Anthony, Corrine, Ricardo, or even Jeanette. Jeanette never shared any photos concerning her personal relationships to social media. Ricardo's page had one photo of him hugging Jeanette from behind, captioned, "I love this beautiful queen, but she doesn't want me," along with a sad emoji face. There were many comments from women suggesting he choose them instead. Then there was one comment posted just that morning from Jeanette, with laughing emojis, telling him she was going to take his phone from him if he didn't behave. He replied to her comment, "I love you, babe!" She responded with a bunch of kissing emojis and a red lip emoji.

I was really fired up. I had my own fire to put out, but Ricardo and Jeanette's relationship was more unnerving in that moment. Corrine's pages didn't have any info about her grand, secret birthday bash from last night, but that morning she did make a post promoting an upcoming yacht ride taking place in New York, in June. She warned everyone to get their tickets quickly before it sold out. I clicked on the ticket link, and it was already sold out. That got me even more fired up.

When my mind finally returned to my own problems, I thought of where Teddy said he worked, and I wondered how I could possibly track him down. I would even track down his ex-wife if I had to, but one way or another, he was going to answer for what he did to me.

There was a knock at my door. I quickly hid the incriminating envelope.

"Daddy! Where have you been? You had Mommy worried sick."

I stood back to let the weary looking man into my room, and he went directly to lay across my bed.

"I know. I just got a bit caught up in all the fanfare. Figured it was a once in a lifetime experience."

"Daddy, that's not cool. You know how Mommy feels about you. Why would you play with her like that?"

"It wasn't like I was trying to play with her feelings. Hell, I came here as a single man, looking forward to getting some action in Rio de Janeiro. Every man looks forward to an opportunity such as this. I wasn't planning on being with your mother. I just wasn't. It happened, and I shouldn't have let it happen."

"Oh my god! This day is turning into one big disaster after another."

"Why is that? What else is going on? You having second thoughts about getting married?"

"I don't know. This whole trip has been stressful. I've been trying to spend some quality time with my fiancé, yet he wants to wait until after we're married, but we check out tomorrow morning. When are we supposed to have quality time? We won't even have time for breakfast in bed or anything; instead we've gotta rush to the airport. And now listening to you talking about how every man looks forward to being with women in Brazil—How am I supposed to feel? So basically, my fiancé hasn't made time for me, because he was trying to get his last bit of freak on before marrying me? What if he picked up some disease? He hasn't had enough time to know."

The hypocrisy of my own actions came to the forefront of my mind. I didn't use any protection with Ted, and there was no telling what diseases he might have had.

"Stop stressing yourself. Dude seems pretty cool. He was on his best behavior last night. Pete was the one acting a fool and taking me right along with him. I ain't gonna lie, we had a blast. As far as I know, your boy was heading back to the hotel. I even remember him saying something about trying to hang out with you."

"I didn't see him. I know I probably shouldn't get myself worked up, but when I dialed his room looking for you, a woman answered. I hung up and dialed again, and that time he answered. I haven't been able to shake that thought."

My father laughed. "Girl, stop it! So now you're going to convict the man because you dialed the wrong number? It's that kind of bullshit that always kept me from settling down. Your mother does the same shit. You don't want to be starting off a marriage like that, with accusations. Nevertheless, if you don't feel comfortable, ain't no one going to fault you if you cancel this wedding."

I became defensive. "So you're saying I need to call off my damn wedding?"

He quickly turned over and sat up on the bed. "Oh no! You're not going to be raising your voice at me like that. And that's not even what I said. You need to be comfortable with a person you're trying to marry. So, either you're comfortable and you should go forward, or you're not comfortable and need to pump the brakes."

Tears formed in my eyes. The truth of the matter was, I wasn't comfortable, but I couldn't see calling off my wedding, and my plan to be married with a baby by thirty would be crushed. My father got up and came closer on the bed to sit on the side of me and held me as I cried into his chest. He smelled bad—horrible—but it felt great to have him hold me as he did.

Another knock on my door. It was my mother and other members of my family. There was so much fussing going on, and I had nowhere to escape to. I was just stuck in the middle of the chaos as my family chastised my father and Pete for their wild shenanigans, which Pete found amusing.

Finally, I heard someone say, "Hey, we're supposed to be getting ready for a wedding. Y'all sitting here bullshitting, got the bride all upset."

Everyone looked at me crying and came to hug on me.

CHAPTER 10

I sat at the vanity in my bridal suite with my head in a praying position. I wasn't praying, though I probably should have been. I was just so overwhelmed. Disgusted. Everything in me was screaming for me not to marry Brandon, but I couldn't see my way out. I heard knocking at the door, but I couldn't bring myself to answer. I was just frozen in my frustrations.

Jeanette walked in. "What the hell? Why didn't you answer? I didn't want to barge in, not knowing if you were dressed or not."

I looked at her through the mirror and tried to force a smile. "I wasn't sure if you would be here or not."

"I ain't gonna lie, I think you need to call it off, but I didn't come here to fight with you or get in the middle of your family mess. I do however, have someone with me that would like to say hello."

I turned to face her. I noticed a thick envelope in her hands, like the one slipped underneath my door earlier. "What's that?" I asked pointing to the envelope.

"Oh, I don't know. It was at the door when I just opened it. She handed it to me."

I wanted to scream. I thought Teddy was gone, but he obviously was still around, lurking. I slipped the envelope in a bag. I didn't dare open in front of Jeanette. She watched suspiciously.

"Who's here to say hello? I hope it's not any more drama, because I've had non-stop drama since this morning. By the way, you look beautiful. I also saw you leaving last night, and you looked breathtaking." That time I genuinely smiled.

"Aww, thank you, Asha."

That was all she said on the subject. I thought she might offer up some details, but she didn't.

"You could let whoever in."

She smiled and went to the door to open. In walked Anthony.

"Queen Asha! What, you're just going to run off and get married and not even send me an invitation? I thought we were better than that."

He came to where I was seated with a look of shock, to give me a hug. I wasn't sure how to feel.

"I'm going to step out and let you two talk," Jeanette said as she headed out the door.

"Are you serious, Anthony? I haven't talked to you in damn near seven years. This is the first time I'm actually seeing you in person since Jamaica."

"And you knew from that time, I stay on the move and rarely have time to talk, especially without some interruption." He took a seat on the sofa and then patted it for me to come sit near him. I was hesitant but did so. "Are you angry with me? I've kept in touch with you through the years. It might not have been on the phone. I've been keeping up with your social media and modeling, proud as hell of you."

I smiled. "I mean, it would have been nice to talk to you sometimes. If nothing more, I needed your friendship. I wasn't sure how to feel. On one hand, people would tell me you were sending modeling gigs my way, but I think I've sent you a DM a few times asking you to call me or to talk."

"Asha, I promise you, I never saw a DM from you, asking for a call. I absolutely would have. Unfortunately, other people typically handle all that stuff for me. I'd just check in on your page from time to time, particularly when I knew you had a new gig. I'd want to see how you did. You've been killing it, and I've been so proud of you." He stood up and held his arms out to the side. "Look at me right now; I don't typically carry phones or anything. Like I said, other people handle that." He sat back down. "I noticed a while back, there was something about you getting engaged. I think I might have even liked that post. I was happy for you. I remembered you saying you wanted to start a family by the age of thirty."

"Damn! You remembered that?" I laughed.

"Of course. You will always have a special place in my heart, and I remember everything. And if you ever, ever need anything, don't hesitate to let me know."

"How? I already tried that."

"I'm not trying to toot my own horn or anything, but it's crazy how many women be hitting my DM asking for calls. My staff probably lumped you in with them. I'll have someone send you my secretary's number, so at least you can get someone live. If I don't call you back within twenty-four hours, just try again. Don't get all prideful. Sometimes I do have the intention to do things, but forget. You know a brother's getting old." He laughed.

"Thank you. I appreciate it." I smiled. "By the way, I heard you're also getting married."

He shook his head. "Yeah, I think it's time for me to take that leap. I wish you could meet her. I think you'd like her. She makes me so damn happy. And more important, she's not insecure and knows to give me enough space to handle my business."

"I met her the other day. She invited us to her birthday party. She thought we were here for her party. I take it she's very popular. There were a lot of people there."

"Yeah, she has a big following. Her family is from different parts of the globe, so that helps her visibility. Of course, when they see she's doing things, they make a bigger deal about it to people they know. As a result, she blew up. She also models while she's finishing up with school. She doesn't have to model, but I like that she wants her own life."

"Oh wow! She's in school? How does she manage?"

"She only has a few more months and then she'll have her Master's degree."

I almost choked. "Master's? She looks super young. Didn't she just celebrate her twenty-second birthday?"

"I forgot to add, she's super smart. Yeah, she hit those books big time. I told her she should share stuff like that on social media so people don't think she's some airhead. I told her our people need to see we are about getting degrees and owning businesses, as well as pulling others up when we get success. She decided she'll share when she's done and have a big graduation event. I liked that idea."

The more he talked, the more I hated Corrine. Even more than I had already hated her.

"So, you have plans for any more children? Didn't you have a few already?"

"She doesn't want any anytime soon. She likes doing mission work, and working with sick and hungry people living in Third World conditions. She wants to start a foundation when she's done with school. So, no time for babies."

"How do your kids feel about her?"

"Everybody's cool, but of course I have to deal with some hate from the mothers. Oh, I don't know if you know, I'm up to twenty-one now."

I looked at him perplexed. "Children?"

"Yep! Got me a whole tribe. You should have had my baby, you know. You would have been set for life."

I laughed and gasped at the same time. "I never heard from or saw you again. How? What, you were going to mail me a semen specimen?" I joked.

He laughed.

"So, will you be giving up all other women once you get married? Or will there be a chance of number twenty-two and twenty-three with someone else?"

He shrugged. "Hey, she knows how it is and will probably always be. I'm not going to lie to her, and she doesn't be questioning anything. She said she'd prefer not to ask, just as long as I treat her as my queen and anyone else know their place."

"Oh my! Wow! Nah, I don't think I could handle such an arrangement. Do you expect her to be faithful while you're out doing whatever?"

"I don't ask her what she's doing. I'm sure there's others."

"Are you freakin' serious?! So, you're okay with your wife—your queen—being touched on by other men?"

"I don't get hung up on shit like that. I'm not going to put barriers on her that's not applicable to me."

"Then why get married?"

"Why do people enter into a marriage knowing they're entering it with a suitcase filled with lies and skeletons? I wouldn't be surprised that you're about to walk down that aisle and got some secret shit you'd hate for your husband to know, and I'm sure he has some just the same. People have to use a lot of energy to hide those lies, and when you think about it, it's a house of cards. I don't want that for my life or my wife. Who knows, I might get married and decide I don't want to be with anyone else ever again. That would be my choice. I wouldn't even make her lie to me, saying she won't be with anyone else. Like I said, I'd rather build my marriage without lies or deception. Speaking of which, when I heard you were getting married today, and you knew I was here, but wouldn't extend an invitation, I wondered if that was because you didn't want hubby to know about me—us?"

I stood up and paced a bit before answering. "No, he doesn't know anything about you, about that. Well, he just knows that you are a business acquaintance from long ago."

Anthony laughed. "Well, I guess that's kind of true. So, he doesn't know you came to Jamaica to see me?"

"He thinks I went to Jamaica for a modeling gig. Technically, that also was kind of true. I just didn't know about the modeling gig before I arrived." I laughed.

"Okay. Well, whatever works for you. Does he think you're a virgin or something? He has to know you've been with other guys before him, right? Or did you lie about that as well?"

I shook my head and laughed. "No, he doesn't think I was a virgin. But since we're on the subject, can I tell you something?" I asked sitting back down.

"What, that nobody has been able to put it on you the way the anaconda put it on you?" He laughed.

My mouth opened. I couldn't believe he said what I wanted to tell him. "That is the truth, though. It's crazy. I guess that's why I've really been wanting to talk to you through these years. I'd try to analyze what you did differently, that made me feel the way I felt." My gaze wandered off to that time as my body reminisced that sensational feeling he provided. "Since then, I have struggled with why you never wanted to be with me like that again. Why'd you friend-zone me?"

"Wow! That's deep. I didn't know you felt that way. I definitely wish we would have talked before now." He sighed and rubbed his excessive forehead. "Asha, there were a few things. One, I knew you didn't really want to be with me and was only there at the urging of your friend. The sex, as I can recall, didn't seem natural. I remember your telling me you didn't even want to, but then next thing, you're on me.

"Another thing was what you told me happened to you the previous night. I ended up watching the footage of who all went into your room that night. That hurt my heart. I was crushed, and all of those dudes got properly dealt with. It was hard to be around you after that or even talk to you, but I always felt like I owed you and had to make it up to you. I just couldn't face you. I won't lie; I probably wouldn't be facing you now if your friend didn't just drag me here to talk. I'm actually glad she did. I will always care about you, respect you, and look out for you. She said you never finished school. I think you need to do that, especially since you're now trying to get married and have children. That's going to cut into your modeling, and you need something to fall back on. The last thing you want is to have yourself in a position to depend on any man. So many women have kids, depend on a man for their coins, and next thing he's beating her ass, disrespecting her, and she doesn't know how to get out."

He paused to dig inside his jacket pocket and pulled out an envelope.

"I was going to have this sent to you, since I wasn't expecting to see you. This is not to relieve my guilty conscience or anything, but I want you to always have your own separate bank account that he doesn't know about. I'm telling you exactly like I'd tell my own daughters. Sit it in the bank and let it draw interest or whatever, but it'll be there if and whenever you have a need."

He put the envelope in my hand. I wanted to wait to open it, but then I couldn't help but wonder. I peeped in the envelope and there was a cashier's check for $50,000. I gasped.

"Oh Anthony, I can't accept this. This is way too much."

"Okay, so you have millions sitting in banks around the globe and don't need my measly chump change?" He chuckled. "Trust me, I spend more than that on bottle service or strippers. Don't make us part on bad terms, with you insulting me now."

I cried. He reached over and hugged me.

"Asha, you're a diamond in the rough. Never forget how precious you are. I heard dude you're about to marry is a bit questionable. Just don't lose focus of how precious and valuable you are. And if it doesn't work out, then chalk it up to an experience and keep it moving. As long as you got me as a friend, your back will always be covered."

Anthony was still holding me when one of my cousins, Martha, just barged in.

"Okay! What's going on in here? Did you forget you're supposed to be getting married right now?" She gave Anthony a dirty look.

"Martha, this is a longtime friend and business associate. That was his fiancée's big birthday party y'all were at the other night." I laughed as I got up to clean up my face.

"Oh! Well, damn! Okay. Anyhow, you need to come on. I'm hungry and getting cranky, and we're waiting on you. When your momma came out long ago, she said you just needed a few minutes and would be right out."

Anthony stood to leave. "Asha, I'm going to get on out of here. Best wishes and congratulations."

"You're welcome to stay, if you'd like."

"Thanks, but I gotta fly out in a few. I need to catch me a quick nap."

I went to hug him. It felt awkward hugging him in a standing position. His head came to my breasts.

"Take care and be safe."

Then he was out the door.

"Asha, who was that ugly creature? Where you know him from? Eew, that is one ugly something."

"Girl, stop it! That ugly creature, as you call it, helps me keep a full modeling schedule."

"Oh, so he's like your agent?"

I hadn't thought about him in that manner before, but I guess that's just what he had been for me. "Yep!"

"Shit! Maybe he could help me."

I laughed.

"You laughing and I'm serious. Shoot, I always wanted to be on TV or something. I think I can act."

"Martha, my wedding. You're hungry, remember?"

"Oh yeah. I'm gonna let them know you're really coming now."

"Thank you."

I couldn't stop smiling after Martha left out. I wanted to hug Jeanette and thank her for giving me the one thing I've been needing for so long. Closure. I even felt guilty about how I treated her. I was having a change of heart and wanted things to work out for her and

Ricardo. I wanted her to be happy. I couldn't remember the last time I've wanted that for her.

My smile quickly faded as I went to put the envelope from Anthony in my bag and found the other envelope still waiting for me to open. My heart was racing. Sure enough, there were even more photos from Teddy. Although I didn't give him a blow job, I had put my mouth down there, in a joking manner, to demonstrate how his dick was too fat to even get inside my mouth. You wouldn't know that from the photo. It looked like I was good into it, and my mouth was wide open. Underneath that picture, there was a caption, "How do you think your husband will feel knowing your mouth was on this just before you kissed his lips to say, 'I do?'"

I had to take a seat. I was about to fall to pieces. I heard a knock and rushed to put the papers back in the envelope and back in my bag. I quickly checked my face and ran out to get married.

CHAPTER 11

oming down the aisle, Brandon looked way more nervous than I did. I felt like I wanted to throw up. Every fiber of my being was telling me to run.

The room was nicely decorated, and the setup was intimate. The hotel had the divider set up, and one side functioned for the ceremony seating, while the other side was set to function for the reception. I noticed Sylvia was sitting in the back, looking as if she was thoroughly pissed about something. I smiled when her eyes connected to mine, but she rolled her eyes and picked her fingernails. I couldn't believe she was still angry with me from the night before. Matter of fact, I couldn't even remember what we argued about. We're family. We fuss and fight and we kiss and make up. I looked to the other side of the aisle and was shocked. There sat Ricardo, smiling. I was half happy to see him. It was time for me to bury my hard feelings, and what better occasion to do so than this one? My mother and father sat on the front row, holding hands. I wanted to laugh at their insanity.

By the time I reached Brandon, he had a nervous smile, but looked like he might have been happy. The officiant asked who gives the bride, and my father stood to give me away. As my father returned to his seat, Sylvia decided to make a very loud departure from the room. Everyone turned and some gasped. Brandon looked really concerned. Her behavior really had me racking my brain to figure out what I might have said to make her that angry. I wanted to stop the wedding and run after her. Then I recalled our fight being about her asking me not to marry Brandon. I rolled my eyes and shook her from my thoughts. I couldn't believe she'd get like that and couldn't be happy for and celebrate me. When she passed her bar exam, I helped throw her a big party, knowing it was cutting into my wedding budget. And now she wanted to do this shit? *Bitch!*

My mind raced while the officiant talked. I was focused enough when it was time for us to say, "I do." But right at that moment, a noise at the door caused us all to turn around. At first, I figured it was Sylvia coming back and was going to ignore it, but I turned just in time to see Teddy leaving. I almost fainted but managed to say, "I do." I was holding Brandon's hand for dear life and tried not to look at his eyes. I figured he'd just assume it was wedding jitters. His hand was clammy. It seemed he was holding my hand just as tight. We had to let go to exchange rings. My hand was shaking terribly. So was his. Some people laughed at our nervousness. We were pronounced husband and wife. After that, Brandon kissed me. He was trying to get a whole, passionate kiss, but I couldn't stop thinking about the photo Teddy sent, and I cut the kiss.

As we turned to exit, I noticed an envelope sitting on an empty seat in the back. It wasn't one of the hotel envelopes like the others. It was a greeting card envelope, undoubtedly left by Teddy. I tried to subtly grab the envelope as we passed, and used it like a fan. It felt like a card, but something was definitely inside the card. Aside from Corrine, I don't think I've ever hated anyone as much as I hated Teddy. Since modeling, I've even had a few stalkers, but this took the cake. I thought about just telling Brandon so Teddy wouldn't be able to blackmail me, but I would wait until we were back home and away from everyone.

Everyone came to congratulate us as we stood in the back. When my eyes met Ricardo's eyes as he approached, smiling, holding on to Jeanette's hand, I realized at that second, I wasn't over him after all. He looked so handsome. He shook Brandon's hand and then hugged me. He smelled delightful. I hadn't realized I closed my eyes, because when I opened them, Jeanette's stretched eyes was looking at me oddly, and her opened mouth looked as if to let me know I had a lot of nerve . . . but she was still smiling.

"Congratulations?" she said as a question, still with a smile. "Hope you get everything you deserve."

"Thank you," I said as I hugged her. Her hug seemed fake and forced, as I could feel her body tense up when I hugged her.

The event manager ushered our guests to the other side of the partition for the reception. Brandon and I hung back for photos.

"Well, Mrs. Harper, we are married. You happy?" Brandon asked in a borderline insulting way.

"Of course I am. Why would you ask me that?"

"Why so defensive? I was just asking if you're happy. You got the wedding you wanted, so I'm hoping you're happy." He kissed me. "Oh, and what was up with that peck you gave me when it was time for me to kiss you? It's not like we ain't swap slob in front of others before."

I forced a smile. "I don't know. I was just super nervous. When I first came in the room, I felt like I was going to throw up. While we were standing up there, I felt like I was going to faint. I also felt your clammy hands." I chuckled to sound convincing. "I guess I wasn't the only one nervous."

"Hell yeah, I was nervous. Never thought in a million years I'd be lassoed."

"Lassoed? You feel trapped?"

"Absolutely not. I asked you, remember?"

"Well, yeah, but I had to pressure you for a date, remember?"

"I got scared after I proposed, but I knew what I wanted."

"Aww, baby!" That time I gave him the real kiss. "And yes, I am very happy. Thank you for helping make this fairytale possible for me."

"Fairytale? I would have figured you'd want to get married in a big church with thousands of people, wearing the biggest dress you could find, and like five outfit changes throughout the night. A limo would have taken us from the church, dragging cans, announcing, 'Just Married,' and we would have been transported to a huge reception, at the convention center or something of that size. I would have expected a band and a deejay. Then we'd ride off in a limo to the airport to head to our honeymoon, while we'd sneak and get busy in the bathroom on the airplane. That's what I figured would be your fairytale."

"Aww, that sounds so sweet and romantic. I kind of wish we did do that instead. I hate that your family wasn't here. That hurts me. Now I'll always feel they hate me."

"It doesn't matter what they think or feel. My feeling is the only one that matters." He kissed me again.

I was still trying to hold on to that envelope for dear life. Each time I'd put it down for a photo, I'd pick it right back up. I managed to slip away from Brandon by telling him I had to go to the bathroom, and I went back to the bridal suite. I quickly opened the envelope and saw a blank card and a folded letter-sized paper that had a close-up shot of my breasts. I was so shaken. I didn't know what to do. I quickly put that away with the other. I couldn't get out of Brazil fast enough.

When I returned to the hallway to meet Brandon for our grand entrance, I was so paranoid. I felt like I was seeing Teddy everywhere. Even as we danced our first dance, I thought I saw him standing in a doorway, wearing a banquet staff uniform. Oddly, who I did not see was Jeanette and Ricardo. Her place setting hadn't even been touched. I imagined them off somewhere having sex before making their entrance. Their entrance never happened. I didn't see her any more that night, and I was getting annoyed with everyone continually asking me where she was and why she wouldn't be there.

CHAPTER 12

I wanted to cut the evening short and hurry to our honeymoon suite, but I was afraid to leave, not knowing if Teddy would be in there distributing envelopes once we disappeared.

I was already worried about being able to enjoy our first night of sex as husband and wife, but what came once we did make it to our suite, I definitely didn't see coming.

I changed into my sexy white lingerie and Brandon was looking hot on the bed in his silk boxers. The room was lit in a sultry glow from the candles placed throughout. Rose petals adorned the bed, and soft Brazilian jazz played in the background. Brandon rose from the bed to greet me and walked around me, inspecting my body as if seeing it for the first time. I was wearing a white bra and thong set, with a white garter and stockings.

"You are so fucking beautiful. I mean, hot!"

I seductively smiled. Brandon had this way of sexually turning me on with his words when he wanted to.

He nuzzled my neck from behind as he wrapped his arms around me and pressed himself against me. He wasn't as hard as I'd expect him to be, but I figured maybe the boxers were too constricting for him to fully engorge. He caressed my breasts before removing the see-through robe I wore. He gently ran his fingertips up and down my body as if he had all the time in the world. He went and sat on the bed, pulling me to him. He started kissing my covered breasts before removing the lace material concealing my nipples.

"Oh my god! This shit is all mine until death do us part."

He used the tip of his tongue to tease my nipples, sucking and alternating a flick of the tongue. His kisses to my breasts became hungrier before he started south.

He leaned back on the bed and pulled me to sit on top of his groin. He still wasn't that hard, so I slowly wined my hips to get him hard. He then positioned me to sit on his face instead. I desperately tried to push the flashbacks of Ted from my mind.

Brandon pleasured me in that position for a while and then stopped to get me to remove his boxers and return the favor. I was sucking and sucking and sucking and licking and sucking some more, but he still maintained a semi-erection. I was frustrated and ready to pick a fight, but I managed to suppress it.

Still lying on his back, he turned me in a sixty-nine position. Finally, he was getting harder. Although it wasn't all the way hard, I decided to try to reverse ride it, hoping that would help. I knew he loved looking at my ass when we'd have sex, so I made sure he could watch my ass hide and unhide his dick. That definitely got him going. Eventually, he got so excited he flipped me onto my hands and knees and took me from the back. He was in full beast mode then, and I was loving it. He was going so long, I laid flat onto my stomach, while he continued to fuck me from behind. Brandon didn't seem to care if I was up, down, standing, sitting, or whatever; he loved fucking me from the back.

I started thinking of my argument with Sylvia. I remember her saying Brandon didn't really love me, and I didn't know his sexual fantasies. As Brandon fucked me from behind, I chuckled at the thought. I definitely knew my man loved it from behind. On the flip side of that, I wondered if thoughts of being married to me caused him to have difficulty achieving his erection when I was turned the other direction.

Brandon ended up coming inside of me from that position. That was our first time having sex without a condom, and I didn't think to ask him about it since we were now married. I was still on the pill but planned on stopping once we got settled with our living arrangements. I was most uncomfortable about him not using a condom because I failed to use one with Teddy the night before, and I wanted to get checked out when we got back home. This night was supposed to be the happiest night of my life, but all I wanted to do was cry. Also, I was pissed that Jeanette was off somewhere fucking the man I should have been with.

Brandon was spent, like he didn't have anything left in him, and the probability of a round two was out of the question. I wanted to protest so bad, but I was desperately trying not to ruin our romantic night. After rolling off of my ass, he laid on his stomach and passed out. I was disgusted with him. On my wedding night, I had to watch television in a different language, or depressing political news on MSNBC. I ended up blowing out all the candles and turning on a nightstand lamp. I wanted to check my phone and see what was going on in social media world, but I didn't want people to see I was online and not getting busy.

I laid on the bed next to Brandon, and started gently rubbing his back in long strokes down to his ass. As my hand ran up and down, it came across some areas that weren't consistently smooth. I decided to inspect closer. His back and ass were loaded with fresh scratches. It was getting harder to breathe. I tried to count to twenty and did some breathing techniques before waking him up.

"Brandon. Brandon, wake up." I started off in a low voice, but increased the pitch. "Brandon! Wake the fuck up!"

He struggled to open his eyes. "What the hell's the matter with you?"

"What bitch scratched you the fuck up like that?"

"What? What the hell you talking about?"

Tears formed in my eyes. "You have fresh scratches. They're still red."

"Didn't we just finish fucking?"

"Bro! You just fucked me from the back. My hands never touched your back. Try again!"

"I don't know what you're talking about. If anything, right before the wedding, your aunt—or is she a cousin, I don't know—scratched my back while we were waiting for you. I kept trying to scratch it myself, and she got up and scratched it for me."

"Hmm, okay, so I guess she had her hand down your pants, scratching both sides of your ass as well, huh? How could you do that shit to me, Brandon?"

"Like I said, I don't know what you're talking about. I don't know what you think I did to you."

"Get the fuck out! Go stay with your boys or whatever. Now you think you're going to sit here and insult my intelligence as well? I'd have more respect for you if you'd just said you were trying to get your last screw in as a single man. Nah, instead you wanna play me like I'm supposed to be so fucking stupid. Even worse, I'm sucking and sucking and sucking, and you could barely get hard. How long did it take before your dick finally came to life? I've been trying for days to be with you. Instead, you're fucking other people? Please get up and get the fuck out of here before I lose it."

"Look, can we just talk about this shit in the morning? I'm tired. You wanna leave, then you leave and tell your people whatever."

Those words made me get quiet. I didn't want them to know. If they saw one of us outside the room, they'd automatically know something was wrong.

"Why'd you even wanna marry me if you weren't ready to settle down?" I yelled as the tears poured.

"Asha, I'm not going to do this with you tonight. This is our last night here together, and you want to fuck it up with some bullshit. And why you blow out all the candles?"

"What was I supposed to do with the candles while you were dead to the world? Go to sleep and let the place burn down? Your ass was passed out, and how are we supposed to be together if I gotta just watch you sleep? Brandon, I desperately wanted and needed you. This night was supposed to be perfect."

"We can finish trying to make it perfect or we can keep fighting. Which do you want?"

"Am I just supposed to forget about you being scarred up? How am I supposed to make love to you and put my hands over the scratches some other bitch left on you?"

He sat up on the bed and shrugged. "You know, I asked if you were happy, because I knew there was no pleasing your ass. You are never satisfied. You get so damn emotional about every fucking thing. You want the truth? Can you handle the truth? Last night I came back early to get you, but you were nowhere to be found. I guess I should be asking where the fuck you were at. I even thought maybe—just maybe—you were trying to get your last little fling in before we lock it down forever. I didn't like that thought, but I knew it was a strong possibility, and I made up my mind I wouldn't ask you any questions, knowing I couldn't handle the truth. I know how you are about condoms, so I imagined that you'd have the decency to wear one. I figured once we said our 'I do's,' we would wipe the slate clean and leave all our dirt in the past."

My mind was screaming for me to tell him about Teddy's stalking ass, right in that moment. Brandon had just given me an opening, but I couldn't. I couldn't bring myself to admit I was doing exactly what he thought—without the condom.

"So basically, you thought I was with someone else, and that thought gave you license to go fuck some other bitch, huh?" I wasn't sure how I had the nerve to switch into angry mode in that moment, knowing how guilty I was. Here was an opportunity to build our marriage on truth. I made a conscious decision to build it on lies.

Brandon sat looking at me for the longest before getting off the bed to go find some clothes.

"What are you doing? Where are you going?" I yelled.

"Didn't you just tell me I had to get out? I can't sit here and fight with you all night. I know you're not going to let me get any rest, and I'm not going to do this with you tonight. When we said our wedding vows, we declared that we'd forsake all others, and I meant that with everything in me." He had tears in his eyes as he was pulling on a pair of jeans.

I got up from the bed to stop him. I was angry, but I couldn't let him go out and show the world we were already fighting. Everyone already felt I should not have gotten married.

"Okay. Don't go."

"What, you want me to stay and fight?"

"I don't want to fight. You swear? No more other women?"

"It wasn't the church that I wanted to be in, but I said it before God and all others in attendance."

I wanted to salvage the night. I half smiled.

He took me in his arms and actually kissed me as if he was truly in love with me. It seemed almost like the first time, because I couldn't remember him ever kissing me like that. When I heard him whisper, "We have babies to start working on," I felt like the luckiest woman in the world. His indiscretion was all forgiven. We had superb sex after that. Every now and then, I'd recall my time with Anthony and that pulsation I felt when he was inside of me.

CHAPTER 13

Thoughts of Teddy pushing envelopes under the door of our honeymoon suite kept breaking my sleep, and I must've gotten up five times to check. I know one thing, I was ecstatic to be headed home. Sylvia and Jeanette didn't fly back with us. I heard Sylvia was out extra early that morning. As for Jeanette, I wasn't sure what she was doing. The front desk staff gave me a message that she wouldn't be flying back with us. She didn't even have the decency to text me or anything.

Even on the airplane, it was difficult for me to relax until they closed the door and I was certain Teddy wasn't going to show up at the last minute. We had a layover in Miami, and I was paranoid that he would pop out like a boogeyman.

"I should have moved my stuff to your house before we left to Rio," I said to Brandon while we waited in Miami. I had my arm locked into his as we sat side-by-side.

"Huh? Move to my house? We're supposed to move to your place. You don't even like being on the south end. Plus, you have the condo to yourself now. I'd much prefer to be there."

"Brandon!" I pulled my arm from his to fully look at him, hoping he was just playing with me. Especially, since we had a previous discussion about my moving into his home. "Are you kidding? I told you we were supposed to all be moving out and then renting the place. You have the big house with a theater room. Our condo doesn't even have separation for when you might have your friends over."

"Well, we'll just find another home for the two of us, that we can pick out together. And don't forget, there's a theater room, gym, and pool at the condo. All your favorite bars and restaurants are within walking distance. I don't know how you would have thought otherwise."

"Okay, that's all fine and good, but we still have to stay somewhere in the meantime."

He gave a heavy sigh and closed his eyes. His jaw was tightened. I could tell he was angry, but I couldn't understand why.

"What's wrong with you? Why're you looking like you're about to blow a gasket or something?"

"Asha, I have to clear out of that house in the next few days. Someone else will be moving in it within the next week."

I was so shocked that I almost forgot we were in an airport. "WHAT? What the hell? When were you going to tell me?" I shouted in a low voice to keep our conversation private.

"I didn't think it was a big deal. I knew you didn't like being on the southside and always talked about how you never want to have to trade in that great view from your place, so I figured it was a no-brainer that we'd be at your place. My stuff is pretty much all packed up. Most of that stuff, I'll put in storage. Just bring my clothes, until we find a place together. It'll also be easier for me to make it to work."

I placed my hand over my mouth to keep from screaming. I couldn't believe he was just telling me all of this shit.

"Brandon, when at any point did you and I talk about this shit?"

"I'm pretty certain we've talked about this a time or two. You were mostly focused on this wedding and all the arrangements. I mean, had we not discussed it, I wouldn't have packed up my home for someone else to move into next week."

I fought the tears creeping into my eyes. "Sylvia and Jeanette are going to expect me to pay the entire mortgage and condo fees if we stay there. That's a lot for a Buckhead address."

Brandon started laughing and shaking his head.

"So, you were just kidding?" I asked getting a sense of relief.

"No, I wasn't kidding. You are sitting here acting like we're not going to be all right. I wish you'd stop worrying about every damn thing. I thought for sure, once this wedding was done, you'd chill. Instead you're all wound up about the next thing. Let's just chill tonight, and tomorrow we can map out the next step of our beautiful journey together. And, wherever we decide to move, we have to make sure it's in a good school district for the baby I'm sure I put inside of you last night."

I was cheesing then. I playfully punched him on the arm, and he turned to give me a quick kiss. The more I thought about it, I concluded his house was not in an area I'd want to raise my children.

"I need to get a key for you," I said to Brandon as we were about to enter our unit.

He passionately kissed me. "I think I'm supposed to carry you over the threshold, right?"

I laughed. "I don't know. Do people still do that?"

He shrugged, took the key from me, unlocked the door, and then picked me up. I was tickled by his gesture, but I was concerned by the lights that were already on. My heart was starting to beat extra hard, as thoughts of Teddy somehow getting into my home raced through my mind.

"Babe, I didn't leave the lights on before I left. I think someone's been in my home," I whispered with terror.

"Are you serious?" He put me down, still on the outside of the doorway. "Stay here and let me go check."

I loved that he was letting me know he was no punk and was willing to go in to see if someone was inside.

I grabbed hold of his arm. "No, we'll go together. I don't want something to happen to you."

We both snuck in. The place was dimly lit, but nothing looked broken or out of place. My bedroom was on one side of the condo, while the other bedrooms were at the other side. I saw a light coming from what used to be Jeanette's room.

"What the hell? Someone's in Jeanette's room."

We tiptoed to that door and could hear music at a low volume.

"You think Jeanette brought someone back here instead of taking them to her house?" he asked in a whisper.

"You know, that might make sense. I guess she feels she's still contributing to the mortgage, and she can come and go whenever. Come on, let's get our luggage from outside and leave them be."

He rubbed my ass as I turned to tiptoe away from Jeanette's room, and I playfully swatted his hand.

I woke up the following morning, so in love with my new husband. He seemed happy, and that made me happy. I hated when he had to rush out to go to work. I wanted to be able to cook for him and just lounge around for the day. I certainly didn't want to be sitting up in Jeanette and Ricardo's face, whenever they decided to get up. It was crazy how she made it home before us, because I assumed she hadn't left Rio, or I figured she was going someplace else with Ricardo.

I looked inside of the empty refrigerator, forgetting I hadn't gone shopping before leaving. Thankfully, I found some granola in the pantry, and I ate that with a bottle of water for my breakfast. I really wanted to go lie back down, but I decided to sit at the dining table so I could see them when they came out of the room. I laughed at the thought of her thinking I would be at Brandon's house, which was why she thought it would be clear to treat the condo as her hotel. I also found it strange that she wouldn't want to take him to her brand new house.

Like clockwork, I opened up Facebook, Instagram, Twitter, and Snapchat to see what Corrine was up to. I thought I might have been able to shake the feeling after having that great chat with Anthony. Unfortunately, I wasn't yet ready to let go. Which reminded me, I needed to get that cashier's check in the bank.

I became excited to see a bunch of photos and videos of the different birthday events in Rio. My heart dropped when I saw photos titled, "Night One," which was an A-list, celebrity-filled event. There were people from the music industry, the movie industry, politicians, athletes. I mean some of everybody was there, but me. The photos showed everyone celebrating her as if she was really somebody. Then there was a video of Anthony's marriage proposal to Corrine. It was a beautiful proposal, but it still made me jealous and aggravated because it was her.

The Night Two photos were from the hotel. I was most interested with Night Three, when I knew Jeanette was there. There was a day set of photos taken at the beach. I looked at Corrine's perfect body and was wishing she'd get pregnant. I flipped through the night photos. It looked like it was some rooftop party with a Miami looking background. I felt my blood boiling when I came across five random photos of Jeanette and Corrine hanging out together. They seemed comfortable with one another. One of them showed Jeanette sitting at a banquet table. Corrine was bent over from behind the chair with her arms wrapped around Jeanette, kissing her on the cheek. Jeanette looked extra happy. In another photo, they were on a chaise lounge together, with Corrine's legs draped across Jeanette's and Jeanette putting up a peace sign in front of Corrine's face as they were cracking up laughing. They were really, really comfortable with one another. I thought it ironic that Jeanette hadn't even mentioned their relationship and acted as if she didn't really know the girl. Then again, she was obviously hiding her relationship with Ricardo. I saw a few photos of Jeanette with Ricardo. Ricardo had a lot of photos taken with many different women, but in a supposed couples photo, he was with Jeanette. Everyone at that event was dressed sophisticated and elegantly. Ricardo was wearing a turquoise tie with his white suit. I couldn't help but wonder if he was supposed to be coordinated with Jeanette, since I noticed Anthony's tie happened to match Corrine's dress. It was almost like the whole wardrobe thing was previously planned.

I decided to open another browser to check out Ricardo's profile. I became really confused when I saw a live video posted thirty minutes earlier, of him and Jeanette jogging along a beach.

"Mi baby say I'm getting fat and I need to get in shape. You see I do anyt'ing for dis woman, mon. She say dat maybe if I get in shape, she say, yes, to mi marriage proposal. I'ma t'ink I migh' need ta buy a bigger ring, 'cause she killing me out here dis morning. I can't eat not'ing till I finish me run, mon." You could hear him breathing heavily, trying to run, and then he turned the camera lens in her direction. "Look at her way up dere, mon. She say if I want to marry her, I must catch her. Woman, slow down nuh, so I can catch yuh! I outta breath, so I hafta turn dis t'ing off so I can catch my love. Peace!"

As I sat confused, trying to figure how Jeanette was on a beach and in her bedroom at the same time, Ricardo posted a photo in that very moment. It was a photo of Jeanette's left hand with a huge-ass yellow diamond. He captioned the photo: I finally caught up to her and she said, yes!

In my confusion, the thought crossed my mind that maybe the woman running wasn't actually Jeanette, although it looked like her from behind. The hand; it definitely belonged to Jeanette. Jeanette had long ago gotten a small tattoo on her hand with the first initials of her parents and herself, which is also the name of her company, MJP.

I was mad, hurt, jealous, confused, and then I became afraid at the thought of a creepy-ass Teddy being camped out inside of my home all night, waiting for Brandon to leave so he could hurt me.

I decided to investigate. I got up from the table and went into the kitchen to grab the largest knife I could find. I eased the door open. The drapes were still closed, making the room a little darker. I looked over at the bed, and someone was definitely sleeping in it, but it looked like a single body. I creeped closer to the bed, about to snatch the covers off of the person, when I heard a gun cock. My heart jumped into my throat, and I dropped the knife.

CHAPTER 14

hat the fuck! What are you doing here—in here?"

"I should be asking you the same. And then you come up in here with a knife? Were you supposed to kill someone with that?" she asked as she hit a light switch on her bed.

"We got in last night. All this time, I thought Jeanette was in here with company. I just saw a live video of her on some beach, getting engaged."

"Oh my goodness, really? That is so sweet."

"Sylvia, could you stop pointing that damn gun at me?"

"Oh yeah," she said as she uncocked it and slid it back underneath her pillow.

"What are you doing here? When did you get here, and why'd you leave my wedding the way you did? That was hurtful."

"I spoke with Jeanette the other day. I told her I was moving back into the condo, and I told her I'd be switching bedrooms. I figured I'd have the place to myself. Why aren't you at Brandon's house? Didn't you say you were moving in with him?"

Sylvia abruptly stopped talking and made a mad dash to the bathroom to vomit. I didn't know much about her dating life anymore, but that had morning sickness and being pregnant written all over it.

I wondered if that had anything to do with her moving back to the condo. I was going to wait for her to come out of the bathroom to ask, but I heard the shower come on, so I figured that was my cue to leave the room. I went back to the dining room and decided to check my emails to see if I had any new modeling offers. There were a couple of emails asking me my availability. I noticed as I got closer and closer to thirty, the calls and emails began to slow down.

In my obsession, I'm not sure why I felt the need to visit Jeanette's page just to see how many followers she had.

"Oh, hell no!" I said to myself when I saw she had over six million followers. "She must have bought them. Those have to be paid followers. There is no way in hell she's poppin' like that."

The day wasn't starting off well, and it was only 9:30. I thought about how Brandon was going to flip when he found out Sylvia moved back in. But then again, we weren't supposed to be there either. I figured the living arrangement might work out well, to help keep our expenses down until Brandon and I could find a new house to move to.

I thought about the possibility of Sylvia being pregnant. I wanted to be happy for her, but she wasn't supposed to be pregnant before me. I was anxious to know who the father might be, or if maybe she did some artificial insemination thing. It seemed like everyone was keeping secrets these days—Jeanette hiding Ricardo and possibly Corrine. Now, Sylvia hiding guys she was dating. I guessed she was still stuck on my fling with Ricardo and was worried I'd go behind her back. *Stupid ass.*

Sylvia came rushing out the room, fully dressed with her work bag on her shoulder and her pocketbook in her hand.

"Where you going? I thought we'd have an opportunity to sit down and talk. You know things are going to be kind of awkward since Brandon's going to be living here now."

She chuckled and shook her head. "I gotta get to the office. We have a meeting at eleven."

"Well, I guess it's good that I woke you up."

"No, you didn't. I was just laying there when you came in. I've been on the phone, checked emails, everything, before your intrusion. But I gotta run."

And just like that, she was out the door, as if trying to avoid any conversations with me. I thought about how I would hardly see her before she moved. I hoped that would be the case now.

I went and hit the shower, ready to start my day and run my errands. I returned calls for modeling gigs. One of them was shooting in Sedona, Arizona in two days, meaning I'd have to leave the next day. I didn't want to just accept it without consulting with Brandon, because I imagined, this is how life would be going forward. When I called him, he told me to never feel I have to ask his permission to take a job opportunity. So, I jumped on my opportunities. I had another voicemail for a third opportunity to shoot a commercial out in L.A. I prayed it led to something even bigger. It would be wonderful to go house hunting in California and have access to acting opportunities.

Brandon called me later to say he'd be late, since he had to stop at his house. I kind of anticipated it, and in between cooking for my husband, I read the hundreds of thousands of congratulatory comments to Jeanette and Ricardo. I probably spent more time and energy going through each of the messages than they spent.

The one that stood out most was from Corrine:

"Yay! We're about to be family for real now! Congratulations to the best, best, best business/brand manager ever. I'm so glad I stumbled into your life. You have definitely changed my life beyond my wildest dreams. I have the love of my life because of you. You mean the world to me. You're better than any big sister I could have ever wished for. Love you for life, fam. Oh, can't wait for your new bestseller, Don't Waste Time with Small Minded People, to drop on June 14th. Signing party at our house! Everybody be sure to snag your copy . . . or two or three. Presales are already available, and they'll be gone."

I sat flabbergasted.

When the subject of Corrine and Anthony came up, Jeanette didn't even breathe a syllable about knowing her or doing business with them. In fact, I clearly remember that day she walked up behind me when I was on my computer and acted as if she didn't know Corrine. She also acted like she didn't know her when we were in Rio. She never breathed a word about having any communications with Anthony all this time. She totally hid her relationship with Ricardo from me. And now I learned she had a new book dropping in a few weeks, on my birthday? I couldn't help but wonder if she was insinuating that I was the small minded one. All that time she was playing me like we were besties, and now I realized I didn't even know this bitch? I was thinking she was in Rio for my wedding, and now I saw she was actually there for Corrine and Ricardo. Wow! Just fucking wow! I remembered when I first told her my wedding date, and she couldn't commit because of some other prior engagement. But when I said Rio, suddenly, she made it as if she'd be there for ME. Now I saw she was there for Corrine and Ricardo, and I was just the afterthought. *Bitch!*

I insisted on torturing myself by continuing to read the comments. There was a post that tagged Ricardo and Jeanette: "Thank you, Daddy, for running a little faster to catch her. Congratulations! Welcome to the family! But then again, you were already part of the family. I love you guys." That was followed by heart emojis and kissy faces.

Curiosity had me then checking that person's page. She looked our age. She used the words "daddy" and "family." Surely that couldn't be one of Ricardo's daughters. It just couldn't be. I saw all the Grambling Alma Mater paraphernalia on her page, and I remembered him saying his eldest daughter attended there. I was even more disappointed to see she was a doctor. I was feeling extra inferior as I thought of all the times Jeanette would encourage me to finish school. There she was, about to have a doctor our age for a stepdaughter.

I started thinking, perhaps I should speak with Brandon about holding us both down financially, so I could go on and finish up with something. If I got pregnant, he'd have no choice. Thankfully, he had a great job and made lots of money.

I was in a deep sleep by the time Brandon made it home. He tried to be quiet, but turning the shower on pulled me from my sleep.

"Brandon, it's four-thirty. What the hell?"

"Hey, babe. I've been at the house trying to get as much as I could done. I almost stayed down there, but I didn't want to make you angry. I guess I'll be in late until I get everything out and cleaned up."

I yawned, trying to fully wake up. "I have to leave for Arizona later this afternoon. Why didn't you call me or something?"

"I didn't plan on being out this late. I kept planning to do one more thing, and that led to the next thing."

"Can I have a kiss?" I asked out of insecurity more than anything.

"As soon as I come out the bathroom. I'm a stinking mess."

"Uhm hmm."

"What's that supposed to—you know what? Never mind." He went into the bathroom agitated and closed the door.

I looked at the clothes he dropped on the floor just before going into the bathroom. I was tempted to go check his pockets and his phone.

When he was done with his shower and brushing his teeth, he crawled into the bed, gave me a peck on the lips and rolled over in the opposite direction on my king size bed.

"Wow! That's it? I've waited most of the night for you and I have to leave in a few hours, and I get just a peck?"

He sucked his teeth. "Aw, come on now. Do you see the time? I have less than two hours to sleep before I have to get to work. I already told you, once I get everything all cleared down there, we can fully relax and enjoy one another. Now please, let me sleep."

"Fine! Could you at least hold me?"

"No, I can't 'cause you think you're slick, knowing that's going to get me excited. Nope. Go to sleep."

He was right, because I sure did plan on seducing him. I needed to be with him. We should still be on our honeymoon, having so much sex I could barely stand it. And his rejection, albeit for sound reasons, played right into my insecurities.

When I woke up in bed alone that morning, it took me a moment to register that I was married and my husband was missing from the bed. I looked at the clock and saw it was after ten. I jumped up like a bat out of hell. I couldn't believe I slept so late. Even worse, Brandon didn't bother to wake me. I found a note attached to the refrigerator, saying he didn't want to wake me before my big job and for me to call him when I was up, so he could say good morning. That made me start conjuring up all sorts of vengeful tactics to someday pay him back. I didn't bother calling him, because I had to hurry up and pack for my trip . . . and check up on Jeanette and Corrine's world.

While I was packing, I saw Brandon's bag from Brazil. I had yet to work out his space in my closet or dresser, and now with Sylvia, I couldn't just put his stuff in that room. I tried with all my might not to snoop in it, but I was weak. I was extra careful so he wouldn't notice I had gone through his bag. Once my hand stumbled upon a huge opened box of condoms, I didn't give a damn about him knowing I went through his bag. I was so troubled, I took a seat on the sofa in my bedroom. I thought of the scratches on his body and cried. I knew he said we were leaving all the premarital violations behind us, but it wasn't that easy.

I got up and continued digging through his bag. I found a sealed envelope in one of the zipper pockets. I assumed he must have forgotten he put it there. It was a hotel envelope. A thick hotel envelope, not addressed to anyone. That time I took a seat on the floor with a hand over my mouth. I looked at the envelope as if it would open itself. I took deep breaths in and would blow it out, trying to calm myself down.

When I got myself together, I ripped the envelope open. Sure enough, it was from Teddy. I boo-hoo-hoo cried. I wondered when and how Brandon got the envelope, and I couldn't even ask him about it. If I asked, he'd want to know how I found the envelope or what was in it.

I packed the pages into my bag, along with the other pages previously delivered. I couldn't leave them in the house, just in case Brandon decided to snoop while I was away. I couldn't understand what it was I could have done so bad to Teddy to make him terrorize me like that.

I was still so livid about the open condom box, I left it on the bed and didn't bother to call him as he requested. Hell, if Jeanette could make a man chase after her, then I was going to make Brandon chase me. I needed to make sure he was trained early in this marriage.

CHAPTER 15

What I thought was going to be a two-day trip turned into a four-day trip. I had a lot of fun with it. A lot of times, my gigs could get stressful and I'd work with other girls that seemed catty or cliquish, often leading me to stay to myself. I don't know if I was just feeling empowered about knowing Brandon was angry, or if unlike most of the gigs I work, the people I was working with on that trip were really cool. Brandon had been calling nonstop since finding those condoms that I left on the bed. He called at least five times before I finally answered. I was satisfied with his persistence. He spent most of his time at the other house. He hadn't mentioned Sylvia being at the condo, and I had yet to let him know.

My return flight was delayed, and it was just about midnight by the time I reached my door. I heard loud arguing. I paused to see if the noise might have been coming from someplace else. It was definitely coming from my unit. Instead of walking in and stopping the argument, I decided to get close enough to listen. At times their voices would trail off as if they were moving about from one side of the condo to the other side, in the direction of my room.

"Yes, you are, you bum motherfucker!" I heard Sylvia yell.

"No, I been told you to take care of that shit. You're just being hateful," he rebutted.

"I bet you better go set your ass down somewhere and figure out what the fuck you're going to say. You better figure something out."

"I hate calling women, bitches, but I swear. This shit ain't cool."

Sylvia laughed in exaggeration. "Not cool! Not fucking cool? Did you just say . . ." Then her voice trailed off and I didn't get to hear the rest. "Well get another fucking job, you bum!" she yelled as they seemed to move again.

"You know what? I ain't got time for this. This is some fucked up shit. You wrong and you know you're wrong."

The voices disappeared again, and I could only hear inaudible yelling. But then it suddenly became quiet. I didn't hear any shots, but I did wonder if Sylvia shot him. She never was too fond of him. Her nor Jeanette. I waited for a few minutes and didn't hear anything else, so I quietly entered the unit. I didn't hear them at all. I went in the direction of my bedroom and didn't see him. I was trying to be quiet, but made too much noise with my bags. I wasn't sure what I was trying to catch them in the act of, especially when Brandon knew I was on my way home. By the time I came from my bedroom, Brandon was coming from the direction of Sylvia's bedroom. He looked angry. Sylvia closed her door and didn't bother coming out to greet me.

"What the hell is going on? And why are you coming from over there?"

"No, 'Hey Babe! How are you doing?' Instead, the first thing out your mouth is another accusation." He brushed past me and headed to the bedroom. I followed behind him. He opened the closet door and dressers. "What do you see?"

I looked, unsure of what he wanted me to see. "I don't know. My clothes?"

"Thank you! And where exactly do you think my clothes should go? I figured I'd put them in the other bedroom, and that didn't go over too well."

I sighed. I felt a weight lift from me when I figured that must have been what the argument was about. I felt so much better.

"I'm sorry, babe. I came up to the door and I heard y'all both just raising hell, and her calling you names. I see I'm going to have to have a strong talk with her, because that shit will absolutely not be tolerated. No one's going to be talking to my husband any ol' kind of way."

"Please! There's nothing for you to say. She's going to clear that stuff out over the weekend."

"Oh? She calmed down that fast? The way y'all were fussing, I thought she might have shot you. I didn't even tell you, she pulled a gun on me before I left. When I realized Jeanette wasn't the one here, I went in the room with a knife, and she pulls out a gun."

"Damn! How'd you forget to mention that to me?" He took me in his arms and held me tightly. He seemed shook.

"Aw baby, why are you trembling? Don't worry, she ain't going to do anything stupid. Remember, she's a lawyer. She's not going to just throw her life away like that."

He shrugged it off. "Anyhow, I tried to fix you a nice bath, but it's probably cold by now."

"Aw, for real? You are simply the best. Thank you so much," I said before kissing him.

I looked in the bathroom and saw the effort he put forth. The bubbles were all flat. "How about I just take a shower and crawl in bed with my gorgeous husband? Or maybe my gorgeous husband can crawl in the shower with his beautiful wife?"

"I like the latter. I need a shower anyhow."

The shower sex was to die for. I was looking forward to finishing up on the bed. What I did not expect was Sylvia to be standing in the opened doorway of my bedroom. Our door was closed before we went into the shower. She stood looking pissed, with her arms folded across her.

"Sylvia! What the hell? Get the hell out of our room." I looked behind me to see if Brandon was naked or not. He had just a towel wrapped around his waist.

Tears flowed from her eyes, her nostrils were flared, and her mouth was pouted. "Man, you must got me all fucked up. This shit ain't gonna be okay."

"What? I know you're not trying to tell me I can't be in my own home with my husband."

"Don't do this. Please don't do this. Let's just sit down and talk this weekend," Brandon tried to plead.

She laughed. "You're out your fucking mind."

"Uh-uh! Oh no! You need to go on somewhere with that shit. You are not going to talk to my husband any ol' kind of way or be disrespecting him like that. As a matter of fact, you're going to get your ass out of my fucking bedroom, so me and husband can finish doing what married people do best."

"Brandon," she said in a low voice, looking at him as if she'd hurt him.

I looked back at him and noticed he was wearing his robe. Guess he figured he might have to break up a fight. Hell, I didn't want to fight my cousin. I hadn't fought anyone since middle school.

She repeated, "Brandon."

I looked at him with his eyes closed and he was shaking his head side to side.

"I don't know what the fuck is going on, but somebody better say something. Why do you keep calling Brandon?"

"Ask him," she said and then turned to leave from my room. "I'll be in the living room when you're ready," she yelled out.

"Brandon, what the fuck is going on?"

"Baby, please just ignore that shit and let's finish what we started."

"You must be out of your mind." I threw my robe on and went into the living room and sat on a seat across from Sylvia. "Okay, here I am."

"You forgot about your dear husband. He needs to bring his ass on out here."

Brandon came out of the bedroom, fully dressed.

"What the hell? Where are you going?"

He said nothing, but just took a seat at the dining table and held his head down.

"You wanna say it or should I?" she asked him.

He just waved his hand and still said nothing.

"I'm pregnant!" she snapped.

"Okay, and? I figured that the other day when you ran off vomiting that morning. So, all this is about you're worried about Brandon using the closet in the other room because you're having a baby? 'Cause all this drama ain't even necessary. We're planning on going house hunting soon. He's renting out the other house, and we're going to take care of business from here on. I understand you weren't expecting me to return here after the wedding, but we didn't expect you either." I rambled on and on, while Sylvia looked at me like I was crazy.

"What? What the hell are you talking about, and what closet?"

I looked at Brandon and he covered his face before saying, "Sylvia, please don't."

"Man, fuck you!" she yelled. "Did you listen to me when I told you, 'don't?' NO! So, shut the fuck up!"

"Oh no, no, no, no! I already told you, you are not going to be disrespecting my husband."

"Oh please! Your whole damn marriage is a sham, and your so-called husband's a fraud."

I didn't know how to respond to that, and Brandon wasn't even trying to defend himself.

"Brandon is the father of my baby, and I don't know what house you think he's renting out. His ass doesn't own shit! He's a sorry, broke-ass bum. The only reason he felt the need to marry you was because you're his meal ticket. He and I have literally fucked all the way up to the wedding, and he wasn't supposed to even go through with that sham of a wedding. And since I'm already pregnant, that should tell you it didn't just happen. I told his raggedy ass to call the shit off. No, I didn't know I was pregnant until yesterday. His ass thinks I'm supposed to run and abort the baby so he and I can keep fucking, while I'm forced to wait for him to be done with you. That shit ain't happening. Brandon and I are having a baby. Period."

I closed my eyes and listened to the sound of blood rushing in my head. I didn't know what to say. I was too stunned to cry. And still, Brandon said absolutely nothing. No effort to defend himself against these preposterous accusations.

She continued. "I remember you saying he was paying for some big wedding here in Georgia. No, he's not, nor was he ever. He got you believing he's paid. No. This bastard makes $47,000 a year. That's it. That home—he was the fucking renter. He's crying to me about how poor he is to afford my baby. I told him he better get a second job then. That degree he told you he had? Motherfucker got a few college credits, just like your ass. That's it."

There was a long silence as I continued to process her words.

"Let me see if I got this right: You had sex with my husband? Your thirsty ass couldn't go find your own man, because you just wanted to share mine? You make him out to be all kinds of pathetic bums, but yet you're trying to plan a whole family with him—have his baby and everything? Okay, and now I understand why you went storming out of my wedding. I wondered what I might have said or done that upset you so much. Nah, you were angry because he didn't stop the wedding. You wanted him to marry your trick ass. I guess you wanted to be that meal ticket, huh? You are so fucked up. You are the worst kind of bitch, and the only reason I ain't hopping over this coffee table to snatch your high-yellow ass is because you ain't worth me going to jail, when I actually have the man that you want."

She laughed hysterically. "Ho, you think I'm the worst kind of bitch? I guess now's a good time to tell you, Jeanette knew all about your delusional ass fucking her man. You had me believing your stupid shit, thinking she was foul and took him from you. She never had a clue that you were even on his radar when she got with him. And from what I understand, he was just one of like ten other guys you were fucking all in the same night, while in Jamaica."

"Hold up! Wait! What?" Brandon suddenly found a voice.

"Oh no, you just finish sitting your ass there quiet, before I spill the tea about you also fucking Jeanette."

His eyes widened. "Who told you that? Where'd you get that shit from? That's bullshit."

"You wanna try and deny it? Please do, motherfucker, 'cause I got receipts. Please deny that shit."

She stood up as if she was ready to go get those receipts.

"What!" I yelled, also standing up.

Again, Brandon was silenced.

Sylvia laughed as she sat back on the sofa. "I thought you'd want to hurry up and shut that bullshit up."

"Brandon, you better deny that shit or something," I yelled at him and then redirected my attention to her. "Where'd you get that shit from?"

"Your friend told me. I told her what you did, calling yourself getting back at her." Sylvia laughed. "Yep, me and Jeanette had us a whole tea party happening. Now, let's talk about who you were fucking before that Jamaica trip. You wanna have that conversation, bitch? You know, at first, I was like, so what, because I didn't really give a damn about him, but then I learn you were serving up all the secrets to your girl. You talked so much shit about me to her, trying to make her not like me, yet you always wanted us to hang together. What kind of sick shit is that?"

Sylvia directed her attention to Brandon before continuing her verbal assault.

"Brandon, do you know this ho has slept with at least four of my exes over the years? And that's just four that I know about. It only stopped because I stopped bringing guys around her trampy, no-self-esteem-having ass." She looked back at me. "The only reason Jeanette fucked your so-called man here was for what you did to her. Crazy thing, you were so obsessed with her relationship with dude, she had to lie to you and make you believe they no longer communicated. Even while we were in Brazil, you were breaking your neck over dude and worrying about what they were doing and where they were going. I already told Brandon how you planned that whole trip because you were all jealous and trying to catch up with both those guys. Speaking of fucking, let's talk about who you were actually fucking in Brazil."

My heart jumped. "What? I fucked my husband in Brazil, but that's none of your concern."

"None of my concern?" Sylvia laughed. "See, that's where you're wrong. Anything and everything concerning the father of my child is my concern. But getting back to the point—you were fucking more than your husband. I'm sure you must have noticed that strange man in that small-ass room. He stopped me in the hallway. He told me how y'all were together until early that morning. Guess that's why Brandon was blowing up my phone all that night, trying to beg me to come get into his bed, because he couldn't find your ass."

"Oh please, someone lied to you," I insisted.

She laughed hysterically again. "Whew! Girl stop! You're making my sides hurt from laughing. You know the lawyer in me ain't just gonna take someone's word. I needed proof. Your ripped thong was definitely proof. I have it in my room, in a plastic baggie. How about I give it to your hussssband?"

Brandon jumped up and stood before me, as if he had grounds. "When I asked you about leaving our shit behind us, you made it as if I was the only one that fucked up? Yes, I did do a lot of wrong, and planned to never do wrong by you again. I never thought that she'd be here in the house with us, and I definitely didn't know about any baby. For all I know, that could be anyone's baby that she's just trying to pin on me."

A crazed cackle burst from Sylvia's mouth. "Your bum ass only makes forty-seven thousand. *Why* on earth would I choose the brokest ninja I could find, to pin my baby on? How many times did we finish and you would brag how you just put a baby up inside of me? Well, guess what? We're about to have that baby you put up inside of me. I wish I would abort my child. Not even for a bum ass like yourself."

"And that's just why I didn't choose to be with you the way you wanted me to, because you don't know how to respect anybody. You think it's okay to talk to me in any kind of way and question why I'm going through with marrying the one I actually love."

"Oh no you didn't go there. You said you didn't love her. Remember?"

"I never told you that. Now you're just making up shit to try to fuck with my wife's head. I guess you're done saying all you need to say, because now I'm going back into the bedroom with my wife, and we are going to talk and work things out. You wanna stand at the door and listen to me make love to my wife every night, then you do that. All that me-and-you shit is done."

"Oh, please! Done my ass. You were just in my room kissing me when we heard her coming in the house. Your dick was brick hard when you ran out. You are so full of shit, and she is so sneaky and desperate that she won't even give a fuck. She calls her friend a backstabber, but she is the true definition of a backstabber. She calls people friends and can't even be happy for them. She's all salty because we had sense enough to get an education and get our priorities in order."

I pridefully took hold of Brandon's hand. I was glad he put her in her place and let her know he chose me over her. I didn't care what she had to say anymore, because the more she spoke, it became more obvious that she wanted Brandon for herself and was hoping he'd leave me at the altar. I was curious as to the length of their affair.

"How long have you been trying to share *my* man with me? I figure it must have been a couple of months, since you're supposed to be pregnant."

"A couple of months?" She heartily laughed. "Uh, NO! That's why I never in a million years saw that proposal coming. We were already in a steady sexual relationship. He came to me and asked what we had planned and wanted in on it. I guess he had something else he wanted to get in on. My pussy."

"Your ass seduced me. What you sitting there lying for?" Brandon yelled.

"Please! You don't need anyone to seduce you. Do you need me to spell out the details of that first time? You know, when you asked me to stop by your house to work on the birthday plans? Then you just so happened to be fixing dinner and insisted I have some, along with the bottle of wine you had just opened. The conversation was cool. We laughed. You put on music and we started talking about music and the whole music industry and the probability of me going that direction in law. Then something came on and you wanted to dance, and shit happened from there. Remember?!"

"Okay, but was it not you pushing your body up against me while we danced? We weren't slow dancing. No, just like you said, you were only trying to pay my wife back for some silly shit you couldn't let go of. You talk about her being jealous; you're the one who tried to break us up. And you want to tell some shit? Why don't you tell her how you've been prancing around this crib, butt naked, while she was away, 'cause you was hoping I'd make a move on you. I told you to cover yourself up, and you said it's your condo."

My mouth was opened from all the shock. "Wow! Really? You're a low-down bitch. I can admit, I've done some fucked up, hurtful shit to you and Jeanette, but I was super young and dumb. You're that mad at me, why would you want us to live together? All that shit was long before we even bought this condo."

"For financial reasons? Duh!" She stood from the sofa and

started heading toward her room. "I'm going to bed. I ain't gonna be sitting out here with y'all all night. Some of us do have jobs—real jobs. And Brandon, I'll see you later."

"Oh no the fuck you won't!" I yelled.

She laughed and finished walking, saying, "Watch!"

I kept shaking my head side to side with my fists clenched. I was so ready to kill her ass. I was beyond angry.

The situation between them was jacked up, but it did happen before we were married. How was I supposed to blame him when he was only a victim of her revenge and Jeanette's? I stared into space for a moment, thinking, *I wish I would just hand my husband over to that spinster. That'll never happen.*

Brandon took my hand and escorted me to our bedroom. As soon as we got inside, I started kissing him. He pulled away.

"So, what about this dude you were with in Brazil the night I couldn't find you?"

I looked at him in disbelief, having the nerve to question me about anything. But for some reason I felt compelled to keep my lie going. "Brandon, don't start. It was obvious that the bitch was angry and bitter, just making shit up. You said it yourself."

"So, there was no other guy?"

"Hell no!"

"I mean, if there was, I'd rather you just be honest and move on. I don't want to be in a store one day and some dude comes up to me telling me how he fucked my wife."

"I am not going to have this conversation all night. You want to believe what she tells you to break us up, then whatever. I'm not doing the foolishness. But speaking of lies, do I even fucking know you? Is Brandon your real name? Maybe I need to go ask my cousin, whom you've been fucking for a whole year, since she seems to know more about you than I do. Forty-seven thousand? What the hell? How are we supposed to survive on that little change? What happened to your big businesses? You keep talking about you want us to have a baby, and now I find out I can't afford to not keep working. And what about that house? It wasn't even your house? I figured you'd be able to show some equity and it would help to get us a new house." I quickly rubbed my temples and asked, "Do I dare inquire about your credit? I can only imagine—No! I don't even want to imagine."

I took a minute to calm down.

"Brandon, why were you fucking my cousin and best friend? You know, I kind of always figured you were out there with other women, but I don't understand why them. Wasn't it obvious to you that fucking them was something you just don't do?"

He sat on the sofa and put his head into his hands. For the longest he said nothing as I just stood watching him. I wanted to slap the shit out of his ass. Eventually, he lifted his head and patted the seat for me to sit next to him. I did as he requested.

He took a deep breath and then exhaled. "You know what? I'm so glad all of this is out on the table. I truly meant that I wanted us to have a fresh start the day I made you my wife. I knew I fucked up, but never in a million years did I think you'd hear about it. Especially not like this. They seemed like they were so supportive of you and our marriage, so I figured I could leave it all behind us without ever hurting you. I saw Jeanette happily moved on with her dude, so I didn't think she'd say anything at this point. And just to be clear, I never actually had sex with Jeanette. Almost, but it didn't happen. I heard what you did to both of them, and I ain't gonna lie, I actually thought it was pretty low-down on your part. But after what I did, I had no right to say a damn thing or judge you, and I had no intention of trying to punish you."

"Uhmm, all of that was long before I met you. Sure, I was wrong, I'll admit that, but you had no right to feel you should punish me."

Brandon stood up and walked to the window and gazed out for a minute before turning back to look at me.

"Asha, I really want to make this marriage work, but I keep giving you an opportunity to be honest with me, and you refuse to."

"Honesty? You're questioning me about honesty, Brandon? All that earful of shit I just got about you? The financially secure man that I thought you were? A man now with a child on the way, with another woman? My cousin."

"In my defense, I knew nothing about any baby until today. I even asked her to abort it because I had no intentions of being with her ever again. But since you want to just sit here and bullshit, I'm going to just put it out there: I know you fucked some dude in Rio. The fact that you keep lying to me when I keep extending an out, is troubling. Close your mouth, because you can't even deny it. Teddy, right?"

My mouth was wide open, and my eyes were stretched even wider. My mind raced, trying to figure out how he knew. I found that sealed envelope in his bag, but I destroyed that evidence.

"But how?"

"How what?"

"How did you know? You set me up to try to justify your actions with my cousin?" I asked, getting angry.

He shook his head and laughed. "Don't you even try to turn this on me. And to answer your question, I had absolutely nothing to do with anything. You went off somewhere before our reception, and this old dude walks up to me asking to talk. He said he wanted to apologize to me man-to-man, because he had no idea the woman I just married was the same woman in his bed that morning. He was pleasant and respectable, so I couldn't see making a scene, causing everyone else to know what you did. You damn right, my first instinct was anger, but I thought about my own shit and made up my mind that I was going to just call it a wash. One of my boys saw I was bothered, and asked if I was good. I told him I was. Crazy thing, you hadn't even picked up on the fact that my demeanor had just changed. Although I wouldn't have gotten into that conversation right then, it bothered me that you didn't bother to see something might have been bothering me. I didn't even want to believe him, and when I asked you that night, and you denied it, I was angry at him for trying to play head games with me. However, to hear your cousin say she got your thong and seeing your expression . . . The fact that you would lie when I kept giving you an out hurts like hell."

I sat leaned forward for a minute in silence, with my hands folded almost in a praying position.

"Brandon, he took pictures of me. I don't know how or where any cameras were, and he was terrorizing me from the time I left his room. I wasn't just terrified about you finding out, I was terrified about what he was capable of. He kept dropping off envelopes filled with compromising, computer printed photos of me. I never told him my room number, yet he delivered an envelope there, to my bridal suite, in our wedding hall. I mean, he was relentless, and I was distracted by the terror he was causing me."

"I found an envelope that morning we were about to leave. You were in the shower or bathroom or something. My bag was near the door, so I just stuck the envelope in my bag. It was on hotel stationary. I thought it might have been the hotel invoice or something. That day when you left that box of condoms on the bed was the first chance I had to empty my bag, and I thought of that envelope. I couldn't find it and was upset thinking I might have lost it. From what I'm hearing now, I assume you removed the envelope to keep me from seeing the contents, right?"

I nodded as tears rolled down my cheeks.

"It was crazy, because I was really looking forward to our wedding night, and I thought it would be the best, most passionate night of our lives. The more you complained about my lack of erection, the more the image of you fucking that old prick would enter my mind. I thought of saying something to you then, but I wanted to start off right. When we had that talk, and I opened the door for you to be honest, you shut that door. That bothered me, but I just made up my mind that I was going to leave it behind us, since it happened before we said our vows to one another."

That time I patted the seat for him to return.

"What are we going to do about Sylvia? We will be living in hell if we can't move from here. I can't share you with her. I won't! That's not even an option. Right now, I don't even know how this marriage can survive. What if I also get pregnant? What if I'm already pregnant?"

Brandon stretched out his legs, resting his head on the back of the sofa, looking at the ceiling. "I don't know. Maybe if she sees us a united front, she'll rethink carrying the baby. Or maybe if your family knew, they'd tell her to get rid of it."

"I'll be honest, I have a problem with her getting an abortion. I did that when I was just a teen, and it still haunts me."

"You did what? You had an abortion?" he asked, quickly sitting up and looking at me with disgust.

I hesitated before answering. "Three times before I even made eighteen."

"Asha? How could you?"

"How could I? You're asking me how I could have done something when I was an uninformed, ill-prepared teen, yet you're asking someone to abort your child, now when she is finally able to manage?"

He shook his head and calmed down. "Okay, you're right. I don't know why I didn't think about it like that. It's just that she's going to try everything to ruin our marriage."

"Maybe our marriage was ruined before it began," I said, staring blankly toward the window.

"Don't speak like that. We're going to make this work."

"Brandon, how do you think I'm supposed to feel when I have to go out of town for these modeling gigs? We obviously need the money, since you're not as well off as you led me to believe. How am I supposed to concentrate on my work, knowing my husband is home alone with my cousin, as she walks around butt-naked, and they're having a baby together? How am I supposed to feel when it's time for you to go to doctor appointments with her, and you two begin bonding over your baby in her stomach? How do you think I'll feel if I roll over on any given night and don't find you here in the bed with me, because you need to check on your baby's mother, right down the hall?

"I love you. I swear I do, but I just can't see how this is going to work. We can't even afford to move unless we totally downgrade. I don't understand, why didn't we just stay in that house you were renting? If you were able to manage that on your own, then surely we could have managed with both our incomes. I guess now it makes sense why she moved back here instead of living in her other house."

"Asha, I want to be honest with you, but if we keep going down this road, there's no telling where it'll take us. I know this is hard, but we just have to work on one day at a time. We have to strengthen our bond. Hell, I'll put bells on the door to alert you when it opens. I'll get a minifridge so I can keep something cold in here and not have a reason to go out there."

"What about when you need to eat?"

"If you're not here, I'll plan on eating out. I won't spend time in the common areas."

I looked at him optimistically. "You really wanna try to make this work with me? Do you really love me, or do you see me as some meal ticket, as Sylvia says?"

He laughed. "That's some crazy shit. I absolutely don't see you as a meal ticket. Yes, I loved the fact that you were—are—a strong, independent woman, but a meal ticket? Not at all. I've thought about if and when you got pregnant, then I would be the one having to provide, and always think of ways that I'll step up when that time comes. Do I love you? With all my heart. I love your beautiful chocolate brown skin and everything within, from the crown of your head, to the soles of your feet. I love you. And I'd be a fool to not want to be married to you and make this work."

That was all I needed to hear. As far as I was concerned, the air was clear and germ-free. I was so relieved to no longer have Teddy in my thoughts, wondering when he would make his move.

I climbed onto Brandon's lap, in a straddled position, and kissed him in a way to let him know I was totally in love with him. I laughed at the thought of Sylvia thinking she was going to win against me.

CHAPTER 16

I did all I could to keep my husband out of Sylvia's eyesight over the few days that followed. I also didn't see her, which kind of had me nervous. I was expecting her to do everything in her power to make me miserable.

I confided in my mother, and she was HOT. She was mad about what Brandon did, but told me I better not let Sylvia have him.

So many times, I fought myself from trying to get in touch with Anthony. I just needed a really good friend, and going through my current dilemma made me realize I had no friends. Somehow, Jeanette and Sylvia became allies, and I, the enemy. I thought of calling Jeanette to apologize to her for betraying her with Ricardo, but I couldn't get past thoughts of her *almost* sleeping with Brandon, and more than likely laughing at my expense as I was about to get married. I also recalled Anthony saying something about hearing that Brandon was kind of questionable. Jeanette probably told him everything, and they had a great laugh behind my back. That could have been the reason he felt the need to give me that money; because he knew my marriage wouldn't last. That thought started causing me ill feelings about Anthony.

I was sitting at the dining table on my laptop when Sylvia came in from work.

"Hey, cuz," she sang as if there wasn't a problem in the world.

"Hey!"

"How was your day?" she asked as she kicked her heels off and bent to pick them up.

"My day was fine. And yours?" I asked dryly.

"What's up with all the attitude?"

I looked at her like she was crazy. This was the first time I was seeing her since that spat we had a few days prior.

"Are you serious? My humor meter is a bit off right now."

"I mean, if you'd prefer I say nothing to you, I can do that. I had some news to share with you, but if you'd prefer not to hear, I won't," she said matter of fact like.

Bitch! I absolutely wanted to know the news, but I didn't know what kind of game she was up to.

Right at that moment, Brandon just so happened to walk in. I couldn't help but wonder if it was orchestrated, where one would enter and the other would wait a few minutes.

I got up from the seat to go greet Brandon with a kiss. Sylvia was still looking like we were all in a happy place.

"Oh good, Brandon, you're here. I was just about to share some good news with my cousin. I'm sure you'd like to hear also."

Brandon wore a confused smile and looked at me as we both went to sit back at the table.

"Just give me a minute. Let me go put my stuff down. I'll be right back," she said and then disappeared to her room.

"What the hell is going on?" he asked.

"The hell if I know. She just came in right before you, being all nice."

Sylvia came back into the dining room. "Umm, Asha, you cooked? You mind if I fix a plate? I'm starving."

I wasn't sure how to respond. I didn't like the idea of her in my food, or eating before my husband.

"I'll fix your plate. I have to fix a plate for my husband, anyhow."

"Cool."

Brandon came into the kitchen to help fix plates. We kept eyeing each other, trying to figure out what was going on.

We got the plates and glasses to the table and chose to eat in silence. I didn't want to have any conversations that would anger me while dishes and silverware were within reach.

"That was delicious," Sylvia said after I began clearing the table.

Brandon helped me take everything into the kitchen.

When we returned she asked, "Have you talked to Jeanette?"

"No. I haven't heard from her since my wedding."

"She's about to marry Ricardo. I think it's good everyone's able to move on with their lives and be happy. I'm glad the two of you are happy. You deserve it."

Now I was really on edge, waiting for the shoe to drop. I also clearly recalled telling Sylvia about the engagement that morning she pulled a gun on me.

"Thank you. That means a lot coming from you," Brandon said, seeming sincere.

I said nothing, because I knew my cousin better than that.

"Anyhow, I spoke with Jeanette, and I'll be moving out. Figure it would be best for all."

I let out a deep sigh. I was ready to jump up and click my heels in the air. But then Brandon had to go and fuck up my euphoria.

"So, where do you plan to move?"

She smiled as if she knew he was stepping into her trap.

"I got a really super job opportunity, making way more money than I could ever earn here."

"Well, money isn't always everything."

"Brandon," I said, getting annoyed by his inquisition.

"Yes, I know, but this will be great. I'll even get to travel to some wonderful places around the world, for work."

"Okay, and didn't you just say you're pregnant? How is that supposed to be good for the baby?" he asked, starting to get an attitude.

She had a smirk on her face as I sat looking at my husband in disbelief.

"We'll be fine. Actually, what I didn't tell you, I'll be moving to Jamaica. To Kingston. That's where I'll be spending the bulk of my time when I'm not traveling. Jeanette helped me get this wonderful opportunity. She talked to your ex, and he set it all up for me. He is definitely a blessing."

I wanted to crawl up underneath a rock and die. I hated her ass. I KNOW she said that shit on purpose.

"Ex? Whose ex?"

"My cousin's ex. Anthony."

He turned to me and asked, "Anthony, the guy you claimed handles all your business arrangements?"

"Yep! Same one!" she answered before I could lie.

"What the fuck?! You fucked him too?" Brandon asked, raising his voice as he stood from the table.

"Okay, I'm not going to sit here and have you raising your voice at me."

"I specifically asked if you ever had anything going on with that dude and you said no. Why'd you lie? Were you fucking him while we were dating or something?"

"No. In my cousin's defense, she hadn't seen him in like seven years. He came by right before the wedding, and she hadn't talked to him before then."

Brandon then looked at me in disbelief. "Hold up! You saw him right before our wedding? You were fucking him too?"

I shook my head with a snarl look on my face. "Brandon, don't you even go there. You know she's sitting here trying to start shit."

"Fine, we'll discuss this in private," he said to me and then redirected his attention back to Sylvia. "And you must have bumped your fucking head if you think you're taking my child and running off to some other country. That shit ain't happening! Hell no! No!"

My mouth opened from the shock and my eyes pierced daggers into Brandon.

"Aww, Sweetie, I didn't think you'd care. I won't deny you your child. I just think everyone would be much happier this way. Wouldn't you, cuz?"

"Absolutely! The sooner the better," I shouted. I wanted to get up and go to the bedroom, but Brandon was heated and had no intentions of leaving without a full-blown fight with the mother of his child.

"Fuck that shit!" He repeatedly slammed his hand on the table. "You are not taking my child any-fucking-where. You better find a job closer if you're not happy with your current job. You can't just waltz up into another country and practice law. You're not licensed there."

"Brandon, you need to calm down! Why are you getting all worked up when she's going to be out of our hair and give us peace?" I asked.

"I'm not sure what to tell you, Brandon. You don't have a say over my life. And who knows, I still might decide to abort the baby, as you requested just a few days ago, remember?" she continued to provoke him.

"An abortion? Oh no! No! I know I said it at first, but I've come around to the idea. You're not killing my child."

Sylvia laughed. "You're funny. Anyhow, I just wanted to let you know. I'll be here for another month, since I had to give my job notice, and I gotta get these two rooms ready to rent out."

I was looking down, and my neck almost snapped with the quickness I turned to look at her. "Wait, what? Rent out? Oh, hell no! I'm not having no renters in my home."

"Well, Jeanette and I figured with Brandon's little income and your modeling gigs quickly dwindling down, there's no way you'd be able to afford this mortgage and HOA fees on your own. We're not going to be footing the bill, so it only makes sense to bring in renters. Unless you want to enter into a contract to assume full financial responsibility. As investors in this condo, that is the majority decision Jeanette and I have come to."

"Sylvia, there is no fucking way that we're going to be able to manage a forty-five-hundred-dollar mortgage on our own. This is some bullshit."

"Well, yeah, we kind of figured that, which is why we think roommates will help. You have the largest of the bedrooms, so what's the problem?"

"What do you mean, what's the problem? I'm not living here with strangers, and you can't make me."

"Okay, well here's your options: One, you can figure out how to pay the entire mortgage plus the condo fees. Two, you can move out into a cheaper place you two could afford and we'll rent the entire unit for fifty-nine hundred a month. Three, you can deal with roommates, paying half the mortgage. Or four, you could see if you qualify for your own mortgage to buy the unit from us at the current market rate."

Sylvia clicked her nails on the table as she stared me down in a daring manner.

"Sylvia, why are you doing this? Tell me what you want."

"Hold up! What?" I asked Brandon. "What do you mean, tell you what she wants? What are you supposed to be doing to pacify her?"

"Chill, I'm trying to work this out so no one is doing anything foolish or irrational. I think this whole moving thing is irrational and out of anger. I think we just need to sit down like adults and try to come up with a resolution."

"Such as?" I asked, ready to ball up my fist and hit him with everything in me.

"So, if I said I wanted dick every night in order to stay here with your child, you'd accommodate me?"

I was about to lose it. I got up and started pacing back and forth while saying a silent prayer.

"Is that what this is all about? All of this is anger because I told you I can't be with you anymore?"

Sylvia cracked up laughing. "Anymore? When did it stop?"

I stopped pacing. "Brandon! What the fuck?!"

"Calm down, Asha! You know she's just messing with your head."

"Okay, so why do you want her to stay? Why not just let her trifling ass leave? Baby or no baby, she needs to go."

"Oh, I'm definitely going, but you're going to have to get that mortgage thing figured out, so we'll know if we need to protect our investment. And since we opted for a 15-year mortgage, and have plenty of equity. Yeah, I'm thinking you might have a difficult time trying to qualify for that on your own."

"How about you buy Asha out?" Brandon volunteered without first discussing with me.

I snapped, "That ain't an option. This is just as much my investment."

"Thanks for the input, Brandon, but buying Asha out is not on the table. She's been afforded the pleasure of staying here when we moved out, keeping us from making money, while she had Jeanette helping her pay a portion. That ship has sailed. Jeanette wants her portion paid through rental income, as do I. Don't worry, you don't have to make your decision tonight. Let me know when you get back from your trip. That way you'll have a better idea of what you'll be able to afford to do." She stood up from the chair. "Anyhow, I'm exhausted. Pregnancy will do that to you. I'm going to turn in for the night. Thanks again for dinner."

After she was gone, I simply pointed my finger toward the bedroom, for Brandon to go to.

"We need to clean up this kitchen," he said, trying to avoid the hell waiting on the other side of that bedroom door.

"I'll handle it when we're done."

He looked like a defeated dog and headed to the bedroom, where I raised hell. He sat in silence for the most part. When I was done yelling, I left to go clean the kitchen as I allowed my tears to flow freely.

Brandon emerged from the room dressed in shorts and a t-shirt, rushing toward the door not saying a word.

"Where are you going?"

"The gym!" he snapped and left out.

But if that wasn't bad enough, Sylvia then emerged from her room, dressed for the gym. Before leaving out she stopped at the breakfast bar.

"Cuz, I know things are very difficult right now, but I am really trying to put space between us so everyone can be at peace. I know the situation is complicated, which is why I'm trying to remedy it. 'Cause at the end of the day, no matter how messy the situation is, we're still family."

"You know what? Don't even go there. You sat your ass right back and let me marry someone you knew you were fucking."

"We tried to tell you not to marry him, but you wouldn't listen."

"You didn't have to fuck him. I could even see if it happened just once, but you kept up a whole side relationship with my husband. That ain't no family shit. Don't you ever call me family again."

"You don't really mean that, I know. I know you're just angry right now. Everything will be all good."

"Answer this: Why would you sit back and watch me marry him if you knew you were involved with him?"

"I didn't. I got up and walked out, remember? I told Brandon's manipulative ass that he needed to call off the wedding. I told him to give whatever reason he wanted, but he needed to call it off. He made that decision to marry you, knowing what he was doing the whole time."

"The whole time? What's the whole time?"

"Cuz, stop asking questions, knowing you don't really want the truth. I could tell you he and I were just fucking this morning, and you wouldn't let him go. Especially now. No, this is now a competition to you, and I'm trying to gracefully excuse myself."

I looked at her to see if she was being sincere. She seemed to be, but I didn't trust her. Especially with her heading to the gym, where my husband said he was going.

"And another thing," she continued, "regarding this condo, I know it's wonderful living here, but I'm sure you have enough in the bank to help put a down payment on a new home for yourself. If you don't, you can find a nice house to rent for less than two grand a month. Surely the two of you could afford that. I looked on Zillow and saw some in this area for that amount. It's a win-win for everyone. I really am trying to be nice, but I'll be damned if I'm going to let Brandon make any decisions for my life. You need to think about your own well-being. Just because I'm not around doesn't automatically make your husband trustworthy. And I don't wanna throw salt on a fresh wound, but I heard there's been a lot of complaints about your weight gain, meaning your gigs are going to get fewer and fewer. What are you going to do for income? And if Anthony's fiancée decides to get in his ear and cut your little career short, then you are really fucked! Right now, you don't have time to be spending your energies fighting me."

"Why?"

"Why? Why what?"

"Why did you sleep with Brandon? Why would you do that? And why wouldn't you tell me that you slept with him? That would have stopped me from marrying him. You've been sleeping with him since before he proposed. You should have thrown a wrench in that proposal."

She sighed and rolled her eyes and then chuckled. "Cuz, you weren't trying to hear shit. First, no, I absolutely wasn't going to ruin the surprise party that Jeanette and I spent thousands of dollars on. I raised hell with Brandon about that. We didn't know he was going to pull that shit. Why do you think he wasn't trying to set any date? Somehow once you came up with that whole Brazil wedding thing, you were a runaway train that couldn't be stopped. I figured you'd go live with him for a while and get to see what he's really all about. You would have definitely learned about his finances. He was often late with his rent. You would have also learned that he did have a better job at the same company, but they phased the position out, and his option was to downgrade to keep a job, or leave. He asked me what I thought he should do. I told him to take the downgrade until he found something else. He wanted to know if it was legal. That's how he told me." She chuckled.

"So, I could see you sleeping with him in the beginning, before the engagement, not that it was okay, but why'd you keep sleeping with him?"

"I'm sure you don't need me to tell you the sex is great, do you?"

I slammed my hand on the counter, feeling like I just got a kick in the gut. I couldn't stop the tears.

"I know you don't like what I'm saying but, Asha, he is no good for you. He's still trying to be with me. He's not going to stop unless I leave. And if I leave, it'll be someone else. Brandon's an opportunist. He's going to roll with whatever serves his best interest. When he realizes your coins are being reduced . . . baby girl, I know you're angry with me, but like I said, you gotta look out for you first."

I deliriously laughed. "Oh, I need to let him go so you could have him, huh?"

"And you stand here and question why no one said anything to you before. You're not trying to hear shit. See, you don't seem to understand, the only reason he is with you is because I allow it. If I told him to leave you right now, he'd hop to it. But whatever! Make it the best way you can. I tried to play nice."

She picked up her towel and water bottle and left out the door.

My anxiety was getting the better of me. I ran down to the gym, determined to catch the pair in a lovers' quarrel. Brandon wasn't even there. Sylvia was there along with other tenants, looking surprised when she saw me.

I tried to play nice since others were around.

"You see where Brandon got to?"

She looked at me oddly. "No, I thought he was upstairs in your room."

I was confused. "He left to the gym before you."

She shook her head. "Well, maybe he went to a different gym. He wasn't in here when I got here."

I looked at Sylvia, believing she was lying to upset me. I didn't respond. I walked outside to the walking trail, figuring I'd find him there. He was nowhere to be found. I then went looking for his car, and that was gone, also.

Sylvia came from the gym as I headed to the elevators.

"You didn't find him?"

"Mind your damn business!" I snapped and went into the elevator door that opened.

She stood laughing and shaking her head.

I called Brandon the minute I got back in the door. He didn't answer, but then I heard his phone ringing. He left it in the bedroom. I never looked through his phone before, but I needed answers. Everything in me screamed to not do it, but I had to.

After trying various combinations, I finally was able to crack his password, which was his mother's birthday. His phone was loaded with photos of naked women. He was having text conversations with many women, and although he had the decency to tell them he was now married, they continued to send him nude photos, and he was saving every one of them. Those were a walk in the park compared to the next text I found.

CHAPTER 17

Asha, that's your husband and things are sometimes rocky in the beginning, but you gotta fight. I mean really fight for your husband. I don't like your father being with other women, but I understand sometimes men just need a little space, 'cause you see who he always runs back to?"

I looked at my delusional mother as if she had really lost her mind. "Mom, Daddy does not run back to you. You're only with him if he happens to be around. All these years, and he still hasn't committed to you."

"Girl, why you come over here with that foolishness? I had errands to run."

"I know, Mom, but I don't know what to do. I didn't say anything about it when he came in yesterday, but according to that text, it's clear as day he's the one chasing Sylvia."

"Maybe you're reading too much into this. He just asked if they could meet up in private. They do need to sit down and talk about how they're going to deal with this baby, and he probably just didn't want to upset you. He's trying to protect you, and you need to let him. Just like you got yourself all bent out of shape when you couldn't find him in the gym yesterday and learned that he left to ride to the park when he saw Sylvia. He's obviously trying to avoid her. He's telling all those girls that's he's now a married man, but they're the ones wanting to disrespect your marriage, not him."

I loved laying on the bed with my mother when I was stressed. That somehow always made my life better. I didn't like her trying to convince me to give him a pass, but I didn't want to just throw him away, especially knowing all those women in his phone were trying to convince him to leave his wife.

I was devastated when I went through his phone the day before and saw playful text messages between him and Sylvia. When he texted her about meeting up, she refused his invitation. I was also devastated to see photos of them together on the beach in Rio. I didn't ask him to delete anything. I took the liberty of deleting anything I felt he didn't need to have in his phone, to include Sylvia's number. Oh, and Jeanette's number. He purchased his current phone since we were engaged. I wasn't sure what he felt he needed to talk to Jeanette about after the party. The thought of them almost sleeping together after we were engaged angered me. Thankfully, Brandon had the good sense to shut down her advances, or so he said. I thought of finding a way to let Ricardo know what she did. I know what I did was wrong, but she should have confronted me about it. That was so many years ago.

"Mom, what am I supposed to do if he convinces Sylvia to stay? Why does he even want her to stay when he and I could live in peace?"

"Baby, you need to put your foot down. Let him know you're not going to sit back and tolerate that."

"Like give him an ultimatum? What if he really leaves me?"

"That man ain't going anywhere. Stop acting like you don't know your worth."

"I want her to go, but he doesn't want to be away from his baby. I mean, how could I blame him? If it were anyone else, I'd tell her she's wrong for trying to take the baby away from its father."

"You tell him you will get joint custody and sometimes the baby will live with you two."

I sighed. "Sylvia would never let that happen."

"You just tell him that. We know she ain't, but he don't know that. Your plan is to first get her out of the picture. Make him think everything will work out. Even tell him the two of you can take a trip there to check up on the baby. He'll fall for that."

I smiled. Sounded like a wonderful plan.

"Thank you, Mommy," I said, reaching over to kiss her.

"You need to get home and put it on your husband good. You leave for your trip tomorrow, and you need to make sure he's satisfied."

"Are they ever satisfied? Remember how Daddy went running off in Brazil?"

"Oh shut up! Stop trying to remind me of what he did. You go worry about your own."

I went home and did as my mother advised. I started off talking Brandon into letting Sylvia go, and then I tried to give him the best night of sex possible before departing the following day.

I always was a glutton for punishment. Someone once said, if you seek, you shall find, and I wasn't sure why I was seeking, knowing I wasn't prepared to do anything about it.

I told Brandon that my trip was going to be for three days, but I knew before I left, it was only going to be for two days. I talked to Brandon through the day to keep him thinking I was busy working. He told me he had been successfully avoiding Sylvia and hadn't seen her since I left. I set a whole plan in motion to catch him with her. If push came to shove and they weren't together, I'd say the shoot wrapped up earlier than anticipated and I decided to surprise him.

My flight was in at three, but I stayed away from home until almost nine that evening. I eased to the door and tried to listen. I heard nothing. I already saw both cars downstairs, so I knew they were home. I eased the door open, and it was quiet, as well as dark. I decided to head to my own bedroom, which to my dismay turned out to be dark and empty. The bed was still made, just how I left it before my trip, with the stuffed animals positioned in the pattern that I purposefully left them.

My heart was thumping, and I even had tears in my eyes, but I tried to keep quiet as I put my bags down. I was sure not to have a rattling bag giving me away, as I had the previous trip. I also made sure not to wear any shoes that would make noise, but when I was in my bedroom, I took them off.

I tiptoed towards Sylvia's room. The door was slightly opened and the television light was on, but there was no sound other than the television. I heard a key inserted at the door, and I quickly ducked down and snuck past Sylvia's room to hide in the room that used to be her room. The lights went on in the kitchen.

"Brandon, is that you?" Sylvia called out.

"Yeah, babe," he responded, calling her what he called me.

She got up and went to the kitchen to join him. I was too far away to make out what they were saying or doing. From time to time, I'd hear them laughing, as if they'd been getting along just dandy in my absence. They were in there a good twenty minutes, and were probably eating, since I could smell take-out food. Since his car was parked outside when I got home, I assumed he must have gone somewhere within walking distance. I heard Sylvia go back in her room and turn on her shower, and I heard Brandon in the kitchen, cleaning.

When the shower stopped, I heard Brandon in the doorway of her room, "Babe, I'm gonna go call Asha and tell her goodnight."

"Whatever! Why you telling me?" She laughed.

"Damn!" I heard him say while still standing in her doorway.

"Go make your call and stop staring."

"I'm trying, but you know you're sure not making it easy. Look," he said.

I wondered what that meant.

"I don't need to see that. Looks like you better hurry up and go make your call so she can handle that for you." Sylvia laughed again. "Get out!"

I panicked because my phone was in my room inside my bag. I had the phone on vibrate. If he went into the bedroom to try to call, he'd probably hear the vibration and know I was somewhere lurking. I was torn about intercepting any possibility of them fucking, so I could remain in denial about the fact that they've been sexually involved since our marriage.

He turned on the television in the living room, I guess to give me the impression that he was in the bedroom watching television. A few minutes later, he returned to Sylvia's doorway saying, "She didn't answer."

"Oh. Well, I'm sure she'll see your call and call you back."

"Yeah, you're probably right."

He returned to the living room.

They seemed to be behaving in a civil manner. It was all confusing. I didn't know what to make of anything. Another half hour went by and he returned to her doorway. "Still no answer or callback."

"Maybe she's relaxing. Modeling is exhausting. She might have just laid down for a minute and conked out."

I was actually surprised to hear how supportive Sylvia was being, instead of trying to make him think I was out messing around.

"Maybe you're right. You need anything else? I need my son or daughter happy. I don't want you lying and saying their dad wasn't shit."

"You ain't shit." She laughed.

"Yeah, okay. I see you got jokes."

He walked away from Sylvia's room and turned off the lights in the kitchen and living room. It seemed as if he might have gone to our bedroom. I was hoping he wasn't in there trying to call me again, because then he'd hear my phone. I had to find a way to sneak past Sylvia's opened door and get to the bedroom before Brandon alerted Sylvia about my bags being home. I got down low and made it past without being seen. I tiptoed to my bedroom where I found Brandon laying on the sofa, watching television. I'm not sure why it hadn't crossed my mind that he could have slept on the sofa in our bedroom.

"Asha!" he said with surprise. "What the hell? Where'd you come from so quietly?"

"I didn't want to wake Sylvia if she was asleep. I saw her door was opened just now. I thought she normally keeps it closed."

He shrugged. "Sounds like an accusation instead of you just coming over here and giving me a kiss."

I walked to the sofa as he raised up to receive my kiss. I didn't really catch him doing anything wrong, but I was still suspicious.

I looked at the bed and then pointed to it. "You didn't sleep on the bed while I was gone?"

"I've been sleeping right here. This is very comfortable. Actually, I'd sit here to watch television and then fall asleep." He looked around. "Where's your bags?"

I felt so embarrassed. I confessed, "I'm so sorry. I snuck in here earlier while you were out, thinking I was going to catch you in the act of messing with my cousin. My bags are inside my closet."

He looked confused. "So you were in here hiding and spying? Asha, really? That's what you think of me?"

"I'm sorry," I cried. "Please forgive me. You have no idea how difficult this situation is for me, and then I hear you two being all nice and you calling her 'babe.' That was hard for me."

He laughed. "You thought you were going to catch us in bed together?"

"I didn't want to, but I had to know what's really going on."

"You lied and told me you were coming home tomorrow, so you could try to catch us in some act? Asha, this shit is insane. Is this what I'm going to have to deal with every time you go away?"

I refused to answer. He shook his head and returned to his lying position to watch the television. That night, he refused to make love to me, saying he was still pissed off with my behavior. I begged and pleaded, and he wouldn't budge.

The next morning while he was in the shower, I decided to sneak into his phone to see what women he may have been with while I was away. I couldn't understand his total rejection.

Unfortunately, he hadn't had an opportunity to clear his phone out before I got to it. He and Sylvia had been texting back and forth. I saw she texted him at the time I came home, saying: FYI, your wife just walked in and she's sneaking around in the house like she's trying to catch us doing something.

He responded: Wow! Thanks!

Later she texted him: Dumbass is hiding out in my old room.

He responded: LOL! You have got to be kidding.

I was puzzled how she knew when I came in and why she didn't say anything to me. There were no messages before that. I was also wondering if she gave him a heads up long before he returned with that food and why he was calling her 'babe' and standing in her doorway, knowing she just got out of the shower. Why didn't he come in looking for me?

I heard the water shut off from his shower and quickly returned his phone to the nightstand and went to play sleep. He tried to prepare for work quietly, but he was actually loud. When he was fully dressed, he didn't try to wake me. Just a quick kiss on the side of my head that wasn't buried in the pillow, and then he left out of the bedroom. I started to jump up to see if he ran to see Sylvia, but I stayed put.

I know one thing; these two were making me batshit crazy.

Everyone was cordial to one another over the next week. I learned of two new gigs that I had lined up, but I wasn't comfortable leaving for yet another gig that would keep me over a weekend. I tried to get Brandon to go with me, but he couldn't get off that Friday, and he refused to call out sick because he was still hoping for a better position with the company.

I had also taken note of the time passing, and there was no more talk of Sylvia leaving. She hadn't even questioned me about our future living arrangement. She was typically not home when I got up or got home late.

I was still troubled about how she knew when I snuck in the house that night. I thought about buying a nanny cam to spy on them while I was away, but then wondered if that was how Sylvia knew I came in. She was into guns, so it wouldn't surprise me if she was into hidden cameras. If she did have a spy cam, she'd be able to see me going around the house planting my own.

I knew Brandon would be about done with me if he found out I was still spying on them. I didn't know what to do. I was especially insecure because it was a weekend and both of them would be off and spending time together. I contemplated cancelling the gig that morning but knew Anthony would never lift a finger to help me again.

I opted for the hidden nanny cam. Actually, I purchased three. I tried to find inconspicuous locations to place them, while also trying to place them discreetly, just in case Sylvia had cameras watching what I was doing. I hid one on our entertainment unit to capture a view toward the sofas and dining area. I put it amongst some knickknacks to so it would blend in. We had a fake plant on top of the cabinet in the kitchen, and I planted one there, trying to angle it to capture the entrance into the kitchen. I planted the third one in a fake tree that sat as if you were going toward my bedroom. That captured a view going toward Sylvia's room. Before leaving, I made sure I could see everything on my laptop and my phone. I was determined to catch them that weekend. I wasn't sure what I'd do, but I needed answers.

CHAPTER 18

was feeling myself as I collected my bags to take off for my trip.
I wasn't sure what I'd catch on those cameras, or what I'd do
when I did. I figured at the very least, if nothing was going on, then
I'd be able to finally fully trust and commit to my husband. I looked
around and stood at the door for a moment, trying to think if I might
have forgotten anything. I opened the door and felt my heart fall,
along with my bags.

An envelope from the hotel in Rio rested on my Welcome
doormat outside my door. I stood staring at it for the longest, as if
that would make it go away. It was one thing to be outside of my
hotel room, but this was my home—on a whole different continent.

I cautiously picked up the envelope. To my surprise, it wasn't
as thick as the previous envelopes, but I was able to feel something
inside of it. I was glad I had told Brandon about the stalker, so I'd
be able to freely tell him the man found our home. I debated going
to file a police report, but I didn't know enough about Teddy to tell
them, nor did I want to tell them about the nature of our involvement.

I was able to collect myself, gather my dropped belongings, and
rush out to meet my waiting Lyft. Once inside, I peeked into the
envelope. There was a flash drive and a single-page letter. I was

desperate to see the contents, but I tucked it into my bag until I could check it out alone.

My mind couldn't stop thinking about the envelope, and I thought I'd get a free moment to investigate it once I arrived at my hotel in Phoenix. However, they were calling for me the minute my plane landed. It was so difficult trying to work and keep my mind off not only the envelope, but what action my hidden video cameras might have been catching.

I had people continuously yelling at me all evening, and I tried to block most of it out. That was, until I heard someone say, "Oh come on, how much longer are we supposed to put up with her talentless, old, fat ass? We're going to have to draw the line with these favors."

Someone else elbowed that guy to alert him that I was looking in shock, and he said, "Oh so what! She needs to know the truth."

It took everything in me not to cry. The photographer looked at me with pity. He mouthed the words, "Smile and keep it together." That made me force a smile and try to focus on my photoshoot. There was an event directly following, and we were to model some of the pieces throughout the event.

By the time I made it back to my room, I was beyond exhausted. I was in a different time zone, I was up early, and it was already four in the morning. That was also my first opportunity to check my phone. There were several missed calls from Brandon. I wasn't sure why he was blowing up my phone like that while he knew I was working, but I had sent him a text earlier, letting him know I received another envelope on our doormat. He didn't respond until I was about to get on the plane, but I told him I was boarding.

After my shower, I called him.

"Hello," he answered, sounding asleep.

"Hey. Sorry I'm just making it back to my phone. I've been

working all night. I hopped in the shower and wanted to call you before I pass out and get whisked away again."

"Uhm," was all he responded with.

"Are you 'sleep?"

"It's just after six. What you think I'm doing?" he snapped.

"Well, I wanted to call and talk to you. This has been a horrendous day. I heard one of the directors call me an old fat ass while I was doing a shoot. He said I had no talent."

"Wow! That's fucked up. But yeah, anyway, we need to talk. I mean a serious talk. I know you're having a difficult time right now, and I don't want to make it heavier, but this shit has got to stop. I understand you're insecure, but hiding fucking cameras? Asha, that's some stupid fucking shit. You didn't think anyone would see them? Once Sylvia saw the first one, she looked and found two more. If you wanted me to stay with my family or something while you were away, you should have just said that shit. I started to do just that, but then I figured you'd be accusing me of doing something out there as well."

I was speechless. I was certain no one would find the hidden cameras. The only logical way Sylvia could have found my hidden cameras was if she already had some watching. I was angry and embarrassed.

He continued. "So, hopefully, this is the last time we're going to have this conversation on the subject. You hear me?"

"Yes," I tearfully replied.

"Stop crying. You just need to stop that shit. I know I fucked up and didn't make it easy, but when I said it's me and you, I meant that. Now, tell me about that envelope you got. What was in it? How'd dude find your address?"

"I don't know, Brandon! Don't you think this shit is terrifying to me?" I yelled. "I never mentioned the part of town I lived in. I didn't have my ID with me, so I don't know. The only thing I can think of, he must have had some connection with the front desk staff to be able to get all those hotel envelopes."

I dug into my bag to pull out the envelope as I spoke.

"What kind of stuff did y'all talk about that would help him figure out where you live? It had to be something. Think!"

I dropped the phone as I read the letter. I didn't read the entire thing, but I saw a demand for $25,000 and fourteen days to get the money.

"Asha!" I heard Brandon yelling when I picked the phone back up and put it to my ear.

"Oh my god, Brandon. This is an extortion letter, demanding twenty-five thousand dollars within the next fourteen days."

"Get the fuck out of here! Are you just bullshitting me?"

"No!"

I wanted to tell him there was also a lengthy website address typed in the letter, along with a note saying that was just a sample of what the world would be seeing and that the flash drive contained a bigger sample.

"Asha! Stop zoning out while I'm trying to talk to you."

I didn't know he was saying anything. My ears were only hearing my heartbeat inside my head.

"Brandon, I have to go," I said before ending the call.

I had to see what was behind that link and what was on that flash drive. There was no way I could listen to a hyped-up Brandon at the same time. He kept trying to call back repeatedly, but I was on a mission.

When I typed the address into a browser, it immediately directed me to a porn site, showing a silent twenty-second clip of me naked on top of Teddy with my hands behind my head. I started hyperventilating. I couldn't stop blinking as the tears flooded my eyes. I pushed my laptop away to make it go away. Right underneath, there was a display of the number of views. 23,673.

I put my face into a pillow and screamed. A few minutes after collecting myself, I pulled out the flash drive and plugged it into my laptop. It was like a whole professional production was put together. It had an intro with words and music, reading "The Night Before, Starring Chocolate Bunny." It started off with us standing outside Teddy's hotel room door talking and touching. It had some audio that was not my voice, but looking at the video, you couldn't tell it wasn't me talking. In the video, I supposedly said, "I'm a naughty whore, and I want you to fuck me with that super big cock of yours before I get married in a few hours." The voice didn't even match. It sounded like some ditsy blonde. Even Teddy's voice sounded different than I remembered. He then played shy, saying he'd never been with a black chick before, and my fake voice responded, "Well, I'm going to break your black girl virginity. I'm going to fuck you like you've never been fucked before."

Here's the worst part—the filming began while we stood outside of his hotel room, having that bogus conversation. It was like he was somehow tapped into the hotel's security cameras, but it was able to zoom in on us in front of his door. Next, it showed the minute we got inside of his room and he ripped my thong off, and his face was quickly buried underneath my miniskirt. Of course, there was exaggerated moaning and groaning. At one point, the camera focused in on the clock, reading 11:47pm.

I again screamed into the pillow but looked back at the screen just in time to see the part where my fake voice was asking him if I could piss in his mouth, and he said, "Yeah, baby, you lay down right there while I suck that piss out." Then the clock displayed 12:52am. I was riding Teddy's face, and then there was the scene when he abruptly stopped and I looked down at his face with him appearing unconscious. I jumped off of him saying, "Oh shit! No!!" Only difference was, the fake voice yelled, "Oh shit! I thought my super fat black pussy lips smothered you to death."

You could then see Teddy with a Cheshire cat smile, saying, "You liked that? You want some of that down there?" pointing toward his bulge. He then showed my hand rubbing on his groin. "You want that?" He used his other hand to open his pants and release his swollen cock. My fake voice exclaimed, "Oh my! I've never seen a cock like that before. It's the size of a log."

Next, I was acting like I was going to give him a blowjob. The fake voice said, "Oh my god! I want your giant cock in my mouth so bad, but it won't fit."

I didn't see any that night, but it would appear as if he had cameras everywhere and a cameraman helping to do close-up shots. The scenes were all just bits and pieces randomly put together. The video ended right when he got around to opening my blouse and freeing my swollen girls from the bra, but then it faded to: "Subscribe to enjoy the full video."

I was so engrossed in that video, I hadn't realized Brandon was still calling repeatedly. I finally answered, hysterical and incoherent.

"Asha! Calm down! I can't understand a thing you're saying."

"He made a fucking video!"

If I didn't know any better, I thought I heard Brandon laugh.

"Who made a video?"

"Did you just laugh?"

"No."

"Yes, you did. I heard you."

"Asha, I almost choked. You did not hear me laugh. Who made a video?"

"Who the fuck you think!" I shot, now angry, because I knew for certain he laughed, and he was denying it. He actually still sounded like he was fighting laughter. "You know what? Fuck it! Goodbye!" I hung up.

He was pissing me off. *Why the hell would he ask me who, like he didn't know what we were just talking about before? Stupid ass!*

Brandon kept calling, and I kept ignoring.

Then he sent me a text: "I wish you would answer the phone. If this guy is demanding $25,000 for some video, then I think you need to pay to get rid of him."

THAT pissed me off. I called him back. "What the fuck do you mean I need to pay him? Pay him with what? You have twenty-five thousand dollars to give to him? No! So, shut the fuck up, telling me I need to just pay someone twenty-five thousand dollars. I just paid for our entire fucking wedding, all by myself, in case you forgot."

"Asha, you better chill the fuck out, talking to me like I'm some punk on the street. First of all, no one told you to pay for any elaborate wedding in another fucking country. I said let's do a simple church wedding, that we could both afford. I'm not sure who you were trying to impress. Second, none of this shit would have happened if we didn't go to Brazil. And finally, it definitely wouldn't have happened if you weren't cocking your fucking legs open to some random motherfucker, a few hours before you were about to marry me. You did all that shit, so stop treating me like the fucking enemy here. We need to figure out how we gonna pay this motherfucker off and get him out of our lives, for good."

"How about I just call the police and report this shit? Why is that not a suggestion?" I snapped.

"So, you're willing to tell them what you did and have them looking at naked pictures and videos of you?"

I thought about that, and the thought was unsettling. "But if I pay him, how do I know he'll go away? He'll keep demanding more and more, and I don't have money like that. You just heard Sylvia talking about we need to move because we can't afford to buy her and Jeanette out. I have no choice but to go to the police."

"I don't think that's a good idea. I think if anything, that might piss him off and there's no telling how much damage would be done before the police can actually catch up to him. You said he wants the money in fourteen days? See if he'll take part now and maybe some more down the road."

"First of all, I don't know how to contact his ass. Second, I'm not doing that. He's not getting a fucking dime, keeping me living in fear for the rest of my life. He wanna release some shit, then let him do it, and when he does, it'll be that much easier to track his ass down."

"So, you just want the world to see I married a whore? You're not even thinking about what this will do to me."

I was about to go off on him, but I could hardly catch my breath, as his words seemed to knock the wind out of me. I just ended the call. I couldn't talk to him anymore that night. I didn't answer his calls for the remainder of my trip.

I desperately wanted to talk to Sylvia, since she was a lawyer. I thought she could give me the best advice on handling the situation, but I made such a mess of our relationship. Well, technically, she did, by sleeping with Brandon. I thought of what I would tell the police if I called to make a report, and I really didn't want them to see the mess I made hours before my wedding.

I replayed that night over and over in my mind, trying to figure out

HOW I came to do something so stupid. I remembered feeling some kind of insecurity earlier that day when seeing Sylvia walking with Brandon. I remembered feeling anger and jealousy about Jeanette going off to hang with Miss Corrine and Ricardo. I remembered nothing seemed to be going right that night, and somehow, while I should have been celebrated by my friends and family, I was wandering off alone, vulnerable, into the bed with Teddy.

CHAPTER 19

I arrived home at almost three, going into Monday morning. Everyone was asleep. I still didn't want to talk to or see Brandon, so I camped out in Sylvia's former bedroom.

The whole ride home, I wondered what would make Brandon think I just had $25,000 to give like that. I never told him about the money I received from Anthony. I wondered if somehow Anthony told Jeanette and Jeanette told Sylvia, and then Sylvia told Brandon. As far as Brandon and I discussed, funds were about to get tight. My gigs were dwindling, and they weren't even high paying gigs. I remembered when we talked about how we'd find another home, I mentioned that I might be able to come up with about $10,000 for a down payment, but didn't think that would be enough, and I suggested that we might just have to rent something.

For him to turn around and suggest I just pay someone $25,000, knowing he didn't have two nickels to contribute, led me to believe he somehow knew about the $50,000.

I heard Brandon and Sylvia arguing that morning before they left out. It was kind of hard to hear what they were saying, but at one point she got closer to her room and I heard her say, "Your broke ass can't afford shit, so no, you don't get a say in my life."

"I have a say in my baby's life."

"No, you don't."

"Come on, babe. I got some money coming to me soon, and I'll be able to afford to take care of our baby."

"Where you got money coming from? You got a new job lined up, paying some real money?"

"Something like that. Please, Sylvia, just give me a chance. You can't do this to me."

She laughed. "You sound like you keep forgetting, you have a wife. Now, leave me the fuck alone. I gotta go, so move," she said before slamming her bedroom door closed.

"Bitch! Both of y'all!"

Both of y'all??? I couldn't help but wonder who the both were. Could he possibly have included me in that both, or would he be talking about Jeanette?

I heard the front door slam. I wanted to get up and go see, but I hadn't heard Sylvia. A few minutes later, she came busting into the room I was sleeping in, almost as if she knew I was there.

"You need to get his ass out of this fucking house! You can go with him or do whatever, but he needs to go."

Instead of me playing it cool and gathering information, I automatically went on the defense.

"He's my husband and he'll live wherever I live. You don't get to decide who can or cannot live here. You have another house, remember? Why can't you stay there?"

"You are so fucking stupid. You deserve everything you get. Dumbass! Oh, and by the way, tell *your* husband to stop hitting on me every time you're away, because I'm not trying to fuck with him anymore."

"Please! He is not trying to hit on you. He told me that's all in the past. And you wanna talk about someone being stupid, keep fucking with me and see if I won't I let the rest of the family know what your backstabbing ass did to me."

She laughed, and then laughed harder. "Tell them. They already know. Hell, they knew before you said, 'I do' to the joker. You're the only one who don't wanna know what a piece of shit he is. Speaking of husband, why are you sleeping in here instead of your own bed? Why didn't you want your husband to know you were home? I heard your ass creeping in here last night. I almost shot your ass, but you lucky I caught a whiff of your perfume. Oh, and the next time your husband creeps his naked ass in my bathroom while I'm in the shower or crawls in my bed with his hard dick in hand, I will shoot him. Too bad you missed him just last night. I shouldn't have to be locking my bedroom or bathroom door. If the shit's closed, that's the first clue to stay the fuck out of it."

I could feel the blood rushing into my head. I was getting dizzy, while sitting up on the bed.

"Why would he be in your room?"

"Because he's relentlessly begging for some pussy?" she stated as a question. "What do you think? And his sad ass is trying to remind me that my pussy belongs to him. Yeah, he's all the way fucked up with that shit. I'm going to get a restraining order if I have to, and if you can't control his ass, then you'll be out right along with him."

She turned and left from the room and then from the house.

I wanted to get up and go check the rest of the house, but I was overcome with grief and depression.

Later that morning, I got up to investigate. My heart sank when I found a set of folded papers resting on top of an envelope from the hotel in Rio. It was obvious that Brandon set it there for me to see. I opened the stack, and I saw a similar typed note, demanding $25,000 in now less than two weeks, that included that same website address. There were several nude photos printed out onto the pages. I sat on the bed and cried and cried and cried.

I later called my mother, and she suggested I speak with the building management to see about getting video of a strange man lurking outside my door, dropping envelopes. Upon her advice, I called, but they told me I would need a police report first. I was trying not to get the police involved. I even called some legal hotline for advice, and they also told me I needed to go to the police to be able to get the material removed from the porn website.

Oddly, Brandon didn't attempt to call me that entire day. Nor did I try to call him. I was still angry, and Sylvia's words were like gasoline on a fire.

On top of all my troubles, I now had to find us someplace to stay quickly, before Sylvia either shot him or obtained a restraining order. I really didn't want to believe he was still pursuing Sylvia, but I heard him with my own ears, begging her to give him some kind of chance. I was also curious about this new job that he had yet to mention to me. Why would he be telling her and not his wife?

I'm not sure why I cringed when I heard Brandon coming home after work. I was sitting at the table on my laptop. He paused long enough to look at me with disgust, and then he headed to the bedroom. I was stunned by his actions. I heard him begging Sylvia with my own ears, yet he was acting as if I had done something.

I got up and stormed into the bedroom. "What the fuck was that about?"

"Asha, don't start no shit with me. You did see those papers I left on the bed, didn't you? I saw them. I also saw that website, along with almost a hundred thousand other people. How could you? That is so disgusting. You—I don't even know what the fuck to say anymore. I mean, it was one thing for you to have some last little fling, but you didn't tell me you were making porno flicks. Are you that desperate to be an actress? First, I find out you been having a bunch of abortions, and now I find out I married a fucking porn whore. Do you know how embarrassing this shit is going to be for me when my family finds out? I'm disgusted, Asha. No wonder you were trying to hide the shit from me. When you told me that shit, you tried to make it sound like you were some kind of victim. Looking at those photos and that website, you were cheesing for the fucking camera, wasn't you?"

When I was able to respond after the shock wore off, I said, "Brandon, that is so fucking unfair. You can see in that letter that someone is threatening me."

He was about to go into the bathroom, but turned back to face me. "Are they now? How do I know you're not in on this shit, so I could feel sorry for you? How do you take pictures or a video like that and no one else is in the room with you? You can't, so cut that bullshit! You've already proven yourself to be a habitual liar."

I gasped and covered my mouth. "Brandon, I swear, I don't know how he did it."

"What exactly do you do on all these modeling gigs you run off to? You make all this money, but I have yet to see you on some big runway fashion show. You're a thick, dark skinned woman, almost a year away from turning thirty with a whole lot of ass. Whose hiring you to model, if it's not porn? I didn't want to think like that before, but now I can't help but wonder. What all are you hiding from me? You obviously like to lie. When I repeatedly tried to get you to tell me about you fucking with dude, you kept lying until I called you out. Is he the only reason we had to be in Brazil? So you could do this, quote-unquote, modeling gig? And it's also a coincidence that your ex, that helps line up these gigs, just so happened to be there. How fucking stupid do you think I am? Were you fucking him also?"

I was too stunned to answer. I just sat on the bed, looking down, trying to imagine how awful it all looked.

"Yeah, that's right. Don't say shit, 'cause you don't know how to tell the truth about a damn thing." He went into the bathroom, closed the door, and turned on the shower.

I had to admit, everything he just said all seemed suspicious. Brandon had never questioned my modeling gigs. It crushed my soul for him to do so in that moment. While I should have been cussing him out, he managed to turn the tables on me, and all I could think about was how I could fix things so he wouldn't be angry with me.

Two days later, when I received another notice with an account number to wire the $25,000, I dug into my secret account and tried my damndest to make this problem go away and fix my marriage. That night I prepared a romantic dinner and set up a candlelit bath for us, hoping to romance him. I even bought him flowers. I didn't tell him I paid the fee. I was just hoping we'd heard the last of Teddy. If that didn't end it, I'd have no choice but to go to the police.

Thankfully, my husband was receptive to my peace offering. He even apologized for saying such ugly words to me. The sex was perfect that night. However, when I had to remind him that I had another out-of-town trip to make, his attitude seemed to return. When I tried to turn the tables by telling him about Sylvia saying he was still trying to fuck her every time I leave town, he told me I was a fool for letting her play with my head like that. He said his only concern with Sylvia was the child growing inside of her, and nothing more. I let that go, because I didn't want us to be in a bad place with one another.

CHAPTER 20

I arrived home early Saturday morning from my gig out in Seattle. I was hoping to get a quick shower and hop in the bed with my husband. However, when I arrived, I found my naked husband in the kitchen, preparing breakfast. When I say "naked," I mean as naked as he entered the world. He didn't seem surprised, and although I hadn't spoken with him that morning, he knew I'd be getting in early that morning. Sure, it was thirty minutes earlier than I expected, but still, he knew to expect me.

He ran to greet me with a kiss as if expecting me and then escorted me to the table to have a seat for the breakfast he prepared.

"Can I at least go put my stuff away and get a shower? I've been flying all night."

"No, I'll go put your bags in the room. You just have a seat."

I did as he instructed and waited on his return from our bedroom. When he returned, he was wearing a bathrobe. I was a bit perplexed why he was naked before my entrance but felt a need to put a robe on once I was home. I didn't say anything, determined not to start an instant fight.

He set a plate of food in front of me and then went to knock on Sylvia's door, asking if she wanted some of the breakfast he prepared.

She had him bringing her a plate to her room. It took everything in me not to go knock the plate out of his hand. Particularly, because I was thinking—hoping—Sylvia might not have been home, since he felt it was okay to walk around naked. Still, I held my peace. He returned to the table, acting happy to see me and inquiring about my trip.

"Brandon, bring me some more juice," Sylvia called out from her bedroom.

Before Brandon could jump up, I did. I was losing my patience. I went to Sylvia's opened doorway.

"You want some damn juice, you get up and get that shit. My husband is not your servant."

Sylvia looked at me as if I was crazy and then smirked. She pushed her covers from her and started getting out of the bed. She was naked. Before she could make it fully off the bed, Brandon came running with the juice container.

"What the—? What the hell is going on here?" I yelled.

It was bad enough seeing Brandon strutting around naked, but then to see Sylvia also naked, and he just so happened to be up preparing breakfast, was unsettling. Brandon actually pushed past me to get the juice container to Sylvia.

"Thank you, babe," she said sweetly.

My eyes were flooded and I could hardly breathe.

I started charging toward Sylvia, but Brandon grabbed hold of me.

"Let her go, 'cause I know this bitch don't think she's about to try to lay a finger on me. I already told you, control your man. You couldn't, so oh well. It is what it is."

"Sylvia, stop that!" Brandon tried to chastise.

"What do you mean, 'stop it?' You need to just tell her delusional ass the truth. I don't know why you insist on the games."

"What is she talking about, Brandon?"

"You know damn well what I'm talking about. I tell you about him always trying to get some pussy from me when you're not around, and you want to make me out to be the liar. Well, if this ain't an eye-opener, I don't know what would be."

"Shut up, Sylvia!" Brandon warned.

"Don't be telling me to shut up! Did you or did you not just wake up in my bed?"

I stopped trying to push past Brandon to actually look at Brandon.

"She's lying, isn't she?" I asked him.

"Let's go and talk," he said, looking defeated as he tried to escort me out of Sylvia's room.

"Yeah, you go do that. Me and our baby need some sleep after all that activity."

I turned to try to push past Brandon again, but he was stronger and quicker. He lifted me up and carried me from Sylvia's room, pulling her door closed as we exited.

I was screaming and crying while he kept trying to get me to calm down.

Once I was calmed, he sat on the sofa in our bedroom with his face in his hands. I sat silently, unsure of what else to say or do. I felt like a prisoner, trapped where I didn't want to be. I wasn't sure if I was supposed to just accept sharing my husband with my pregnant cousin, or if I was supposed to walk away. She wasn't going away, ever. With the baby involved, he wasn't going to let go of her.

"Do you love her?" I asked, breaking the silence.

He hesitated a long time before shrugging his shoulders.

"At least have the decency to look me in my fucking eye and tell me the truth. I asked, do - you - fucking - love - her?"

I wasn't sure why I was pressing him for an answer, knowing I wasn't prepared for one.

He looked me in my eye. "Yes."

"Yes? What the fuck do you mean, *yes*? Why would you marry me if you loved her?"

"I swear, I didn't know at the time. It was something about the baby that made me realize how much she meant to me."

I had to catch my breath from that gut kicker.

"Asha, I swear I didn't mean to hurt you."

"So what am I supposed to do? Just share my husband with my cousin?"

He covered his face again. "No. I don't want you to share."

"You say you don't want me to share, but you'll sleep with her every chance I turn my back."

"No, I said I don't want you to share," he repeated. "I decided it's best for me to be with Sylvia. She's the one I belong with. Not you. I think we need to end this marriage. I want to be with the mother of my child, and I want to raise my child properly, without any confrontations or confusion. I also don't want the mother of my child stressed, and frankly, my marriage to you is stressful to her. Hell, it's stressful to me."

I sat stunned. I was trembling. I couldn't believe what I was hearing. Here, I was simply worried about my husband sleeping with my cousin, but instead, he was flat out telling me he preferred to be with her and not me.

"Brandon, you don't mean that. Please, tell me you didn't mean that. I promise, I won't hound you anymore about Sylvia. Please, I'll do whatever you want."

"I paid to watch your so-called porno the other day. I realized, you are definitely not wife material for me. Sylvia would never do something so despicable. And, she has never lied like you do."

"What? What do you mean you watched the porno movie? I paid that bastard the money."

"You paid it? Why didn't you tell me? Where'd you get that kind of money from? You told me you didn't have that kind of money."

I looked down in shame as I debated on telling Brandon about the money I received from Anthony. "I had a rainy-day fund. I dipped into it to pay the guy off. I did it because I didn't want any stress or tension between you and me. I wanted us to be happy. I want us to be happy."

"How can I be happy with the 'Chocolate Bunny,' knowing she's a habitual liar? For fourteen ninety-nine, the whole world can see my so-called loving and faithful wife. After watching that movie, all I can see is a dirty whore. And I didn't see you use condom the first, yet you made me use one until after we were married."

I gasped. "Brandon, please." I got down on my knees to beg him.

"It's pointless, Asha. I'm in love with Sylvia, and that's who I'm going to be with. I'll be moving into the bedroom with her."

"No! No! You can't do this to me, Brandon. I showed you that I was a victim. Why won't you believe me?"

"Because I watched the entire hundred and twenty-six minutes with my own eyes. There was nothing 'victim' about it. You are a whore. Plain and simple. You are a liar. A lying whore."

"I thought you said we would forgive each other for anything that happened before our vows? I forgave you for getting my cousin pregnant. Now, you say you want to leave me for her? Right in the next room? I can't live like that."

"Yes, we talked about forgiving the prior infidelities, but your lying is endless."

"What have I lied about?" I stood from my knees and yelled.

"The fact that you even had twenty-five thousand dollars to pay the guy. When we talked about moving, you claimed you didn't have any money. Now I find out you had twenty-five thousand dollars just sitting around. Like I said, you can't be trusted."

"I can't be trusted? You're the one that has been sleeping with my cousin throughout our entire relationship. Aside from that one fuck-up, I have never cheated on you."

"My decision is made. I don't feel like arguing anymore. I haven't had much sleep, and I just want to rest right now."

"What?"

"You heard me. I'm going to rest now." Brandon stood up, leaving the bedroom and walking in the direction of Sylvia's room.

"Brandon! Brandon! Don't you do that! I swear, don't you do that!" I screamed.

"I'm sorry. It's over. We're done," he calmly replied.

"You are my fucking husband! Brandon!"

I was still calling out long after he disappeared behind Sylvia's door. I was still in disbelief, hoping I was having a bad dream. I banged on Sylvia's locked door, and neither of them responded. I thought of getting a knife and kicking the door down, but remembered Sylvia had a gun. I ended up sitting outside her—their—door, wailing like a wounded animal. I couldn't believe Sylvia could be so low-down, particularly after just complaining about Brandon being a bother to her.

After a while, I managed to get up and go finish crying in my own bed. I still was hoping that Brandon would come into the room, declaring he'd made a horrible mistake. I no longer cared about him having sex with Sylvia whenever he felt like it. I was even willing to share him, if that would make him still want to be with me. The thought of having no part of him had me contemplating suicide. I was also troubled to learn about the video still being sold online, despite me paying the $25,000. I was kicking myself for not telling Brandon about the money I received from Anthony.

At some point I dozed off and was jarred from my sleep when I heard Brandon in the bedroom.

I quickly sat up on the bed. "Brandon. Baby. You're back. I'm so sorry. I've learned my lesson. I'll do whatever you want. I promise, I won't complain about your spending time with my cousin. Please, just don't leave me."

Brandon was obviously trying to quietly gather some of his belongings and was startled when he heard my plea. He took a seat on the sofa, looking confused. I took that as a good sign. I jumped off the bed and went to kneel before him, to beg him to stay with me. I tried to remind him how much he loved me and all the great times we shared. When I reached up to kiss his lips, he didn't fight it. He was actually receptive. I didn't even complain about the pussy I was smelling on his mouth, which made it obvious his face had been between Sylvia's legs. I actually tried to seduce him into bed with me as his hands ravaged my body. His fingers were exploring between my legs and then he abruptly stopped.

"No! I can't do this. I'm committing myself to my child's mother. I meant what I said. It's over."

"Brandon. Brandon, please don't do this. It's obvious you're not ready to let go. I don't want to let go. Please. We can find a way to make this work."

Sylvia appeared in the doorway but remained silent. Brandon jumped away from me as if I had the plague.

"I said, no!" he yelled. "Get it through your head, we are done."

Sylvia turned and walked away. Brandon quickly grabbed the items he gathered and chased behind her.

I tortured myself that night, constantly going near her door to see if I could hear them having sex. I wasn't sure how I was going to live like that, although I expected Sylvia to live the same way before Brandon dumped me. That went on for the next few days as Brandon tried to make it clearer and clearer that he was done with me. It was also odd how he seemed like he was buying a bunch of new stuff. I naturally assumed Sylvia must have been buying him to keep him away from me. When I had to leave the following weekend, it seemed like it wasn't fast enough. They frolicked all over the house as if I wasn't even there, and I could do nothing but hide in my room.

To my surprise, I returned from my latest gig to find all of Brandon's belongings back in our bedroom. I wasn't sure what to make of it. Neither he nor Sylvia was home that Monday afternoon. I was half hopeful that Brandon came to his senses and decided to fight for our marriage, and I was half angry, thinking of his audacity of blatantly going back and forth between me and my cousin.

I was already in bed when Brandon waltzed in that night. He went straight to the shower and then crawled into my bed as if there was nothing to be discussed. When he started humping on my ass and fondling my breasts as I laid on my side, I put up no resistance. I was just happy Sylvia didn't have him. Eventually, he was penetrating me from behind, and I was thankful for the attention he gave my desperate body. I had a thousand questions, but I was scared to ask any.

That next morning, Brandon got up and prepared for work like normal, avoiding any conversations. After he was gone, I battled my mixed feelings. I was angry that he felt he could just crawl back between my legs without any discussion. I didn't know how or where things stood, nor what to expect with regards to our marriage.

I wasn't sure what made me realize I hadn't been checking social media for the usual suspects, but when I checked Corrine's page, I liked to died. I found a new photo of her and Sylvia. I attempted to check Sylvia's pages and found that I was blocked. Even Jeanette and Ricardo had me blocked. Jeanette and Sylvia had my fake Rachel profile blocked as well. However, I was able to use my Rachel profile to see Ricardo's page. Guess they must have forgotten to block me there, or maybe they left open only what they wanted me to see. Sylvia was in Jamaica. They were all pictured together at a restaurant.

Seeing that caused me to look inside Sylvia's room. It wasn't cleared out, but it was obvious a lot of stuff was gone. I couldn't help but wonder if that was the reason Brandon returned to my bed. In the very next thought, I could care less how Brandon ended back up in my bed, as long as he was there. I didn't dare rock the boat by questioning him. Instead, we carried on like nothing ever happened. Neither of us mentioned Sylvia's name, although he seemed irritated.

CHAPTER 21

A month passed, and I was in a blissful place. Sylvia was gone and I had my husband to myself. Or so I thought.

"Is your name Asha?" some strange woman asked when I came outside to go to the walking trail.

I looked her up and down before answering. "Uh, yes."

"If you have a moment, we need to talk."

I wasn't sure if I wanted to hear anything she had to say. She was an equally tall, attractive woman with a great body, and I was absolutely certain she wanted to discuss her sexual relationship with my husband.

"I'm not sure. What is this about?"

"Brandon."

"Well, yeah, I definitely don't want to talk about my husband with anyone."

"I plan to get the police involved, and I'm thinking you might not have anything to do with anything. That's why I wanted to speak with you first—to find out how much you know or don't know."

She really had my attention then. "The police? What is this all about?"

"Your husband is a crook. He's an extortionist. I'm not sure how, but he managed to make a sex tape without my knowledge or permission, and then he blackmailed me. Despite my paying the extortion fee, he went forward with posting the video online for anyone willing to pay."

As I felt my legs about to give out on me, I looked around for a seat and didn't see any. I sat on the ground to try to catch my breath. I couldn't believe what I was hearing, but it was hard not to, since the same thing happened to me.

"I'm sorry to upset you like this," she continued. "I happened to notice a video of you was posted on the same website. I remembered him mentioning having a wife named Asha, who was a big-time model. I was angry, because he didn't mention anything about having a wife until after we slept together a few times. When I saw your video, it was with a different guy, so I wasn't sure what to make of it, since he said you were supposed to be his wife."

"Well, how did you know it was me in the video?"

"I googled you and I saw plenty of photos with your image and name. The name on the video was different, but it was clear that it was you."

"There are plenty of Ashas in Atlanta. How did you decide it was me?"

"When I found your IG page, I saw you with Brandon. You had photos talking about you being a married woman. And you have your career listed as a model and actress."

"So, where did you sleep with my husband at? In my home? How did he make a sex video without you knowing it? How did you find my home or where we live at?" I was totally worked up and was desperate for answers, while trying to fight to defend my husband.

"He took me to a hotel one time. The other times we'd be at my house. I should have known something was up when he insisted on going to the hotel after we usually met up at my house. I didn't see any cameras or anything, but I definitely recognized the hotel when I saw the video I was being blackmailed with."

I stood back to my feet. "Okay, but how did you find my home?" I snapped at her unsympathetically.

"It took some doing. I wouldn't have been able to find him, because he's not tied to this address. He's tied to an address down in Jonesboro. It was easier to track down your address, and then I was able to track him to this address because he posted a video of him walking on this trail, maybe two weeks ago and showed his building. I was here a little over a week ago and saw him with a different woman. I started to approach him, but I lost my nerve."

"What do you mean you saw him with a different woman?" Insanely, that was the only thing my mind seemed to register.

"Yes, I saw him kiss her before they both got into their cars and pulled off."

"What did she look like?" I asked, trying to figure out if it was Sylvia. She was supposedly long gone, so I couldn't understand who would have been leaving my home just a week ago.

"I don't know. It's really hard to say. I didn't get a good look at her. I was more focused on seeing him. She was a light complexioned woman. Kind of tall. I remember seeing him feeling on her bottom before she got into her car. She was shapely. He'd always do that to me before we'd part ways."

Sylvia instantly came to mind. I couldn't understand. According to various social media pages, she was in Jamaica. I even remembered one day hearing Brandon on the phone, telling someone she was in

Jamaica for her new job. He turned around and called her a bitch. I didn't bother to question him, as long as she was gone out of our lives.

"So, what do you want of me? Why track me down?"

"I wanted to have a civil conversation with you. I was hoping you could help me get that video taken down and stop your husband from sending blackmail photos to my home and job. I wanted to appeal to your sense of decency. I have a family, and if they catch on, it would destroy me. I paid the requested fee to stop it, so I don't know what else to do. If I go to the police, then the whole thing would be out, probably in the news, and then my family would find out."

"When you say 'family,' do you mean a husband?"

She looked ashamed. "Yes. I have a husband and two children. I need this video to go away. I need the photos to stop. I need this to all go away."

"You knew you were married and decided to take up with my husband, but now you want my help? Even worse, you said you had him in your home?"

"Asha, I swear, I didn't know he was your husband when I was with him."

"But you knew you had a husband, didn't you?"

Tears trickled from her eyes. "I was going through a difficult time back then. My husband and I have since worked things out. It's one thing for me to tell him that I cheated on him, but it's totally different if I tell him I was out there taking pictures and making sex videos that I didn't know about."

"You say you didn't know. How did you not know?"

"I can't explain it. It's like there were cameras everywhere. I didn't see any. There was no one else in the room. I don't know how he did it, but when I saw the video, it looked like someone else was there."

I was deeply troubled by her accusation, since her experience was so identical to my own.

"I can tell by your reaction, you know what I'm talking about. Please help me," she cried.

I stared at her for a minute, wondering if the entire conversation was a setup. I wondered if Teddy sent her to lie on Brandon.

"I don't know what you think you can tell, but I don't believe a word you're saying. I don't believe you've been with my husband. I don't believe you saw him kissing some other woman. And frankly, you come across as some stalker, and I will call the police if I ever see you anywhere again."

The woman looked at me as if I were crazy. "Are you serious? Are you freaking kidding? If you want to know if I slept with Brandon, you could see the damn video for yourself. When you subscribe to their site, you can see a bunch of different videos, which also includes Brandon with other women. I absolutely am not trying to stalk you. I'm here trying to see if you too are a victim. There're several other videos, and I can't help but wonder if they were all made in the same manner. That would mean Brandon and these other guys are secretly recording women and then possibly extorting them."

"I'm sorry. This is all too much for me. I can't. I just can't wrap my head around my husband being a part of something like that."

The woman pulled out her cell phone and did some quick typing and pulled up the video of her with my husband in a hotel, carrying on. I could even see the fresh tan he got while we were in Brazil, letting me know he was with this woman after we were married. I could even hear that her voice was also altered, as was done on my video.

"Now will you believe me?" she asked.

I covered my face, hoping to make it all go away. "I can't do this. Please, just turn that off. Leave me alone! I can't." I wanted to show my strength, but my escaped tears showed I wasn't as strong as I tried to let on.

The woman wrapped her arms around me to provide me comfort, and I totally sobbed on her shoulder. A part of me was crying because I didn't want to be crying on some strange woman's shoulder. Particularly, one who slept with my husband.

"Please, Asha, help me put a stop to this. I'm sure we're not the only victims. I'm pretty damn certain you were also a victim, because I heard your voice was substituted the same way they did mine. There are almost a hundred videos on their channel. All of those women are probably victims."

"I don't know what you want from me. I don't know anything. None of this makes any sense. He's my husband."

"He's going to take you down with him. What do you think's going to happen as soon as I go to the police and let them know that your husband is a part of some extortionist sex ring, victimizing women? They'll look at you both living in this swanky condo, and no doubt, charge you right along with him. How do you think you'll be able to prove you weren't in on this scheme?"

She made a very valid point. However, I loved Brandon with every fiber of my being. I couldn't imagine my life without him.

"Do you have a card or something so I could reach you? I don't even know your name."

"My name is Lena. Lena Duncan. I live in Lithonia. I have a son and a daughter. If you walk with me to my car, I can give you one of my business cards."

I hesitantly walked Lena to her car. I still didn't trust her. After getting her card, I thanked her and let her know I'd be in touch. She told me she would see if she could identify some of the other women and get them to help build a case to take Brandon and his crew down.

CHAPTER 22

B randon, we need to talk."

He closed his eyes and shook his head. "Asha, I haven't even got in the door good. I don't feel like any nonsense."

"Really? You don't feel like any nonsense. I didn't feel like any nonsense either, when your bitches started stalking me."

"What the fuck are you talking about?"

I was sitting on the sofa, but he decided to just head to the bedroom, as if he wasn't interested in hearing what I had to say. I sat on the conversation I had with Lena for three days. I tried to weigh out all the pros and cons, as well as determine the best approach without really alienating my husband.

I remained seated on the sofa. After a few minutes, Brandon reappeared and headed into the kitchen to get his dinner plate from the microwave. When he took his seat at the table, his eyes made contact with the business card I intentionally left on the table, but then he pretended not to see it. He ate his food in silence as I watched him from the sofa. I watched his demeanor, and he seemed irritated. He had been irritated over the last few days, which was part of the reason I tried to avoid the conversation with him.

He only ate some food, and pushed his plate away from him. He rose from the table and started back toward the bedroom.

"Was something wrong with the food? You barely touched it."

"It doesn't taste right. I don't want any more."

"What do you mean it doesn't taste right? So, now you have a problem with my cooking?" I asked, following on his heels.

He stopped and gave a look that gave me chills before turning away and continuing toward the bedroom. Something about his look had me feeling fearful, and for the first time, I was wishing Sylvia was around. I thought about the possibility of Brandon being dangerous. I waited a while and decided to head into the bedroom.

"Did you clean that kitchen up or did you waltz up in here to bother me with some bullshit?"

"I will get the kitchen. I figured I'd come in here and see why you're in such a bad mood."

"You try immediately walking through the door and being greeted with some nonsense."

"Nonsense? I said we need to talk. How is that nonsense?"

"Well, I don't feel like talking. I just want peace."

"If you don't talk to me, then your friend Lena will be going to the police."

"Who? Who the fuck is Lena? See, that's why I didn't want to talk to you, because I knew you'd be on some insecurity shit. Save it, 'cause I ain't trying to hear the shit."

"Lena is the one that tracked me down outside of my home to let me know she's going to have you prosecuted for some kind of illegal video recording."

"Oh please! That sounds like someone else trying to rattle you. I told you, you need to stop letting these bitches get to you like that."

"No, she wasn't just trying to rattle me. She actually showed me the video of you and her fucking, and the video just so happened to be posted on the exact same website as the video that I was in. This woman basically came and told me everything that I personally experienced with that asshole, Teddy. I couldn't help but wonder, do you personally know Teddy? Are you a part of some ring that extorts women? And based on the tan you had in the video she showed, it was definitely after we were married. Even worse, why would you tell her my name? Why would you tell her you are married to some supermodel named Asha? That's how she found me and then found you. She told me she saw you leaving out of this building a week or so ago with some different bitch. What the fuck is going on, Brandon?" I was trying not to cry, but again, the tears came pouring out.

"Asha, leave me alone with that bullshit. I don't know why you believe everything you hear." He waved me away and spoke as if I was bothering him with something trivial.

"Hear? No, I saw that shit with my own eyes. I met someone being blackmailed and extorted in the exact same manner I have been."

"I don't know who this bitch is, but I promise you, I ain't into making any videos. Maybe she was behind the extortion. Maybe she made a video of me without my knowledge, and she's playing with your head, trying to make you think it's me."

"You think?"

"I can't believe you would doubt me, your husband, like you do. Why would I marry you if I was trying to do some crazy shit like you suggest?"

"Why were you having sex with her? I saw you."

"That shit could have been old. I don't even know this person you're talking about. Personally, I think it's someone fucking with you. Why would she confront you outside the building? I come out every day. Don't you think if she had a beef with me or I did the shit she claims, she would have confronted me instead of you? No, she confronted you because she's fucking with you."

"She said she didn't approach you because she was afraid."

"Okay, well, why didn't she send the police if she knew where I live and I did these things to her? Asha, sometimes you need to think. You let people get in your head."

He was sounding really convincing. He almost had me believing what he was saying.

"In my head? You were fucking Sylvia, and you swore she was messing with me. You even tried to leave me to be with her, until she left your ass, and suddenly you want to rebound back into my bed."

Brandon had a look as if he'd spit fire any moment. "What did you just say to me? What the fuck did you just say to me?"

In all this time, I hadn't attempted to rock the boat. I still didn't, but it was out there, and I couldn't pull it back.

"You came crawling back in my bed, in between my legs, just because Sylvia left your ass and went to Jamaica."

He laughed but still had a deranged look. "Girl, you done lost your fucking mind. So, is this not my bed as well? Did you not freely open your fucking legs and beg me to fuck you? Wasn't that you begging to come back and was even willing to share? Now you're complaining?"

"If this is your bed, then why were you sharing a bed with my cousin when she was here?"

"That's my baby's mother. I didn't want her upset. I told you that."

"So, she's more important than your wife? You said you were divorcing me for her."

"I didn't say all that." He spoke as if he was ashamed. "I was just trying to keep her from doing the stupid shit she ended up doing anyway—taking my baby away to some other country."

"Are we supposed to be working on this marriage or what? Are you trying to be with them or are you trying to be with me?"

"I lay down and wake up with you each day. Why would you ask me such stupid shit? Asha, I'm really beginning to lose patience with you. I can't deal with your insecurities."

"You keep saying my insecurities as if they're not actually facts. You were fucking Sylvia. You were almost fucking Jeanette, whatever almost is. Now I learn you were fucking Lena, and whoever the other bitch you brought up in this house, presumably when I was away on a gig. Then you call me insecure. You're wrong for that shit, Brandon."

Brandon closed his eyes, shook his head, and smiled. When he opened them, he grabbed his sneakers and said, "You want to be insecure? You want to have a reason to bitch and moan? I'll see you later then. I'm heading out."

"Where are you going?" I asked, becoming frantic.

"Wherever! You wanna talk shit about me crawling into *your* bed, in between your legs? Then you want to talk about who I'm fucking. I can't win with you, and I'm not going to keep trying. I'm going to go crawl between some legs that'll appreciate my ass."

I followed Brandon to the door, grabbing the back of his shirt.

"Brandon, don't you go out that door. I'm warning you. Don't you dare."

He quickly turned around and grabbed me by the throat. "Threaten me again! Hear, bitch?"

He held my throat so long and tight, I began feeling dizzy. When he finally let me go, I dropped to the floor like a ragdoll. I continued to lay lifelessly on the floor, long after he was out the door. At that point, I didn't want to live. I didn't feel like I had anything left to live for. I was wishing Brandon would have just finished the job, since he was all I had left, but then he left me yet again.

As I laid on the floor, I thought of Lena. Anger started setting in. I was angry that she would try to convince me that Brandon did to her, what was done to me. She was obviously in on it with Teddy. That's the only way she could have said and known as much as she did. I decided I was going to find her and beat her ass when I did find her. I tried to call the number on the card she gave me, but it kept going straight to voicemail.

It was after midnight when Brandon came home, and I was determined to find a way to fix things. I was so angry at myself for letting women get to me. I wasn't going to question him, because I knew whatever dirt he did was my fault. He was right; I had no business bothering him the minute he walked through the door from work. I realized that I need to be thankful I had a husband who came straight home from work, and came home to me.

And when he wanted to crawl in between my legs, I didn't question him about who he might have been with immediately before me, or why he still smelled of sex. I decided I was going to fight for my marriage and never again make him so angry that he'd put his hands on me.

CHAPTER 23

For two weeks, I had been checking my phone and emails, looking for new gigs. There were none. The one I was scheduled to do cancelled me without explanation. The event wasn't cancelled. Just me. I kept checking my bank accounts, as if funds were going to miraculously be added. It was during that moment that I realized Brandon had never paid a single bill the entire time we'd been married. He'd tell me to go online and pay his car note and insurance, but never bothered trying to reimburse me, and I had been too foolish to ask for him to pay me back. With things being so tense lately, I was definitely afraid to ask him to start helping to pay bills. Even Sylvia left without coughing up a dime for the entire time she was here.

My birthday came and went, and my husband barely made it home that night. When he did, he went straight to sleep, still smelling like he was between someone else's legs.

I had left two messages for Anthony, hoping to find out why my gigs seemed to suddenly dry up. I had yet to hear from him. They were probably too busy celebrating Jeanette's new book release. To date, she had yet to tell me about it or her engagement. Funny thing, my "Rachel" profile was also blocked from Ricardo's multiple social media pages. Anything I wanted to know, I had to find on Corrine's page, which was how I got to see Jeanette's book celebration. I was also able to see the reminder of the upcoming boat ride in New York. I thought of riding up and just showing up, sure Anthony wouldn't turn me away. However, looking at my remaining funds, taking recreational trips definitely was not in the budget.

I quickly closed my laptop when I heard Brandon's key inserted into the door. I ran over to the large window to act like I was just looking out of it, deep in thought. Crazy thing, I heard the door open and close, but I didn't hear a word from Brandon. I turned to see him, but I didn't see him. I walked into the bedroom and found him lying on the sofa with his arm draped across his head, as if he were exhausted. I quietly walked over to him, sat down, and attempted to kiss his lips.

He jerked away. "Damn! Don't be doing that. You know I hate people sneaking up on me like that."

I jumped up. My feelings were crushed. "I'm sorry. I didn't hear you come in. Why didn't you say anything to me?"

"If you didn't hear me, then what the hell are you doing sneaking here in the bedroom? You're so full of shit. You don't think I heard you running over to that window just before I came in that door?"

"Why are you biting my head off? What did I do wrong now?"

"Don't fucking be trying to sneak up on me, that's what."

I took a seat on the bed and just looked at him as he resumed his position with his arm over his forehead.

"Can I do anything to make things better?"

"You can get the fuck out of here and leave me with some damn peace."

"Wow! Get the fuck out of here? Out of my own room? I can't be in my own bedroom anymore?"

"Don't you have a gig or something to go to? When are you going to be leaving out again?"

I was crushed. I was already feeling bad about not having any gigs, and then this blow from my darling husband. Instead of answering, I got up to leave the bedroom.

"Bitch! Don't you walk out on me when I'm talking to you. You fucking answer me when I ask you a question." He was sitting up looking as if he'd jump up and hurt me.

"Bitch? Is that what I am to you now? A bitch?"

"Oh, don't start that fake tears shit again. I asked you a fucking question."

"Well, when you find a bitch, maybe she'll answer your questions, because I'm not that bitch."

I turned to walk out, and within seconds, Brandon was on my ass, snatching me by the back of my head. I could feel some of my tracks being snatched. He put his other hand across my face and threw me to the floor. Everything was happening so quickly, but I caught a glimpse of his eyes, and knew I fucked up. He started kicking me and punching me in my head as I tried to use my arms to shield my face.

"Say something else smart to me! Hear, bitch?"

I wanted to beg him to stop, but I could only cry. I was too afraid to scream for help, doubtful anyone would be able to hear me.

When he finally stopped beating on me, he stepped back, out of breath, and ordered me to get up, undress and get on the bed. I tried to quickly do as he ordered. He turned the television on, and maxed out the volume. Before that, I thought he was going to just try to fuck me. Particularly when I saw him opening his belt buckle. However, he didn't open his pants. He just removed his belt. I knew what was about to happen, but never in a million years would I have believed it would happen to me. Brandon preceded to whip me as if I was some really out-of-control kid. I screamed and screamed. He didn't care. The whipping seemed endless. My skin felt like it was on fire.

"Get up and go get my fucking dinner, bitch!"

I stumbled, falling off the bed, but quickly got up to run for his dinner plate. After heating his plate up and turning to leave the kitchen with his plate, I saw him standing with the belt still in his hand. I was terrified. He stepped to the side to let me by. I quickly placed his plate on the table. As quick as I set the plate down, he hit me three more times across my back and legs. He then ordered me to sit on the sofa and not make a sound. I did as he told. I was pretty certain I had to have some open abrasions from the belt, and I worried about blood getting on our white sofa. I didn't dare say a word about my concern.

He ate some of the food and then lifted the plate of food to throw at me.

"You can't cook worth a damn. I think your ass is trying to poison me. Is that what you're trying to do? Why all of a sudden your food tastes like shit? You used to know how to cook."

I didn't know if I should answer or not. I didn't want him to get angry for not answering him again.

"I'll do better. I promise."

"You better!"

He went into the bedroom for a few minutes, came out all put together, and left the house without saying a word. I sat still on the sofa, afraid to move. When it was obvious he wasn't coming right back, I got up to go nurse the many wounds my dear husband inflicted upon me.

As I nursed my wounds, my phone rang. I ran to it, afraid of not answering fast enough for Brandon.

"Hello."

"Asha?"

"Hey, Mom! What's going on?" I said, trying to sound normal.

"You tell me. Why you sound out of breath and like you were crying?"

"I'm not crying. I think I might have a bit of a cold, but I was in a different room from my phone and ran to catch it when I heard it ringing."

"That must have been some running. It only rang one time."

Her interrogation was getting on my nerves. I wanted to tell her what happened, but I knew she'd tell my father, and there would be no telling what they'd do to my husband.

"I was in the bathroom about to fix a bath, and my phone was in the bedroom. I didn't have too far to run." I tried to laugh to ease her mind. "Anyhow, what's up?"

"I was just calling to check up on you. You usually call me and tell me about your modeling jobs or something, but I haven't heard anything lately."

I couldn't believe that first it was Brandon questioning me about my gigs, and now my mother.

"I haven't had any to call about. The one I had was cancelled."

"You think Sylvia might be behind this?"

"Behind what?"

"All of a sudden you're not getting calls."

"No, Ma, I don't think she has that much control over anyone," I said, but I had also wondered the same myself. "This was pretty much to be anticipated the closer I got to thirty."

"Speaking of which, where did your hubby take you for your birthday? I know he must have done it up big. Hopefully, y'all can make it over this way during the weekend and I can fix your birthday dinner."

"Oh wow! Mom, that sounds wonderful. I'm sure Brandon would love that. We actually stayed in for my birthday. He was trying to be the romantic one, you know." I fake laughed.

"Y'all over there having all that sex, I'm sure you'll be pregnant with your own child before long."

"That would be nice. I'm sure that would make my husband so happy."

"How does he feel with Sylvia being gone?"

"I don't know and don't care. Good riddance! We don't waste our time speaking about her ass."

"I wish she wasn't pregnant, so you could whoop her ass. She deserves it. I guess she's mad your husband didn't chase behind her."

"Probably. Yeah, she needs her ass beat," I said, looking in the mirror at my wounds, which were more than likely a result of my husband's inability to get over my stupid cousin.

"Well, I'm glad you got your husband back to yourself and she's out of the picture."

"Yeah, so am I."

"I bet he can't keep his hands off of you." She laughed.

I fought the tears and chuckled. "Yeah, you can say that again."

There was a long pause.

"Are you sure you're okay? You don't sound like yourself. Should I come over and sit with you for a while?"

"No, Mom. I'm fine. Brandon just went out to the gym and should be back in a few. Hopefully, he'll help me nurse this cold."

"Oh, okay. If you want to come over, I'll make you some soup."

"I'd love that, any other time. Mom, I'm married now. I have to make sure my husband is taken care of."

"Being married doesn't mean you're supposed to stop living while waiting on his schedule."

"It's not like that at all. I just feel this is the first time we've really had to be completely together without all the other distractions or me being on the road. I love being here when he gets home."

"I guess. What would I know? No one ever bothered trying to marry me. I guess you gotta do what you gotta do to keep that man happy."

"Exactly. Thank you for understanding."

"Well, I'm going to get off of here. I'll be looking forward to seeing y'all this weekend."

"Sure thing. I'll let Brandon know."

After hanging up, I was dreading even asking Brandon about going to my mother's for my birthday dinner. Once upon a time, not so long ago, I was feeling like I won the prize when Sylvia left. Now, I was wondering if it was a prize at all.

It was almost 11:30 at night, and Brandon was just sending a text. He made it sound as if all was well between us.

"Hey babe. My car and insurance need to be paid before midnight. I need you to take care of that for me before it's late. See you soon."

I cringed thinking about how much I had left in the bank. I wasn't sure how much longer I'd be able to keep up carrying us both. I was also cringing at the thought of what he'd do to me if I told him I'd need him to pay me back. I sucked it up, remembering I still had the other $25,000 in that emergency account.

Nonetheless, I jumped to it and got the payments made before midnight. I sent him the confirmation, but he didn't bother to respond.

Brandon still hadn't made it home when I eventually dozed off. When daylight hit my eyes, I woke up and saw he hadn't been in the bed or on the bedroom sofa. I grabbed my phone and called him, worried something might have happened to him. I heard his phone ringing from the living room. I got up and put on a robe to see why his phone was in there.

Brandon strolled from Sylvia's original room, naked, as if just waking up.

"Babe, what are you doing in there? Why didn't you come to bed? I was worried something happened to you."

"Don't start with me so early in the morning. Go back to bed." He picked his phone up from the breakfast bar to check it. "You called me?"

"Yes. I was worried. I hadn't heard from you. I sent a text last night to let you know the payment was made, but then I didn't hear anything. When I didn't see you this morning, I got worried."

"Yeah, whatever. Go back to bed."

I felt like I was in a bad Twilight Zone episode when I saw the dried up cum covering his pelvic area.

"How about I fix you some breakfast before you leave for work? It's already getting late for you."

"GET YOUR ASS BACK TO BED! DAMN! How many fucking times do I need to say it to your dumb ass?"

"But, babe—"

He ran up on me as if he was about to hit me in the face. I quickly ran back to the room. He followed behind me.

"Now stay your ass there until I say you can come out." Then he slammed the door closed, leaving me alone.

I picked up my phone at least ten times, about to call my mother or the police. Pride got in the way. All I could think about was making headlines regarding my failed marriage. I definitely didn't want Sylvia or Jeanette to find out.

From time to time, I'd sneak to the door to see what I could hear. Although I couldn't really hear anything, I definitely smelled food cooking. I was starving. I never ate dinner after getting that beating. I hated tap water, but had no choice but to drink from the bathroom faucet, since my permission to leave the room hadn't come. It was after eleven, so I couldn't understand why he hadn't left for work yet.

After a while, I heard the front door close. I thought for sure Brandon would be in to let me know I could come out. He didn't. Shortly after two, he sent me a text telling me to go clean up the kitchen and the back bedroom before he returned. When I checked both, I wanted to cry. The mess was beyond ridiculous, and then seeing three dirty plates on the dining table was even more unnerving. Glutton for punishment, as always, I somehow felt a need to search the back bedroom and bathroom for any remnant of condoms. For some reason or another, I needed to know if Brandon was using condoms with these women. I didn't see any. I did see a nasty mess in the bathroom. Dirty washcloths were just thrown inside the tub. Towels on the floor. Towels in the bedroom.

I sat on the floor in the hallway, thinking about my out of control life and where it went wrong. I thought about what I could have done to bring this travesty upon myself. I thought about how my best friend and cousin did me dirty, yet they were off to their happy lives.

Just as quick as that thought entered my mind, I began having flashbacks of all the different men I went behind both of their backs to have sex with. Sylvia only knew about four, but there were way more. I had been stabbing them in the back since middle school. I remember this guy, Taquan. He was Jeanette's first. He was 18 or 19, maybe even 20. I just know he wasn't in school and had a job and a car. She bragged about how gentle he was and how good he made her feel. Hell, I wanted to feel it too.

Taquan wasn't my first. My first was more than one. Actually, three boys, when I was just eleven. People used to tease me about being dark skinned, and these boys from my neighborhood liked me. We snuck into this abandoned apartment, and I let each of them take turns on me. None of them made me feel good. Neither did the several that followed.

In hindsight, none of them knew what they were doing with their pre-puberty penises, but they wanted to be with me, and that was all that mattered. That's why I wanted to get with Taquan. Taquan had a way bigger dick than any of the others, and I loved it. I snuck off with him a few times, until he dumped me when I got pregnant.

Crazy thing was, when my father started coming around, and I'd always hear him fucking my mother I'd become aroused. I was always looking for someone to make me feel as good as my fingers were making me feel from touching myself while listening to my parents. I didn't find that satisfaction until Taquan. After that, any time Jeanette or Sylvia would brag about how great the sex was with whatever guy, I was going for him.

After Taquan, I no longer had an appetite for boys my age. I preferred them in their twenties. I was probably 16 when I got with this guy in his thirties, but sex with him wasn't gratifying. Even worse, I got pregnant by him as well. He was determined to teach me how to master blowjobs. Before him, I thought I knew how, but he'd tell me I was giving head like a silly kid. Looking back now, I was just a silly kid, and he had no business with me. However, I was determined to give him as many blowjobs as it took to finally make him explode—in my mouth. He also was the one who told me I needed to learn to swallow, because it was disrespectful to a man to see his sperm being spit out. After him, I was like the blowjob queen. That was all I needed to snatch any man I wanted, once they showed the slightest interest in me. Unlike Jeanette, who went after what she wanted, I'd wait until I knew they were dog enough to want me, despite them fucking my friend or cousin.

My third pregnancy was one of Sylvia's boyfriends. I was 17, and he was a college guy, maybe a year or two older. His bed skills sucked. I couldn't imagine how he held Sylvia's attention for as long as he did. He was going back and forth between us, until I got pregnant. Then he dumped us both and went on with his life.

I already had a pretty decent body and plenty of boobs, and boys and men seemed to love it. I only got cosmetic work done because I was following Jeanette. I listened to her talking about how we could make so much money with the modeling thing. Although I didn't think I needed it at the time, I absolutely loved the attention we got once we had modifications. I loved how guys would go crazy when Jeanette and I would enter a room. Not sure if it was because she's light skinned, but I didn't get the same attention when walking into a room with just Sylvia. Guys always gravitated to her when we'd be together. The resentment would make me go behind her back to make them want me instead of her. Not one has ever turned away the pussy I was offering. They might have talked shit and tried to say how fucked up I was to do that to my cousin, but they always took the pussy before having anything to say on the subject.

I sat there wondering if karma was coming for me.

CHAPTER 24

That little trip down memory lane was all I needed. Suddenly, I felt empowered, like I could have or do anything I wanted. My momma didn't raise me to be anyone's victim.

I didn't clean a thing. I packed a few things and left. Got into my car and drove to Washington, D.C. I didn't know what I was going to do once I got there, but one thing I knew, I wasn't going to sit around and be anyone's punching bag or cleaning lady. I also wasn't going to sit around waiting to see what diseases my husband would bring me. That one shot of penicillin I had to get when I was 18 was all the convincing I needed about protecting myself. Well, almost convinced, since I didn't protect myself or get checked after messing around with Teddy. I figured if I got something, I would have heard it from my husband by now. I was kind of wishing I had caught something, so he could have passed it on to Sylvia.

Brandon was calling and calling and calling. Eventually, I stopped to buy a whole new phone with a new number and powered off my old phone. I was sure to give my mother the number. I eventually told her what Brandon did. Surprisingly, she wasn't outraged like I thought she'd be. She didn't say she'd tell my father or anything. She just told me to be safe and keep her posted on my whereabouts.

I found a nice hotel right outside of D.C. on the Virginia side. I was hesitant about using my credit card for the room, not knowing if Brandon would somehow track me down. As I stood on line to get a room, the manager, who was a decent looking brother, stopped what he was doing and called me over to a different terminal. He looked to be around my father's age, or close to it. He was nice looking, but there were plenty of gray hairs in his neatly trimmed beard. For some reason or another, I felt comfortable with him. I shared with him that I was fleeing an abuser and was worried about my name being on the registry with my credit card. He was kind enough to change my name to Betty Williams. He also advised me to park my car on a different lot, just in case Brandon somehow tracked my credit card to the hotel. Although I never gave Brandon any of that information, I kept a box filled with credit card and bank statements up in my bedroom closet.

When I made it to my room, I logged into all of my financial accounts and changed the security information I had written down in my desk drawer at home. I kept my old phone turned off to keep Brandon from possibly tracking me with it. I was sure to let my mother know where I was at and that I was safe. I didn't have any real plan, nor did I know how long I'd be where I was at.

Somehow, despite all the madness I was dealing with, once I realized the date, I became focused on how I could get to New York and make it to that boat ride in a few nights. Now more than ever, I needed to speak with Anthony. I needed to understand how or why my meal ticket got cut off, with my modeling gigs. I was even hoping maybe he had some goons that might put the fear of God in Brandon, so he'd never lift a finger to me again—nor would he leave me or be with other women.

I still desperately wanted to be with my husband. I was hoping my abrupt departure would shake him up and make him think twice about how he treated me. I wanted him to love me and treat me with respect.

A knock at the door interrupted my thoughts. Actually, it scared the hell out of me.

"Miss Woodard, it's me, Calvin, from the front desk."

My heart was thumping so hard, thinking Brandon found me that quick.

I opened the door for the manager. He had a tray of food and two bottles of water. I was stunned.

"I brought this for you. I figured you might not feel comfortable going downstairs for food, not knowing what's what."

"Oh, my goodness! Thank you so much. That was really kind of you. And you're right, I was worrying about how I'd get food. I thought of calling room service, but even that made me nervous."

He came in and set the tray on the table.

"Glad I could help out. I was off and about to head out. I wanted to check up on you before I go."

I'm not sure why that seemed to be my cue to breakdown and start crying. All that time, I was pumped up with adrenaline, feeling invincible. Right in that moment, my reality hit me. Calvin took me in his arms and held me tightly. It was just what I needed.

"Everything's going to be fine. You're here right now, and you're safe. You can eat, take a hot shower, get a good night's rest, and regroup."

With Calvin's arms wrapped around me, it caused me to remember all the wounds Brandon left on my body. Suddenly, I felt the physical pain. I stepped away from Calvin and pulled my top over my head.

"Look what he did to me."

Calvin inspected the whelp marks. "Oh my goodness! Did he hit you with a belt? These look like belt marks."

I nodded my head as a fresh set of tears began flowing. He took me into his arms again.

"Is it just on your body or is it on your legs as well?"

"It's on my legs and arms. It's everywhere."

"You have to report him to the police. Did he break the skin? Not that that should matter much."

I sat on the chair to pull my pants off. He had me stand closer to the light to inspect the additional damage.

"You definitely need to call the police. Next time he's going to kill you. He's beating on you like you're some child. He shouldn't even be beating a child like this. Do you mind if I asked what caused him to do this to you?"

I closed my eyes and hesitantly answered. "I am a model. I usually go away on the road. Yesterday, he just started flipping out because he realized I hadn't been going anywhere lately. He started calling me names and next thing I know, he grabbed me by the head and started beating on me. He stopped long enough to make me remove my clothes and then he removed his belt and turned up the volume on the television."

I became so overwhelmed with grief, I had to take a seat on the bed. Calvin sat next to me.

I managed to pull myself together. "I don't know how long it lasted. It felt like forever. Next thing I know, he's gone. This morning, I got worried when I saw he hadn't returned home. I called him and heard his phone ringing inside the home. I went to see how that was happening, and then he appears from another bedroom. He demands that I return to my bedroom and not come back out until he tells me I can. He forced me to stay in there for hours. Eventually, he sent me a text, ordering me to clean up the kitchen and the bedroom he was in. I saw three plates with leftover food sitting on the table. The bedroom and bathroom were atrocious."

"Wait a minute. Are you saying he had two other women in your home?"

I shrugged my shoulders. "I don't know."

"You are way too beautiful to be dealing with something like that. I'm glad you knew to get the hell out of there. You have to call the police. He needs to be locked up. Why are you trying to protect him?"

"He's my husband," I answered before crying again.

"And he'll be someone else's husband when you're dead and buried from him killing you. I hope you're not thinking of going back to him and working things out in a few days?"

I didn't say anything. I was too embarrassed to admit that that was exactly what I was thinking.

"Oh come on!" Getting excited, he stood from the bed and became very animated. "You have to think more of yourself than that. You are absolutely gorgeous and could probably have any man you choose. You don't need to put up with that nonsense. Let him go be someone else's problem."

"I didn't tell you the worst part."

"I can't imagine it being any worse." He closed his eyes and shook his head as he returned to his seat next to me.

"It is. He's expecting a child with my cousin. After our wedding, I learned that he had been sleeping with my best friend and my first cousin. He'd pretty much been in a relationship with my cousin the entire time he's been with me. I'm not sure why he chose to marry me. My cousin told me I was nothing more than his meal ticket. Just a day or two after my wedding, my cousin is throwing up. Next thing she's telling me that it's his baby. All that time, I thought she couldn't stand him. No. Her only issue with him was that he went forward with marrying me."

Calvin shook his head. "Why in the hell would your cousin do something like that to you? That is so pathetic. Where is she at?"

"Believe it or not, she was briefly living with us when we first returned from Brazil, where my wedding was at. They continued sleeping together every time I was away. Eventually, he got so bold and decided he was leaving me and declared his love for my cousin. He moved into her bedroom. That was only for a couple of weeks, because she up and left him, moving to Kingston, Jamaica. Once she was gone, he moved right back into my bedroom. He's been furious since then. That's probably when his temper really started showing."

"But why would you stay with him? Were you living in his home and had no place to go?"

Calvin's questions were so embarrassing to me. The more I answered, the dumber I felt.

"Actually, my cousin, my friend, and I bought that condo for investment purposes. I thought he was doing well financially, and I would be moving into the nice house he was living in once we married. Instead, I learned he was only renting and had to move out. He moved most of his clothes into our home. We had just gotten married, and I didn't know what to say at that point."

"You just got married?"

"Yes. In April."

"Oh wow! That's terrible. Do you think maybe you can get the marriage annulled? I'm thinking you should be able to with him expecting a child with your cousin, and you've never really had a whole marriage."

I started crying again. "I love him. I just want him to love me. I thought he loved me."

"How? You say he's been with your cousin and friend the entire time. That man never loved you. There is no way a man could love you and be in a relationship with your cousin and friend. There is no way a man could love you and beat on you or disrespect you like he's done. He's having a baby with someone else, for crying out loud. What are you supposed to do, sit around and wait for your turn?" He stood up in front of me and pulled me to my feet. He took me in front of the large mirror. "Look at that gorgeous woman. She can have any man that she wants. She doesn't have to tolerate no kind of foolishness. You are very beautiful and desirable."

He was standing directly behind me with a hand on each side of my arm as he spoke, looking at all of me through the mirror. Although I had on a bra and thong, he had a look of hunger in his eyes. I could tell he wanted me. I stared at his eyes through the mirror, until they made contact with mine. There was an obvious mutual attraction. He rubbed his hands on each of my shoulders, and I stepped backwards, toward his body. I was longing for him to slide the bra straps from my shoulders. The silence was deafening. He removed his hands when he realized my eyes made contact with his wedding band.

"Okay, beautiful, I guess you better eat your food. I'm sure you're starving. I need to get going, anyhow," he said with a cracked voice. "It's pretty late and I'm sure you're exhausted."

I don't know what the hell came over me. I just turned and started kissing him. I needed to feel desirable, and he told me I was. His desperate kiss let me know he wanted me just as much as I needed him in that moment. I loved how he kept telling me that I was beautiful, especially when I was feeling very unattractive.

My bra was off of my body in no time. He devoured my breasts as if he'd been waiting a lifetime to have them. With his mouth all over my breasts, we managed to make our way back over to the bed. Insanely, his lips remained fastened to my nipple as we maneuvered back to the bed. I tried to grab for his belt buckle, but then my recent trauma caused me to decide to get his shirt unbuttoned instead. I let him undo his own pants.

As we laid spent, trying to catch our breaths, I wanted to kick myself. I couldn't believe I fucked this strange man raw, after just worrying about what diseases I'd get from Brandon. The salty sweat from our bodies that seeped into my wounds reminded me of all the fresh injuries to my body. I was then convinced how really crazy I must be, only hours later, laying with a man that is not my husband, but someone else's husband. But hell, I needed to feel desired in that moment, and Calvin made me feel all of that and then some.

"Wow! That was way better than I could have even imagined."

I smiled, still looking up at the ceiling, trying to block out thoughts of how stupid I was feeling.

"You know what's crazy?"

"What?" I turned my head slightly to face him.

"Your voice sounds way different."

I chuckled. "Way different? Different from when I came in?"

He laughed, while fondling his still saturated penis. "No, silly. From your movie. I actually like this voice better."

I was confused. "This voice? Movie? What movie?" I raised up and rested on my arm, to turn in his direction.

"In the movie, it sounds like a white woman's voice. I prefer your natural voice. It's much more sultry and seductive."

I thought about what he could possibly be talking about. "I think you might have me confused with someone else."

He rolled onto his side, facing me, and placed his hand over his mouth. "Oh shoot! I am so sorry. You look just like her—the woman in the movie. Your body is as gorgeous. I spotted you when you first stood on line. I just had to help you myself. I wanted to get to know you better. I really wanted to be with you. You are so perfect. I swear, when I checked you in, never in a million years did I think I'd actually get to be with you like this."

He was gawking at my breasts, and I sat up on the bed to cover them. "Calvin, you have me really confused. Did you just see me as a beautiful woman and wanted to get to know me when I stood on the line, or did you think you knew me from somewhere?"

"Truthfully, I wasn't sure if it was you until I was up here and you mentioned your modeling. Then I knew for sure."

I smiled. I felt better because he must have recognized me from some of my videos or photo shoots. Only thing is, I never had speaking parts on any of those videos.

"You follow me on social media?" I asked, assuming he must have heard me speaking on one of the videos there.

"No, but I probably should. I'm sure you have some wonderful content."

He got up and started getting dressed. I wanted to ask if he needed to wash himself before going home to his wife, but his confusing me was making my brain hurt, and I wanted him to leave. Not only that, I was hungry and had yet to touch the food he brought up.

When he was fully dressed, he pulled me up from the bed by the hand and had me walk him to the door. He stared at my breasts before bending to kiss them again, and then stood up straight to look at me with a smile.

"I'd like to maybe stop in and see you in the morning before I start work. Would you like that?"

"I think I'd like that." I smiled.

He started kissing me again and kept squeezing my wounded ass for dear life as he pressed his pelvis against mine.

"This booty is so awesome. I absolutely love it. It's not okay to be abusing you in any way, but I can now understand why your husband might be crazy. Hell, I think I'd go crazy having you for a wife, just the same." He laughed.

"I must not make him that crazy. He's the one out there with other women."

"Not saying it's all right, but I'm sure it can't be easy being married to a model, knowing other men have their hands all over her body."

I looked at him as if he was crazy. "It's not like that. I mean, not really. We have people helping with our wardrobe changes, but it's so quick, you hardly think anything of it."

He started kissing me again and then nursing on my breasts again. "Damn, I'm going to have a hard time sleeping tonight. All I'll be thinking about is that delicious cream center of the Chocolate Bunny." He chuckled and then pecked my lips again before heading out the door.

I stood stunned. I was already confused by his conversation, but that Chocolate Bunny part made me think of—*OH MY GOD! NOOOOOO!*

The movie. The voice. He was talking about that fucking movie with Teddy.

My legs became weak. I looked for something to grab hold of, to keep from falling.

This motherfucker thought he was fucking a porno chick. That was the kind of modeling he was talking about. How could I be so fucking stupid to not realize what he was saying to me?

"I got to get out of here. There's no way I can be here in the morning when he returns," I said to no one.

I started grabbing my bags, but then I figured I had better wait a while to make sure he was gone. I couldn't believe how stupid I was. Once again, I opened my legs for the first man calling me beautiful. It seemed I'd never learn.

I waited about an hour before sneaking out of the hotel and getting back on the road. After grabbing some fast food, I just found a rest stop somewhere in Maryland and camped out there for the night. Even in the midst of my latest troubles, I still considered trying to make it up to New York for that boat ride Corrine was having.

CHAPTER 25

I must have been dog tired, because I managed to get a deep sleep in that car. I was annoyed the ringing phone woke me. I couldn't understand why my momma would be bothering me so early. At least I assumed it was still early. I had a deep sleep, but it didn't seem that long.

I reached inside of my bag to find my phone. The ringing had stopped and then started again. I figured something must have been wrong if she was calling back to back like that. When I got the phone out and saw Brandon's number, and not my mother's, I started freaking out. I started thinking the worst. I wondered if he broke into my mother's house and hurt her to get my number.

Once the ringing stopped, I quickly dialed my mother's number.

"Hello," she answered, as if I woke her up.

"Momma! Did you give Brandon my new number? He's calling repeatedly on my new phone." I started crying.

I was frantic, and my mother seemed calm.

"Asha, that's your husband. We had a long talk, and he promised not to touch you again. He said he's going to do right by you and your marriage. You need to go home to your husband. Don't let that bitch take your husband from you. For all you know, that's not even his baby. What if you hand your husband over to her, and then find out it's not his child? You have less than a year to have your own baby. It ain't going to happen if you leave your husband. Go home."

My mouth was open, but I was too stunned to speak. I couldn't believe my mother betrayed me the way she did. I confessed to her about him beating me and mistreating me, and she was trying to convince me to go back to him? I was so devastated, I was shaking.

"Asha, are you listening to me? I know things started off rough, but it'll all work out. He knows if he lays a finger on you again, I'm going to tell your father. He doesn't want that."

"I'm not going back to him, Momma. I can't believe you'd even suggest something so insane," I yelled into the phone. "What, you want him to kill me? Your only fucking child? Do you have some life insurance policy where you'll get rich if he kills me? Why would you tell me to go back into that hell?"

"Don't you speak to me like that! Do you want to be alone for the rest of your life?"

"At least I'd be alive! If I go back, I'll be dead. How long do you think he could go without putting his hands on me again? Do you seriously think he's just going to suddenly be faithful to me? He's been unfaithful for as long as I've known him. I can't go back there."

"So, what, you just gonna be out there making porno movies?"

"What?! What the hell are you talking about? Where'd that come from? What does that even have to do with anything? I told you someone was blackmailing me."

"I saw that movie, Asha. Well, I saw as much as I could stand. I had to know if you were telling me the truth. You lied to me. I saw you doing all those things, and there was no way you didn't see any cameras. I even saw a close-up of in between your legs. It was so close, you could see the stuff coming out. You're going to try to sit there and keep lying to your own mother? I don't understand what would make you resort to doing that shit. I know you wanted to be in movies or on television, but when have you seen women from porn making it in Hollywood?"

"Momma, are you calling me a liar? Are you accusing me of voluntarily doing that movie? Why would I lie about something like that?"

"I don't know. Why are you lying to me?"

I was at a loss for words, so I screamed into the phone and ended the call.

The phone started ringing again. I thought it would be my momma calling back, but it was Brandon calling again.

"What the fuck do you want?"

"Asha, you need to come home, babe."

"Oh, fuck you! You need to be cleared the fuck out of my house before I do get back. Otherwise, I'll be having you locked the fuck up. You must be stupid if you think you're going to beat on me the way you did, bring bitches into my fucking home, to which you have never contributed a damn dime to, and I'm supposed to stay with you. You need to be the fuck out. I've already been to the police station, and they've taken pictures of all the marks and bruising you've left on my body. Stay there and see won't you go to jail."

I lied about the police, hoping that would make him go away.

"Babe, could you just hear me out? I've been so stressed lately, and I just needed to be able to talk to my beautiful wife. Each day you've been giving me a hard way to go. I know I fucked up, but I'm willing to do whatever to fix things."

I hesitated before responding. "Really?" I asked in a softened tone.

"Yes, baby. I'll do anything for you—for us. I love you. You love me, and we belong together. I just want to wipe the slate clean and give your mother that grandbaby she's been wanting. You know we only have less than a year now." He chuckled.

I chuckled. "Yeah, I do love you, but you know what?"

"What?"

"You still better be out of my fucking house before I return and have your ass locked the fuck up. We are so done. Go have your baby with my cousin. Be her fucking problem. Beat on her ass so she can shoot you."

"Asha! Stop being like that. I didn't tell you why I was so stressed. That girl has been trying to blackmail me. She said she didn't give a damn where I got it from."

"What girl? What are you talking about?"

"That Lena chick. She approached you because she had already been demanding money from me. I didn't know what to do. I didn't have that kind of money. I tried to play the tough guy role, but the truth is, I was scared."

"But why couldn't you just talk to me about it? I tried talking to you. I told you she said she'd go to the police."

"No, she's talking about going to the police and saying that you and I are running this racket. She's been demanding twenty-five thousand dollars. I took all my frustrations out on you, and I'm sorry. I don't know what to do. It's one thing for me to go to prison, but she's trying to destroy my queen in the process."

"Brandon, I think we both need to go to the police."

"Asha, no one's going to believe us. You look happy as hell in that video, constantly appearing to look into the camera. You'll never be able to convince anyone that you didn't see any cameras. You didn't see them, like I didn't see them."

"Brandon, are you telling me the truth? Are you just trying to trick me to come home?"

"I don't want to trick you to come home. I want and need you to come home. I need my wife. You are my everything."

"Then what about all those other women? You had two women in our house the other day."

He laughed. "No, I didn't, babe. I was just trying to mess with you. No one else was in there. I just put those extra plates on the table to make you think that. I made all that mess. I would never do anything like that to you."

"You had dried up cum on the front of you. I saw it with my own eyes."

"Baby, I jerked off in a towel and then fell asleep with it laying on me."

That seemed almost plausible.

"Why'd you beat me like that?"

"I was so frustrated. I had no business touching you like that. Between all this blackmail, the baby situation, my job stressing me . . . I was just losing it. Asha, please come home. I can't survive without you. I don't even want to live if I can't have you."

"Brandon, I don't have a job anymore. All of my modeling gigs were cancelled or just disappeared. I have nothing to look forward to. I am almost out of money, and I don't know how we're going to pay for anything, anymore. We'd have to move out and let people rent our home. I don't have enough money to carry us both. I'm scared. I have never been in this position before."

"Aw, baby. Just come on home. We'll figure something out. We're going to be all right. I'm going to make sure you're taken care of."

I couldn't stop smiling. It was like that was all I needed to hear.

"I'm somewhere up in Maryland. I'm going to run in here to the bathroom and then I'll be heading home."

"Maryland? How'd you end up there?"

"I don't know. It was either go north or go west."

He laughed. "Well, hurry home, babe. I can't wait to see you and make love to my wife."

I know I probably should have made him suffer a bit longer, but I believed he had learned his lesson. He'd know better than to push his luck with me in the future.

CHAPTER 26

I won't lie. I was scared as hell when I pulled up in front of my building. Brandon's car was there. I was really hoping he was being sincere. I was still angry with my mother, so I didn't bother calling her with any updates. I figured I'd just let her worry.

My heart thumped harder with each step to my door. I took a deep breath before sticking the key into the door. He scared the hell out of me. He was standing right near the door when I opened it, wearing glasses. He had this wicked smile that let me know I should have run when I had the chance.

The way he pulled me into his arms seemed somewhat forceful, but he acted as if he was so happy to see me. He immediately started kissing me and trying to peel my clothes off while still near the door.

"Brandon! Can I get inside the house good?"

"I miss my wife."

"When did you get new glasses?"

"I been had these. You just never see me when I wear them."

Despite my protest, he continued stripping me naked there in the living room as he spoke. I wanted to stop him, but I didn't want to start a fight. I was happy that he was happy to see me, but something in my gut was making the situation uncomfortable. I tried to get him to the bedroom, but he seemed hellbent on staying in the living room.

He opened his pants and reached in for his limp penis to pull out. "Suck this!"

"What?" I was about to get an attitude, because I didn't appreciate his tone.

"I said, suck it. I need you to help get it hard."

"Brandon, can we go into the bedroom? Can I relax a bit, first? I've been on the road all those hours, and I'm really tired."

"Well, let's just do this so you can get you some rest."

I wanted to cry, but I just went on and gave what he wanted. He had me down on my knees, sucking him for a good twenty minutes, and he didn't get hard. Finally, I stopped.

"Why you stop? That was feeling really good."

"One, my knees hurt on this hard floor. Two, you're not even getting hard."

"Okay, well come over here. I got something else for you."

He escorted me to the sofa and laid me on my back. He took one of my feet and draped it across the top of the sofa, while my other foot was on the floor.

"What are you doing?" I asked, afraid.

"I'm about to make you feel really good."

He dug between the sofa cushions and pulled out this long metal vibrator. It had to be at about twelve inches long. I tried to close my legs as quick as my eyes saw the thing, but he quickly sat in between them.

"Baby, don't be afraid. I'm not going to hurt you with it. I'm going to make you feel really good."

"No, Brandon. I don't want that thing inside of me."

"I'll use it on the outside."

He turned the thing on and placed it against my nipple. My nipple came to immediate attention. He laughed and then set the vibrator against the other nipple. Although my nipples were stimulated, I still didn't like the idea or feeling of it.

It's not like this was my first sex toy experience, but it was my first time using one with Brandon. His whole demeanor was off, and that was making the experience so uncomfortable.

He slowly took the vibrator down to my navel and lingered there as he used his tongue to tantalize my breasts. I was beginning to relax just a little. I kept my eyes closed as he rubbed the vibrator along the insides of my thighs. I could feel the anticipation building. He left the vibrator along the inside of my thigh as his mouth made its way to my navel. He took his time there, licking and gently sucking as if it was a delicate flower. My body began twitching from the sensation. He brought the vibrator closer to my hotbox, while his mouth remained on my bellybutton. Although the vibrator wasn't actually touching me, it was close enough to excite me. I tried to inch my hips closer to it. That amused him.

He began holding the vibrator inches away from my clit, as he watched my hips jerk to get it nearer. "Go on and get it," he said, laughing.

I was already moaning, wanting the stimulation.

He used his fingers to open my lower lips. "Wow! Would you look at that pretty pussy? That's what you call chocolate-strawberry." He leaned down to quickly lick inside and sat back up. "Uhm, tasty." He brought the vibrator back closer to my tunnel and let it make slight contact to my entrance. My whole body jerked, as I released a loud moan. "Hmm, I think she likes that. Let me try that one again."

He did it again, and again my body jerked.

I know I originally didn't want that thing inside of me, but he had me so desperate in that moment. I wanted to feel all twelve inches of that metal vibrating more than I wanted him inside of me.

He put the vibrator back up against my inner thigh, while he began inserting one finger and then two fingers, and then three fingers, and eventually four fingers. "Damn, look at all this juice. I mean, this pussy is milky as hell." He bent to spend a few seconds licking my wetness. When he lifted up again, he placed the vibrator tip at my entrance, eventually easing it up inside of me. "Wow! Look how this pussy is opening up and taking this piece of metal up inside. Amazing. A beautiful sight. Damn, look at this—it's all the way up inside of her. All twelve inches, and she's going fucking crazy."

I didn't know what all of his commentary was about, but it was getting on my nerves. I sure as hell was going crazy, but his talking was interfering with my orgasm.

"Shit! Would you look at all that pussy juice shooting out of there? I think my dick is finally getting hard. Let me see if I can taste some of that juice while it's squirting out." He bent again to lick my pussy. "Oh yeah, tasty as hell. Delicious."

After my orgasm, I wanted the vibrator out, but he wouldn't take it out. I kept trying to back up away from it, but he kept pushing it in, further and further. Then he changed his position, while keeping the vibrator inside of me, to make me suck on his dick again. He was gagging me, as he tried to push it deep into my throat.

The vibrator was getting really hot inside of me, almost like it was burning me. I began trying to struggle to get Brandon's dick out of my mouth to tell him to remove that vibrator. He stuck with me each move I made to get up and away. I could still hear him giving some kind of commentary, but at that point, I was becoming hysterical, and couldn't make out what he was saying. I was beginning to realize that he was trying to hurt me. Or so I thought.

His dick was brick hard and he quickly pulled me from the sofa and pushed me onto my knees, with my upper torso bent over onto the sofa. He tossed the vibrator to the side and used both hands to spread my ass cheeks.

"My lord, would you look at all this beautiful black, chocolaty ass? This is what you call a beautiful ass. Even the asshole is beautiful." He bent and licked my asshole. "Damn, even her asshole tastes delicious."

I was about to ask him who the hell he was talking to, but at that moment, he rammed his dick up inside of me from behind. He used a hand to firmly press my head into the sofa. He fucked me like an animal, and then he'd pull out.

"Look at all that cum on my dick. This pussy is soaking wet." And then he was back inside.

That was the moment that I thought something very sinister was going on. I thought about those mysterious glasses I had never seen before.

As he pounded from behind, suddenly I felt the vibrator buzzing up against my rectum. I started trying to use my ass to push him off of me, but that seemed to excite him more.

"Should I or should I?" he asked as if someone was watching. "That's a virgin booty hole." He laughed like a madman.

He began attempting to penetrate my rectum with the vibrator, while his dick continued stroking—pounding—my pussy. I tried to scream, but he used his free hand to grab a sofa pillow to press over my head. It seemed the more I tried to fight, the deeper the vibrator was going.

"Oh shit! It's halfway inside already. Look at her going crazy.

Can you imagine having two dicks inside of you? Damn, looking at this asshole taking in that vibrator got me ready to bust. Oh shit!"

He quickly pulled his penis out of me and shot his hot liquids on my ass, near my asshole.

He laughed hysterically. "Look at this! That vibrator is all the way in. Twelve-fucking-inches up the ass. Don't tell me I don't know how to pick 'em."

I felt my body going limp, like I was falling unconscious. I can't remember everything after that, but I knew he was continuing to have sex on me, with me passed out. I remember praying to die. I hated myself for being so stupid and returning to him after what he had already done to me. I was mad at myself for not letting my mother know where I was at.

I'm not sure how long I was out, but when I came to, I couldn't see anything. I attempted to put my hands to my eyes, but couldn't because my arms were tied behind my back to something firm. I was sat in an upright position. I felt a sharp shooting pain in my rectum area. I eventually realized that my eyes were covered and my mouth gagged. I tried to listen, uncertain of where I was. My body was numb, and I could feel pins and needles in my butt, legs, and hands, as if they were losing sensation. I couldn't feel any clothes on my body. I tried to wiggle my fingers to touch the floor and determine if I was even in my own home, and which room. I felt some slight weight on top of my head. I move my head to see if the weight moved. I eventually realized that I was inside our coat closet in the living room.

I wanted to try to scream, but I had no idea why I was there or how I got there. I figured it had to be Brandon's doing, but I wasn't certain. I didn't know if maybe someone came in and did something to him as well. I couldn't tell if it was night or day. I had no idea how long I was locked up in that closet. I wondered what he planned to do with me and how long he planned to keep me locked up. I was foolishly still hoping that this was just him trying to teach me a lesson, and we'd be able to move forward after this. I tried to rationalize that I must have caused him a lot of grief, running off the way I did.

I made up my mind. Once he untied me, I would let him know I wouldn't run off again and I'd definitely stop with all the insecurities.

My thoughts were interrupted by voices. I could hear Brandon's voice, but I was unable to hear what he was saying. The blindfold was covering my ears. I heard another voice, that sounded as if it was a woman's voice. Then I heard the television. It seemed like it was up loud. I began smelling the scent of food cooking. I was starving. I waited and waited and waited, but food never came.

After a while, it was quiet again. At some point, I dozed off.

CHAPTER 27

The sound of the front door jarred me from my sleep. It sounded like a bunch of people, or maybe I was becoming delirious. I had no idea how much time had passed at that point. I heard the closet door open. I was too weak and numb to move. It sounded as if someone was calling my name, but I was having difficulty processing my thoughts.

I felt the blindfold and gag being removed, and I heard my name being repeatedly called. Although the blindfold was off, I still couldn't open my eyes. I heard several people yelling and fussing. Even sounded like someone crying. My body was very numb still, but I felt someone wrapping me in a cover. In my delirium, it seemed as if I was hearing Sylvia and Jeanette's voices. It even sounded like Corrine's voice.

"Wake up, Asha! Asha! Wake up!"

I was absolutely certain that was Jeanette's voice.

"Is the ambulance on the way?"

That definitely sounded how I remembered Corrine's voice. I really felt I was going crazy then. I wondered if I had made the trip to New York, after all. *Did I make it onto the boat and pass out?*

"They're on the way," I heard Sylvia say.

I felt a wet towel applied to my forehead. I wanted to speak so bad. I couldn't believe we were all together again.

I may have been going in and out of consciousness, but I next remembered an oxygen mask over my face and a bunch of people talking. It felt like I was moving. I heard a machine beeping. The voices I was hearing no longer belonged to Sylvia, Jeanette, or Corrine. I began wondering if I ever heard their voices or was I dreaming.

When I finally awoke, I found myself in a hospital hooked up to two IVs, oxygen, and a heart monitor. Eventually I realized I also had a catheter. Just looking at my surroundings caused tears to flow, as I tried to recall the events that led up to me being in a hospital.

I began remembering another beating from Brandon, after I was passed out. I remembered the pain he inflicted upon me from that vibrator. I remembered him talking as if someone was in the room watching. I remembered waking up in the closet. I remembered being happy to hear my best friend and cousin, but then sad because I didn't know if it was just a dream or not.

I must have dozed off, because my sleep was jarred by a technician attempting to get blood from my arm.

"Oh great! You're awake. I'll be sure to let the nurse know."

"How did I get here?" I asked in a whisper.

"I really can't say. I only collect blood in the morning. I'm sure your nurse will talk to you."

Shortly thereafter, a nurse came in. She started checking all my vitals instead of speaking. She seemed rude and unsympathetic as if she was there just to do a job, collect a check, and go home.

"Could you tell me how I got here?" I asked.

"Well, I'm assuming an ambulance probably brought you. That's how most unconscious people get here."

On any other day, I would have cussed her out, but I was desperate for answers. I tried to remain polite, despite her rudeness.

"Do you know how I might have got into the ambulance or who called the ambulance?"

"We don't get paid to monitor how people get into ambulances nor who called them. Our responsibilities begin when you come onto our ward."

I closed my eyes tightly, as my patience with her was running out. Thankfully, the bitch walked out before I could say anything else. I saw the clock on the wall when I reopened my eyes. It read 6:46. I was hoping that meant someone new would be on duty shortly.

About thirty minutes later, two doctors showed up. One was probably a student, since he stayed quiet and just nervously waved.

"Good morning, Asha. So glad to finally see you're fully awake. You gave everyone quite a scare."

"Good morning," I responded. "How long was I out? How long have I been here?"

"It's been a few days. By the way, I'm Doctor Lassiter. I'm the chief neurosurgeon. I handled your surgery."

"Surgery? What surgery?"

Crazy thing, right when I asked that question was the first time I attempted to put my hand to my forehead. My entire head was bandaged. He could tell I was shocked by my gasp.

"We had to relieve the swelling on your brain. When I say you are very lucky to be here, you are very lucky. I think if you weren't found when you were found, you wouldn't be with us today."

I was really confused. "What happened? How? Who found me? When was I found?"

"From my understanding, you had been locked inside of a closet, tied up, for a few days. You had been badly battered, sodomized, dehydrated, and possibly left for dead. I believe it was some of your family members that found you."

"Oh, my goodness! How?" I cried.

"The perpetrator was said to be your husband. At least you'll never have to worry about him bothering you again."

"Brandon? What do you mean?"

"He's deceased. I believe one of the family members who found you shot him. A single gunshot wound to the chest did him in."

I cried out loud. I couldn't believe any of this was real. I was hoping I was simply trapped in a bad dream and would eventually wake up.

"I'm so sorry to have to give you such devastating news. You do have some family members that have been camped out these past few days, very anxious to see you. I'm sure they'll be happy to learn you are awake and alert. I just need to do a quick assessment before I can clear you for visitors. I believe you can only have two visitors at a time. Also, you'll probably be having other doctors coming to check you out. No one could really do much until your neurological condition stabilized."

I had a million questions, but I decided to hold them for my family. After he finished his assessment, he let me know I'd be in the hospital for a few more days and then would have to go to rehab. I wanted to cry all over again, thinking about how much damage Brandon must have done to me to cause me to need rehab after being hospitalized.

It seemed like forever, but eventually, my mother and father were allowed into my room. No one else was allowed. My mother came running in crying and plopped her body over mine.

"Oh, my baby! This is all my fault. I am so sorry."

My father rolled his eyes at my mother. "You damn right it's your fault. Why the fuck would you give that asshole my daughter's number after you knew he had already beat on her? And the fact that you would try to hide it from me. Now look at my baby girl."

"Arthur, please don't start that shit again. I said I'm sorry," she snapped.

"You're the one that brought it back up, and I was just reminding you."

"Would the two of you stop it and help me remember what happened to me? I'd appreciate that."

"Listen to her speech. It's all fucked up, and it's your fault," my father scolded.

I hadn't realized anything was wrong with my speech. I thought I was speaking normal. The doctor hadn't mentioned anything about my speech being off.

"It's going to be all right. We're going to make sure you get a great speech therapist, and you'll be talking like your old self in no time." My mother started crying again.

"What's wrong with my speech? I'm talking just fine."

My father came and hugged me. "Don't worry, baby. It's going to be all right."

That didn't quite answer my question, but it underscored the fact that something was definitely wrong with it.

"What happened to me? I can't remember."

"Your mother gave that lunatic your new phone number after you had just ran away from him, after he beat you. Somehow, you ended up back in your place, and Sylvia and your other friends found you tied up in the closet. Supposedly, you were there for a few days. Thankfully, they had been in the states for some boat trip in New

York. Your mother got worried after a few days of not hearing from you and called Sylvia, hoping she left a key someplace so we could go to the condo to check on you. Instead, Sylvia went. Your so-called husband had the nerve to be in there with another woman. Police said the woman kept asking him where you were at, and he lied to her saying you left him. Your car was downstairs. Your friends were searching the home and ended up checking the closet. Brandon tried to charge at Sylvia and your friends, and Sylvia shot him."

Those words caused my mother to hysterically cry again. My father rolled his eyes at her again.

"If that's guilt, you should feel guilty," he said to her.

"What friends found me?

"Your friend Jeanette, and I think the other lady was Karen, Corrine or something like that."

"Really?"

I heard myself ask that question, but my father just looked at me and didn't respond, as if I hadn't actually spoken. I kept asking over and over again, but he didn't say anything. Next thing I felt him gently rubbing my head and face. I'm not sure when my eyes closed or how I just drifted into a slumber, just like that. I had so many questions and needed answers.

I was in the hospital another seven days, and I had yet to see Sylvia or Jeanette. I was even anxious to see Corrine. I couldn't believe she accompanied the others to see about me. That actually meant a lot to me. A few days after his first visit, I learned from my father that Jeanette and Corrine had returned to Jamaica after my first few days in the hospital, while I was still unconscious. Sylvia was dealing with legal battles regarding the shooting, although she was licensed to carry. They didn't like the fact that she was living out of the country.

When I left the hospital, I had to go to a rehab facility. Between the surgery to my brain and the damage caused by Brandon, my motor skills were impaired. I was still having difficulty holding things, standing, speaking, and with incontinence. The therapists said I'd be better in no time. However, I just wished I had died.

I couldn't understand why, despite what he to me, I still loved Brandon. A part of me resented Sylvia for killing him. I wondered if she only did so to make sure I couldn't have him anymore.

CHAPTER 28

I had been at the rehabilitation facility for about two weeks when I was told I had some visitors. My father drove trucks, so he had to get back on the road. My mother had to get back to work and maintain her normal life. However, when either of them came, the staff didn't bother to make any announcements like this.

I was sitting up in a special chair when Jeanette, Ricardo, Corrine, and Anthony walked in. I was beyond ecstatic. I was also embarrassed, thinking of all the foolishness I had done to them.

"Hey, beautiful!" Corrine said, looking super happy to see me. She came and hugged me as if we were besties.

The others also came to hug me. They didn't look as bright and cheerful as Corrine. As a matter of fact, Anthony looked like he would hit the roof.

"He's lucky he's dead," he said to no one in particular.

"Exactly!" Ricardo added.

Jeanette grabbed a stool that the therapist was using and sat in front of me. "How are you feeling?"

I shrugged. I was embarrassed to answer, knowing my speech was impaired. "Okay."

Tears fell from her eyes. "That stupid motherfucker. I can't believe he did all this shit, and now Sylvia gotta fight for her fucking freedom. Grimy bastard."

"Huh?" I asked, still trying to keep my speaking to a bare minimum. I wanted to ask what the hell she meant about Sylvia fighting for her freedom.

"Damn Georgia bullshit. They've been holding Sylvia since she shot Brandon. They're not buying that self-defense line."

"Why?" I asked. I was getting upset.

"He was with a woman and was still on the bed when Sylvia shot him in the chest. The woman says Brandon didn't make any attempt to attack her or me and Corrine. We were in a different part of the house, so we didn't see what really happened. We tried to say it was self-defense, as well."

"She was the one that told us to look inside the closet for you. I didn't understand how she knew that. She said that she could smell an odor coming from the closet. We smelled the odor as well but had no idea where it was coming from," Corrine added.

"The same time she was telling us to look in the closet, she was telling us to call the police. Then she disappeared. Less than a minute later, we heard the gunshot but couldn't run to see what happened, because we spotted you tucked in the back of the closet with a bunch of clothes and mess thrown on top of you," Jeanette told me.

My tears began falling.

Ricardo came and stood behind Jeanette. "I know dis is hard for you, queen, but just t'ink, you survived and you're going to have a great life in front of yuh. Dat mutafucker can never hurt you again."

Anthony got some tissues from near my bed and gave them to Corrine, and she wiped my tears.

I had so many more questions but struggled to get them out.

I somehow was jumbling my words and thoughts together and had difficulty communicating. I wondered if they thought Sylvia's actions were sinister. I also wondered how she knew to tell them to find me in the closet.

"Hey lovely, we're going to head on out so you can get some rest, but we're going to keep a check on you until you're all better," Corrine said. Inside I laughed, because I remembered a time I hated her use of the word "lovely," but now I was embracing the term of affection that she showered me with.

"Unfortunately, I have to fly back out. But I'll be back soon," Anthony said.

Ricardo nodded. "Yeah, I gotta fly out as well. My beautiful queen will look after yuh, for certain."

Jeanette stood to hug Ricardo with a big smile. Looking at her, you could tell she was beyond happy. I couldn't remember ever having that look the entire time I knew Brandon, let alone while I was married him.

"We'll try to stop by tomorrow or the next day."

I kept trying to say, "Thank you," but they seemed to struggle to understand what I was saying. Eventually Corrine caught on, and told me I was welcome.

I didn't know what was happening, but it seemed that my ability to speak was getting worse instead of better. As a matter of fact, it seemed that everything was getting worse. It seemed as if I was doing better when I first arrived to the facility. I was able to stand better and hold myself up longer. The past few days were more of a struggle. I would also tire out more.

Jeanette and Corrine came back two days later. Jeanette tried to fix up my hair, but she mostly talked to Corrine, or they'd speak about what was on the television. I remember hearing her tell Corrine how she had to get back on the road for her book tour. The book she had never told me about. Even in that moment, I was fighting my feelings of resentment.

Two days after that, Corrine returned without Jeanette. It was crazy, because I didn't even know her. As a matter of fact, I remembered hating her, yet she was the only one able to carve a moment of her time for me. I appreciated the company, but at the same time I was thinking I wouldn't have been in that position if she hadn't kept Anthony away from me. It was all her fault. I could have been with Anthony instead of Brandon and could have had a happy life.

She loved to hear herself talk, because she went on and on and on about the various places she had traveled and talked about me visiting those places when I got well. I'd just smile. She annoyed me so much, I was happy when a technician came to take me for an MRI of my brain.

"Is she going to be all right? Should I go with her?" she asked the technician.

"No, ma'am. No one can go with her. It should only take about thirty minutes."

She looked at her watch. "Oh shoot! I have to get going. I didn't know it would take so long," she said to the technician. She turned to face me. "Asha, I have to fly out of the country, but I'll be back as soon as I can. I have an event. I'll be continuing to pray for you."

She bent down to hug me. I felt partially guilty, knowing that she was praying for me, but since it was all her fault, she should feel guilty.

My mother was present the following day when Dr. Lassiter came to visit me at the facility. I was still feeling some kind of way with her because of her disloyalty. If I had a lot of visitors, I would tell her not to bother coming at all. However, despite my big modeling career, it seemed like I was but a mere hiccup in the world.

Even the article that one of my caregivers shared only mentioned, "A woman was severely beaten and left for dead in a closet, as her husband laid in the home they shared with another woman. The woman's pregnant family member, a licensed-to-carry attorney, Sylvia Bordeaux, has been held in connection with the shooting death of the woman's husband, claiming self-defense, despite him being in a lying position on the bed with the other woman. Ms. Bordeaux claimed the male victim attempted to charge at her, but the evidence and witness state otherwise."

That was the end of the story. Not any mention of my name.

My mother showed me the ten people who posted prayers on my Facebook page. That was it. She also showed me Corrine's post about me, asking everyone to keep me in prayer, without giving specifics. She was gracious to tag my Instagram page, and I was able to see the thousands and thousands of praying hands posted underneath *her* post. For some reason or another, I still found a reason to be offended.

"Good afternoon, ladies," the doctor said when he entered my room. He looked tired. I had another doctor since at the rehab center, but he didn't come in with Dr. Lassiter. "How is my patient doing today?"

I tried to smile, but as of late, it seemed everything was becoming increasingly difficult.

"I guess you're wondering why I'm here," he said as he pulled the stool to sit in front of my chair. "Asha, we're going to have to try to operate again. I understand you have been having diminished neurological functions, which certainly is not the direction we want to be heading. Your MRI is concerning, and your EEG has been showing seizure activity. The seizure activity is sometimes expected after any operation to the brain, but it tends to correct with time and medication. Instead, it seems your seizure activity is impairing your motor skills, and I'm sure you've probably noticed that speaking is becoming more and more difficult. That's due to intermittent paralysis occurring in your central nervous system. We're going to have to try to fix that before it gets worse. However, I must tell you, unfortunately, there is no guarantee that this will work, but at the pace your motor skills are diminishing, we need to do something sooner rather than later. We're going to have you moved back to the hospital and prepped for surgery within the next day or two."

"I don't like this," my mother protested. "What if she doesn't survive or gets worse?"

"Ma'am, with all due respect, at this pace, she won't survive without it. Trust me; I wouldn't dare consider another surgery this quickly if it wasn't a matter of life and death. I'm sure you've noticed that Asha was able to speak some before leaving the hospital, as well as use her hands and briefly stand. As you can see, she's losing her ability to swallow her own saliva, let alone speak. She still seems pretty coherent, and I can see the emotional reaction through her eyes, which lets me know her brain is still capable of registering and processing information. That's not going to be the case for too much longer. At this pace, I'd give it another week or two."

"What?! What do you mean another week or two?" my mother yelled, and I thought the same, but was unable to speak it.

"That's pretty much how much time we're looking at. Maybe even less. If she gets to the point where her brain forgets to command her heart to beat or her lungs to pump oxygen . . . Let's just not even mention that, but it wouldn't be good."

Tears spilled from my eyes. I couldn't cry like normal, but I was still able to process thoughts as he had mentioned, and I didn't like what I was hearing. A part of me did want to just die. I didn't want to have to live with memories of all that was done to me. I was losing functions, but unfortunately, not my memory.

"I don't know. I don't think I want you messing with my baby anymore. I think we need to get a second opinion first. How do we know it wasn't your first operation that caused all of this damage?"

The doctor looked at her, offended. Hell, I would look at her too if someone made such an accusation.

"Ma'am—Ms. Woodard—frankly, I don't need your permission. I'm only speaking in front of you as a courtesy since you are her mother. You are entitled to find all the second opinions that you'd like, but this operation will indeed be happening within the next forty-eight hours."

"I'll go to court to get an emergency order to stop you. You're not just going to do whatever you feel like to my child."

He looked at her as if she was stupid. I was annoyed with her as well and tried to yell for her to shut up. Particularly since I felt it was her fault that I was currently fighting for my life.

Dr. Lassiter went and pushed the call button. A nurse came into the room within minutes.

"Sarah, could you do me a favor and get the video equipment for a consent to treat?" He spoke as if he was very agitated.

"Sure, doctor," she replied and hurried back out.

"And what is that supposed to mean?" my mother rudely asked. "My daughter can't speak or write, so what kind of consent are you supposed to get?"

He smugly smiled at her. "Just sit and watch."

Sarah returned with a technician and some kind of video

equipment to include a monitor that I could look at. When it was all set up, Dr. Lassiter went on to explain my condition in both scientific and layman terms.

At the conclusion of his speech, he asked me, "Asha Woodard Harper, are you able to comprehend everything I just said to you?"

I tried to speak the word, "Yes," while nodding my head.

"Is anyone here forcing you to do anything against your will?"

I attempted to shake my head, while answering, "No."

He then said, "Your mother is present with us and is requesting your procedure be postponed for a second opinion and possible judicial actions. Is that your opinion as well?"

I looked at my mother as if she was crazy before again attempting to shake my head and answered, "No."

As much as I wanted to just die, I wasn't going to let my mother have a drop of satisfaction, thinking I was on her side.

"That being said, and understanding all the risks associated both with the surgery, as well as the risks of not going forward with the surgery, do you give permission to perform the necessary surgery that may or may not save your life as well as your deteriorating neurological functions?"

I slowly attempted to nod my head and answered, "Yes."

"Thank you, Asha. That concludes this video consent to treat, which is being witnessed by the patient's mother, Joy Woodard, Nurse Sarah Smalls, as well as the licensed video technician, Gary Simmons."

He then signaled for Gary to terminate the video and left the room. The nurse and technician followed.

"Asha, you're making a big mistake. Why would you give your consent without a second opinion?" my mother scolded as quickly as they were gone.

"Go!" I tried to yell. It probably sounded like "O" since she looked as if she couldn't understand what I was saying. I wanted to use my hands to point toward the door, but I was unable to. Instead, my mother just remained seated in silence, watching the muted television with tears in her eyes. I just let her be after that.

CHAPTER 29

A month after the second surgery, I was actually improving. I was still in the hospital instead of the rehab facility, but I was doing better with forming words and moving my hands and feet, and I was getting close to moving my legs. They were ready to upgrade me back to solid foods. They said it would still only be soft foods, but not only liquids. In over two months, I hadn't had a full meal. I remember my last meal being a chicken sandwich I picked up before I returned home to Brandon on that fateful evening.

I was sitting up in a chair watching television. Thankfully, my mind was fully able to function and understand, to help me to communicate properly. I was able to laugh at funny things on television or get angry if the situation was appropriate. The doctor said that was a good sign that my neurons were working.

Jeanette walked in with a shy smile. For the first time I looked at her and realized she was absolutely gorgeous. I remember often looking at her and wondering why any guy would be interested in her over me. It wasn't like she was all dressed up. As a matter of fact, she was dressed in jeans, a hoodie, and a baseball cap with her hair pulled into a ponytail. It didn't take me long to notice the sparkle from her left hand. I hadn't noticed when I last saw her. It was her engagement ring. It actually looked larger than I remembered from the video Ricardo had posted a while back. As a matter of fact, it was a white diamond and not the yellow from the video.

She came and gave me a hug. "Hey, beautiful! How's it going? I heard you're doing a lot better. I came a few weeks ago, but they had to keep you sedated for a while, I guess to help you heal. They had you on a ventilator and everything, so to see you sitting up and breathing on your own now is quite a blessing. Everyone's been praying for you."

I was shocked. I didn't have any memory of the ventilator, and I definitely didn't have any memory of her being there.

I smiled. I wanted her to see my eyes happy. I tried to say, "thank you," but I wasn't sure how she might have heard what I was saying.

She understood. "You are so welcome. I'm just glad to be able to see you on this side of life. I'm glad we have this moment alone, just you and me. You know, I have thought about all the petty foolishness that has been building between you and I over the years, and I couldn't think of absolutely anything that was worth never having the opportunity to see or speak with you again. All of that needs to be behind us so we can move forward."

"I sorry." I was saddened by her words.

"So am I, sweetheart. So am I. I found out some crazy shit and didn't say a word. I allowed my anger over pettiness, to rule my better judgement. I allowed your cousin in my ear, and she was steadily pouring gasoline on the fire—no, steady throwing grenades is more like it. With the stuff she shared, I couldn't believe I was ever friends with you. It was crazy to learn that before your marriage, while she was enlisting my support to get you away from Brandon, she was doing everything, and I do mean everything, to get him for herself."

"Huh?" was all I could manage to say. I was definitely confused and wanted her to elaborate on all she was saying.

She had been standing all that time, and she let out a big sigh before taking a seat.

"Sylvia told me about how you would go and sleep with whatever guy I was seeing since we were kids—teens. She said you'd always question why guys wanted my ugly ass over you, especially with my complexion being darker. She told me about your trip to see Ricardo, but by that time, he had already told me all about it. When he told me, I really didn't want much to do with you, but I wasn't all that serious about him at the time, and lord knows I wasn't his only."

She shook her head and laughed. "So, I swept that under the rug and just stopped letting you know all of my business. He also told me about how y'all first connected in your room when we were in Jamaica and wondered if you were just trying to get back at him. I learned from Sylvia that you felt like I took him away from you. I didn't believe her when she told me that nonsense, because you knew we hadn't had a single discussion about you being with Ricardo. He didn't even mention it back then. When I got with Ricardo back then, you knew I was strictly there to have fun." She laughed again. "That's another reason I didn't take him serious. I didn't question who or what he was sleeping with. We were still kicking it about a year later, and then he started visiting Atlanta to see me. I was impressed. Eventually, he started showing up to some of my events and making greater efforts to pursue me, and that's probably where I began catching feelings." She paused to chuckle, thinking back to that time in her mind. "Despite my feelings, Ricardo was the *king* of flirting. He'd talk so much junk to other women, even while I was with him. He would tell every one of them that I was his woman.

I didn't know how to take him seriously. I started channeling most of my energies into my business and wasn't looking to pursue any relationships. Turned out, Ricardo was the only guy I was sleeping with over the years. At that point, he already told me about the experience with you, so I definitely wasn't going to let you know, nor have him around you.

"I always swore to myself that I'd never let a piece of dick come before my best friend. I loved you more than a sister. I didn't even want to be successful without you by my side. That's why I couldn't understand where this jealousy or rivalry came from. I think the first time I picked up on any kind of rivalry was when we took that first trip to Jamaica, over seven years ago. According to Sylvia, it's been the entirety of our friendship. When I first picked up on a problem, I had yet to meet Ricardo. I remember telling you about a guy I was interested in meeting, but I hadn't even told you who. I think I remember asking you what was up that night. So much about our relationship changed from then on. I didn't know why. Each time I'd offer some kind of help or to shop together and buy similar outfits, it was like you'd always decline. I would ask if you needed help with your schoolwork, and you'd say you got it, when in fact you dropped out without even telling me. Hell, I was crushed about that. I just knew we'd be sitting on stacks of paper together. Black queens, sitting on our throne of dollars. Of course, I recently learned from your cousin that all that pulling away was because you felt I was trying to control or manipulate you. There was no way I was believing that bullshit, but then aside from that, I have no explanation why. Hopefully, when you get well, we can have a sit-down and you could tell me, from your own mouth.

"For the most part, that's why I started hiding my life from you—because of this unspoken rivalry and knowing you slept with

Ricardo. Oh, let me clear up one thing: I did not sleep with Brandon. Never. I thought about doing it to pay you back for what you did, but I didn't. Not only that, I couldn't stand him, and I just couldn't sink to that level. When Sylvia came to Jamaica, she said you knew all about me sleeping with Brandon. I asked her how, because that never happened. She said even Brandon confessed. Like I said, that never happened. I did flirt with his ass one time after he hijacked your birthday party. I didn't like him and I didn't trust him. I didn't want him with you, because he was shady as hell, and I felt you could have done better than him. I asked him something about his mortgage on his house and he didn't know what the hell I was talking about. I asked him then, how did he own a home and have no clue what I was talking about. He responded by cussing me out. That was when I tried to flirt with him. Trust, there was no skin or slob involved. I just baited him to see if he'd be willing. He was willing, and I told him I was going to tell. I didn't tell, but I did tell you to drop kick his ass to the curb.

"But enough about that, them, him, and me—oh, but before I move too far on, let me mention Corrine. She was one of my earlier clients. I met her at one of my conferences in L.A. It was a casual meeting. My first impression of her was that she was drop dead gorgeous, but she was super smart, humble, and meek. She wasn't modeling at that time. She was in school, already working on her Bachelor's degree. I asked to represent her, and she said, yes. I had Ricardo get me some contacts through Anthony, since I remembered him putting all that stuff together when you and I went there. Although I didn't see Anthony, he provided me all kinds of contacts, and I took it from there. I was on my 'boss' shit." She laughed. "Before you know it, Corrine was a household name, and most folk couldn't even tell you why. I hated that I was giving all of that to Corrine and not to you, but you were still rejecting my help. Even worse, you were rejecting the validity of my business or any of my endeavors. I remember it tripped me out when I came home that time and saw you on your computer, using a fake profile. I probably should have told you about her being my client then, but by that time she was with Anthony, and I didn't think you'd take too kindly to that. So, I sat on it. And if you're wondering how she got with him, it's because Ricardo was trying to support me, showing up for the events I put together for Corrine, and one time he brought Anthony. The four of us hung out after the event and were just having friendly, fun conversation. Ricardo pulled me away, leaving them two together, and the rest is history. I didn't tell you about it for a few reasons. One, I wasn't sure how you were feeling about Anthony. One minute, you'd be calling him all kinds of assholes, years after that one event in Jamaica, and the next minute you'd be saying you were just social media friends. And since I hadn't mentioned that I was still dealing with Ricardo, I didn't tell you about them coming to Corrine's event to show support."

She stood up.

"Whew! I done talked so much, my throat's drying out." She laughed. "You need something to drink? I'm going to go find something to drink."

"No, thank you." I slurred some, but I think she understood.

"I'll be right back." She grabbed her purse and was out the door.

I was glad for the moment, because with all that she was saying, I realized that parts of my memory were a bit off. I was trying hard to recall all of the things she mentioned. I vaguely remembered Sylvia saying something about Brandon sleeping with Jeanette. I also had to remember a time when she caught me on the computer. I remembered a lot of things, but every now and again, some memories were fragmented.

She eventually returned. It seemed like a long time, but there was a commercial on the television when she left the room, and although a different commercial, commercials were still on when she came back. She had a bottle of Pepsi in one hand and a cup with a straw in the other. She set the Pepsi down.

"The nurse said you could have some of this. It's just juice. I know you love your Pepsi just like me, but she said you can't have that right now."

She held the straw to my mouth, and I was so grateful for that juice. Sometimes I'd forget to close my mouth, and it would dry out. That juice was right on time. I choked a little and she took the cup away and cleaned up the juice that escaped my mouth.

"You're going to have to take smaller sips, lady. You'll choke. We'll just wait a few minutes before I give you some more." She affectionately rubbed my back.

I felt happy. I had yet to fully process the memories of all that I had done to her, but I was happy that whatever it was, she was big enough to forgive me and be by my side in my time of need.

She picked up her bottle of Pepsi, opened it, took a swig, closed it back up, and set it down. Suddenly she looked sad.

"I heard about and saw a little bit of that ridiculous porn movie. Only a fool would believe that was supposed to be your voice." Jeanette rolled her eyes and shook her head.

I sat trying hard to recall the porno movie she spoke about. The memory was vague. Actually, the word *porn* seemed to be stuck in my mind, but I wasn't sure why.

She sat back down and continued. "But then again, I don't think they'd give a shit about the voice. I remember when we were in Brazil, I saw Sylvia in the lobby speaking to that guy. They were near the bar together. I didn't think much of it. Even after the movie, I told Sylvia that it was a good thing she didn't go off with that nut. At first, she was agreeing. Eventually, after she moved to Jamaica and was blowing up my ear with all the dirt you did to me and to her, she confessed to setting that whole thing up with the guy in the hotel. She said she recruited like four stupid guys to bed you the night before your wedding. In hindsight, it was probably to get Brandon to herself. She even paid for that room he took you to. Whichever one of the four guys that was able to snag you, was supposed to take you to that room. She said they didn't even know about the cameras set up in that room. They just figured they were getting some pussy as part of some bachelorette party scheme.

"I remember wanting to take you with me to the birthday party I went to that night, but you were acting soooo ugly with me. I didn't get it. I had no idea what you felt I did to you. I mean, I was definitely wrong for not telling you about my relationship with Corrine, but I felt you were dead wrong for seeming to plan your wedding around Corrine's event. The minute you mentioned the place, day, and time of your wedding, I laughed to myself. I was convinced you hadn't gotten over Anthony, but I didn't understand why. He told me he hadn't spoken with you in years and said he just tried to look out for you over the years, throwing gigs your way to keep you eating well. I remember also being concerned about how you'd act around Ricardo. Instead, I said nothing about inviting you, kept the drama to a bare minimum and went on about my business.

"I told Ricardo about what Sylvia was telling me. Of course, he agreed I needed to keep my distance from you, but when I shared her confession about the video, he wanted me away from her as well. We didn't completely alienate her, with her being pregnant and all. We just needed a bit of distance and knew not to trust her. I did warn

Corrine to keep an eye opened. Corrine spoke to Anthony about it. He was pissed. Right before we were about to head to New York for Corrine's boat event, Anthony got all up in Sylvia's ass. He didn't give a damn about her being pregnant. He was even angrier when he learned that Sylvia's baby belonged to your husband and that she had been with him since before your engagement. I remember her trying to defend her actions, saying it didn't matter because Brandon was still a dog with a bunch of bitches all up in the house. I think for the most part, everyone took it as speculation on her part. No one gave a second thought to how she'd know that. Anthony let her know that he wouldn't be able to keep her in his employ but would make sure she wasn't financially hurting. He said he didn't want that kind of energy in his circle. He also told her to get that video off the net.

"We were in New York when your mother called Sylvia, saying she was worried. There was a bit of an argument, with Sylvia telling Joy how y'all talked so much shit about her and treated her like shit, but now needed her help. I only caught bits and pieces of the conversation, but when I heard her say, 'Maybe if she wasn't out screwing around with random men, he wouldn't be beating her ass.' That's when I was like, Whoa! Wait a minute. Who's beating whose ass? She told us Brandon had beat you up and you ran away, but Joy foolishly gave him your new number a few days earlier and hadn't heard from you since. I called Joy back asking if she'd called the police, but she hadn't because she didn't know if you were just mad that she gave Brandon your new number or if something actually happened. I told her to at least make a report. Next thing I see Sylvia pulling out her laptop and looking at some kind of video feeds into our condo. I was like, 'what the—?' Then she says we need to hurry up and get to Atlanta. The whole shit was so crazy. The guys weren't with us, but they managed to get us a quick flight to A-T-L. While we were flying back, I asked Sylvia about how she was able to see inside the condo. She said she been had the place wired up, because we were always away from home. She had cameras placed inside different light fixtures. That shit pissed me off, especially knowing she was the one that set up that whole Brazil video. I learned that day, her ass was certified crazy. She didn't see that it was a big deal. She also told us that day how she got some chick to go to a hotel with Brandon, and she was able to record that and let the girl show you the video so you'd leave Brandon alone, but it still didn't matter to you. As she spoke, I wondered what she saw that made her feel we needed to rush to Atlanta in that exact moment. She didn't see you on camera, but she said she saw your keys sitting on the coffee table. She said she did see Brandon with another woman, but couldn't understand where you would be without your keys.

"I'm trying to tell you, that bitch went up in there, straight Rambo style. She went up into my old bedroom, and within seconds, Corrine and I heard a single gunshot. We had just opened that closet door and saw your tightly tied feet sticking out from underneath a pile of clothes. Anthony had bodyguards for Corrine and I, and they came running in. They were standing in the opened doorway, but they came all the way in at that point, grabbed me and Corrine, and pulled us out the house. The bodyguards went inside to check things out, next thing we go back inside, Sylvia's in the kitchen, the other girl was sitting at the dining table, and you were laid out on the floor, barely conscious. One of the bodyguards got you out of the closet. That fool had your arms tied to that pipe inside the closet.

"Girl, you wouldn't believe all the dirt that has come out since that day."

Right at that moment, a nurse walked in and interrupted Jeanette.

"Okay, visiting hours are over. I need to get the patient out of that chair and cleaned up so she can get her meds and rest for a bit."

"No!" I said.

I was desperate to hear anything else Jeanette had to say about the events leading up to the point where my thoughts were fragmented. I remembered some things as she spoke of them, but other things, I had no recollection of what she was saying. I remembered something about New York, but I wasn't sure why it was important. I had forgotten about Sylvia shooting anyone. I kept trying to remember who Brandon was. Insanely, I clearly remembered Anthony and Ricardo. Well, I knew they were important in my life, but I wasn't sure why.

"Oh yes, yes. Your friend can come by later for the next set of visiting hours, or I'm sure she'll be back tomorrow."

"Ugh! Okay, I'll try to get back tomorrow. I won't be able to get here later today. Plus, I don't like being here when her mother's here. You know that never goes well." Jeanette rolled her eyes at the thought of dealing with my mother.

Could you imagine being engrossed in a good suspense movie or novel and they just abruptly cut you off, saying, "stay tuned," and then you have to wait to find out what happened? At times, I was forgetting I was the victim in the story, but it was sounding like a page-turning novel for a minute. It was definitely better than the home rehab television program I was watching before Jeanette showed up.

"Honeybunch, get you some rest. I'll try to make it back tomorrow. Maybe by then, I'll have even more info to tell." She leaned over and hugged me. She held onto me tightly before kissing the top of my head. "Love you, girl."

I wanted to cry, watching her leave.

I really wanted to cry when she didn't come see me the next day. I don't know if it was because of my mother or what. My mother showed up that next day, and I didn't see a sign of Jeanette.

CHAPTER 30

A few weeks later, I was taken back to the rehabilitation facility. My mother was still giving Dr. Lassiter a hard way to go. He'd try checking on me early in the morning to avoid her, but even then, she'd be at the nurse's station raising hell for one reason or another. If my father was around, she'd find a corner to keep herself set in, while cheesing and grinning, still hoping for my father's affections.

I was so glad when my father came to visit me at a time he knew my mother wouldn't be there.

"Damn, I thought I'd never get to see you without an audience."

"Momma?" I asked.

"Who else? At least anyone else, I could ask them to step out for a few minutes of privacy. In all these months, I don't think I've saw your mother leave to go to the bathroom while I'd be with you."

I laughed. It was still a little painful, but it felt good. When my mother wasn't around, some of the staff members at both the hospital and the rehab facility would try to keep my spirits lifted, saying laughter is good for the soul. They just didn't know, in my case, laughter was a bit physically painful.

My father picked up on the grimace on my face.

"Baby, does that hurt you?"

"A li'l bit."

"Oh, I'm sorry. Is that normal? Should I call someone?" he asked, looking frantic.

"It okay. They know."

I was like a child, learning how to speak all over again. I'd hate when my mind was conscious enough to know I wasn't speaking properly yet. But I was at least happy to be able to communicate to the point others could figure out what I was saying. At times, I'd take a long time to respond, because my brain was struggling to force my mouth to speak correctly. I'd get so frustrated. My speech therapist told me not to worry about trying to speak perfect right away. She said I'd get there as my brain continued to heal. She said it's more important to focus on communicating than pronunciation. That was very difficult. However, I saw people were able to comprehend what I was saying, so I was good with that for the time being. Everyone but my mother was happy about my progress. She was always finding something negative to say or telling me I wasn't trying hard enough.

My mother is a tall, thick, black woman, and most of the nurses and other staff members acted like they were afraid of her. Her voice is very commanding, and capable of intimidating people. Instead of confronting her, most people try to avoid her. She bragged to me about one time when a nurse threatened to have her permanently banned from the hospital, she looked down into the nurse's eyes and said, "Try it!"

I was mad the nurse didn't have her banned. So many times I wanted to tell them not to let my mother back in, but I was worried about her finding out that the order came from me. I figured if I managed to survive this whole ordeal, shit would hit the fan if she found out.

"Not sure if you've been brought up to speed, but Sylvia was finally granted bail. One million dollars, though. Not sure who's going to cough that up for her to be released. Supposedly, they were worried about her fleeing the country. They already took her passport, so I'm not sure why they figured she'd be a flight risk. You know your mother is trying to make sure she's not released, all because she had been having an affair with your husband. Yes, I agree, that is a horrible thing to do to someone, and then it being a family member. I don't understand Joy's anger. That girl saved your life. For that, I'll be forever grateful. Maybe she didn't have to kill the guy—I don't know because I wasn't there. I would think she was highly enraged to know some guy was doing that to her family. That's the way I see it and how the rest of my family sees it. Your mother and the prosecutors see it as a crime of passion, saying she flipped when seeing him with another woman."

"I doe-no. Nette tell me some'in, but I doe see her no mo."

"Jeanette? Your friend Jeanette?"

I nodded my head. "Yea."

He rolled his eyes up and sucked his teeth. "Your silly mother. She gave orders to the staff that none of your friends were allowed back to see you. She said they all played a role into what happened to you. She couldn't say exactly what it was. I think she said something about Jeanette also sleeping with Brandon. She said the other girl—I can't remember her name—stole some other guy from you and Jeanette stole your boyfriend from you. I don't know. It all sounded crazy."

"Oh no!" I said getting upset. "It a mi-take. It a mi-take. I wrong."

He looked at me oddly. "So, you told your mother something? Is that what she's holding against them?"

I nodded my head. I was so frustrated and ready to cry. I wanted to tell him the whole story, but I already knew my speech wasn't capable yet.

"It all a mi-take. I wrong. I told her wrong."

"Oh, baby girl. Those people saved your life. Why would you tell your mother anything against them?"

"Befo'. I dead . . . said it before I hurt. I wa' mad."

He seemed to struggle to make out what I was saying. "So, you told your mother stuff before all this craziness happened?" he asked.

I nodded, glad that he understood what I was trying to say. "Yea."

"Should I try to override your mother's wishes and allow them to come back to see you?"

I smiled as best as I could. "Yea. Yea, p'ease. 'Ank you."

"I'll do anything for you, my baby girl. I just wish I wasn't so nice to that guy when we were in Brazil. Your mother bragged about how great he was and begged me not to do anything to scare him off. She talked about how we'd probably be holding our first grandchild within a year, and I got caught up in her foolishness. I was actually looking forward to being a good granddad, since I wasn't that great of a dad to my daughter.

"Speaking of which, I have been wanting to tell you something for the longest. I could never get a moment away from your mother to tell you."

I looked at him worried, since his expression changed to that of worry.

"You have a little brother. I didn't find out about him right away, but I have been wanting you to meet him." His jaw tightened and his lips pursed. "I also have a wife now."

My eyes stretched as far as they could without causing pain. "Dad!"

"I know. I'm sorry to spring it on you like this. I was always trying to find the right time to tell you. I figured there would never be a right time to tell your mother. I had been seeing this woman in Las Vegas. Her name is Shelly. I really liked her. She owned a big company there in Vegas as well as in Los Angeles. Neither of us had much time to spend with the other. She was busy with her business, and I was on the road. After a while, we kind of drifted. Then it got to a point when I'd just call to see how she was doing, and she'd twist every conversation into a commitment conversation. I knew I needed to settle down, but guys tend to make you feel foolish when you let a woman snag you. I knew I loved that woman, but I thought I had something to prove to the guys. One day I called to check up on her and she told me I wasn't allowed to call her again until I was ready to commit, because she wasn't going to be living her life in limbo waiting on me. We're on the phone and suddenly I hear a kid whining. She rushed me off the phone. She was in L.A. at the time, and I hopped on a plane and flew to see her. I can't even explain what made me do that. At first, she wasn't going to allow me to come see her when I let her know I flew in, but then she said, okay.

"As quick as I saw him, I knew he was my kid." My father paused to smile. "He's beautiful. She let me get a DNA test, just so there would be no doubts. He's definitely my kid. I was beyond happy and excited, but then suddenly I was feeling trapped with her. That was two years ago when I met him. It's been over five years since she and I first met. When we were in Brazil for your wedding, and I was with your mother, there wasn't a doubt left in my mind that I wanted to spend the rest of my life with Shelly. When I got back to the States, I took Shelly to Vegas, and we got married, and I've been happier than I have ever been. Only thing is, I'd look at my son—your brother—and I'd feel a bit of guilt for being in his life early on, but not yours. And now with everything that's happened, I feel guilt for not giving you that stable home you wanted and needed while growing up. I don't want to completely blame everything on your mother, but as many times as I have tried to make it work for your sake, it just wasn't working."

I sat staring at him. I wanted to smack the hell out of him, and I thought had he told me any of this before, I would have definitely smacked him. I was angry and jealous. At the same time, I understood the part about him trying to make things work with my mother, because I did remember him coming back and forth, but my mother would always want to monopolize his time.

"I can see that this is making you angry. Especially, since I should have told you long before now about having a brother. The time just never seemed right, and even now, I hate telling you and upsetting you like this. Shelly is really anxious to meet you and anxious for you to meet your brother. I was working on a plan to make it happen before all this happened. Now, we have to wait until you're well enough to travel, to keep your mother from going ballistic. I doubt she'll handle the news well."

"Go!"

"Go?"

I tried to gather the strength, lifted my hand and pointed toward the door. "Go!"

"Are you asking me to leave, Asha?"

"Go!" I closed my eyes as if that would make him disappear.

"Asha, you want me to go away?"

I refused to say anything else and kept my eyes closed.

He came and kissed me on my forehead. "I'm so sorry. I really wanted you to know. Hopefully, you'll give us the opportunity to talk about this again in the future."

I remained silent until he was gone. Then I opened my eyes and let the tears flow.

Perhaps I was behaving childishly, but when looking for people to add to the blame list, his name just moved closer to the top. He was so busy trying to appease my mother, Shelly, his dick, and whoever else that he didn't have time to be the father that I needed, when I needed him.

You damn right, I'm mad. Especially with you bragging about how you're the happiest you've ever been. No, the day I was born should have been your happiest day, but you weren't happy until you found out you had a son with some new chick, twenty-whatever years later. Keep being the absent father you've always been, while I kept making excuses for your absence.

In my rage, I let the next nurse entering my room know my mother nor father were allowed back to see me. I still couldn't believe my mother's gall to cut off my visitors, after she was the one that pushed me back into Brandon's hell. I even recalled asking her, "What if he kills me?"

That night in Jamaica, Anthony told me I needed to stop being a follower and come out of Jeanette's shadow. With the help of my mother, I completely took that the wrong way and fell into my mother's dark shadow instead. I allowed my mother to make me think the world was out to get me and they really hated me because of my dark complexion. Yet, somehow, I ended up hating my best friend, who wore an even darker complexion. Guess it never crossed my mind that Jeanette might have experienced some of the same rejections based on complexion that I experience. Instead, I felt a need to steal away any boy or man willing to accept a dark-skinned girl.

I was hoping after two brain operations, the doctor managed to get most of my stupidity out.

CHAPTER 31

Three more months went by and I was beginning to feel like I might have cut off my own nose to spite my face. No visit from my mother. No visit from my father. None of my family would come, and I didn't really understand why. Hadn't heard a peep from Jeanette and company.

There had been so many staff turnovers at the rehab facility. Low wages, is what I heard. Patients have come and gone. Some have all the way gone—on to meet their maker.

I still had a ways to go, but I was doing so much better. The good thing about improvement is it makes you that much more determined. I was standing for longer periods of time. I could grip the door handle—just couldn't pull it open yet. I'd been doing a lot of reading, and I worked on my speech even when the therapist wasn't around. My speech therapist brought me this recorder to speak and listen to myself. That was like the best contraption ever. I used a mirror to help me form my lips and tongue to put words together.

One of the staff teased that I seemed more determined to run my mouth than to walk. The thing about losing your ability to speak, is you realize all the times in your life when you should have spoken up but didn't. You think about all the conversations you should have had but didn't. You think about all the times you should have been singing that song, but were too insecure. I lived my life quietly in the background, always doing what others told me to do and losing sight on what it was that I wanted to do.

I look at the media these days and the wonderful celebration of dark complexioned women, even with nappy hair. I grew up with a mother always reminding me of how much the world hated us just for being dark-skinned with nappy hair. I remember my mother sharing that while she was pregnant with me, she had hoped I took my father's lighter complexion, just so I'd have a better chance at life. And when my father didn't hang around, she'd always talk about how she wondered if he would have if I'd come out lighter.

Looking back on life, I realize that my dark complexion wasn't my stumbling block. It was my mother—the one always feeding me insecurities for breakfast, lunch and dinner. Always reminding me that the world didn't want me to have anything, and how I needed to take whatever I wanted, when I wanted, because no one was going to simply let me have it.

And during this rehabilitation time, I've had the opportunity to consider my life, which ran parallel to Jeanette's. She didn't have my problems, despite her dark skin. She had a voice, and even a loud voice, and never shied away from attention. She owned her dark complexion and made the world applaud it, while I tried to stay quiet to hide mine. I remember Jeanette speaking to me as if she was my motivational coach, but I tuned her out because I thought she was trying to make me look dumb, so she could look like the smarter one. She was always so positive and uplifting, constantly celebrating our black beauty, telling me how people were paying to look like we did naturally. They were trying to darken their complexions and thicken their lips. They were getting nappy weaves sewn into their heads. When we started community college, she said one day there would be so many little black girls looking up to us. She said they were depending on us to be successful, so they too could feel good about themselves, embrace their blackness, and carry the torch.

Looking at how very different our lives turned out, I guess it would be safe to say that I'm the poster child for everything NOT to do, and she would be the poster child for everything to do to be successful. Being jealous of your best friend is definitely the thing not to do. I see now, I have been jealous of Jeanette our entire life and sabotaged my own success as a result. That jealousy and the fruits of that tree, I can't even blame on my momma. That was all me.

I knew one thing; when I was finally discharged, I was going to find a way to make it all good. I was going to use my voice and say all the things that needed to be said to fix my friendship with Jeanette. I was going to use my voice to take ownership of my transgressions against her and her fiancé. I was going to do my all to celebrate, support, and lift my friend up so she could shine brightly for other little girls to see.

That thought made me smile. It made me determined to get better and get discharged.

My heart leaped with joy when one of the staff came to the lounge area to let me know I had a visitor. At that point, I was almost desperate enough to want to see my mother. However, when I got to the visiting area, it was Corrine. She smiled, but she didn't look happy. She leaned over to my wheelchair and gave me a big hug, almost like she didn't want to let go. Then the tears fell from her eyes.

"What's wrong?" I asked.

I wanted to know where the others were, but figured Jeanette might have rethought her position about resuming our friendship. Or maybe she discovered something else I might have done to hurt her.

Corrine couldn't stop crying. She'd try to speak and pull it together, but then would cry again.

"They're gone."

"Huh?" I knew my speech was a bit impaired, but not my hearing. "Who? What?"

"Jeanette and Ricardo. They're gone." She rested her face into the fold of her arm onto the table and sobbed.

"What? Gone? Gone where?" I asked, not trying to accept what I was thinking, based on her behavior.

"They were in a boating accident. They were out there during the storm . . . a hurricane," she answered when she collected herself. "It's been almost a month, and they haven't been found. We refused to accept the reality. Anthony still hasn't accepted it. He's not eating or taking care of himself. He is devastated. I'm devastated. She heard from your father one day, and he told her that he opened up the visitor list for us to be able to visit again. She was excited about it. She said she had stuff to tell you and never got to. Our schedules got so busy, and the same week we talked about all getting together and flying here to see you, that was the end."

"But how? Why? Why were they on a boat in a hurricane?"

"The hurricane hadn't fully moved in just yet. It was still sunny and beautiful. The waves were coming long before the storm. Going out on the yacht was one of their favorite things to do. I remember Ricardo saying it would probably be the last run for the season, because they'd usually get back-to-back storms. Anthony and I were about to go, but then he said the water looked kind of rough. Ricardo laughed and made a joke—something about a Gilligan's Island. That was the end. The waves became so rough, Anthony worried and had a helicopter sent out to rescue them if needed. He felt the water was too rough to try to sail back. The helicopter went out, but there was no sign of the boat. With the hurricane approaching, the governor would not order any search and rescue missions. We had to wait for days to get someone out there. Maybe a week later, pieces of the boat were found, but still no sign of Ricardo, Jeanette, or the crew that went out with them. Anthony was hoping someone kidnapped them and was holding them for some ransom, but no demand was ever made, nor were there any other boats out when the helicopter went searching.

"It's been a very, very rough month for all of us. Jeanette's mother is still in Kingston, expecting someone to find her—them."

I sat shaking my head side to side, not accepting what was spoken to me. Even my hands were trembling in my lap. I thought back to when we were growing up. I tried to recall Jeanette's sense of humor and if I thought she'd be capable of trying to fool everyone. That was not her personality. She was the fun one, but she was also no-nonsense.

Corrine took hold of my shaking hands.

"She was pregnant. She couldn't wait to let you know. They were going to be married on New Year's Eve and wanted the ceremony to cross into the new year."

I jerked my hands from Corrine. It was an involuntary reaction. I think if I wasn't sitting in the wheelchair, that would have been the point I would have fell. I was having a hard time catching my breath. My hands began violently twitching, and then my feet.

"Nurse! Please, someone! Help! Help!" she screamed. "Asha! Asha, please! Someone, please help." She ran to an alarm button on the wall and pushed it.

I didn't get to see Corrine again, because I was rushed back to the hospital. All of my progress went out of the window, just like that. I remember sleeping. It seemed like such a long sleep. I wanted to wake up. I could hear conversations in my mind. I saw a tsunami of memories. Some good. Some bad. I remember seeing happy memories and being wide awake, but then I'd see these visions of Ricardo and Jeanette on a boat in the middle of the ocean, overtaken by waves. Each time I'd see that memory, it was like I wouldn't see anything else, and the voices would stop. The images in my mind would stop. Life just became a blank wall.

CHAPTER 32

"AJ, that's your big sister, Asha. I figured it's time you finally get to meet her."

"Why does she look like that? Can she hear? Is she retarded?"

"Don't say that. That's not nice. No. Several years ago, she was in a very bad accident and it caused some swelling to her brain. She had to have surgery, but the surgery didn't go to well, and then she had to have another. She was doing really well after the second surgery, but then she got bad news about her best friend dying in a boat accident, and she started having really bad seizures after that. Eventually, she fell into a coma. She was in a coma for just about a year. She's been in a nursing home all these years. I've been trying to get her released to my care and fly her here to our home to live with us."

"Mommy said she could live with us?"

"She sure did. And Mommy is going to see to it that your big sister has the best of care, and hopefully one day she'll get better, so you two can get to know each other. I'm sure she's going to be excited to get to know you."

"Her eyes are open. She can't hear you talking? Can she hear me?"

"I don't know, AJ. That's why you can't be saying mean things about your sister, or things that could hurt her feelings. You wanna give her a hug?"

"No. She looks scary. She doesn't blink her eyes. Plus, her hand keeps moving in a circle. No, I don't want to hug her. Will she always look like that?"

"I don't think so. Your mom is going to have a team of doctors flown in to see about helping her get better."

"Okay then. I'll hug her when she gets better. If she's my sister, why is her skin way darker than mine? She doesn't look like me."

"AJ! That's not nice. She is your sister. I'm her father just like I'm your father. You two just have different mothers."

"Who's her mother? Where does she live?"

"Unfortunately, her mother went to heaven two years ago. Her name was Joy."

"How did she die?"

"You ask so many questions. Her heart got sick and then she died. She died while your sister was in the hospital."

"That's really sad. I'm sorry for saying she's retarded."

"I'm sure she forgives you. Just make sure you're nice to her."

"Hey Mommy! Look, Daddy says she's my big sister."

"Yes dear, Daddy told you correctly. But right now, you need to come and eat your lunch before your soccer practice."

"Okay. Is Asha going to be here later?"

"No. She's going to be staying in a place where there will be lots of nurses and doctors to care for her."

"A hospital?"

"No, not quite. But she'll have round the clock care. It's a nursing home."

"Daddy, I thought you said she was going to live with us?"

"Stop giving me that look, Arthur. I told you she could come here, but never said to live inside this house. I arranged a nice facility for her to go to. Surely, they'll allow home visits from time to time."

"Shelly—"

"Arthur. Don't Shelly me. I said what I said. I found a facility for her, and she'll have plenty of doctors and nurses to care for her. As much as we travel, she needs to be someplace stable where she's well cared for."

"I guess you're right."

"I always am. Come on and get your lunch so you can take your son to his soccer practice."

CHAPTER 33

I've lived trapped in my mind for almost ten years now. When I had the chance to speak, I blew it. I'm trapped in some nursing home, where I'm expected to die. Forgotten.

Over the decade, I have heard so much and have never been able to respond. Then again, I started wondering if I remained in this state by choice. I wanted to die so long ago, but it just never happened. My husband. My best friend. My mother, and now my father. All gone.

I remember the day that bitch, Shelly, came to the nursing home to tell me my father was dead. Involved in a truck accident. I remember her telling me that I'd probably have to get state medical assistance, because I wasn't her responsibility, and she wasn't going to pay another dime for me. She told me that she told her twelve-year-old son that his big sister also died so he'd stop asking to see me. She called me all kinds of retards. She said something in either German or some other language and then asked if I knew what that meant. She said it means, retard, and then she laughed hysterically. Thankfully, she never returned.

After hearing about Jeanette and Ricardo, I had a series of seizures that led to a coma. I heard a lot of conversations when people didn't know I could hear them. I recalled a time before my father died. He was talking about how Sylvia was selling sex videos she had collected of me and Brandon online through some international channel. The police uncovered a bunch of emails, text messages, computer files, bank records, and other evidence that she thought she covered her tracks on. They even found a video that she saved of both times Brandon put his hands on me, including when he sodomized, beat, and tied me up in the closet then threw clothes on top of me. She had the whole moment captured on video and then had the nerve to try to use it in her self-defense case. That defense failed because she saved the video three days before receiving the call from my mother. Basically, she was just waiting for me to die.

All that time when I thought it was Teddy tormenting me, the evil was right under the roof with me. Not that it made any difference anymore, but it then made sense how an envelope kept showing up, even across continents. I remembered at one point I thought it was Brandon, when that Lena lady came to confront me about her and Brandon being together and told me how she was being extorted in the same manner. I really thought it was him, on that last night together, when I thought he was speaking to an audience as he sodomized me.

I guess Sylvia was able to listen to all of our conversations and knew exactly how and when to hit. That's also probably how she knew I had that $50,000 from Anthony.

Her stupid ass puts in all that time and energy into law school, and then throws it all out the window for literal dick. I'll be in my grave still wondering why she didn't just tell me she was sleeping with Brandon to keep me from marrying him, instead of inflicting so much pain and throwing everything away. What a fool. Can't help but wonder where her and Brandon's child ended up.

The End

Keep reading for a preview of
MR. & MRS. JENKINS

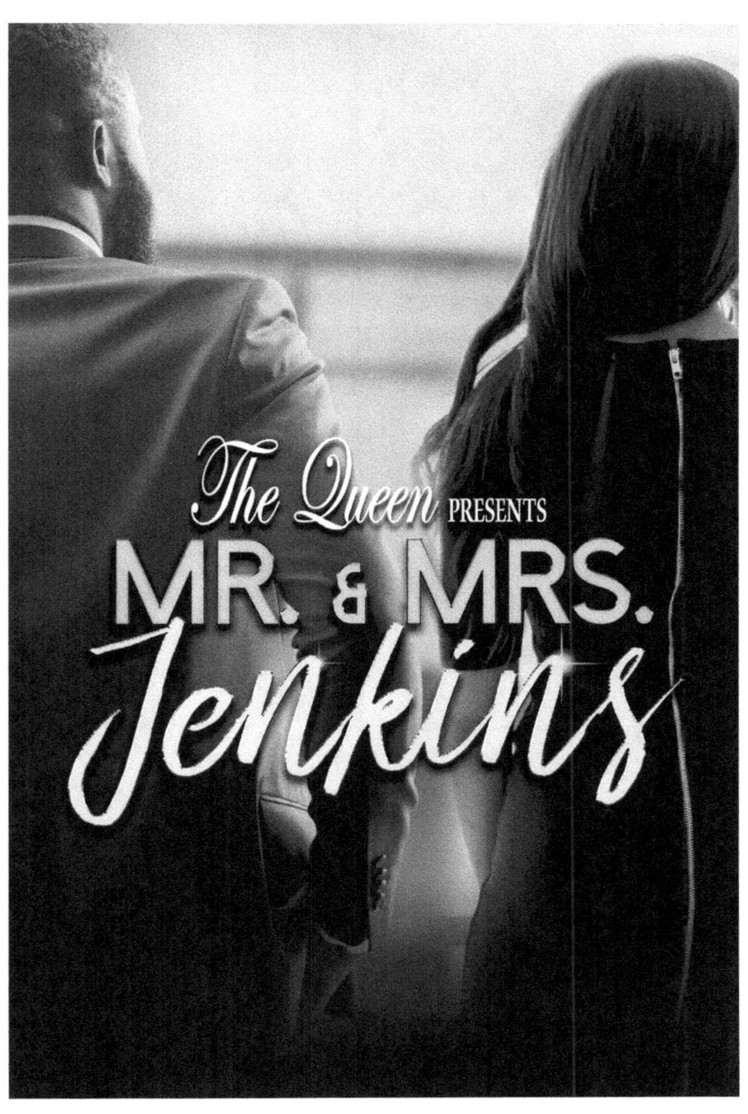

1

JENKINS & JENKINS

In a huff, Monica walked into the spacious white office she shared with her brother-in-law, Anthony, and slammed her bags down on her desk as he looked up from his computer and watched as some of the items fell from her desk.

"FUCK!" she yelled, as she stooped down to collect some of the files that had scattered.

"Well, good morning to you," Anthony said, trying to lighten the moment.

"It's anything but," she snapped as she continued trying to gather the fallen items.

"Not sure if this will help, but I stopped by and picked up some of your favorite pastries this morning," he said, nodding his head in the direction of where a box of pastries sat on their meeting table.

That caused Monica to soften up, and tears formed in her eyes. "Aww Anthony, that was so sweet of you. I really needed it. This entire morning has been a mess."

"You want to talk about it before we get to work?"

"It looks like you've already been hard at work." She pointed to his cluttered desk.

He chuckled. "Yeah, I've been here since six-thirty this morning, but I could use a little break. Besides, I have some ideas I want to bounce off of you for this new campaign, and I need your mind cleared of all the junk first."

After collecting everything from the floor, Monica stood from her squatting position and stared at him for a moment without speaking.

"I bet your ass is cold," he said, catching her off-guard. "That's probably why you're so angry."

"Ha ha. I see we got jokes." She chortled after snapping out of her trance.

"Monica, it's like twelve degrees outside. You have that skimpy leather jacket on, and that skirt is made of what—nylon?" Anthony scolded, pointing toward the wall-to-wall windows.

After putting the files back on her desk, Monica went for the hand sanitizer on the wall. As she rubbed her hands together, she took her daily inventory of the collection of successful ad campaigns on the wall before going to open the box of fresh pastries.

"For your information, my coat is in the car, but I was just too angry to realize I left it. And, if you must know, there is about forty percent nylon in this skirt. It's a cashmere blend that my well-paid stylist selected for me."

"About that. When are you going to get rid of the dude and go do your own clothes shopping? I know how much you make, and we're not banking the big bucks like that."

"How many hours a day do we spend stuck in this office or in someone else's office? When am I supposed to go shopping for myself? Hell, you *need* to hire my stylist to shop for your wife, because that is one sad looking chick. The way my sister dresses makes *you* look bad. If I didn't know any better, I would think your business was struggling to make ends meet, and she was getting paid minimum wage on her job. Hell, I'm the one with a barely working husband that doesn't contribute to the fucking household," Monica said, getting angry all over again. "Do you know, every dime he gets paid from the church, he's always giving right back to pay the ten different offerings that corrupt-ass church collects, or he's using it to travel with that crooked-ass pastor of his?"

"Hey! That used to be my pastor, once upon a time. We grew up in that church. Well, sort of. There were only about five hundred or so members back then. Now, they went and got all mega."

"Tell me Pastor Wade ain't shady as shit," Monica said before swallowing a bite of bear claw pastry. "Oh my god! This is so fucking good. Thank you. This just made my day—but that motherfucker is still shady as hell."

Anthony laughed as he got up from his desk to get a pastry for himself and took a seat across from Monica at the round meeting table. "How do you take the Lord's name in vain and cuss all in the same sentence?"

"First of all, I didn't take the Lord's name in vain, because when I said, 'god,' I was speaking in the lowercase 'g' sense, and not the capital 'g.' Big difference."

Anthony laughed so hard, he almost choked on his cruller. "You can't be serious, right? I guess that 'g' makes all the difference in the world."

"It does. It really does. The same as when we say 'Lord' and 'lord.' One has a lowercase 'l' and the other has an uppercase. When we use the uppercase, that's the same as talking about the uppercase 'g' God."

Anthony covered his face and shook his head. "Okay, you win. I'm sure the man upstairs knows your heart." He laughed again.

"Whatever!" she said, rolling her eyes while a laugh escaped her. "And getting back to your brother—my dear husband—don't they teach you that the man is supposed to be the provider in the house? Could you imagine if we had kids? We'd be homeless, because I wouldn't be able to work as much *and* care for a baby. Speaking of babies, is my sister still trying to get pregnant and doing all that extra fertility stuff?"

"Pfft!" Anthony turned his focus to the windows to keep Monica from seeing his deep-seated frustration. "You have to have sex in order to get pregnant. Now she's talking about going to a fertility clinic to see if something might be wrong with me because she hasn't gotten pregnant."

"I always tell you, she should have married Aaron. They would be perfect for each other. No matter what I do, he's always too tired or too busy or gone."

"I know. I'm sorry," Anthony said, placing a hand over her hand resting on the table.

"What are you sorry about? Hell, I'm sorry for you. I hate what Mya does to you. She's always trying to give everyone advice on how to fix their lives, but she doesn't have sense enough to know that a man has needs that should be taken care of."

Just then, Monica and Anthony's eyes locked, and they both became uncomfortable.

"Yeah, I guess we better get back to work now," Anthony said as he quickly shuffled back over to his desk with the rest of his pastry.

At times, Monica got a kick out of making Anthony uncomfortable, especially when her hormones were raging and she was being neglected by her own husband. That was the reason she had their office set up with their desks facing each other from across the large space. She'd often catch Anthony staring at her when he didn't think she knew, and when she'd look up at him, he'd quickly turn away. Sure, it was cold outside, and the wind quickly whipped through her flimsy fabric, but her hormones wanted Anthony to take notice of her panty-less derriere. Monica had curves for days compared to her sister, who barely had hips or breasts. She couldn't understand what Anthony could have found attractive about Mya.

Monica thought she was getting a good deal by getting with Anthony's identical twin, although their facial hair and weight made them easy to tell apart. Anthony stayed well-groomed and had a lush, neatly trimmed beard that made Monica moist between her legs at the mere thought of it, along with his perfect white teeth and thick lips.

Despite also having the same perfect teeth and thick lips, Aaron, on the other hand, wore no facial hair, and his barber was any student at the beauty school on $5.00 Haircut Day, diminishing her attraction to him. He had facial hair and was better groomed when they were in college, but without having a full-time job over the years and Monica's weariness of providing for his grooming needs, he resorted to the beauty school.

While Anthony sported dapper suits or name-brand dress shirts, Aaron got many of his items from the second-hand store or hand-me-downs from other men in the church. The only time he'd ever have something new was at Christmas or his birthday. Anthony took pride in his body and made an effort to stay fit, while Aaron never passed up a meal offered by the church parishioners, adding to his continually growing waistline. Monica dressed in mostly name-brand items, while her sister bought her clothes off a rack in Walmart, Kmart, TJ Maxx, or Burlington's clearance section.

Monica and Anthony Jenkins started their successful ad agency almost five years ago after graduating from Howard University, which they attended with each of their twin siblings. Anthony's brother, Aaron, was working to answer the ministry calling that he received several months before their graduation. Monica's fraternal twin sister, Mya, opted to further her education to pursue her dream job of being a social worker. Monica spent many years fighting the undeniable chemistry between she and Anthony, because of her marriage to his brother.

When Monica and Aaron married straight out of college, she had no idea that he would forego having a real job as he pursued a ministry career. She had no idea that he'd be leaving her home alone most nights while he followed the pastor of his church on his travels, in hopes of one day filling those shoes. However, being married to her business partner's brother wasn't the only reason Monica had to fight her desires to be with him; her business partner was also married to her sister, Mya.

Anthony met Mya in their sophomore year of college when they shared a sociology class and had to work on a group project together. They often bumped heads on the project, but somehow, Anthony found Mya's "know-it-all" logic both annoying and attractive. Although the pair began dating that semester, it wasn't until the following semester that Anthony found himself sharing just about every class with Monica. The two had a great number of things in common, but Anthony didn't feel comfortable pursuing anything with Mya's twin sister. Instead, he introduced her to his twin brother, who was an accounting major before he switched to theology in his last year.

Aaron proposed marriage to Monica at the time he received his ministry calling, because he felt that was the right thing to do. In the back of her mind, she knew she was most compatible with Anthony, but since her sister was dating him, she went on to accept Aaron's marriage proposal. Not to be outdone, Mya pressed Anthony to get married as well. She wanted to have a double wedding, which consisted of a quick trip to Las Vegas.

Despite being twins, Anthony hated the fact that he found Monica to be so much more attractive that his wife. Actually, had they not told anyone they were twins, no one would have ever guessed it. Monica took her father's mellow yet humorous attitude; height; full, heart-shaped lips; and cocoa complexion along with her mother's sensual curves. Mya inherited her mother's fiery personality, short height, thin lips, and pale complexion, along with her father's thin frame. Even though they were twins, Mya always behaved much older than Monica.

While most twins typically have close relationships, Monica now despised her sister because she had the man Monica wanted. She and Mya weren't all that close by the time they made it to high school, because Monica resented Mya's authoritative demeanor.

Their mother was a biracial woman with a British mother and a Senegalese father who was absent during her upbringing. She'd often tell Monica that Mya meant well and only had her best interest at heart. Mya was their mother's pet, while Monica was their father's pet. Although their father cheated on their mother more times than a few, he could still do no wrong in Monica's eyes. She adored the ground he walked on. Mya, on the other hand, would team up with their mother on holding grudges or finding ways to punish him for his infidelities. Despite the numerous infidelities, their mother was determined to hold onto him and not allow some other woman the benefit of saying she took him. Although their mother possessed a beautiful light-golden complexion, somehow Mya took on a pale complexion. Monica would often joke and tell Mya to stay out of the sun or that she needed a blood transfusion to get some color and would often ask Mya if she needed to borrow some ass or tits. However, when Mya managed to snag Anthony, knowing Monica was wishing she had him, there were no insults that Monica could hurl to cause Mya any insecurities.

"So, what's new? Tell me about this new campaign you have," Monica said once she got situated at her desk and turned her computer on.

"It's for a political fundraiser. I received this email asking if we could handle the ads."

"Wow! Really? That's great. We're gonna finally get to add some political campaign ads to our wall now. A senator?" she asked, pointing to the wall filled with their photos and posters.

"Not quite." Anthony laughed. "Just city council, but it's a start. If we do well on this, it could open up the gates for many other political ad campaigns."

"True, but what type of budget are they talking about? I don't want to waste our time handling charity cases—I already have one at home," she said, rolling her eyes at the disgusting thought of her freeloading husband. "We make our best coins dealing with corporations, and Momma needs a new pair of shoes."

"Momma or you?" Anthony laughed. "You have a different pair of shoes for every day of the year."

"That's not true. I don't even have fifty pairs of shoes."

"Fifty! I only have a total of fifteen, and that includes my sneakers."

"That's because of who your wife is. You make all the money, and she's always ragging on you when you buy something nice for yourself. She'd rather have you live like poor people while she saves a college fund for a baby that hasn't even been conceived. That's just ridiculous."

"I can't even argue with you on that," he responded, looking off into the distance.

Monica shook her head. "That's crazy; you two have been living in that cramped up apartment since you've been married. With her little salary and her trying to bank every one of your dimes for a baby, y'all will never move. What I don't understand is, why won't you just get a backbone and tell her how it's going to be? Why do you let her control everything?"

"I tried that, and it didn't work. You know how your sister is. I told her I was going to start searching for a house for us, and she told me I couldn't buy a house without her signature, and she didn't feel we needed to begin a house search until she becomes pregnant."

"It's five damn years later!"

"I guess that's why she's now insisting that I go see what's wrong with me. We only have sex when she thinks she's ovulating, and she thinks I'm the problem. Even then, there's no romance or anything. It's just, 'I think I'm ovulating. Come on and let's do it'."

"Why don't you just take the initiative? You're the man. Stop letting my sister treat you like a punk."

"Stop acting like you don't know your sister. You do remember that time when she went crying to you, talking about she felt like she was raped by her own husband that time when I decided to be the man and take initiative? She told your mom, and your mom told my mom, and it was all kinds of disasters. So now, I just wait."

"You don't think about just getting yours outside of the marriage? I mean, it doesn't seem like you'll ever be fulfilled in that marriage."

"Of course the thought has crossed my mind, but I am a married man. If I'm going to stay married, then it is what it is. I just try to focus on this business and how we can make it grow. We have seventeen employees right now. Eventually, I'd like us to have our names on the building in lights and have several layers to our management team. The last thing we need is my marriage problems creating waves for our business."

"Yeah, I guess. It just seems so tragic for you to have to work so hard to make everyone else happy, but you have no life of your own. You don't even have any real friends."

"I still have friends from Howard that I keep in touch with."

Monica waved her hand. "Keep in touch with is all you do. You don't get to go hang out with them. When is the last time you just went out and it wasn't job-related or networking? I mean, just went and hung out with your boys and talked shit while ogling over some hot-ass women?"

Anthony took a moment to think about it. Monica was right. Although he maintained phone conversations with his friends from college, he never spent any time with them, because Mya would always accuse him of wanting to go out and open up the doors for problems in their marriage. To keep the peace, he'd decline the offers from his friends. "Again, I can't even argue."

"You know what really makes me sad when I think about you two? The only time you two spend a night on the town is when it's her birthday, and you would plan some beautiful surprise that she'd always manage to jack up with her fucked-up attitude. When it's your birthday, what do you get? She'll invite the family over to your little-ass apartment for a dinner she sucks at cooking."

Anthony laughed so hard. "Stop ragging on my wife like that. Her cooking ain't that bad."

"Oh, it's that bad and then some. You ain't fooling anyone with that smoothie diet bullshit. I know you do the smoothies because you can't get a good meal at home. We've been at your mom's house, my mom's house, and my house for dinner, and trust me—I see the difference when it's time for you to sit down to eat. That bitch can't cook worth a damn, and since she's my sister, I can say anything I want about the stuck-up bitch. Not sure if you know this or not, salmon is NOT supposed to be dehydrated when cooked. I'm not sure why she bothers steaming broccoli. She might as well serve it raw since hers is so hard and flavorless."

By this time, Anthony had tears in his eyes from laughing so hard.

"Look at how you're laughing. You know I'm right. Tell me I'm lying." Monica laughed.

Anthony held his hands up while still laughing. "I'm not saying a thing."

"I thought so. Anyhow, let's get back to this new campaign. Are we going to assign it to one of the others or is it something you're going to work on personally?"

"Uh . . . Well . . . I think it's something *we* are going to be working on. They are under the impression that we are a husband-and-wife team, and they said that was something that helped influence their decision to choose us for this campaign."

"Huh? Why would they think we're husband and wife? What does that have to do with anything?"

"I guess it might have something to do with our business name, Jenkins & Jenkins, as well as our picture together on our website.

Honestly, even Mya had a problem with our photos and wanted me to have the website changed."

"Oh, really?" Monica twisted her lips and rolled her eyes. "We were just having fun during our photo shoot, and that was the image we wanted to portray—that we are a fun and creative bunch. She's so stupid. Don't tell me anything else about her today. She gets on my damn nerves." Her eyes narrowed. "You know, I do remember a while back, Momma had something to say about why you and I were so close up on each other in photos. I asked her if she had a problem with the photos we took with the rest of our core team as well, because we were just as close. Now that you're telling me this, it must have been Mya that went to Momma to get her to say something to me, because that bitch knows better than to come to me with the bullshit."

"Okay, I see you're getting yourself all worked up again, and we did a good job of calming the storm that blew in here this morning. Speaking of which, what had you in a huff this morning?"

"Your brother. What else?"

"What happened?"

"Same shit as always. Last night he's too tired, and this morning he needs to save his energy to work on the church's Valentine's Day music festival."

Anthony looked confused. "That's like three weeks away. He wants you to wait until that's over?"

"I don't know, but I do know I'm getting sick and tired of begging his fat ass for a piece of dick. He ought to be glad I'm willing to fuck his fat ass. I'm trying to figure out how the sexy, 185-pound man that I married is 330 pounds now. I know all them bitches in the church keep feeding him, and he don't know how to say 'no' to food. Even your momma keeps telling him he needs to cut back and go on a diet before he has a heart attack like your father did. Y'all are supposed to be identical twins. How could this be?"

"I keep telling him as well. I told him to do the smoothie diet with me. Dad hasn't been the same since he had that heart attack, and that was four years ago. He just sits around like he's waiting to die."

"I know. That's sad. My dad always goes to see him and swears he's not going anymore but ends up there the following week." Monica chuckled.

"Yeah, I like your dad. One of the perks to being married to your sister."

Monica laughed. "Hang around my dad enough, he'll help you find all kinds of side pieces. And you see, in all these years, my mom ain't letting him go. Teeth falling out, and starting to look like a pregnant pencil, and she ain't letting none of them bitches get to keep him."

Anthony burst out laughing. "A pregnant pencil? Damn! He don't look that bad. He got a little pot belly, but that's it. He's sixty, sixty-one, right?"

"No, he's going to be sixty-five in May. He did so much drinking all those years that his liver's all fucked up now, got him looking like a pregnant pencil."

"Your mom still looks good for her age."

"I guess she would. She's only forty-three. You know my dad was a dirty ol' man all of his life." Monica laughed again. "He only married our mother because he didn't want us growing up without a father, like she did."

"You ever wonder if he might have some other seeds out there?"

"I doubt it. He might be a dog, but he's big on family unity. If he had other kids, he'd want them to be a part of our lives. I don't think he'd hide it from us. Not only that, I remember Daddy telling me a long time ago that after us, he knew never to mess with anyone without some birth control, because he couldn't afford any more twins."

"Well, I guess we can't be mad at him if your mother isn't."

"Please, my mother harasses every young girl he messes with. Even about a month ago, she was talking about going and fighting some nineteen-year-old girl he messed with."

"Damn! A nineteen-year-old? I could see what he'd see in them, but what do they want with him? No disrespect to you. He's old, married, his wife takes all his money, and like you said, he's missing a few teeth. I don't get it."

"Probably some young, dumb ho with 'daddy syndrome.'"

"So, what was so special about this girl? Why not try to fight the others?"

"My mother tries to fight all of them, but the nineteen-year-old happens to be the latest one."

"You ever ask your dad why he does what he does, with the cheating?"

"Yeah. You know he and I are very close, so he tells me just about everything. My mother is always putting him on sexual punishment and making him sleep on the sofa for one thing or another. She always wants to try to control him, and sometimes he just wants to be somewhere where he could have peace . . . and sex. I tried talking to Momma about her controlling ways, but then she'll clap back, saying that's why she still has her man and not some other bitch. She feels if she doesn't control him, he would have *been* left."

"Hey, I guess I can't knock it. He's still there after all these years."

"Funny, I see you following down the same path when I look at you with my sister."

"Please! It ain't even like that with us."

"Oh? And why haven't you been able to buy that new house that you've been wanting? That condo you're in used to be nice when y'all first bought it a few years back, but now that thing is a hiccup away from being called the ghetto."

"Ha ha, I see we back with the jokes again."

"You know it's true. You better man up and take what you want out of life before you become my father. Oh, and in case you didn't know, he lost his first tooth when my mother smashed him in the mouth with an aluminum foil box after one of his cheating escapades that kept him out for two or three nights. I think we were like fifteen at the time. I loved my daddy, and he could do no wrong in my eyes. I remember hating my mother for doing that. I felt like she didn't want him to be attractive to other women anymore. I also remember that next time he stayed out, I was glad, because I felt my mother deserved it based on what she did to him."

"You still feel the same?" Anthony asked.

"No. I mean, she didn't have to do that to him, but I see that he was wrong for what he did. I remember I used to ask Daddy to leave Momma and take me with him, but to leave miserable Mya to be miserable with Momma." Monica laughed. "Daddy would always say that he'd never split his babies up like that, and he would never leave us. Guess he kept his word, at all costs."

"Yeah, that he did do," Anthony responded, staring off into space, thinking of his own marriage.

"Well, we need to get back to working on this new campaign. So, are we going to let these people believe that you and I are married?"

"We are married."

Monica punched Anthony in the shoulder. "You know what I mean."

Anthony laughed and played like he was afraid. "Oh, violent like your mother."

"No, that's my sister. She's the violent one."

"Yeah, I've seen that temper." He chuckled. "Anyhow, I say we let them believe whatever they want to believe. I doubt if they'll ever ask if we're married to each other. And if the truth ever comes up and they think we lied, we can honestly say we didn't."

"Hey, it works for me. They just better have a decent budget, or else they'll only be getting just you on this campaign. I've never heard of any city council members having a whole lot of money. As a matter of fact, they're usually broke and live in public housing, or close to it."

"Girl, you are too much." Anthony laughed heartily and shook his head. "I think we can just work on this fundraiser and see where it goes from there. I'm sure it'll open up plenty of other doors to people who are well connected. Broke people don't typically attend fundraisers."

"You have a point there. Okay. I'll follow your lead on this one."

"See, that's why you and I make such a dynamic team."

As quickly as the words left his mouth, Anthony was filled with regret for saying it. He could see that look in Monica's eyes that said she wanted to be more than a dynamic business team.

After Monica snapped out of the momentary trance induced by Anthony's words, she made her way to the office door. "I'm going to go check on the others and see where everyone's at."

"Good deal," Anthony responded.

2

ANTHONY

Anthony sat in the parking lot of the apartment complex for a good fifteen minutes after turning off the ignition. The thought of going home was becoming more and more unbearable. He'd leave extra early in the mornings and tried to return as late as possible to avoid the daily drama he received each time he stepped inside of his home.

Earlier that morning, he left before six in the morning, because his attempt to get sex from his wife escalated into an argument of sex being pointless since he couldn't seem to make the baby that she so desperately wanted. That turned into Mya demanding he find time in his busy schedule to go see a doctor about his possible infertility. So many times he thought about going out and finding another woman to impregnate just to prove that he wasn't the problem. He was already medically checked when his wife first made the accusation that he must have a problem. His tests came back fine, but three years later, she was questioning the validity of the previous results.

Another big problem he was struggling with was his growing feelings for his sister-in-law. Monica was everything he could possibly want. She had a sensational sense of humor. She was compassionate. She was super sexy and beautiful. She was talented and smart. She was creative at the drop of a hat. She wore her blackness regally. She was stylish, yet financially savvy and business-oriented. She always smelled good. She was a homeowner. She could cook. She knew good food and wines. She loved the arts. But, she was his brother's wife and his wife's sister, and that meant she was off-limits.

There were many times when Anthony considered cheating on his wife, but he was not as concerned that Mya would find out as he was about Monica finding out. He didn't know what would become of their friendship and their working relationship. Although Monica suggested he go out and find him some action on the side, he didn't believe she really meant it, and he thought she'd be crushed if he did. Basically, he found himself being faithful to his wife more for his sister-in-law than for his wife.

In the back of his mind, Anthony didn't want to have any children with Mya, because he wasn't sure how much longer he'd be able to tolerate her. On the other hand, the thought of having a daughter or son to come home to each day would bring a smile to his face. The other thing that would make him smile was each night before going to bed, he'd pull up the company's website just to look at the photos. He could remember the jolt of lightening that shot through his entire body while he and Monica played around on the set, and the photographer captured most of those moments. Only a person with their head in the sand would deny that there was chemistry between the two. He'd sleep peacefully each night with Monica's smile etched in his mind. Unfortunately, that same smile caused him to wake up horny and wanting sex from his wife.

Oftentimes, when he'd look at Mya compared to her twin sister, he couldn't understand how she looked so undernourished while Monica had every curve, perfectly set where it needed to be. Although Mya wasn't albino, she was very sun-sensitive and would never be caught wearing a sexy bikini at a beach or pool, as her cocoa-colored sister would.

Frostbite started nipping away at his toes as he sat in the car, letting him know it was time for him to go in the house to face whatever drama awaited him. He got out of the car and made his way up the walkway to enter his building. There were a bunch of kids sitting out there smoking weed, and he was reminded of Monica's words about them living in a ghetto. He acknowledged the teenage boys as he did each night when he got home. However, this night one of them had something extra to say.

"Yo, Mr. Anthony, I sure hope you ate before you got home. Your wife had the whole hallway lit the hell up with whatever she was burning. That was hours ago, and the hallway still stinks. My moms was about to call the fire department, but we decided to go check first. She burned your dinner." The boy laughed, and the others joined in. Even Anthony laughed.

"Thanks for the heads-up. I usually make my smoothie at night, so I can stay in shape," Anthony said, patting his flat abs.

"You gonna stay in shape just from missing meals," another boy added, and again they all laughed.

Anthony went into the building and made his way to the elevator. Although their apartment was on the fourth floor, he could already smell the burnt smell from the ground floor. The fourth floor smelled even worse. But that was the least of his problems.

"What the hell are you doing ordering another credit card?" Mya yelled as quickly as he turned the doorknob and opened the door. She had been sitting there waiting for him. "And what the hell were you doing sitting in that car for all that time? You didn't think

I saw you pull up almost twenty minutes ago? Were you on your phone talking to some bitch?"

"I'm doing well. My day was just fine. Thanks for asking," Anthony responded.

"I didn't ask you all of that. I want to know why you would apply for another credit card, knowing we are trying to save money for this baby."

"What baby, Mya? We don't have any baby. We don't even have sex to have a baby, and I figured it would be good if we took a nice vacation or something, just to get away for a few days. I wanted to do something romantic with my wife, and I ordered that credit card for that purpose."

"And I cut the shit up for the purpose of our child, when we do have one. We don't need to be racking up debt and wasting any money on any stupid trips. You saw one beach, you saw them all. I don't drink alcohol, so I don't need any of those fruity drinks, and I can't stand when you drink, because then you want to get all freaky and do stupid shit."

"Me wanting to make love to my wife is stupid shit? Really? Stupid shit is you almost burning the house down and having the neighbors ready to call the fire department."

"They need to mind their business. They only knocked on the door to see what I was doing, just to have something to talk about."

"Mya, I could smell the shit down on the first floor before I reached the elevator. But getting back to this credit card thing, what do you mean, you cut it up? Did I hear you right?"

"Yes, I cut it up. We don't need any extra debt."

"What debt? This condo is paid in full. My student loans are paid in full. You only have a small balance left on your loans, which should be finished by the end of this year. My car is paid for. Your car is paid for. So what extra debt are you talking about?"

"Well, we need to stay debt-free. I don't want our child struggling through college and having to take out loans. What if he wants to become a lawyer or doctor? That's over $100,000 right there for his education."

"And what if he or she decides they don't want to go to college? Are you going to tell him or her that they can't enjoy life today because they might need some money tomorrow?"

"You know, you sound just like my stupid father. That sounds like some stupid shit he'd say."

"Are you calling me stupid? Because you certainly are not sounding like any social worker I've ever known of—belittling people instead of trying to build them up."

"That's because your arrogant ass needs to be brought down a notch or two sometimes."

"*I'm* arrogant?" Anthony asked in disbelief. Every fiber of his being was telling him to just walk away from her because things would get worse.

"Yes, you are arrogant. You have the nerve to park right outside of our window, not giving a damn if I could see you on the phone with some bitch."

"Okay, so now you saw me on the phone, huh?" Anthony laughed. "I give up with you. You're a piece of work."

"So now you're saying I'm lying and I don't know what my eyes saw? I saw your ass on the phone while you were sitting in your car."

"You're right. I was sitting there trying to line up some ass for tomorrow night, since I can't get any from my wife."

Mya stood and stared at Anthony for the longest. "Let me tell you something, I am NOT my mother, and I would cut your dick off while you sleep if you think I'm going to just let you cheat on me and get away with it."

That time Anthony stood and stared at Mya before responding. "So now you're threatening to mutilate me in my sleep over your foolish insecurities? You know what, Mya? I should have done this a long time ago. I think it's time for us to go our separate ways. This marriage ain't working. I've tried to be everything you needed me to be, so much to the point that I don't even know who I am anymore."

"Divorce? A divorce? You can't divorce me. I won't let you."

"You won't let me? And how do you plan on stopping me? The only way you can stop me, is to try being the wife that I want and need. Other than that, I can't do this with you anymore. I should have left your ass that time you went around telling people I raped you."

"You did. I told you I didn't want to have sex, and you just took it."

"Okay, it is what it is. I'll be moving out this weekend," he said, walking toward the bedroom.

She ran to get in front of him. "So where are you going this weekend? You going to stay at some bitch's house? That's the only reason you're suddenly talking this divorce shit. How do you go one minute from talking about 'let's have a baby' to 'I want a divorce'?"

"First of all, it's only been you obsessed with this whole baby thing. I'm not in any rush for kids, truth be known. I want a house to have friends and family over for barbeques and hang out. I want to travel the world before I have kids."

"You're so full of shit. You wanted kids just as much as I wanted them."

"Mya, you don't want any damn kids. We'd have to have sex in order to have kids. You and I don't have sex unless you think you're ovulating—once a fucking month. You keep buying all those stupid test kits to tell you when you might be ovulating, and that's the only time you want to give me some pussy."

"Well, if you didn't want a baby, why go along with it? Why run to have sex when you think I'm ovulating?"

"Has it ever occurred to you that I was just simply horny as fuck? You keep me waiting and waiting, and that's the only time you throw me a bone." Anthony threw his hands up in the air in disgust. "Damn, the more I think of it, I can't believe I hung around this long. I should have *been* left your manipulative ass. I'm done. There's nothing left to talk about."

"We have lots to talk about. I don't want a divorce. My parents didn't divorce, and I'm not divorcing. We made a vow to one another, or did you forget that?"

"No, I didn't forget that, but you obviously did."

"Anthony, we can't divorce. I'm sorry. I won't do it."

"Goodnight, Mya."

"That's all you have to say? No! We need to talk about this shit. You're not going to have me out here looking all stupid to my coworkers, wondering what happened to my husband."

Anthony shook his head and laughed. "Your coworkers? You're worried about what your coworkers might think? What a fucking joke. Tell your nosy-ass coworkers to mind their fucking business. How about that? And on that note, we have nothing else to discuss. It is what it is."

"Then if you're going, go! Get the fuck out of here right now. There's no need to wait for the weekend. Go see your bitch now. I know that's what this is all about. This has nothing to do with me.

This is all about you wanting your dick greased."

"I want my dick greased by my wife, but she decides when or if it will be greased, because she wants to control every fucking thing. As for leaving now, I'm tired. It's late. It's cold as hell outside, and I'm not going anywhere until I leave for work in the morning."

"Close your eyes up in here if you want to. I guarantee you won't have a peaceful moment of rest in here tonight. You're not going to just fuck me over and toss me to the side and think I'm going to just take it laying down. You try to make me look bad, I'll make you look bad to all of your business clients."

"You have a problem with me—whatever that is—but you'd try to destroy a business that has provided well for you, a business that your own sister helped build, and you'd try to destroy the livelihood of our clients who depend on what we do for them because you're feeling jilted? That's some sick shit. The more you speak, the more I see I need to get out of here."

Anthony went into the closet to pull out a suitcase and went into the second bedroom, where he kept his clothes, along with his home office, and began packing.

"So you're really doing this? You really want to declare a war with me?" Mya asked when she saw him quickly packing to leave.

He remained silent. She snatched the frame off the wall that held his college diploma, and smashed it against his glass desk, startling him.

"Mya, if you don't stop this shit, I will call the police, and you will be carried out of here in handcuffs, and your job will find out, causing you to lose your license. Now, I'm trying to get out tonight like you told me to, but I will not stand by while you destroy my property and think that's going to be okay."

"Oh, you're going to call the police on me? How about I call the police on you? They'll believe me before they believe you, and they'll carry you off to jail after they tase your ass, and you won't get to skip over to your bitch's house after all."

"Go ahead, call them if that'll make you feel better. And all the neighbors will look at you and laugh at you every time you go in and out of the building. You want them in your business, call the police."

"Fuck you!"

Anthony continued to stuff as much as he could in his suitcase and another duffle bag. He took the stuff out to his car and came back in for his home computer and files, which he was pretty certain that Mya would sabotage the minute he left. He also went into the master bedroom to collect his toiletries.

By this point, Mya was sitting on the sofa sobbing. She begged him not to leave and promised she'd do whatever she had to do to fix their marriage. He almost fell for it until she said, "Do you know how embarrassing it will be for me when the neighbors realize that you haven't been home? How am I supposed to explain that?"

"I don't know, Mya. Tell them whatever suits you. I don't give a shit anymore. I can't live my life according to what others might have to say about it. Let people believe what they want to."

"You know what? You're such a bitch. I can't believe you'd just walk out on your marriage rather than be a man and deal with the issues. Every marriage has problems. I don't believe for a minute that Monica's marriage is all perfect like she tries to pretend. You don't see them running away. They deal with their issues and move forward."

Anthony wanted to laugh at Mya's perception of Monica trying to portray a perfect marriage, but this wasn't a time for laughing.

"Well, if you're done now, I'm going to take my *bitchness* on out the door now, so you can reflect on where things went wrong with our marriage. I'll be by in a day or two to get the rest of my belongings."

"They'll be destroyed if you walk out of this door tonight."

"You told me I had to leave tonight, now you're telling me I can't, which is why I really have to get the fuck up out of here. If it makes you feel better to destroy my belongings, then you do that. I don't give a shit anymore. Bye!" he said, rushing out the door with the items he collected on his second trip.

He could hear Mya screaming as if someone was killing her by the time he made it to the elevator. Some of the neighbors opened their doors to see what was happening.

He rode around to find a decent hotel he could crash in for a few days until he figured out where he would go. He thought about calling his brother to see if he could crash there, but he didn't feel like answering a bunch of questions that night. However, by midnight, Aaron was calling him. Mya had called her mother and her mother called Monica to tell her about Anthony walking out to be with some other woman and how things got so heated that the neighbors called the police, but he was already gone when they arrived.

The Queen PRESENTS
ENTANGLEMENT

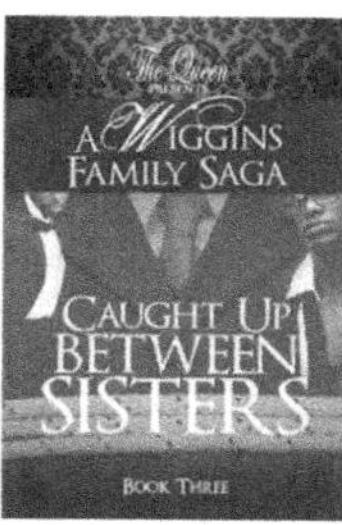
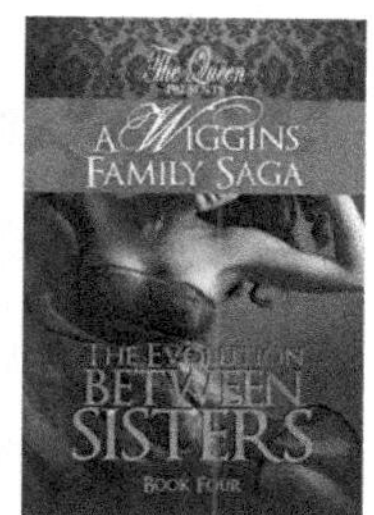

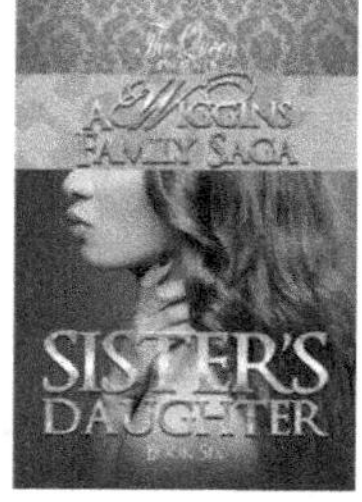

Queendom Dreams

ABOUT
The Queen

The Queen has been writing for many years, ranging in short stories, poetry, plays, professional and other writings. She is a native of (Queensbridge) Long Island City, New York. Her debut novel was *Between Sisters* (of the Between Sisters series). Her education includes Business and International Business Administration, as well as Travel & Tourism. When she's not writing, she loves to travel to sunny climates with clear and turquoise waters or near mountains for inspiration.